ADVANCE PRAISE FOR
HAVANA HARVEST

"Robert Lonsdale, the protagonist in *Havana Harvest*, tries hard to defend against treachery within the ranks of his colleagues in his quest to save an innocent man from certain death. He is a very 'simpatico' figure to whom it's easy to relate. This story would make a damned good movie."
—André Link, former chairman, Lions Gate Films

"*Havana Harvest* is a riveting page-turner full of exciting action that plays out against a very sophisticated international background. I couldn't put the book down."
—Ivan Smith, award-winning actor

"Robert Landori writes marvelously intricate international intrigue thrillers . . ."
—Louise Penny, *New York Times* best-selling author of *The Brutal Telling*

"*Havana Harvest* gives an exciting, fictionalized insight into how the Castro brothers attempted to perpetuate their control over Cuba. A page-turner, it is very topical, given what is happening within the Cuban leadership today."
—LaFlorya Gauthier, author of *Whispers in the Sand*

"Landori writes with the authority of someone who has been there. He is skilled at character development, portraying the passions and philosophies that motivate the protagonists."
—Willa McLean, *The Kitchener–Waterloo Record*

"Landori, you are a writer—yes!"
—J.T.W. Hubbard, author of *The Race*, professor emeritus of journalism, Syracuse University

HAVANA HARVEST

ROBERT LANDORI

EMERALD
BOOK CO.

Published by Emerald Book Company
Austin, TX
www.emeraldbookcompany.com

Distributed by Emerald Book Company

For ordering information or special discounts for bulk purchases, please contact Emerald Book Company at PO Box 91869, Austin, TX 78709, 512.891.6100.

Design and composition by Greenleaf Book Group LLC and Publications Development Company
Cover design by Greenleaf Book Group LLC and Base Art Co.

Publisher's Cataloging-in-Publication Data
(Prepared by The Donohue Group, Inc.)
Landori, Robert.
    Havana harvest / Robert Landori.—1st ed.
        p. ; cm.
    ISBN: 978-1-934572-55-9
1. Generals—Cuba—Fiction. 2. Cuba—Politics and government—1959-1990—Fiction. 3. Intelligence officers—United States—Fiction. 4. Espionage—Cuba—Fiction. 5. Political fiction. 6.Spy stories. I. Title.
PS3612.A536 H38 2010
813/.6   2010930971

Part of the Tree Neutral™ program, which offsets the number of trees consumed in the production and printing of this book by taking proactive steps, such as planting trees in direct proportion to the number of trees used: www.treeneutral.com

TreeNeutral

Printed in the United States of America on acid-free paper

10 11 12 13 14 15 10 9 8 7 6 5 4 3 2 1

First Edition

To: Adam, Eliana, Jarek and Daimen

CAST OF CHARACTERS

Robert Lonsdale: Deputy director Counter-Terrorism and Counter-Narcotics Division, CIA

Patricio Casas Rojo: Brigadier general and commander of Cuban Forces in Africa

Oscar De la Fuente y Bravo: Cuban deputy minister of the Interior

Micheline Beaulieu: Lonsdale's friend

James Morton: Director, Counter-Terrorism and Counter-Narcotics Division, CIA

Lawrence Smythe: Acting director of Central Intelligence and former Florida senator

Filberto Reyes Puma: Miami immigration attorney

Reuven Gal: A retired Mossad officer

Francisco Fernandez Ochoa: Cuban Army captain and aide to General Casas

Ivan Spiegel: A British businessman

Abraham Schwartz: A coin dealer

Raul Castro Ruz: Cuban minister of Defense

Maria Teresa De la Fuente: Wife of Oscar De la Fuente

PREFACE

This novel is based on events that took place in the late 1980s, embellished to make the story more exciting.

In the mid-1960s Fidel Castro made it his business to support leftist guerrillas in the trouble spots of the world because he had to—his masters, the men in the Kremlin, insisted that he do so. To please them, Cuba created a superbly trained and well-equipped mercenary army that it rented out to those who needed it.

Fidel's soldiers fought side-by-side with the locals in Ethiopia against the government, in Angola against the South Africans, in Nicaragua against President Somoza's forces, and in Grenada against the United States.

Cuban military advisors were also present in Jamaica, and among the guerrillas in Argentina, Venezuela, Bolivia, Peru, and Ecuador.

In 1984 rumours reached the CIA and the DEA that the Cubans had become involved in narcotics and money laundering. At first these were discounted; Castro was still considered by Western intelligence agencies to be a man of scruples.

Then, on June 14, 1989, the state-controlled Cuban press announced the arrest of an army general, a deputy minister of the Interior, and twelve accomplices. All stood accused of high treason and of having participated, for their own personal benefit, in drug and money-laundering operations involving Colombian, Panamanian, and U.S. citizens.

In early July the accused were tried in public by a special military tribunal and found guilty without exception. Sentence was passed on July 10. Four of the accused, including the army general and the deputy minister of the Interior, were condemned to death by firing squad, six were sentenced to thirty years in prison each, three to twenty-five years in jail, and one to ten years of "deprivation of liberty."

The death sentences were appealed to the Cuban National Assembly, which upheld them. On July 13, 1989, those condemned to death were shot.

PLANIFICACIÓN

CHAPTER ONE

Friday
George Town, Grand Cayman, British West Indies

Captain Francisco Fernandez Ochoa recognized the woman sitting behind the counter as soon as he entered the stationery store. She was striking, even more attractive in real life than in the photo he had seen of her.

"Buenos dias, Señorita." He tried to make himself sound as Mexican as possible.

"Buenos dias, Señor." She gave him a friendly smile. "How can I be of assistance?"

"Do you have a *special* hardcover copy in Spanish of *A Businessman's Guide to the Cayman Islands*?"

Her eyes flickered. "What year?"

He held his eyes on hers and replied, "1985."

She stood up and locked the drawer of the cash register. "Let me see what I can do for you," she said and headed for the racks.

"*Puta madre*, but it's hot," Fernandez murmured as he wiped his face with the large handkerchief he kept in his back pocket. He was wearing a T-shirt with "Team Mazda" emblazoned on it; long, baggy shorts; and loafers. He looked like a typical tourist visiting from Florida, except that he hailed from Matanzas in Cuba.

The woman was back in less than a minute.

"I am sorry, Señor, but I could only find an English version. Will it do?" The smile was gone; her look was professional, cold.

"I suppose so," Fernandez pulled out his wallet. "How much do I owe you?"

"Thirty dollars," she replied in English.

Fernandez paid without a word and left.

After the store's air-conditioned coolness, the midday heat seemed almost too much to bear, but Fernandez had to make sure no one was following him. He walked about downtown George Town for a quarter hour, sweating while he pretended to window-shop. "Downtown" in Grand Cayman meant a group of buildings measuring ten blocks by eight, a small area, yet containing the headquarters of more than three hundred banks and innumerable lawyers' and accountants' offices.

"*Ladrones todos,*" he muttered under his breath, then thought about it and added, "but what do I care? In a way, I'm a thief too."

He passed the Cayman Arms, the pub favored by local professionals and expats, and then turned right and headed toward the waterfront. By the time he reached the parking lot where he had parked the rented Honda Civic, he was satisfied that no one was following him. He got into the car and drove back to the Holiday Inn where he had stayed the night.

He waited until he was inside his hotel room with the door locked securely behind him before folding back the front flap of the book's dust jacket. There, in the lower left-hand corner of the cover, in small, neatly penciled script resembling a catalogue listing, was the number he needed: 02-110-7063-3214.

It took him only a few seconds to decipher the coded information. The first set of numbers indicated the type of currency in the account. The "02" meant U.S. dollars. The following three numbers stood for the account owner's domicile; 110 meant Venezuela. The next set of numbers indicated the account number, and the last four digits corresponded with the number of one of several passports he was carrying. As he had expected, the designated bank was the Bank of Credit and Commerce International in George Town.

Fernandez tore the number from the cover and flushed it down the toilet. He slipped into his swimsuit, and headed for the pool. A powerfully built, well-tanned, thirty-nine-year-old, his body formed straight lines from his barrel chest through his powerful hips to his muscular, stocky legs. His deceptively mild-looking dark brown eyes gazed out of a pleasantly square face with a well-defined jawline. Thick, black hair and a bushy mustache rounded out the Latin American look. Five feet eight inches tall, he had the fluid grace of movement of a well-conditioned athlete, which in a way he was. Twelve years of professional soldiering in Cuba's mercenary army, with tours of duty in Ethiopia, Nicaragua, and Angola, had made him tough, focused, and savvy.

Barely winded after a vigorous fifteen laps, he toweled down then ordered a club-sandwich and a "Greenie," the local name for a Heineken beer. When his meal was finished, he collapsed into an easy chair at the poolside with a satisfied groan. The temperature was in the high eighties, but a cool ocean breeze made the air feel comfortable. Fernandez relaxed, luxuriating in the tropical sun.

Too young to have fought in the Sierra Maestra with Fidel, Fernandez was nevertheless a child of the Revolution, having known no regime but Castro's. The precocious son of a garage mechanic, he had enrolled in the communist pioneer movement at age ten, on the first anniversary of Fidel's coming to power, motivated neither by economics nor politics. He was simply tired of watching *los ricos, los gusanos*, in their fancy cars whizzing past his father's garage on their way to the luxuries of *la playa*: sun, sand, good food and drink, and the companionship of beautiful women.

He, too, wanted to see the world.

The remarkable leadership qualities that he developed in high school got Fernandez elected class president. Politically reliable, physically strong, with excellent eye-hand coordination, mechanically gifted, and able to score consistently high marks, Fernandez was given the option on graduation of going to university or enrolling in Cuba's regular army, a great honor. He signed up for ten years instead of five and was promptly sent to university to study engineering as part of his army education.

He finished university with fine grades, was assigned to a logistical unit, and was sent overseas, first to Nicaragua, then to Algeria, where he demonstrated exceptional organizational abilities, and finally to Angola, where he showed himself to be a tough, brave soldier and a good leader. Having re-enlisted, he was in the second year of his second ten-year tour of duty in the army and well on his way to becoming a major.

By two o'clock, Fernandez was en route to Grand Cayman's imposing Bank of Credit and Commerce International building. The modern, four-storey edifice housed one of BCCI's most important branches on the ground floor, and the bank's western hemisphere headquarters on the two floors above.

Worried about being identified as a regular customer of the BCCI—in fact, worried about being taken to be a "regular" of anything—Fernandez left his car in the nearby parking lot of Thompson's Bakery rather than in the bank's. He walked back to the town library, crossed the street, and was in the manager's office at exactly quarter to three, as arranged. Though perspiring lightly, he felt confident wearing the Cayman businessman's de rigueur uniform: designer slacks, long-sleeved shirt, and tie.

"May I see the statement for account number 02-110-7063," he said in flawless English.

"Certainly, Sir," Mr. Chowdry, the manager, replied after consulting his computer. "But, first, may I see your passport?" Fernandez obliged. The passport he had been given was authentic, but with a phony name and a doctored photograph—his. The manager inserted the document into the decoder on his desk, smiled, and handed it back to Fernandez. He made a few quick keyboard strokes and then said, "I'll have your statement printed in a jiffy."

"Great," said Fernandez, beginning to relax. "What's the latest I can transfer money?"

"Four, Sir."

Fernandez looked at his watch. "Then we still have time to get a transaction done today."

"By all means."

"And when would the money reach its destination?"

"That depends on the payee bank."

"The payee bank?"

"Yes, Sir, the bank to which you wish to transfer the money."

"I want to wire some money to your branch in Panama."

"Oh, that's easy." The manager smiled warmly, happy that BCCI would not lose a depositor. "Panama will have the money almost instantaneously. We'll send it by coded telex."

"Could you get it there by three-thirty?" Panama was an hour behind Cayman and there would still be time in the Canal City to secure the funds before closing time there.

It was the manager's turn to look at his watch. "I think so, but I'll have to charge you for rush service." He smiled engagingly.

Fernandez nodded. "That's OK, as long as the charge is reasonable."

"One-eighth of one percent of the amount to be transferred." The manager tore off the printout, glanced at it, and then looked back at Fernandez.

"That's too much." The Cuban was angry. "One-twentieth of one percent is the maximum I'm willing to pay."

"That is impossible, quite impossible."

Fernandez got up and held out his hand for the statement. "There's no rush. We'll do it the regular way." He made as if to leave.

The manager caved in as Fernandez had known he would. "Let's make it one-tenth of one percent." That was a thousand dollars on a million dollar transfer, requiring all of ten minutes' work.

"Let's make it a flat seven hundred and fifty dollars," Fernandez retorted.

The manager handed him the two sheets. "It's a deal. Now, can I please have the details so we can make sure the money gets there before closing?"

Fernandez was surprised when the banker handed him the information for two accounts and not one; the primary account and a recently opened sub-account.

He took his time examining the documents. The sub-account held a million U.S. dollars, which had been deposited in cash the day before. This concerned him greatly because he had been told that he was the only person who could access the 7063 account, and the account was supposed to be set up to accept money via wire transfers only, never cash deposits. Obviously, someone using the same name printed in the fake passport he was using had opened and deposited a million dollars into a sub-account. The question was, why?

The number of the sub-account also drew his attention. Unlike the numbers of his other accounts, which were all made up of numerals, the sub-account number included letters: 4321ETEV. Suddenly, he realized the letters in the account number were a message: "ETEV" backwards was "VETE," Spanish for *go away*!

Whoever had put the money into the sub-account wanted him to defect, to run, and they knew that a man on the run needed to have money, and lots of it.

Without betraying the turmoil and confusion brewing within him by as much as a twitch of a facial muscle, Fernandez enunciated his words with care. "Thank you. Now here is what I want. Transfer a million dollars to your branch in Panama and give me a million dollars in cash."

The manager was annoyed. "One million dollars? But . . . but . . . it's almost three o'clock!"

"Five to three to be precise, Mr. Chowdry." Fernandez's voice was cold. "Plenty of time to phone downstairs and make the arrangements."

While the clerks counted and assembled the money, Fernandez struggled to appear calm and relaxed though inside his nerves were screaming and his mind racing to figure out what was going on. Usually calm in a crisis, he was beginning to panic. He alone was responsible for running the Cuban government's supersecret drug-money bank account, and the secret was now obviously out. *They're going to kill me*, he thought. *Either Cuban Military Intelligence or the Colombians, whose money I'm in the process of taking, or the G2.* Of the three, he probably feared the G2, Castro's notorious secret police, the most.

After almost an hour, the banker announced that his withdrawal package was ready. All of the money would not fit into Fernandez's briefcase, so the banker had provided him with a nondescript paper bag in which to carry the remainder. As he walked back to his car with fear twisting his innards, his head spun with what he had done.

When he reached his room, he threw his gear into a duffle bag, put the money on top of his clothes, and checked out of the hotel.

He sat inside the rental car in the hotel parking lot for a while, toying with the idea of returning the money. Whoever had set up the account would see that he had withdrawn the money, but they would also see that he had returned it. He would just need to come up with a reason for the unusual transaction. Then he remembered that he was possibly in danger, and quickly dismissed the idea of trying to come across as the nice guy. This was not a time to think about others, but to concentrate on saving his own skin. He needed to disappear, which required money—lots of it.

It was also necessary to slow down possible pursuit and for this he required further information.

CHAPTER TWO

The clerk locked up the store and left at six sharp. Fernandez followed her along the road toward the airport, first to a gas station, and then to a grocery store. With the engine running to keep cool, he waited in his car and tried to make sense of what was happening.

After twenty minutes had passed, the woman emerged carrying bags of groceries. He trailed her to the Caribbean Paradise condominium complex on the beach south of George Town, and parked far enough away so that he could see into her second-floor condo, which, conveniently, faced the parking lot. He watched for a half-hour before he felt sure she was alone.

It was dusk when Fernandez left his car, the air filled with mosquitoes out in force during their evening feeding frenzy. He sneaked up the stairs and walked slowly by the woman's door. The kitchen window was open and he listened intently, but noise from the TV drowned out all other sounds from inside.

He tried the apartment door. It was not locked; very few doors in Cayman ever were. He slid inside and stood stock-still, listening to the woman rummaging about in the bedroom. When she came out, he grabbed her from behind, his left arm around her throat, his right over her mouth.

"Don't scream or I'll break your neck," he whispered. She kicked him in the shin and he tightened his grip. "One more stunt like that and you're dead." She gave up; she was choking.

"Listen to me. I won't hurt you if you help me. I need a few answers, that's all. You tell me what I want to know and you'll never see me again. Understood?" She nodded, and he swiftly shifted his right hand from her mouth to the back of her head. She was a pro; she knew she was beaten. Maybe she could get away with the beginnings of a scream, but he would break her neck a millisecond later.

"What do you want to know?"

"Did you give the account number to anyone else?"

She didn't answer and he increased the pressure. "They'll kill me. You know I'm not supposed to tell anything to anyone," she finally managed through quick, shallow breaths.

"Who was it?" He began to choke her again.

"I don't know his name. He didn't say."

"What did he look like?"

"Tall and thin and gray."

"Did he have an accent?"

"He sounded Venezuelan."

"And who told you he'd be coming?"

"Nobody."

"Then why did you give him the information?"

"He had the password."

"When was he here?"

"Yesterday."

"Can you remember anything else about him?"

The woman shook her head, and Fernandez tightened his hold.

"Answer me," he whispered fiercely. "Your life depends on it!"

"Wait, wait," she gasped. "There was one thing. He had a big burn mark on his wrist."

Fernandez felt his heart sink. His worst fear was becoming reality. "Above his watch?"

"Yes, above his watch."

Fernandez spun the woman around. "Are you sure?"

"Of course I am sure." Out of breath, she was massaging her bruised throat. "He was tall and thin and gray and had a Venezuelan accent. And he had this burn mark, or skin graft, above his watch on his wrist. He tried to hide it."

Things suddenly snapped into focus. The man who had made the deposit, the man with the burn mark on his wrist, was his superior officer, General Casas, who was telling him to get out while the getting was still good.

But why? Had Fidel lost confidence in General Casas? Had something gone wrong with the drug operation? Had the Colombians sold Cuba out? Was General Casas leaving Fernandez to hang out to dry, to be *the* scapegoat?

Fernandez tried to overcome his confusion, but his brain, slowed by stress and fear, could supply no logical answers. One thing was certain though: he was finished in Cuba and had to flee.

Ruefully, he thanked his lucky stars that his parents were dead, that his estranged wife had remarried, that he had no family left in Cuba through which Fidel could exact revenge for whatever shortcomings the *Lider Maximo* might attribute to Fernandez, his trusted soldier and revolutionary.

Fernandez had known months ago that it would come to this— as soon as he accepted the assignment to help General Casas organize the Cuban government's drug-running joint venture with Colombia's Medellin cartel.

He should have declined to participate, but he hadn't and now it was too late for self-flagellation. He had to get away as quickly as possible, but not before covering his tracks somehow to delay pursuit for as long as possible.

The feeling of helplessness over having allowed himself to be trapped by his own stupidity infuriated him to the point where he lost control. In a fit of blind rage he lashed out and, with the edge of his right hand, hardened by countless unarmed combat exercises, hit the woman in the throat, crushing her windpipe.

She died within minutes.

Fernandez wiped all surfaces he remembered touching, then cautiously let himself out of the apartment and headed for the airport to catch the last flight to Miami.

The BAC 111 lifted off precisely at half-past eight. Fernandez sighed with relief when he saw the Cayman coastline disappear beneath the aircraft's wing. Uncomfortably wedged into a middle seat four rows from the rear, he managed to ignore the fat Middle Eastern–looking man to his left and the equally fat woman to his right, burned pink by the island's brutal sun. His tortured mind was too occupied by more important things.

Getting through exit formalities at Owen Roberts International Airport was always easy. You showed your passport to the immigration officer who stamped it after you surrendered the landing card you were given when you arrived. You then went through security, which also doubled as customs. Nobody gave a damn about what you were taking out of the country as long as you were not trying to walk away with coral or conch shells, so a million bucks' worth of dollar bills in your briefcase was no big deal.

Importing that kind of money into the United States was another matter.

Then there was the problem of the Colombian woman. *I didn't want to kill her, but I had to*, Fernandez rationalized. *I couldn't leave a witness behind, que los Dioses me perdonen.*

Though the Cuban regime frowned on religion, old traditions die hard, and Santeria, a mixture of Catholicism and voodoo, was widely practiced in Castro's Cuba. Fernandez felt more than ever that he could do with a little help from the gods. He knew he had to appease them for having done wrong.

Vehemently against drugs, Fernandez had become so upset when ordered to act as liaison between the army and Cuba's Ministry of the Interior in a cocaine-smuggling operation that he threatened to resign his commission and leave the military.

No way was the army going to let that happen. It needed Fernandez, and a motivated Fernandez at that.

It had taken the deputy minister of the Interior's personal intervention, during which he had explained how desperately Cuba needed the hard currency that the drug deals would generate for *la Patria*, to convince Fernandez of the justness of the cause. Fernandez had given in and then, true to form, had given his all.

The operation had been four months old when he had gotten involved in it. Communication with the Colombians was unreliable, rendezvous were not being kept, money had gone astray, large quantities of drugs had been lost, and quarrels had been frequent. Just about everything had been hit-and-miss.

Fernandez had changed all that by applying his formidable organizational skills. He found a way to communicate with the Colombians in real-time via two-way shortwave radio bursts using equivalent computer-generated random frequency rotations at both ends of the conversation. This eliminated missed rendezvous by allowing the implementation of last-minute changes in scheduling as circumstances dictated.

Since none of the parties involved trusted the others, there was a need for a foolproof way of getting paid. Fernandez had solved the impasse by making the Colombians open a number of bank accounts at the BCCI in Grand Cayman to which they would wire money randomly. They would then tell their representative—the woman in the stationery store—which account was being used on any given day. She would pass this information to the Cuban courier who could then take control of the money on presentation of the right passport at the bank.

Once the courier had possession of the money he would call Havana, give the password, and the Cuban Coast Guard would allow the Colombian drug ship safe passage through Cuban waters.

No password, no passage.

The whiff of kerosene-spiked air hit Fernandez's nostrils as he emerged from the Cayman Airways jet into Walkway G12 at Miami International Airport. The smell was comforting and reminded him of home, of the Santa Clara Military Air Base where he had lived with his wife while acting as Air Force liaison with the Russian MIG fighter unit stationed there.

Home. What a strange concept!

"Home" now that he was about to become a refugee, was the good old US of A.

Fernandez figured he had two ways to play his hand. He could use his Mexican passport, go through U.S. Customs and Immigration, and then walk away, or he could identify himself as a Cuban citizen to the first immigration officer he met and claim automatic landed-refugee status under the law governing Cubans entering the United States.

He decided on the first alternative because it left his options open. If he got busted for trying to enter the country illegally or for carrying too much money, he could still gain entry by revealing his Cuban identity. '*Y si me tratan a matar?*' he whispered as he took his place in the line of non-U.S. passengers waiting to be processed for entry. *Who is going to protect me if they come after me and try to kill me?* He shuddered. Whichever way things went, he had to contact the CIA as soon as possible and ask for protection in exchange for information.

Don't fidget with your hands, he reminded himself. *That's what they watch for, that's how they spot that you're nervous.* He stepped forward with confidence, smiled, and handed the official his carefully completed immigration form and Mexican passport.

He sailed through without being challenged.

Immediately after clearing customs he called his first cousin, Filberto Reyes Puma, who had left Cuba in 1960 and was now practicing law in Florida. His luck held; Reyes Puma was home.

"Filberto, it's your cousin Francisco from Havana."

Dead silence. Then: "Francisco Fernandez?"

"Si, Francisco Fernandez Ochoa."

"Captain Fernandez?"

"Si, si, Filberto. What's the matter with you? How many cousins named Francisco do you have?"

"It's . . . it's that it's such a surprise. Where are you calling from?"

"Miami International Airport. I need to see you at once."

Fernandez hardly recognized his cousin when Reyes Puma, nervous and perspiring, arrived half an hour later. The man, whom Fernandez had not seen for a decade or so, was grossly obese, weighing at least three hundred pounds.

It took Fernandez another half-hour to spell out the details of his predicament. "I need to get protection right away, Filberto. When I get found out they're going to come after me and try to kill me."

"Who will?"

Fernandez was becoming increasingly agitated. "The Colombians, Cuban Military Intelligence, the boys from the MININT—you know, our Ministry of the Interior—and who knows who else."

"Take it easy, take it easy. Let's have some coffee, and we'll make a plan." His cousin led Fernandez into the cafeteria near the Delta counter and found an isolated table. Reyes Puma ordered coffee, Fernandez a double vodka and soda and a ham sandwich.

"Filberto, the people who are after me play for keeps, they don't play games. I want to contact the CIA tonight. Maybe I should turn myself in to U.S. Immigration since I don't dare to leave the airport."

The attorney said nothing for a while. Then, with a shrug, he made up his mind. "Maybe that's not such a bad idea. You don't know this, but I practice mainly immigration law and know most of the senior people at the Immigration and Naturalization Service in Miami."

Fernandez finished his food and gulped down his drink. "Let's go then." He grabbed his bag and stood up.

"Wait, wait. Let me make a few calls first."

Fernandez became suspicious. Why was his cousin stalling?

"No calls."

"OK, OK, I'll go with you."

By two o'clock on Saturday morning, Fernandez was in INS custody, secure in the knowledge that this situation was only temporary since his cousin really did seem to know his way around the immigration people.

CHAPTER THREE

Lonsdale couldn't remember the last time he'd been woken up at four a.m. by a call from the office. It was only after the duty officer had given him the security password that he began to take the man seriously.

"Sorry about that, McDougall," he had grunted, "but I'm old and crotchety and not used to this middle-of-the-night cloak-and-dagger stuff, especially not on a weekend."

"I understand, Sir, but Mr. Morton is on his way to pick you up," the duty officer had replied, "and he thought you might want to pack a few things for your trip."

"What trip?" Lonsdale had no idea what the man was talking about.

"I understand you are going to Miami for a few days."

"What for?"

"That's all I know, Sir. Have a nice trip." The line had gone dead.

Robert Lonsdale and his boss, James Morton, worked for a secret division of the Central Intelligence Agency, created to fight drugs and terrorism, so hush-hush that it was not housed in Langley, but in Bethesda, Maryland.

In addition to Lonsdale and Morton, a team of more than thirty analysts, translators, electronics experts, secretaries, and guards worked in shifts 24–7 to counteract the rise in international terrorist activity. The responsibility for drug interdiction was added later by a concerned administration, fearful of allowing the CIA to become involved in narcotics, yet recognizing that, more and more, drug dealers and terrorists were working hand-in-hand.

Lonsdale heaved himself out of bed and after a lightning-fast shower was ready to go within minutes. On the way out he grabbed his "ready bag" and beat Morton's black, standard CIA-issue chauffeur/bodyguard-driven limousine to the corner by about fifteen seconds.

"What is all this about, Jim?" he asked irritably as he clambered in beside his boss. In spite of the ungodly hour, Morton was dressed elegantly in stylish black slacks and a light, beige worsted jacket over a short-sleeved black Polo shirt, his feet in comfortable-looking black moccasins.

In contrast, Lonsdale wore jeans, a nondescript long-sleeved shirt, an old windbreaker with a hood tucked into the collar, and loafers. He wasn't wearing socks either; he hadn't had time to put them on.

"Please shut the door and simmer down. We're going to Miami for a few days."

"On a Sunday morning at four-thirty a.m.?"

"You've got it ace. And we're going by private jet."

"In the *Challenger*?" The Canadian-made jet was yet another standard toy of the Agency.

"You've got that right too!"

"Oh shit," said Lonsdale. He hated flying in small aircraft.

"Come on, cheer up. The trip is only an hour and a half."

"Damn," said Lonsdale again and lapsed into surly silence, which he did not break until they were somewhere over Georgia.

"What gives?" he finally asked Morton, sipping the hot water the steward had given him. When Morton didn't answer he asked again, but got nowhere, so he leaned back in his seat and dozed off.

The Immigration Detention Center is located in the lower bowels of Miami's International Airport. Lonsdale and Morton were shown into a windowless room, one wall of which was covered by a huge two-way mirror.

"Mr. Quesada will be with you shortly, sirs," the guard told Morton. His uniform was crumpled and he had bad breath.

"Quesada?"

"Yes, Sir, Mr. Quesada. The senior man from INS downtown."

Morton nodded. He realized that the 'senior man' from the Immigration and Naturalization Service was the CIA liaison officer. "Can we get some coffee?" he asked.

"Right away, Sir. Two regulars coming up."

The guard was about to leave when in walked a squat, fit-looking man of medium height with a full head of silver hair combed straight back. He wore a lightweight, grey summer suit and looked like a middle-aged Cesar Romero, neat in appearance and handsome.

"Jorge Quesada," he said, taking Morton's outstretched hand. "I presume you're Jim Morton." His handshake was firm and businesslike.

"Glad to know you," Morton replied, showing Quesada his Agency identification card. "And this is my grouchy associate Robert, but we call him Bob." Lonsdale shrugged a greeting. If Morton wanted him to be a Bob, he'd be a Bob. He sure as hell wasn't going to make waves. He was still too sleepy.

The guard returned with three Styrofoam cups of coffee that smelled vaguely of kerosene.

"Serve yourselves," he said, placing the tray on a table that was pushed up against the mirror. "I brought you sugar and Coffee Mate and half a dozen doughnuts." He left, taking his bad breath with him.

"Not a bad guy," Lonsdale mumbled as though trying to convince himself, his mouth full of sticky dough.

"Yeah. Well, rank hath its privileges." Quesada remarked, taking a gulp of his coffee. He had a very slight Spanish accent.

"You from Cuba?" Lonsdale wanted to know.

"Originally, yes. I came here when I was thirteen."

"So you speak Spanish."

"Of course. Do either of the two of you?"

"I wish I did." Morton bit into his doughnut.

"And you?" Quesada fixed Lonsdale with a baleful look.

Lonsdale decided to lie. "I speak English and a little French, that's all."

Quesada sighed. "That's a pity. Spanish sure would help."

"Let's just see how things play out, shall we?" Morton's voice was hard, cold, and dispassionate.

Quesada shrugged, pointed to the chairs facing the mirror and switched off the lights. The mirror turned into a transparent pane of glass, on the other side of which in a windowless, but brightly lit cell an unkempt, unshaven man lay sleeping in slacks and a long-sleeved shirt on an army-type cot. His shoes were on the floor beside the cot, his jacket under his head doubled as a pillow.

"He says his name is Fernandez and that he is a captain in Fidel's army. He had a million dollars in cash on him when he arrived." Quesada spoke matter-of-factly.

"Counterfeit?" asked Morton.

Quesada shook his head. "He also says that for the last little while he has been coordinating the movement through Cuban waters of Colombian ships carrying drugs. He gave me some interesting information, but stopped talking, because first he wants assurances from the CIA that it will protect him."

"From whom?" Morton was curious.

"The Medellin cartel and the Cuban secret police."

"Did he say who his boss was?" Lonsdale was suddenly very much awake.

"He says he reports directly to a Cuban Army brigadier general called Patricio Casas Rojo, who commands all Cuban troops in Africa. This general is also supposed to be the quartermaster general of the Cuban Army."

"Who fixes things with the Cuban Coast Guard?"

"I suppose the general."

"And with the air force?"

"Also the general, I guess."

Lonsdale wouldn't let go. "And with the coastal defense people?"

Quesada threw up his hands. "I suppose the general does that, too."

"That's bullshit and you know it, Quesada." Lonsdale feigned indignation. "Only someone high up in the Cuban Ministry of the

Interior would have pull strong enough to coordinate all this. I'm sure this must have occurred to you while talking to Fernandez, so do us all a favor and start over again, but this time give details and be specific and accurate."

It took a miffed Quesada an hour to oblige.

"Do you believe all this?" Morton asked Lonsdale after the man had finished.

"I believe that Fernandez believes it."

"But why?"

"Because he's either scared shitless or crazy."

"Why do you say that?"

"Look, Jim." Lonsdale was pacing back and forth, his eyes on the sleeping Cuban. "This guy is a foot soldier who's supposed to follow orders no questions asked. But he now feels he's being left to hang out to dry. None of his orders are in writing. No one, except this General Casas knows about what he's doing, so if something goes wrong or some money goes missing the guy who would get the blame, who'd be made to take the fall, would be him."

"But there's no money missing, just the opposite: there's too much money." Morton couldn't help looking puzzled.

"What do you mean by too much money?"

"You heard Quesada. He said Fernandez told him there was an extra million bucks in the sub-account that should not have been there."

"Which he took," added Quesada.

"Which he was made, no, ordered, to take."

Trust Morton to start splitting hairs, Lonsdale said to himself

"This, in turn," Lonsdale picked up where he had left off, "could mean the Colombians, or a friend of theirs, were sending a bribe to parties unknown and that Fernandez may be the unwitting messenger to deliver it. Fernandez is right to be scared shitless. One way or another someone not particularly friendly will be calling on him soon to collect the money." Lonsdale shrugged.

"But why should that worry Fernandez? He could have given up the money, got paid for his troubles, and then gone back to Cuba. He'd have been safe there. He's in the army and his boss knew what he was up to." It was obvious Quesada was not buying any of Lonsdale's analysis.

Lonsdale gave Quesada a jaundiced look. "If you were in the recipient's shoes would you want a potentially dangerous witness against you to be wandering around alive?" He headed for the door. "There are two possible explanations for Fernandez acting the way he is, but before I lay them on you I want to think them through once more."

"Where are you going?" asked the bewildered Quesada.

"First to freshen up, then to have a chat with our friend here." He nodded toward the prisoner.

A glance at his face in the bathroom mirror surprised Lonsdale. He didn't look as bad as he felt. He smiled when he saw an athletic-looking man with short sandy hair, a generous nose, and an expressive mouth looking back at him. Obviously, his regimen of jogging five miles at least three times a week had paid off. He looked vital and slim and much younger than his fifty-five years.

He took off his bifocals, washed his hands, and splashed his face with cold water. The lines around his speckled, hazel eyes, however, suggested a deep-seated weariness no amount of sleep could cure.

After his wife's tragic death Lonsdale had taken up residence in Georgetown, a fashionable district of Washington, and gradually changed from a fast-living, fun-loving socialite to a reclusive, quiet loner. He was not lonely, just alone, and he enjoyed being so. His job required ferocious focus and this meant that, essentially, he needed solitude.

Not that he was without social contact. On the contrary. He played squash and breakfasted with his acquaintances at least twice a week, and the women he bedded (of whom there were quite a few) invariably fell in love with him. He could be a real charmer when he wanted to be, and his aura of mysterious suffering fascinated them.

But he belonged to no club or church or organization, attended very few social functions, and kept his thoughts and feelings to himself. The only person Lonsdale allowed an occasional glimpse into his private self was Jim Morton, his immediate superior, whom he considered to be not only a colleague, but also a friend.

Though Lonsdale had pretended to Quesada that he could not speak Spanish, he was very much at ease in the language. Nonetheless, he conducted the interview with Fernandez in English.

"And you say you were afraid to return to your posting because there was too much money in the account? I don't find that credible." He'd been baiting Fernandez for some time, but the Cuban would not be shaken.

"I told you already, and I will tell you again," he said. The man had a deliberate way about him, and his speech reflected it. "I am exposed, I am unprotected. If General Casas wants to destroy me, he can. Nobody else can back up my story. If he says I am a liar, I am a liar, and I am dead." His slightly accented English was just about flawless.

"But why would he want you dead?"

Fernandez shrugged. "I don't know. I have been trying to figure this out ever since I found the new account and all the money. Everything was going really well. There were no problems; the operations were being conducted with military precision—"

"They were military operations, remember?"

"Yes, and we were operating like clockwork. The money was good too."

"Where did the money go after being transferred to Panama?"

"Nowhere. It stayed there in a special account, ready for use by Department Z."

"Department Z?"

"Yes, the Ministry of the Interior set it up to circumvent the U.S. blockade."

"How?"

"Originally certain officials in the Ministry of the Interior were given some dollars, which they were allowed to smuggle out to Panama. They used the money to buy medicine and essential spare parts that they smuggled back to Cuba. That's how it all started."

"And then?"

"Then they ran out of money and someone, I think Comrade De la Fuente, suggested the drug idea to them."

"Tell me again who Comrade De la Fuente is"

"Mr. Bob or whatever your name is," Fernandez was getting exasperated. "I've already told you about him three times."

Lonsdale gave the man a bleak smile. "Then tell me about him for the fourth time," he said, his voice icy cold, "and leave out none of the details."

Fernandez sighed and started again. "General Casas told me that the idea of Department Z was Fidel's. He put comrade De la Fuente in charge of creating it and he got General Casas to help."

"Why?"

"Comrade De la Fuente is a deputy minister in the Ministry of the Interior. In this new situation he needed the cooperation of the armed forces. The Ministry has no authority over the army."

"Go on."

"General Casas also told me that De la Fuente then went to Raul, Fidel's brother, who is also our secretary of defense. Raul appointed General Casas to act as coordinator between the Ministry and the army to make Department Z work." The Cuban took a sip from the glass of water on the table, and then continued. "We started to operate in the mid-eighties, buying sensitive materials wherever we could find them."

"Where?"   .

"Everywhere, but especially in Canada, Holland, and Germany." Fernandez stopped talking. He was an old hand at the interrogation game. By making Lonsdale prompt him he would tire Lonsdale and give himself a rest. But Lonsdale, recognizing a professional, would not play. He got up and left.

"Found out anything new?" Morton was anxious to hear.

"In a way, I guess I did, Jim. Fernandez confirmed what I was beginning to suspect: there can be only two explanations for Fernandez's behavior."

"Namely?"

"General Casas is either a very decent human being, ashamed that Fidel Castro's morals have degenerated to the point where he is willing to deal in drugs, or Casas is a front for the Cuban security people in a sting against the CIA."

"Explain."

"Assume that Casas is straight. He wants to tell us about the drug thing, but he's closely watched. He can't order Fernandez to defect and come to us. Doing so would irrevocably damage Casas's position if things went wrong. So he scares Fernandez into doing so by compromising him through messing around with his bank account and practically ordering him to take the extra money and run."

"Got it."

"Now let's assume that Casas is not straight and that he is trying to sucker us into denouncing Fidel for being a drug dealer. He'd make Fernandez do the exact same thing as if he were an honest injun, except that, in such a scenario, *Fernandez would be in the know*."

Morton nodded. "I understand this too, but where would the sting part come in?"

"After our having denounced Fidel, the Cubans would provide irrefutable proof to a five-star international panel of neutral observers that they weren't in bed with the Medellin cartel and that what we took for being drug-transport ships were in reality vessels carrying some innocuous material such as medicine or foodstuffs."

"And Uncle Sam would have egg all over his face."

The long silence that followed was broken by Quesada. "What do we do with Fernandez now?"

Lonsdale bit into a stale ham sandwich and washed it down with tepid coffee. It was past one o'clock in the afternoon, and everybody was edgy. "Leave him alone in there for a while, but turn off the lights and the air conditioning. Let him stew."

"What about his civil rights?" Quesada was concerned.

"He has no civil rights. He came in on a forged passport—remember?"

"He's a Cuban refugee. He's seeking political asylum. He's protected by special laws." Quesada had been the one with whom Reyes Puma had negotiated Fernandez's surrender and it would be Quesada whom the lawyer would crucify if Fernandez were maltreated.

"So we had a power failure." Lonsdale wanted Fernandez to sweat.

"Ease up fella." Morton spoke quietly but with authority. "You know very well Quesada is for the high jump if Fernandez turns out to be valuable and word got out that we roughed him up. Besides, what else can he tell us just now anyway?"

Morton's logic was unassailable, but Lonsdale was not ready to give in. "I need a week to check on his story, and by then I'd like our boy to be really insecure. Babying him won't help me."

"Let's leave that problem to our people downtown," Morton said with finality.

CHAPTER FOUR

Saturday
Havana, Cuba

The little garden was just as Patricio remembered it: cool, cozy, and suffused with the heavy scent of white lilies. The hard-bodied, graying, and distinguished-looking quartermaster general of the Cuban Army and commander of all Cuban forces in Africa, Patricio Casas Rojo, had been given the house and garden on Calle 28 in Vedado by a grateful Fidel Castro at whose side Casas had fought in the Sierra Maestra for three tough years.

Now well into middle age, Patricio could still vividly remember the day when, as a wiry boy of sixteen, he had first met his leader. "So you're the holy terror everyone's been talking about," Fidel had said to him. "The fearless fighter, ambushing Batista's men left and right."

He had stood his ground, waiting for Fidel to stop joshing, embarrassed and much too aware of the people around him in the sunlit clearing, laughing with him . . . or was it at him? He hadn't been able to tell, but it hadn't mattered. In those days of trial by fire, his dedication to Fidel and to the Revolution had been absolute. And he did have a special kind of talent, an instinct that always told him where to position himself in battle for maximum effect, for the greatest firepower, for the most startling surprise. Within six months of having joined the Rebel Army he had been named platoon leader and allowed to initiate operations against the enemy without supervision from headquarters. He was a born soldier, and Fidel had been quick to recognize the youngster's special skills.

Casas had been nineteen the year Batista had fled Cuba, but there had remained much to be done and Casas had volunteered to stay on in the army for a while. Though Cuba was at peace, the ever-present threat of invasion by the United States required that her fighting forces have talented, competent, and devoted leaders. In the end, Casas, who qualified on all counts, was persuaded to make soldiering his career. He married a girl he had met in the Sierra, settled down in Havana, and became the father of two beautiful little girls.

A captain at the time of the Bay of Pigs, he had driven to the battle zone in a taxi, ahead of everybody, and had immediately taken charge of the eastern front. The nation and its leader had been grateful.

When he was sent to Russia for further training and to become a good Communist, his wife, who didn't like his being away so often, left him after a few years. She took the kids with her, but he'd kept the house and moved his widowed mother in to look after it.

His mother greeted him as he walked into the house: "Go wash your hands, Patricio." She still treated him as if he were a child. "You want to set a good example for your daughters." Casas laughed and hugged the gnarled old woman lovingly. His daughters were in their mid–twenties and unlikely to be impressed by their father's clean hands.

He considered the multiple meanings of clean hands as he removed his watch and began to scrub in the downstairs bathroom, carefully avoiding the scar on his wrist. It was still tender, although the accident with the phosphorous grenade had happened more than a year before.

Clean hands indeed, the hands of a murderer, a drug dealer, a cheat.

The Revolution had been pure and noble—all for the people. Casas had seen that. The son of a foreman on a tobacco farm in Pinar del Rio, luck had been with him during Batista's reign. There had always been food on the table and a roof over their heads because his father had learned to read and write and do arithmetic.

Casas had started work at thirteen, backbreaking work in the tobacco fields and lofts. He had been a good-humored boy with a friendly, open smile, always ready to help. The smile and the good humor had stood him in good stead in the Sierra, and later on as well. Soldiers sought to serve under him because he was approachable, brave, and fair.

Batista had been a murdering liar and cheat and a corrupt puppet of the U.S. national crime syndicate run by Myer Lansky. In the forties and fifties there was misery in Cuba; prostitution and drug dealing were rampant, government officials were corrupt, and there was no medical help for the poor. Twenty-five percent of the population couldn't read or write since schooling was available only in the towns and cities; *los campesinos*, the farmers, in the villages and on the farms were condemned to live in ignorance, neglect, and abject poverty.

Along came Fidel Castro and the nation united behind him. He and his followers believed that it was not power that corrupted, but misery. Fidel had tremendous popular support, and in the end, the rule of the army and police thugs, the *gorillas*, came to an end.

Deeply insulted by the Eisenhower administration's dismissive attitude toward him, and egged on by Che Guevara, who was constantly haranguing him about the United States's intention to try to reimpose its will on the people of Cuba, Fidel turned to Russia for help. The Americans responded by blockading the island and the country's economic situation deteriorated because help from the Soviet Union was insufficient to counteract the effects of the blockade.

Casas shrugged as he wondered yet again why Fidel thought that, however brave, an Argentine doctor was qualified to take on the job of being president of the Cuban National Bank and then, having screwed up, become minister of industry.

"Che never really understood that our basic industries were agriculture and tourism. We're not, and never will be, an industrialized nation," Casas had kept repeating to his colleagues at meetings of the Central Committee of the Cuban Communist Party.

Nor did they listen to him when he pleaded against state-directed economic planning, even after he had told them about what he had seen in the USSR while studying at the Staff College in Moscow: the quickest way to destroy individual initiative and wreck an economy was to give bureaucrats the power to make decisions that should be made by entrepreneurs.

Everyone, even his idol Fidel, had thought of him as just an ambitious, talented military commander, without ideas and opinions about anything other than matters military.

If they only knew how wrong they were.

The arrival of his daughters brought Casas back to the present. As he embraced each in turn, he held her a second or two longer and tighter than usual, praying that what he was attempting to do would work out well, at least for his children. As for himself, he saw with clarity that he was in a lose-lose situation. Whatever the outcome, he would be forever disgraced.

Casas doted on his daughters. They were the light of his life, his main reason for continuing to struggle on in hopes that he could make a difference and that their life would be easier than his had been. They were young—Maria eleven, Rebecca sixteen—not old enough to be married.

With his father dead, and no brothers or sisters, Casas's entire family consisted of the people present in his house that fateful Sunday afternoon.

Deputy minister of the Interior, Oscar De la Fuente y Bravo, came by the house an hour after Casas's daughters had left. De la Fuente was one of Fidel's confidants, and like Casas, he had distinguished himself in *la clandestinidad*—the revolutionary underground. But there the similarity ended. People meeting Casas for the first time would come away feeling that he was tough and principled while De la Fuente left the impression of being pliable and a bit of a buffoon because he was short and rather podgy and blinked often behind glasses with very large frames that made him look like an owl.

Nothing could have been further from the truth. De la Fuente was tougher than Casas, more focused, more self-centered, and more ruthless.

Dressed in regulation *verde y olivo* summer fatigues and combat boots, the balding, middle-aged De la Fuente was sweating.

"Café?" he asked De la Fuenta then led his guest to the kitchen, the safest room in the house for private conversation, which Casas had electronically swept that morning to neutralized the listening devices G2, Castro's secret police, routinely installed in prominent people's homes.

"*Si, por favor—y fuerte.*" It was clear De la Fuente was upset. "And while you're at it, make it a double."

"What's up?" Casas asked, as he took two coffee cups from a cabinet. When De la Fuente had called earlier, requesting an immediate meeting, Casas had known very well why, but he pretended complete ignorance. "I didn't expect to see you before Tuesday, and especially not in my home. I just got in from overseas and was hoping for a quiet day or two with the family since I seldom have the opportunity to be with them."

"It couldn't wait, Patricio." De la Fuente's tone was unfriendly, curt. "Fernandez has gone missing."

"What!" Casas, expecting the news and relieved to hear that his plan was working, spun around to face his guest and feigned great consternation. "Are you sure?"

"Sure, I'm sure. He has failed to make the scheduled contact in Jamaica."

"Maybe he's just late, gone off whoring somewhere." Casas tried to sound hopeful. "He's been late before."

"But not by forty-eight hours. Besides, our Miami contacts report they think they saw him there. Apparently he came in from Grand Cayman on Friday night."

"Why the hell would he do that?"

"Who knows? Maybe for money, or because he's chicken, or fed up, or just confused."

"Confused?"

"Yeah, confused. You should know; you're his commander, not me." De la Fuente never missed an opportunity to needle.

The cheap shot hit home, but Casas forced himself to stay cool. "Come off it, Oscar! Now's not the time for the two of us to get into a pissing contest. If Fernandez has gone AWOL then we are all in danger."

"All of us?"

"Yes, all Cubans, our revolution, and our country. Think of the propaganda value of the information he can give the Americans.

Fidel the drug dealer, Cuba the drug center of the Caribbean, Medellin and Matanzas: sister cities of sin, members of the international
drug cartel." He shook his head in disgust. "What a disgrace."

De la Fuente said nothing. Casas put some sugar into his guest's
cup then poured himself a generous helping of rum and topped it
off with Coke. *What a joke*, he thought. *I'm drinking a Cuba libre
while calmly discussing the event* I'm *orchestrating to bring down Fidel's
regime.*

De la Fuente took the steaming cup from Casas then watched the
general gulp down the stiff drink he'd poured himself. "Ease off on
the booze, Patricio. We've got some hard decisions to make." De la
Fuente was already working on a plan to extricate the two of them,
or at least himself, from a potentially very dangerous situation. "The
way I see it we have a maximum of a month's grace."

The general was incredulous. "As long as that? How come?"

"Before doing anything, the Americans will want to double-
check everything Fernandez tells them."

"Or might tell them. We don't even know for sure where he is, or
whether he's telling them anything."

"Assume the worst. Assume he's been singing like a canary since
Saturday morning."

"OK then, one month."

"A month during which we have to find Fernandez so we can
neutralize him. The Americans will then have no credible witness
to back up their story. His death will slow them down and give us
more time. Besides, killing him while he's in the care of the U.S. security people will signal other would-be defectors that the Revolution's
reach is long and that there is no way of betraying it with impunity,
not even by running to the CIA for protection."

"Big deal." Casas persisted. His plan did not include the death of
Fernandez. On the contrary: he needed very much for the captain to
remain alive. "The information from Fernandez will allow the CIA
to retrace then reveal our activities and they'll find enough people to
corroborate the story, even with Fernandez dead."

"Ah, but they will not be able to prove complicity by the Cuban
government."

"Why not?"

"Because of the second thing we will have to arrange to happen."

"And what's that?"

"We have to arrange for a number of mid–level operatives under my command to become aware of the drug operation. Men friendly with each other, sort of a buddy network, so that when the Americans go public with their story we can say that the operation was conceived and executed by a group of greedy, disgruntled midlevel employees of the Ministry of the Interior, who, motivated by the promise of huge sums of money, betrayed the Revolution, La Patria, and Fidel. We will also have to plant damaging evidence in their homes, their bank accounts, and with their friends."

Casas was skeptical. "What about the army?"

"Who gave you your initial assignment?"

"Raul, when Department Z came into being."

"Consider this then, Patricio," De la Fuente lowered his voice to a conspiratorial whisper. "From the outside the drug operation will appear to be just an extension of Department Z, an unauthorized extension created by a bunch of selfish traitors to the cause. It will be easy for Fidel to dissociate himself from this illegal extension created by a group of disloyal officials."

"But we both know that this is not so!" Casas was incensed. "The drug operation was authorized by the Revolutionary government itself, to speed the downfall of the United States"

"And for the foreign currency it generates, which we need so badly to keep Department Z going."

"Department Z is a success thanks to the few dedicated men who have worked in it from the beginning." Casas insisted. "Now you're proposing to involve more people, totally innocent people, so that in the end you can throw them to the wolves." Angry now, Casas slammed his glass down on the marble counter. It shattered.

De la Fuente took no notice. "Remember the Sierra Maestra, Patricio, and the sacrifices our people were required to make in *la clandestinidad*. We have fought hard and are fighting still to show that our way is the right way. You, as a soldier, know that in a fight one is at times required to sacrifice the lives of innocent men."

"But not to save one's own neck!"

"Patricio, stop and think for a moment. We have to achieve two things that are mutually exclusive. Somehow we must try to save our own necks while, at the same time, saving the reputation of the Revolution."

"And you think your way will achieve this?" Still upset, Casas kicked at the shards of glass at his feet.

De la Fuente, sensing that he was winning, continued the conspiratorial approach. "Be reasonable, *socio*," he said quietly, pretending to have overlooked the other man's emotional outburst. "You were appointed liaison to Department Z by Raul. The link to Fidel and to the Revolutionary Council is thus through two people only: you and me. It is our duty—and there are no options here—so I repeat, it is our duty to make sure this link never comes to light."

Casas said nothing for a while. Then he began talking, as if to himself. "I guess Fernandez must die." He pretended to agree because not to do so would have aroused suspicion. "Fernandez was present, at least once, when drugs were discussed by me at the highest levels of the army command, the highest levels, Oscar!" Casas wiped the palms of his hands on his jeans and looked pensively at his guest. "How about your people Oscar, how many are involved?"

"About half a dozen, a third of the original group in Department Z. They're all middle management. The rest know nothing about the drugs, but will be gradually sucked in during the month to come; I'll see to that."

Casas waited. He knew what De la Fuente would have to say next, but he wanted him to have to say it the hard way, without help. De la Fuente did just that. "The third thing we have to do, perhaps the hardest, is to make sure we, ourselves, are covered. If the action is traced to us, and it might be, we have to be prepared, first to deny knowledge of it and then to swear, once it is proven that we did definitely know, that Fidel and the government knew nothing."

"Our word will carry no weight. Nobody will believe us." Casas was bewildered. The conversation was taking a turn he did not expect. "More will be needed than pious protestations of innocence."

"You are right." Leaning close to his colleague De la Fuente fixed him with a merciless stare. "We will have to persuade Fidel to put us on trial, an open trial, well-publicized throughout the world, in which we will say that we were the ones to have thought up and organized the scheme."

"You mean we are to volunteer to take all the blame? The world will never believe that a lowly brigadier general and a deputy minister of the Interior could carry out such a complex operation without Fidel and the revolutionary government finding out about it." Very concerned, the general stopped talking.

De la Fuente moved in for the kill. "Think about it, Patricio." His face was very close to Casas's now. Both men were sweating nervously. Beads of perspiration stood out on De la Fuente's balding head. Casas's hands were clammy and he felt mildly sick. He was beginning to realize what his comrade-in-arms was getting at. "The government will own up to creating Department Z in a flash but will deny knowledge of the drug operation and will be glad to find two scapegoats—us—on whom they can blame the whole thing. More so if there are no witnesses to contradict."

Casas's face turned chalky, and he could hardly restrain the urge to gag. "Whichever way we play this we're dead men," he whispered.

"Not quite. We have a month during which to buy insurance."

"Insurance? What the hell are you talking about?"

"We have to make sure we have irrefutable proof that people at the highest level know about the drug thing and have known all along. That way, if they refuse to allow us to go into exile quietly, we'll go on trial, and, at the last moment, we'll bring in a surprise witness to destroy their case."

Casas was lost. "Oscar I don't follow your thinking. The government and Raul for sure, and also Fidel, know everything. By neutralizing Fernandez we cut one of the threads of proof we need to save ourselves."

De la Fuente interrupted swiftly: "Fernandez adds nothing to our position. His saying that Raul and the rest of the government knew about this thing will be dismissed as baseless slander, lies to save his life. Killing him is necessary to slow down the American investigation and to discredit the CIA even further." De la Fuente was derisive. "Their only witness . . . dead, killed while in their custody."

"But—"

"No buts." De la Fuente was adamant. "All he can testify to is that you knew about the drugs and maybe Raul, not that Fidel did. If we could get someone other than us two to corroborate what Fernandez will say—if he will say it—that might do the trick, but there is no such person." De la Fuente thought for a while then added "No, Patricio, to save the government Fernandez has to die. We don't want anybody reliable around who can swear Raul knew everything." Sweat was pouring down De la Fuente's flushed, red face in rivulets. Casas got him a glass of ice-cold water. "Calm down, Oscar, you'll have a heart attack."

His guest took a gulp. "If nobody, not our government and not the *yanquis*, can prove that Raul knew about the drugs, we're halfway home. All we have to establish is that *I* didn't know about it either, but that's going to be a bitch. Too many people know that I know. They've gotten relevant orders from me directly."

"In writing?"

"Don't be silly. But there's more than one of them and they'll corroborate each other's stories." De la Fuente wiped his face and hands with a dishcloth he had picked off the oven door handle. "No, Patricio, there is only one way to save the Revolution, and that's through having us tried in public if necessary. And there's only one way we can save our own skins."

"How?" Casas's question was a whisper.

"We need to have proof that either Fidel or Raul or my father-in-law or all three of them have been in this from the beginning! I know they have and you know they have, but do we have proof? Do we have irrefutable proof?"

The question troubled Casas. "We have proof that the government has known about Department Z from the word go. It's in the secret minutes, in writing, and everybody signed it. As for the drugs, I never saw anything in writing." The meaning of what he had just said jolted Casas. "Jesus, Oscar," he whispered, his eyes wide. "You've compartmentalized this thing so well that even I don't have direct proof of the drug thing being an officially authorized operation." He gave his guest a hard, no-nonsense look. "Tell me, Oscar," his voice had a steely edge. "Tell me truthfully since you're the one who recruited me. Are you on the level, or have you been fucking with us all this time?"

"What if I have?"

Casas, beside himself with rage, yanked De la Fuente out of his chair with a swift, merciless movement, tearing the man's shirt in the process. De la Fuente stood his ground silently, until Casas released him.

"You ought to watch that temper of yours, Patricio," he finally managed to croak, massaging his throat. "It no longer matters whether the operation is legit. What matters is believable deniability." He turned on his heels and headed for the door.

"Oscar!" The word cracked like a pistol shot and made De la Fuente whip around to face his host. "You leave this house now and you're a dead man."

The Minister smiled deprecatingly. "Don't be a prick, Patricio. You want me alive, not dead. To keep up the appearances of business as usual, come to the office Tuesday morning as planned, and we'll talk some more. By then I'm sure you will have calmed down." De la Fuente left before Casas could think of a suitable reply.

Casas tidied the kitchen and then headed for his favorite spot in the garden, under the mango tree. He needed to think. It concerned him that De la Fuente had not answered the key question of whether the government really knew about the drug operation.

It was vital that the government know. Believable deniability was of no use to Casas. On the contrary, he wanted the world to see to what depths the revolutionaries had sunk. He wanted it known that they were drug dealers, merchants of death, the allies of pimps and whores. And for this, he needed Fernandez's testimony.

Casas's disillusionment with the regime had been slow to mature. He had heard the gossip about Che Guevara's excesses as commander of Morro Castle prison, where the Argentine had, supposedly, presided over the execution of a large number of alleged counter-revolutionaries. This had troubled Casas, but he had dismissed the matter because the Bay of Pigs happened and it had been necessary to protect the gains of the Revolution.

He heard the complaints when he returned from Russia: excessive bureaucratic meddling, the venality of the CDR presidents, cronyism in high places, the rise of a new elite (members of the Cuban Communist Party), inefficient production planning by the state. The list went on and on.

Give it time, he had told himself, *it takes patience to build a new society*. But then the suicides began. Close to a dozen of his erstwhile comrades, all idealistic populists, killed themselves, one after the other. In the end, the drug thing had been the proverbial last straw that had broken the camel's back.

Oscar was unfortunately right for all the wrong reasons. To succeed in what he was planning, Casas had no alternative but to help De la Fuente to obtain proof that Fidel and Raul and the whole damn lot of them, were up to their necks in drugs and guilty as hell.

Whether Casas liked it or not, he and De la Fuente were allies in this. Though motivated by different reasons, they wanted to achieve the same end result. Why then did the deputy minister want Fernandez dead? It just did not make sense.

CHAPTER FIVE

De la Fuente got into his Toyota and forced himself to sit still for an entire minute. He knew he was a bad driver under normal conditions, and anger seemed to affect his eye-hand coordination, which made him even more of a menace on the road.

"Two-and-a-half years' work down the drain," he seethed. "I'm so near to success that I can smell it." He desperately needed concrete evidence linking Castro to the drug operation, even if he had to manufacture it. Fernandez's testimony alone would never be enough.

But allowing Fernandez to remain alive would jeopardize the big picture. It would blow Operation Adios. He had no choice: to allay Casas's suspicions he had to insist that Fernandez be eliminated.

Like most of Fidel's early supporters, De la Fuente had been a student on July 26, 1953, the day Castro and his comrades had attacked the Moncada barracks. De la Fuente had been well aware of Batista's corruptness, his henchmen's cruelty, his cronies' indifference to the suffering of ordinary Cubans in a land where the rich had all the privileges and the poor were exploited without mercy. His relief was sincere when he heard that Fidel had been sent to prison for what he had done rather than condemned to die.

Castro and his fellow freedom fighters were released after serving two of their ten-year prison sentences and left for Mexico soon thereafter to organize the Cuban revolutionary movement from abroad.

De la Fuente suspected that several of his fellow students at the University of Santiago belonged to the clandestine 26th of July Movement, as Fidel's revolutionary group became known, but his discreet inquiries seemed to fall on deaf ears, and for good reason. De la Fuente's father, a magistrate, was known to be a strong Batista supporter.

Three years after the Moncada incident De la Fuente was taking math tutorials at El Preparatorio Flores in Santiago de Cuba when, one evening, he ran into Roberto Cisneiros, a classmate, who was dating Professor Flores's daughter. They got into an animated discussion, and De la Fuente was invited for dinner at the teacher's house. Thereafter, Cisneiros and De la Fuente met frequently for drinks and coffee. At these meetings Oscar made it clear that his sympathies lay with the rebels and not with his father's cronies. Then, one day, Cisneiros disappeared. His girlfriend told De la Fuente that he had gone underground to help prepare the way for Fidel's return.

De la Fuente was mortified. How could his friend have left him behind? Why was the opportunity to help rid his country of the tyrant Batista being denied to him?

A few days later De la Fuente was abducted by two men, blindfolded, and driven into the countryside to a *fidelista* safe house. There he was trained in clandestine work: operating shortwave wireless equipment, mastering methods of encoding, and assembling mines and other explosive devices. At the end of his course he was given the addresses of a number of safe houses located in the principal cities of the country, and then driven in the dead of night to Holguien, a town in southeastern Cuba, to start working for Fidel's underground.

Under Cisneiros's direction, De la Fuente carried out his duties with dedication, verve, and great effectiveness.

When Fidel decided to return to Cuba in the *Granma*, a rundown luxury yacht the revolutionaries had purchased in Mexico, he sent word that he needed a guide familiar with the targeted landing beach near Niguero in Oriente Province. Cisneiros, who knew the area, volunteered to meet Castro and to guide him and his companions into the nearby Sierra Maestra mountain range.

The *Granma* landed in the wrong place, and its occupants were ambushed by Batista's forces. Of the eighty-two revolutionaries on board, only thirty—including the two Castro brothers and the wounded Che Guevara—made it to the relative safety of the mountains with the help of Cisneiros and his adjutant, De la Fuente.

By the time the rebels triumphed in January 1959, De la Fuente had become one of Castro's trusted collaborators and was rewarded for his loyalty and hard work by el Lider Maximo with a post in the Ministry of the Interior.

But within five years De la Fuente was asking himself serious questions about the direction in which Fidel was taking the revolutionary movement. He understood that to make an omelet one had to break some eggs, but he thought there were altogether too many eggs being broken, some without reason.

On the seventeenth anniversary of the Triumph of the Revolution, a public holiday, De la Fuente got to his office early. He needed to attend to urgent business before joining hundreds of thousands of his compatriots on the Plaza de la Revolucion to hear Fidel speak.

He was hurrying through the composition of his second memo when the phone rang. "Oscar," said a familiar voice he could not immediately identify. "It's me, Roberto."

Who the hell is Roberto? De la Fuente asked himself, *and how does he have this number?*

"Roberto?"

"*Coño, pero que te pasa?*" The voice insisted. "Don't you recognize my voice? It's me, Roberto Cisneiros." His former comrade in arms sounded awful.

"I did, I did. It's just that I wanted to be sure. Security, you know," he added lamely.

"I need to talk to you."

"All of a sudden, after a couple of years? What's up?"

"I've been sick, Oscar, but you know that. I'm better now, and I need some advice."

He is looking for a job thought De la Fuente. Cisneiros had been captured and brutally tortured by Batista's secret police a week before the rebels' coming to power. As a result, he had required intermittent psychiatric care during the past decade and was unable to cope with the demands of a steady job. De la Fuente had heard through the grapevine that Cisneiros's wife had divorced him because he was beating her, and that she had taken their two small kids, whom he adored, with her when she moved out.

"When do you want to get together?" De la Fuente felt strong loyalty toward Cisneiros, who had saved his life on more than one occasion.

"How about meeting at the Copelia at eleven? It won't take long, not more than half an hour."

De la Fuente consulted his watch then looked at the stack of papers in his In basket. "OK, let's do it, but be there at eleven sharp." The arrangement left him ninety minutes of working time, certainly not enough to finish what he had hoped to accomplish during the day. But a friend was in need of help so he had to reorganize. He figured he'd spend half an hour with his erstwhile comrade and get home by noon for lunch with his wife and kids. Then he'd go back to the office and do some more work, hopefully finishing most, if not all, that was left to do in time to hear Fidel speak.

The Copelia Ice Cream Palace, on the corner of Calle 23 and N, opposite the Havana Libre Hotel, formerly a Hilton, was within two blocs of the Ministry of the Interior. Cisneiros was waiting for him at the entrance.

They lined up to make their choice from the thirty-odd varieties of ice cream the Copelia offered, and then took a table in the section reserved for the *nomenklatura*, important officials of the government.

Cisneiros looked awful. Dressed in a worn, long-sleeved plaid shirt and faded slacks, his face unshaven, his complexion sallow, his lusterless eyes ringed by dark shadows, he gave the impression of a tortured man down on his luck who had gone without sleep for days.

De la Fuente was so concerned that he could not help blurting out: "Roberto, you look terrible. Are you ill?"

Cisneros grabbed his arm. "It was all for nothing, Oscar, all for nothing," he whispered.

He spent the next half hour telling De la Fuente about how the Revolution had failed the people, how corruption was rampant, how the populace was suffering as a result of Fidel allying himself with the socialist camp, how there was no hope for a better future for the children of Cuba.

"Even those in whom we had placed our trust," Cisneros's voice was hoarse with intensity, "have become selfish, venal, and unjust. We're lost my friend, we're lost—and so are our leaders. We're in the process of betraying every principle we stood for."

Shocked, De la Fuente held his tongue.

"Why are you telling me all this?" he finally asked.

"Because I had to tell an old revolutionary comrade about how I feel before I die." Without saying another word Cisneros stood up and walked out the door of the ice cream parlor.

That evening, sitting on the podium behind Fidel, while as el Lider Maximo rallied the immense crowd in front of them, De la Fuente could not stop thinking about his meeting with Cisneros. By the time he got home that night he knew for certain that he agreed with everything his old friend had told him. This frightened him.

Ten days after meeting with De la Fuente, Roberto Cisneros, an idealistic early member of the revolutionary movement and veteran of the struggle against the tyrant Batista, immolated himself in front of his two children. He left a letter addressed to De la Fuente in which he reiterated what he had told him during their meeting.

The impact on De la Fuente of such a devoted revolutionary's suicide was profound.

A few weeks later, Dr. Oswaldo Dorticos Torrado, president of the Republic of Cuba, was relieved of his post and Fidel Castro named himself president.

Castro's blatant move to reduce the influence of the voices of reason in his entourage tipped the scales for De la Fuente. Though a deputy minister in the Ministry of the Interior, which was headed by his father-in-law, he decided to change sides. He found his chance at a reception where he met the third secretary of the Canadian Embassy, and through him, arranged to be recruited by the CIA.

Three years later he came up with the drug-smuggling idea with the aim of discrediting the Castro administration, and had managed to convince his handlers at the Agency to give it a try. Thus it was crucial that he generate evidence of the Castro regime's complicity in the drug-running operation because only three other people in the world knew about his brainchild.

CHAPTER SIX

Monday
George Town, Grand Cayman

The Monday after he had interviewed Fernandez Lonsdale flew to Grand Cayman.

The BCCI branch in George Town was a freewheeling institution, just as Fernandez had said, aggressive in looking for new business and determined to maintain clients already acquired.

Karim Chowdry, the bank manager had been very cooperative. The CIA maintained large account balances at the branch and Lonsdale had come well recommended. The envelope containing one thousand U.S. dollars, which discretely changed hands during their preliminary chitchat, also helped. Lonsdale had no trouble obtaining a copy of Fernandez's most recent bank statement and, having reviewed it, concluded that he was none the wiser. The Cubans had, it appeared, planned to use the account for a single operation only.

"Who opened the account?" he asked.

Chowdry consulted the file on his desk: "A Venezuelan national by the name of Francisco Raban."

"Do we have an address?" Lonsdale figured the name and the address would be false, but he jotted them down anyway. "I suppose you ask to see passports when someone opens an account."

The manager shrugged. "Yes we do Mr. Robinson, but we can't guarantee the authenticity."

"Of course not, but you do make a note of the number, don't you?"

"That we do."

"May I have it then?"

The manager sighed and obliged. "Is there anything else I can assist you with?"

"Would you know if this Francisco Raban opened any other accounts?"

"Let me see." After consulting his computer the banker shook his head. "Of course, he may have done so under a different name, but we show no link."

Lonsdale got up to leave. "You've been very kind," he said, extending his hand. "May I come back tomorrow if something else occurs to me?"

"Of course, Mr. Robinson." The man was all smiles. "I love chatting with our *good* customers." The emphasis on the word "good" spoke volumes.

Lonsdale had leased an air-conditioned Ford from Cico Car Rentals and was glad of its cool comfort as he drove back to his apartment on Seven Mile Beach. He knew renting an apartment was extravagant, but he preferred the arrangement to living in a hotel. It gave him the solitude and privacy he needed.

Grand Cayman had changed a great deal since his first visit fifteen years earlier. Both sides of West Bay Road were fully built-up now, and the numerous hot-dog stands and strip malls made the landward side look gaudy. He remembered how peaceful the place had been. In the early days, the Caymans had truly been the islands that time had forgotten. No more. On the narrow highway the traffic out of George Town had backed up for miles behind a sanitation truck and the hot, humid air was blue with gasoline fumes. Progress was slow and the dust pervasive.

After what seemed like hours, he managed to reach the driveway of the Islands Club and pulled up in front of Apartment 1. He changed into a swimsuit, smeared his body with a generous amount of Coppertone 4, and then headed for a walk on the beach.

Soon, Lonsdale was lost in his thoughts. Fernandez had told him that the security-conscious Colombians set up a different account for each shipment. He had not been able to remember past account numbers, so Lonsdale had decided to visit Cayman to find out how many accounts there had been and which way the money had flowed. Unfortunately, the task was turning out to be more difficult than anticipated. The main account provided little information; the account owner's name, address, and passport details were certainly false.

As for the four entries in the latest account, he knew all about them. The first deposit was from the Colombians for a million dollars. The second, also for a million, was allegedly deposited by General Casas. The million-dollar transfer to Panama had been made by Fernandez as had the million-dollar cash withdrawal from the subaccount. The main account had also earned a couple of thousand dollars' interest, from which various bank charges had been deducted.

Lonsdale figured the second deposit had to have been made personally by General Casas. But he couldn't figure out how a Cuban communist general could lay his hands on a million dollars—and how he transported it to Cayman. Surely, he had not gone through the States.

Lonsdale decided to visit the offices of Cayman Airways to find out what airlines operated flights in and out of the islands and at what times of the day. After that, he intended to have another talk with Chowdry the BCCI manager. Million dollar cash deposits were rare, even in Cayman banks, and Lonsdale needed the details relating to how and by whom the money had been handled.

CHAPTER SEVEN

Wednesday
Washington, DC

Lonsdale owned a penthouse apartment overlooking Washington Harbor on the twelfth floor of a building on Canal Street in Georgetown, a fashionable area of the Capital equidistant from Georgetown University and Foggy Bottom and near the shops at Georgetown Park. He liked the location even though the drive to the office was long, especially when he had to make the trip during rush hour, but he didn't mind. It gave him time to think and strategize while his driver-bodyguard fought the traffic.

Back in his office after his visit to the Caymans, Lonsdale briefed Morton on his trip while sipping a cup of hot chocolate, his favorite breakfast.

The lanky, six-foot Morton, a meticulous dresser, was forever fussing about the crease in his trousers, the wrinkles in his jacket, or the knot of his tie. Lonsdale found Morton a bit of a stick-in-the-mud at times, while Morton considered Lonsdale too temperamental and brash on occasion.

Morton was a dedicated man who had made the CIA his first and only love. The middle son of a successful Boston liquor manufacturer, he had attended the right Ivy League schools and was at ease with wealth and privilege. But his background had not made him vain or hardened his heart. He felt he owed his country for having given his family a wonderful break, and he devoted his life to repaying the debt. His rise through the ranks of the Agency had been remarkable for a man with almost no experience in the "wet" end of the business. He had earned his promotions through brainpower: he was a superb analyzer and motivator of people.

Morton and Lonsdale ran the CIA's counter-terrorism and counter-narcotics division in tandem. Morton was the titular head, Lonsdale the visionary planner and field commander.

"There's a charter flight from Montreal to Grand Cayman every Thursday. It gets in at eleven thirty in the morning and the same plane returns to Canada at eight at night. That leaves plenty of time for a man like Casas to come in, get the account number from the girl at the stationary store, make a deposit at the bank, and then dash back to Montreal."

"The hell you say! You sure of this?"

"I went back to the BCCI branch on Tuesday and had another talk with the manager. He confirmed that the cash deposit had been made just after lunch on a Thursday, the day before Fernandez showed up at the bank."

"So we have corroboration of Fernandez's story."

"I wouldn't go that far just yet. But there's more, so let's just say that the situation is developing in an interesting way. By the way, where is Fernandez?"

"Still in Miami, still in Quesada's care. Why?"

"I may have to talk to him."

"Now?"

"No, but in a few days." Lonsdale continued. "I asked the manager if he still had some of the dollar bills that we suspect Casas had deposited. He said that the Cayman banks ship most of their cash back to the States as quickly as possible, but the BCCI is an exception. Its clients regularly make large cash withdrawals so the branch hangs on to any U.S. bills deposited. I asked him to give me some serial numbers, and he managed to turn up an intact bundle that had been brought in for deposit to the Fernandez account, but it didn't include the paper band that kept the bundle together. He said they had thrown it out after counting the money. But the clerk who had done the counting remembered the information printed on the band, and she told me where the cash had come from." Lonsdale waited for Morton to ask the obvious, but Morton, used to Lonsdale's theatrics, continued looking out the window. After a few moments Lonsdale gave in.

"The money came from the BCCI in Montreal."

"So when are you going to Montreal?"

"Tomorrow afternoon. I'll use the text of the letter of introduction you gave me for Cayman, but I'll have Mrs. Weisskopf change my cover name and the address and the account numbers." Karyn Weisskopf spoke, read, and wrote seven languages fluently and knew her way around the Agency's labyrinthine administrative setup. In her eighteenth year of service with the CIA, she ran the organizational side of Morton's department with admirable efficiency.

"You think we ought to go fully operational on this thing?"

"Not yet. The topic is very delicate and we don't want any leaks. We shouldn't go fully operational before I've gotten hard evidence."

"What's your timing?"

"It'll take me 'till Monday or Tuesday of next week to go positive on Casas and the mystery depositor being one and the same."

"How do you propose to do that?"

"I'll get some pictures of Casas and show them around Montreal." The expression on Lonsdale's face changed. He dreaded going back to Montreal and ripping open old wounds.

"Are you going solo?"

"For the time being, yes. Do you mind?"

Morton thought about the question. He was beginning to perceive the immensity of what Casas was trying to achieve—if Casas *was* behind the whole thing. If Fernandez was real, if the whole thing was not a reverse sting.

Lonsdale seemingly read his mind. "Scares you, doesn't it?" He gave Morton one of his cynical smiles that the Bostonian so hated. "If we call this one wrong we're screwed, but royally!"

"Why?"

"Why? For Christ's sake, Jim, there are only two alternatives. Either this thing is on the up-and-up, in which case Uncle Sam has a first-class chance to topple Fidel's regime, or we're looking at an elaborate sting against us, which could make us the laughingstock of the world if we allow ourselves to get sucked in."

"When I get back from Montreal, we'll do a preliminary report and the Wise Men can tell us which of the two alternatives looks more likely." The Wise Men were a committee who oversaw the activities of the CIA's Plans Division, the "wet" end of the Agency, without whose permission no meaningful operation could be initiated.

Morton was still not convinced. "But why would you want to solo? Why not arrange for full back-up from the word go?"

"Jim, I don't much care what happens to me anymore, not career—wise, not any—wise. If I solo, and I call the shots wrong, they'll can me and disown me. They'll be in a position, and so will you for that matter, to deny any connection between me and the Agency. Rogue agent rises from the dead, hell-bent on revenge, demented with grief and rage, that sort of thing."

Morton felt awkward. "Are you telling me you'd be willing to lay your career on the line for this? That you're—"

"What career, for God's sake? I'm at a dead end and have been for years, and I'm very happy about it. I've been eligible for retirement for a long time. I've stuck around because I've got nothing better to do."

"That the only reason?" Morton asked softly.

Lonsdale looked away. "At the beginning there was this desire to revenge my wife's murder, but even that faded after a while."

A decade earlier, almost to the day, Lonsdale had been in a Montreal hospital under guard, recovering from a bullet wound in his shoulder, the result of an Islamic terrorist's failed assassination attempt.

It had started to snow early that day and, by evening, a full-blown storm raged outside the windows of the Royal Victoria Hospital. Lonsdale—his name had been Bernard Lands in those days—had eaten dinner with his wife, Andrea, and they had turned in early, he in his hospital bed, she in the room adjacent.

He had been restless, tossing and turning until he dozed off around two, and had slept fitfully for about an hour and a half, awakening in a cold sweat, trembling. His spare pillow and bedcovers were on the floor, the bed sheets all rumpled. He looked at his watch: three thirty-eight in the morning and, from what he could see, a blinding snowstorm still blowing outside. He got up awkwardly, favoring his wounded shoulder, picked up the pillow and bedclothes with his good arm, and threw them onto the bed. He walked over to the window and looked out; the storm was so bad that all he could see was a white glow: the diffusion of the parking lot lights off the sheet of snow in front of his window.

He trotted over to the bathroom to relieve himself then wiped his face and neck with a wet towel. It was at that moment that he heard a noise, as if someone had thrown a snowball against the mosquito screen covering the window.

He thought it was the wind. But then he heard the noise again and looked over to the window. An immense shadow was sliding into view from above. His instinct and training alerted him right away to what was happening, but he was powerless to defend himself. His pistol and walkie-talkie were on the night table beside the bed. He screamed for help.

The window exploded into a thousand splinters of glass. Bullets and the smell of cordite filled the room. He crouched down between the toilet bowl and the bathtub, and watched, frozen in place, as the assassin's weapon raked his bed with long bursts of gunfire. The good Lord must have been looking after him, because he did not as much as get nicked by flying glass or the ricocheting bullets. The firing stopped as abruptly as it had started, and he knew very well what would come next: the familiar thud and rolling noise. He screamed "Grenade" at the top of his voice and dived into the bathtub.

And that's where they found him, temporarily deaf, stunned, and with a nose bleed from the concussion. His head and injured shoulder were aflame with pain, but otherwise he was all right.

Pandemonium had spread across the fifth floor of the hospital. The guard in the adjacent sitting room, hearing his charge's screams, had sounded the alarm on his walkie-talkie, but had time for nothing more. He was under strict order to protect the patient first and to worry about capturing any would-be assassin later.

In theory, it was impossible for anyone unwanted to get near the patient; however, reality often creates screw-ups.

The attack was over in less than a minute. It wasn't much time, yet it was time enough for many terrible things to happen. Andrea, awakened by the gunfire, had rushed to her husband's room, and was killed instantly by the grenade.

Lonsdale shook his head to chase the image away and noticed with surprise that the pain of remembering the past was no longer as sharp as it once was; the years were slowly grinding away at the edges of his grief. He heard Morton ask, "So what drove you to work ten hours a day, six days a week for the last decade?"

"I've told you. I had nothing better to do, and I needed to keep active. I needed something to occupy my mind."

Morton relented. He did not want to cause more grief for his deputy. The man was still hurting. "OK, so you'll go solo. Call us when you've got something. Call us even if you've got nothing. Keep in touch."

"Don't I always?" At the time, it seemed the right thing to say.

CHAPTER EIGHT

Wednesday
Havana, Cuba

Because Oscar De la Fuente was a very bad driver he was also a cautious one, something his wife, twenty years his junior and highly temperamental, could not abide. Whenever possible she would manipulate her husband into letting her drive by insisting that they take *her* car. Because he was head over heels in love with her and could deny her nothing, he would give in most of the time even though it riled him to be chauffeured around by a woman.

But Oscar always drove on Wednesday evenings, when they ate dinner at the Marina Hemmingway's best-known watering hole, El Viejo y el Mar.

The Marina Hemmingway, an agglomeration of hotels, restaurants, and summer residences, is a seaside resort about a half-hour's drive west of central Havana along the coast, and *the* in-place of the capital. Government leaders, important party officials, senior civil servants, as well as distinguished foreign visitors, mainly European businessmen, congregate in the area at night, less for the expensive meal than for the high-octane atmosphere. Oscar would not have been able to bear his colleagues seeing his wife driving on their weekly outing.

"Oscar, you're driving me crazy, crazy, crazy." As usual, Maria Teresa made no bones about how she felt. "You drive like an old woman. At this rate I, too, will be an old woman by the time we get there." De la Fuente gave her a quick sidelong glance and she pouted. They both burst out laughing.

"You are an impatient wench, Tere. I'm at the speed limit, and we only have a maximum of five more miles to go. We'll be there in less than ten minutes."

"You're the only man I know who takes a whole hour to drive ten miles on a first-class highway. I wouldn't be surprised if Ivan got fed up waiting for us and left with one of the girls."

Her husband gave her another glance and she pouted again, but De la Fuente knew better than to say anything. The trick was to get his wife to the restaurant in as good a mood as possible; otherwise she'd ruin the evening for everyone and, to add insult to injury, deny him his conjugal rights later.

De la Fuente had married Maria Teresa Montalba two years previously, after a year of intense courtship during which she had made him suffer plenty. The daughter of Cuba's Minister of the Interior and also a member of the Revolutionary Council, Maria Teresa, a striking beauty, was thirty and spoiled rotten. Born a year after the triumph of the Revolution to parents who doted on her, Tere, as she was known to her family and friends, was denied nothing. Her teenage excesses were forgiven, and her promiscuity in her twenties never mentioned: not in the press, not on radio or TV, not even by word of mouth. Nobody dared talk about Tere's exploits—her father was too powerful.

Though Mrs. De la Fuente kept complaining about being late, she was actually very happy when people had to wait for her. It gave her the opportunity for a grand entrance to show off her new dress, created exclusively for her by her dressmaker who, safe in Cuba, had no scruples about knocking off Thierry Mugler's latest collection numbers. Petite and curvaceous, she had the ideal figure for this famous designer's outfits.

With all eyes on her, Tere headed for the bar at the entrance to the dining room while her husband, three steps behind her, did his best to ignore the lascivious glances cast in his wife's direction by every man and woman in the place.

As De la Fuente expected, Ivan Spiegel, the British businessman, dressed in a blinding white, intricately embroidered guayabera, black mohair slacks, and Gucci loafers, was at the bar, accompanied by two beautiful women. At five-foot-six in elevator shoes and reminiscent of Dudley Moore, he was an impeccable dresser, wiry, excitable, and funny. Plus, he was living testimony to the adage that opposites attract. He loved tall, well-endowed women, and probably because he treated all his dates generously and with great courtesy, he was much sought after in Havana.

"Tere," he called out, rushing to meet her. "What a striking ensemble." He bowed and kissed her hand. "You look beautiful as ever!" Then he grabbed De la Fuente's outstretched hand and pumped it vigorously. "Nice to see you, Oscar, you old rascal. What'll you have to drink?"

In spite of himself De la Fuente laughed. Spiegel's good humor was infectious. "We'll have margaritas, as usual," he replied, and Spiegel turned to the bartender, "And make them doubles."

He helped Maria Teresa hop on the barstool next to a stunning redhead, smiled, and bowed again. "This is Gladys. They call her *Zanahoria*, carrot-head, because of her natural, beautiful hair color." He looked at Tere suggestively. "All over, I might add."

She gave a throaty laugh and smiled at the girl. "How do you do," she said, and then turned to the blond on her other side. "And you— what is your name?"

Ivan was quick to answer for her. "Regina is Gladys's colleague." He grinned and winked. Tere laughed. "You're incorrigible, you know that?"

Ivan threw up his hands in mock resignation. "Can I help it that I'm a great success with women? I love them all."

The margaritas arrived and the maître d' came around with the menus. A quarter hour was spent chatting, choosing the food and selecting the wines. It was close to ten by the time they sat down to dine and they continued to eat right through the floor show.

When the lights came on again the ladies excused themselves, and Ivan turned to Oscar. "Alone at last," he said loudly with a sigh. His mouth was smiling, but there was no humor in his steel grey eyes. "What's up?" he asked quietly.

De la Fuente guffawed, pretending to have just heard a great joke. "Operation Adios is blown," he stated in a matter-of-fact voice.

"How?" In spite of his considerable self-discipline, Spiegel, who was De la Fuente's CIA control, turned a sickly grey.

✪

Spiegel had started dealing with the Castro government as soon as the U.S. embargo had come into effect. Through his Spanish company, Celsa, he supplied Cuba with goods of U.S. origin obtained in Canada, in Holland, in the U.K., and wherever available. Celsa was, in a way, a predecessor of the Ministry of the Interior's Department Z, which Spiegel helped create when it became apparent that Celsa could supply only a fraction of Cuba's needs.

Celsa continued to flourish not only because it provided very efficient service, but also because it supplied difficult-to-obtain non-humanitarian goods: tires for Havana's aged police Harley Davidsons that required specially constructed Firestones, reliable spare parts for Fidel's fleet of Oldsmobiles, replacement parts for the industrial culinary equipment at major hotels . . . The list was endless.

Fidel's people considered Spiegel to be totally reliable because they thought his economic well-being depended heavily on the Cuban government's good will toward him. Did he not demonstrate his loyalty time and again by paying in advance for material destined for Cuba and then absorbing the loss when these were seized? At least that's how the Cubans interpreted the situation. The truth was that the losses were always made up to Spiegel by the Agency, since the "seizures" were pure theater, arranged to make Spiegel's "legend" seem even more authentic.

Spiegel had been put in place by the CIA in anticipation of the emergence of an influential mole, a deep-cover asset. De la Fuente, the mole, was hypervaluable to the CIA and arrangements to keep his identity secret were commensurate with his importance. His existence was known only to the director of Central Intelligence, to the chairman of the Intelligence Oversight Committee, and to his control, Spiegel.

Spiegel's father, a talented Jewish tailor from Hamburg whom polio had left with one leg shorter than the other, was forced to flee Germany when Hitler came to power. He crossed into France and ended up in the mess that was Dunkirk where the British were trying to save hundreds of thousands of their troops before the Germans drove them into the sea. A kindly sergeant had thrown his coat over the trembling young refugee's shoulders and helped him get on board one of the evacuation vessels.

In London, Spiegel senior got a job as resident tailor at a well-known West End men's wear shop. A year later he married his assistant, a Spanish seamstress. Their son, Ivan, was born ten months following their wedding.

Ivan Spiegel was lucky. He had a great talent for languages and as a child, picked up English, German, and Spanish with ease. He was also very intelligent. This prompted his parents to send him to the best "public" school they could afford and then worked their fingers to the bone to keep him there. They hoped their son would win a scholarship to either Oxford or Cambridge thereby ensuring his social and economic success.

But a life of hard work was not for Spiegel. He breezed through high school with excellent marks then took a year off to live with his mother's family in the south of Spain. There he found his true vocation the year the Americans tried to invade Cuba: smuggling.

The Bay of Pigs fiasco meant that the Castroites were cut off from most of the U.S.-made goods they needed to keep their country's infrastructure going. Spiegel recognized the opportunity and began to sell such goods to the Cuban government through Celsa.

By the end of the decade, Celsa had become well established and very profitable. Spiegel turned the running of the operation over to his uncle and returned to England where he started Delta Transport in the UK. Delta became a huge success within five years, then the roof caved in on Spiegel.

Spiegel was the most unlikely CIA agent, which is what made him so valuable. The way he was recruited was equally atypical.

After one of his frequent business trips, mellow and somewhat tipsy from the excellent wines and liqueurs he had consumed with his midday meal on board a Lufthansa flight from Frankfurt to London, Spiegel headed for the immigration lane at Heathrow reserved for British subjects. He stepped up to the desk of the Immigration officer whom he knew by sight from previous trips and handed him his passport and landing card.

From his perch, the official squinted down on Spiegel and gave him a warm smile. "Mr. Spiegel, welcome home." He beckoned to a commissionaire standing against the wall near the exit. "I understand you have been corresponding with the Airport Authority about speeding up admission procedures at Heathrow by establishing a 'fast lane' for first-class and frequent-flier passengers. The Authority finds your suggestion has merit and would like to have more input from you on the subject."

Flattered by the compliment and impressed by the unexpected bureaucratic efficiency, Spiegel responded expansively. "Any time old boy, any time."

"Splendid," the Immigration officer continued, holding on to his passport. "The Authority wishes to inconvenience you as little as possible and has arranged for a limousine to give you a lift to London. Someone from the Authority will accompany you so you'll be able to exchange views without having to give up any of your precious time." He handed the passport to the man who had come up behind him and then turned back to Spiegel. "Please follow the commissionaire."

Somewhat bewildered but pleased, Spiegel surrendered his roll-on and stumbled along behind the man. Since no one was waiting to drive him home, the arrangement suited him fine. His guide knew his way around the labyrinth that was Heathrow. Within minutes Spiegel found himself being helped into a shiny, black, vintage Rolls Royce.

The person waiting for him in the car, dressed with the casual elegance of a country squire returning to London from a weekend's shooting, greeted him with friendly formality. "My name is Samson and, contrary to what you may have been told, I work in the Foreign Office, not for the Airport Authority."

"What does the Foreign Office have to do with the airport?" The bewildered Spiegel was baffled.

"Very little, actually." Samson pressed a button to raise the glass partition to separate them from the driver.

"What am I doing here with you then?" Spiegel was sobering up rapidly.

"Forgive the subterfuge, but I had no other way of arranging this meeting without tipping my hand."

"You could have called me at the office or at home—I'm in the book."

"Mr. Spiegel, the Cuban intelligence services are regularly monitoring your calls. I did not want them to know about my wanting to meet you."

"You must be joking." Spiegel was aghast and suddenly very sober. "What do you want from me?"

"A small favor."

"Such as?"

"Our cousins, the Americans, may need a go-between, a sort of reliable messenger, through whom to maintain contact with one of their people in Havana. They're looking for an intelligent, Spanish-speaker with no visible ties to the States who would have logical reason to visit Cuba on a regular basis. We were asked to help find such a person and we thought of you."

"Who is 'we'?" Spiegel asked, though he had realized, as soon as Samson had called the Americans "cousins," that he was dealing with a representative of the British Secret Intelligence Service, people he had been trying to avoid all his life.

His first reaction was to try to find a way out. "I don't think I'm suitable for this kind of work. I'm a chatterbox, and I don't know how to keep secrets."

Samson rewarded the feeble attempt at weaseling out with a baleful look. "On the contrary, Mr. Spiegel. As far as we can tell, you've been a paragon of discretion with regard to your affairs." Samson's words had an ominous ring that sent shivers up Spiegel's spine. MI6, or whoever the hell Samson was working for, must have been delving into Celsa's activities, and that meant trouble.

Spiegel was trapped and he knew it. "Suppose I decline to cooperate?"

"That's entirely up to you, Mr. Spiegel. We certainly do not wish to, and we cannot coerce you into helping our cousins. We're asking for a favor, a favor—if granted—that will have beneficial effects on the operations of your company."

They must need my services badly, Spiegel thought, and then asked, "Really. Such as?"

"You will have no difficulty having your company's truck transportation licenses in the United Kingdom renewed, your goods destined for Cuba, presently in bonded warehouses in Rotterdam and Rijeka," Samson consulted the file on his lap, "valued at about six hundred thousand dollars and three hundred thousand dollars respectively, will not be seized under the U.S. Trading-with-the-Enemy Act, the vessels on which Celsa's goods are being transported will not be put on the U.S. blacklist. As far as your person is concerned, you will not be denied entry into the United States." Samson stopped talking and looked at Spiegel expectantly.

Spiegel got the message. *We know all about you. If you don't cooperate, we will make sure that everything I have just enumerated* will *happen*.

"How long do I have to give you my answer?"

"Why don't you come around to the office tomorrow afternoon for tea?" Samson dug into his pocket for a business card and handed it to Spiegel. "Shall we say around three-thirty?"

The card read "B. Samson, Group Head, The Foreign Office" and gave an address near Downing Street and a telephone number.

After a sleepless night at his luxurious Belgravia flat, purchased recently as a step toward social respectability, Spiegel came to the conclusion that not cooperating would mean economic disaster and an end to his social ambitions. So he made sure to be at Downing Street the next day at the appointed time, expecting to meet again with the low-level bureaucrat he took Samson to be.

He was surprised by the speed with which he was processed through reception formalities, impressed by the waiting room to which the commissionaire showed him and blown away when a woman, whom he characterized as a member of the horsy set and who turned out to be Samson's secretary, announced that Sir Brandon was looking forward to meeting him again.

Spiegel suddenly realized that the Rolls and driver of the previous day were Sir Brandon's own, not government issue as he had assumed, and that, since knighthoods were not doled out to any Tom, Dick, or Harry, Sir Brandon Samson's card had completely misled him. The man was a senior civil servant with a touch of commendable modesty.

Once Spiegel had told his host that he was willing to accept the assignment, tea with Sir Brandon turned into a very civilized half-hour's affair during which Spiegel was told to be patient. Someone would contact him from the cousins' side in due course.

As he was being shown out, Sir Brandon remarked in an off-hand sort of way, "You might find that you'll start receiving invitations to cocktail parties at foreign embassies. If I were you, I'd go to as many of these as I could."

Spiegel got the message once more and made sure he did.

Six months went by during which Spiegel attended more than two-dozen diplomatic functions. In the seventh month he got his third invitation to the U.S. Embassy. Half an hour after his arrival he was discretely collared by the commercial counselor, taken upstairs, and handed a bulky, heavily sealed envelope marked "I. Spiegel, Eyes Only."

A couple of hours later a fully briefed and very tired Spiegel left the embassy in deep shock. He had just discovered that the CIA mole he was to service was none other than his friend, Deputy Minister of the Interior, Oscar De la Fuente, with whom he had been dealing for the last two years.

Under his Celsa cover, Spiegel continued to have frequent meetings with De la Fuente. On these he reported directly to the Director of Central Intelligence via scrambler. Since Spiegel's London office communicated with his fleet of trucks and ships by radio telephone, the scrambled messages—always transmitted as ultra-high-speed "bursts" during the time of day when radio chatter was at its peak—aroused no suspicion. In fact, they went undetected. Spiegel never talked to the Director face-to-face or directly by telephone. His high-speed bursts, transmitted in code and lasting no longer than a second or two, were duly recorded then decoded at Langley on an "Eyes only Director" basis. Spiegel was kept abreast of developments and given instructions the same way: via scrambled radio messages.

This way of communicating was very safe, but had one major drawback. De la Fuente was constantly playing catch-up ball since the information he was working with was always at least a week old.

De la Fuente put his arm around Spiegel in a gesture of relaxed friendship, but the hoarseness in his voice betrayed the turmoil within him. "One of Casas's people, a Captain Fernandez, has bolted. He's believed to be in Miami."

"In Miami?" Spiegel was aghast. "You mean he's speaking with our people there?"

"I believe so."

Spiegel's mind began to race. "Can the situation be salvaged?"

"Depends on how quickly you can contain things at your end."

"How much time do you need to complete your arrangements?"

"At least another month." De la Fuente was sweating and had difficulty keeping his phony smile in place.

"I'll do my best," Spiegel said and clapped his companion on the shoulder in a great show of bonhomie. "We might still pull this thing off if we're lucky."

CHAPTER NINE

Thursday and Friday
Montreal, Canada

Lonsdale dreaded the thought of having to visit Montreal, a city that, for him, held too many bitter memories by half. He was also concerned about being recognized, though he was pretty sure that the plastic surgery he had undergone at Bethesda, and the passing of ten years since he had last been there, had altered his features enough to make such an eventuality unlikely. Still, one never knew.

Instead of approaching Montreal from the south as usual, Air Canada flight 321 from Washington came in from the northeast to accommodate prevailing winds. Lonsdale, alone in his row, moved over to the window to watch the landing.

He saw the shadow of the descending aircraft bump across the buildings as it headed toward its destination. He could not stop his heart from skipping a beat when the form raced up and down Mount Royal. The hospital in which Andrea had died so tragically over a decade ago stood on that mountain's southern slope.

Stop that, Lonsdale commanded his heart. *Be cool and concentrate on the job at hand. Remember you are Frosty the Snowman.* He often used his operational name when talking to himself.

Using the alias of Don Jackson, he checked into the Hilton on Dorchester Boulevard, a short distance from BCCI's main branch in Montreal and then went for a walk. The late October weather felt cold after Cayman and Washington, but he had come prepared. His

Burberry trench coat, complete with matching cashmere scarf, had a removable lining for which he was now grateful. Under it he was wearing what he called his "traveling uniform," a dark-blue blazer from Gieves and Hawkes of Saville Row, grey slacks, and Bally shoes with rubber soles.

He walked west on Dorchester to Crescent Street, up to Sherbrooke, doubled back to Peel, and then back down to his hotel. He found Montreal much changed. His old haunts had new names, there were fewer people around, and the city seemed less prosperous. Somehow, this restored his composure and helped him to calm down. Or perhaps it was the cold.

On Friday he called the bank manager early and requested an immediate appointment. Akhtar Siddiqui, vice president and assistant general manager in charge of yet another prestige BCCI branch, reluctantly agreed and granted Mr. Jackson a half hour of his precious time.

"I cannot tell you how grateful I am," Lonsdale lied as he took a seat opposite Siddiqui in the man's sumptuously appointed office. A short, rotund man, Siddiqui came across as well educated and somewhat standoffish, but his initial reserve evaporated as soon as he saw Lonsdale's letter of introduction. "My dear chap," he intoned, trying to ingratiate himself, "had you told me a little more about yourself over the telephone I wouldn't have created such a fuss about being busy."

Lonsdale smiled engagingly. "No bones broken," he said and laid Casas's picture on Siddiqui's desk. "Tell me, have you seen my colleague lately?"

Siddiqui was taken aback. "What an unusual question to ask a banker," he murmured and looked at Lonsdale with renewed interest. "Are you a policeman?"

"No, I'm not. I'm an internal auditor checking on our organization's account security arrangements." Lonsdale knew that Siddiqui knew that the answer was evasive, but the letter of introduction had done its magic. Besides, everybody loves intrigue. The banker picked up Casas's picture, examined it with care, then looked up and smiled. "I'm afraid that I have no recollection of ever having seen this man. As you've probably guessed, I do not see every customer."

"Not even one wanting to withdraw a million dollars?"

Siddiqui smiled again. "Above all not one who'd want to do such a thing."

"Oh? How come?"

Siddiqui looked Lonsdale in the eyes. "Let's stop this silly game, shall we Mr. Jackson? You're after information and I shall do whatever is within my power to secure it for you. I cannot help you unless you tell me precisely what you want to know."

"I'm glad you came to the point without delay." Lonsdale was beginning to like the rotund banker; he was cooperative. "Last week a man withdrew a million U.S. dollars from an account in your branch. He did nothing improper or illegal. The money was his to do whatever he wanted with it." Lonsdale held up his hand. "I need to know three things." He ticked the items off on his fingers. "One—was the man who withdrew the money the man in the photo? Two—who is the owner of the account from which the money was withdrawn. And three—where did the money come from."

Siddiqui became very businesslike. "I'm afraid I do not have the answers to any of your questions. But I shall introduce you to our current accounts manager who will, I am sure, be able to provide further details."

"Current accounts manager?"

"Mr. Jackson I'm pretty certain that if the money was, indeed, withdrawn from an account in my branch, then it must have been withdrawn from a current, rather than a savings account. The current accounts manager has access to the details affecting all such accounts in this branch. *She* is the logical person for you. We'll tell her that you are a hush-hush investigator from our internal audit department, and she'll extend you her most enthusiastic cooperation. We often have surprise inspections," Siddiqui added by way of explanation.

"I'm sure," the banker went on, "that she will be able to provide the answers to your first two questions without delay, and once you have them I shall be in a position to provide the answer to the third." He picked up the telephone, but Lonsdale stopped him. The idea of having to reveal his interest to yet another employee of the BCCI did not sit well with him.

"Why is it necessary for me to meet this person? Do you have that many people cashing million dollar checks?"

Siddiqui was taken aback. "You'd be surprised how many substantial cash transactions take place in our branch each week. By law we are supposed to keep track of and report all cash transactions in excess of ten thousand dollars, and I'm sure we do, at least most of them. But I'm also sure that we cannot keep track of all of them. That is why I, personally, try to keep away from cash transactions." Siddiqui's meaning was clear. "Ms. Beaulieu, though, is right on top of the situation."

"Ms. Beaulieu?"

"Yes, Ms. Beaulieu, my current accounts manager." Siddiqui picked up the telephone again and began to dial. "Mr. Jackson don't worry. Ms. Beaulieu is efficient, but, above all, she is very discreet." Lonsdale had no choice but to listen while the banker asked the woman to come to his office.

After replacing the receiver, Siddiqui turned to Lonsdale. "How long are you planning to stay in Montreal?"

"Depends on what this Ms. Beaulieu comes up with."

The manager looked at his watch. "It is unlikely that we shall be able to provide the answer to your third question before Monday. I dare say, you may be stuck here for the weekend."

"Unless, of course, I go back home tonight, and return on Monday." Lonsdale dreaded the thought of having to endure a solitary, grey, wintry weekend in Montreal.

Siddiqui took out his business card and scribbled something on it. "Here's my home telephone number, just in case."

Before Lonsdale could thank him for the courtesy there was a knock on the door, and Ms. Beaulieu walked in. He rose to meet her, and had to fight hard to hide the shock of recognition. The woman was Micheline Beaulieu, his girlfriend of a decade and a half ago!

Prior to Lonsdale becoming part of the CIA's protected employees' program, when his name was still Bernard Lands, he had operated undercover pretending to be an international financial consultant. Hungarian born, he had immigrated to Canada in the early fifties, and had lived in Montreal for over two decades.

A statuesque woman, Micheline had held an irresistible attraction for him right from the start. He had met her in the restaurant she managed, on the ground floor of a building in which Lonsdale was thinking of renting an office.

Using his search for office space as an excuse, he struck up a conversation and, under the spell of her sex appeal, made up his mind on the spot to rent an office in the building.

He had moved in and had often watched her from his office window as she waited for the bus at the end of her shift. One day, he timed his own departure to coincide with hers, and after offering her a lift home, he had talked her into having dinner with him.

They had eaten well, drunk well, and had danced to the music of an excellent Mexican trio in the east end of Montreal, near where she lived. They had laughed a lot, and he had ended up at Micheline's place for the night.

Their lovemaking had been spectacularly passionate and savage, and he was delighted to find that not only was she an accomplished lover but also intelligent, interesting, and genuine.

Lonsdale had driven her to work the next day. That night he had given her a lift home again, and they had picked up where they had left off the night before.

He had ended up living with Micheline for two years. Then, by mutual consent, they began to drift apart. On the third anniversary of their first date, she announced that she intended to leave both him and the country.

"Now why would you want to do that?" he'd asked, pretending indifference.

"Because we're not in love, and we're not going to get married."

"But we're comfortable with each other," he'd protested.

"That's not enough for me. I want to settle down. I want a family. I want a home. And you're not ready for that." She had sounded very firm.

He had given in. "I agree. But why leave Canada?"

She had bitten her lip so hard that it had begun to bleed. "I hate the winters in this country," she had finally replied.

Within a month, Micheline had landed a job in the Bahamas. They'd wished each other a good life and had promised to keep in touch, neither of them believing that they would. But they had, occasionally.

He'd been pleasantly surprised to receive a Christmas card, in which she had written that she was working for the Bank of Nova Scotia in Nassau and that she wished him the very best for the New Year. Because he had been out of the country on assignment over Christmas, he had read her card only in February. By then Micheline—who knew nothing about his covert activities and took him for just another brighter-than-average accountant with international connections who traveled a lot—had written again saying that yes, really, she did wish him the best and would he please write.

Instead, he had called her at work, and they had spent ten minutes catching up. Thereafter, he would call her from time to time, even after she married the Swiss owner-chef of a Nassau restaurant. Lonsdale had been invited to the wedding and had attended with great pleasure.

A few years later the chef returned to his native land, taking his wife with him. Contact between Micheline and Lonsdale ceased, and Lonsdale didn't force the issue since, by then, he, too, had married.

Lonsdale took the woman's outstretched hand and bent over to kiss it without his lips touching her skin, like his mother had taught him to do in the days of his youth. "Bonjour Madame," he murmured. *"Enchanté de faire votre connaissance."* Micheline, startled, gave him a piercing look, and then glanced away.

Siddiqui beamed, oblivious to Lonsdale's discomfiture. "How nice. You speak French." He turned to his colleague, "Madame Beaulieu, this is Mr. Jackson from our Special Audit Department. He needs your help. Will you oblige?"

"Mr. Jackson? Of course." Then she addressed Lonsdale "How can I be of help?" She avoided looking into his eyes.

"Madame, we are checking on the activities of one of our Latin American colleagues." He raised his hand in a gesture of reassurance. "He's done nothing wrong you understand, but his job is delicate, and we're trying to give him as much backup as we can." He reached for Casas's picture in Siddiqui's hand. "This is the man I'm talking about." He gave the photograph to Micheline. "Have you ever met him?" He watched her intently.

She shook her head. Then she looked up and her emerald green eyes blazed into Lonsdale's with such intensity that he had to lower his gaze. "Non." she shook her head again, her eyes never leaving his. "*Je ne pense pas*, I don't think I've ever met this gentleman. But, perhaps, my staff . . ." she let her voice trail off.

Siddiqui cut in on cue. "Madame Beaulieu, why don't you take Mr. Jackson back to your department. Perhaps there, surrounded by your colleagues, you will be able to find a way to make it possible for Mr. Jackson to complete his inquires." He began to shepherd Lonsdale and Micheline toward the door.

"Quite right, Mr. Siddiqui." Lonsdale was surprised by Micheline's willingness to cooperate. "If Mr. Jackson can provide further details about this gentleman," she waved the picture in Lonsdale's face, "we'll be glad to give him all the information we have on him." She opened the door and Lonsdale, about to leave, remembered his manners at the last moment. "Thank you for your time Mr. Siddiqui," he said and bowed in the manager's direction. "May I call on you should I need further assistance?"

"Of course, my dear fellow, any time, even during the weekend. You have my home number, so please don't hesitate to ring should something occur to you."

Lonsdale bowed again and followed Micheline through the door.

Her office was a little cubbyhole in the bowels of the branch, surrounded, almost crowded out, by the desks of her clerk assistants trying to keep up with the day's activities. She slid behind her desk and pointed to the chair in front of it. Lonsdale sat down without a word.

Micheline studied Casas's picture for a while then, all of a sudden, turned on Lonsdale. "What do you want to know about this man? If he hasn't done anything wrong why are you showing his picture around like a criminal's? What are you anyway, some sort of a cop?" Her eyes blazed up at him again.

Lonsdale, troubled, stood his ground. "Madame Beaulieu, Mr. Siddiqui told you who I am and what I'm trying to do. I'm sorry you're having difficulty believing his explanations, but there is precious little I can add to what's been said."

"OK, so you're one of the bank's security officers and you're trying to find out what this man has done."

Lonsdale looked hard at Micheline and decided to take charge. "No, Madame Beaulieu, I already know what this man has done."

"Then what do you want from us?"

"I want you to show me the man's bank account so I can see where his money came from, how much there was of it, and where it went."

Micheline was relieved. "Is that all? Give me the account name and number, and I'll get you your information right away." She picked up a pencil and held it at the ready.

"It's not as easy as you make it sound—"

"What do you mean?"

"I believe that last week—Monday, Tuesday, or Wednesday—a man came in here and withdrew about a million dollars, in cash. I think that man is the man in the photograph you're looking at."

"We had no cash withdrawals that big last week."

"How do you know?"

"All withdrawals in excess of twenty-five thousand dollars are automatically referred to me for approval, and I can tell you that last week there was no withdrawal in excess of two hundred and fifty thousand dollars."

Lonsdale was surprised. "And were there several large withdrawals that could add up to a million dollars?"

"I remember four, all made by the same person: a Mr. Abraham Schwartz, and no, they do not add up to more than a million dollars. He's in the rare coin business and buys and sells them for cash. He and his people are in and out of here making large deposits and cashing large checks all the time."

"Tell you what. Why don't you make me a list of the people who've withdrawn one hundred thousand dollars or more in one shot during the last sixty days. Once we have the list we'll see where we go from there."

"Hold on." She hit a few keys on her computer terminal and within minutes he had his list. There were thirty-seven entries, twenty-two of which related to Mr. Schwartz and his coin business. The rest showed a total transactional value of only a quarter of a million dollars, give or take, working out to about fifteen thousand dollars per transaction on average, not enough to make up the sum he was after.

"Tell me about this Mr. Schwartz," he said, and she became flustered.

"Mr. Schwartz is a coin dealer, as I told you. He really does know his business—a very interesting business. I've become friendly with him, and he has told me a lot of stories about it. Would you believe he does business all over the world? Africa, Europe, Russia . . . even South America—"

A little bell went off in Lonsdale's mind. "Whereabouts in Africa does he do business?"

"I have no idea, but I can ask him."

"Are you friendly with him?"

Micheline blushed. "Mr. Schwartz is an elderly gentleman who has a crush on me. I've been alone since my mother died, and he has been kind to me. Every now and then he takes me out to dinner."

"When is the next time do you think?"

"As a matter of fact, Mr. Schwartz has invited me to go to a concert with him tomorrow night. We'll have dinner before."

"Great. Then, perhaps, you could ask him about his business in Africa and his contacts there. I would like to know where he does business in Africa."

"Sure. I'll be glad to ask him—"

"But, please be circumspect. The BCCI's business is nobody else's business. I don't want Mr. Schwartz to find out that I've asked you about him."

"I haven't reached my present position by being indiscreet. Leave Mr. Schwartz to me, and I'll have your information for you by Monday."

"Not before Monday?" Lonsdale was disappointed. His hopes for a quick confirmation of Casas and the mystery moneyman being one and the same were fading fast. He was reduced to playing a long shot, and he would have to wait sixty long, boring, and lonely hours in a city that continued to wrench his heart before finding out whether the gamble had been worth taking.

Suddenly, he had an idea how he could reduce the waiting time. He turned to Micheline. "There's not much more we can do today, except to show my man's picture to your people to see if anybody recognizes him. That should take about half an hour." He smiled at her. "We started off on the wrong foot, and I have to make amends. Have dinner with me tonight."

Micheline turned crimson. "All right. For old times' sake."

It was his turn to become flustered. "What do you mean by that?"

She took a deep breath. "Cut the crap, Bernard, and stop pretending that you think I don't know who you are. I recognized you in Mr. Siddiqui's office as soon as I laid eyes on you even though someone had messed up your face a bit, and you have grown a beard. I almost had a stroke." Furious, she shook her head repeatedly. "I thought you were dead," she snapped.

Lonsdale, shocked, realized that there was no way out. He had to give in; he needed the woman's help. "Micheline, I didn't know you were back in Montreal, and I certainly did not know you were working at the BCCI. I was sent up here to do a job, a delicate job, I might add, and the Fates would have it that I bump into you."

"That's all you have to say to me after twenty years? After making me and everybody else believe that you were dead? Have you no shame, no decency?" She was furious.

"What can I say Miche? We don't have time just now for my story. I need to know about this man very urgently."

"Why is this matter so urgent?" She would not relent. "Why can't you take five minutes to tell me what's really going on around here? I think I deserve at least that much consideration!"

"You deserve much more and I'll tell you everything I can, but later. Just now, I must try to find out as much as I can about this man's banking activities."

"What do you mean by 'just now'?"

"Before the weekend."

Still seething, Micheline grabbed Casas's picture and stormed out, leaving Lonsdale to cope with two difficult problems. He had to establish a clear link between Casas and the Fernandez bank account in Grand Cayman, but tangible proof of the general and the mystery depositor in the islands being the same had thus far eluded him. His gut said that he was on the right track, but his brains warned that without proof the Wise Men at Langley would not believe his theories about Castro being a drug dealer.

That was the first problem, the solution of which seemed to hinge on the outcome of the Schwartz lead, which was a long shot, besides which it involved Micheline. And therein lay his second problem: what to do about Micheline.

The assassination attempt on his life in Montreal years earlier had deeply affected Lonsdale. He had emerged from his ordeal an ice cold, ruthless, introverted loner, to whom nothing mattered except revenge. He had mounted operation after operation against the world's terrorists, each daring and brilliant, and soon established a reputation as one of the Agency's outstanding, intuitive tactical planners. His handlers would have made him head of the Agency's Anti-Terrorist Division, but they saw the fatal flaw: in the process of overcoming his psychological problems, Lonsdale had dehumanized himself; he had made himself into a machine. And so they anointed Jim Morton instead.

Racked by guilt and self-recrimination, Lonsdale continued to soldier on even after the killer urge for revenge had dulled. Nowadays he went to work because he had nothing better to do, challenged only by his own reputation. He did a good job because he expected it of himself. He kept social contacts to a minimum, reveling in his almost absolute independence, and seeing no one other than trusted friends, of which there were very, very few. The old ones, the real ones, he had needed to leave behind in Montreal when he had "died."

The only emotional vestige of his previous "life" that he had allowed himself to carry over into his new existence was his love of the classical guitar, an instrument he played whenever he could. He also attended concerts on the occasions when one of the instrument's virtuosos—Julian Bream, John Williams, Laurindo Almeida, or Liona Boyd—was in town and spent many a night listening to the performances in his considerable record collection.

During these sessions, he would become totally immersed in the music. With his defenses lowered he would allow himself to feel and would then have to pay dearly for what he considered to be a lapse in self-discipline. His old hurts would surface again and he would have to deal with them once more.

Micheline's reappearance in his life had given him a nasty turn. It had taken all his self-control to hide the turmoil within him from Siddiqui:

her presence was threatening to bring down the walls he had so carefully constructed around his emotional aridity. He tried to take careful stock of the situation and be objective about it.

What did he know about Micheline anyway? She was in her late forties and living alone, she had said. Her parents were dead, but what had happened to her husband, the chef? And had she ever had children by him? Or, by anybody else? That she must have had pain and disappointment in her life was obvious. There were fine lines of suffering around the eyes that no amount of make-up could cover. Her manner had changed too. She was calmer, more self-assured, and she seemed more sophisticated. Had it been only the passage of time that had changed her? A stanza from the Desiderata sprang into Lonsdale's mind: "Give up with grace the things of youth." It seemed Micheline had done just that.

What about Mr. Schwartz? He had been relieved when she had referred to him as an elderly gentleman. Obviously a platonic relationship, or so he hoped. Was he feeling pangs of jealousy?

CHAPTER TEN

It was half-past five by the time Micheline got through her tour of the office. "Sorry to have kept you waiting, but it took longer than I expected." She sounded weary and still very upset. "I have bad news. None of the tellers or the clerks recognized the man. I also asked the security guards, and they say they haven't seen him either. So, as far as I'm concerned, that's it. There's nothing more I can do to help."

Though disappointed, Lonsdale was not ready to give up. "That's not true. There's still the Schwartz angle because of his coin dealership."

"I can't see any connection there." Micheline was adamant.

"Let's forget about work for a while. Where do you want me to take you to dinner?"

"On second thought, I'm not sure I want to go to dinner with you."

He would not accept her refusal. "Come on, Miche, why not? As you say, for old times' sake."

Back at his hotel Lonsdale took a quick shower. Under the spell of the city in which he had lived decades earlier, he could not help but recall a life in Montreal full of hope and idealism—a life he had hoped to devote to the fight for freedom, for democracy, for justice, a life that had, instead, been spent scheming, cheating, intriguing, and killing.

They'd been clever about how they had enrolled him. The CIA makes a point of recruiting individuals with real or potential clout in their communities: political leaders, captains of industry, scholars, artists, and scientists. Since it's difficult to recruit a successful and well-established personality, the Agency is forever scouting for "comers," men and women in communities outside the United States who show promise of becoming influential one day.

Lonsdale was spotted while attending university in Montreal. He had later found out that it had been his language skills that had initially attracted the CIA spotters' attention. He took no credit for these. Some people were good at sports, others made beautiful music or sang or danced. Lonsdale had a gift for mimicry, a trick of the inner ear that allowed him to learn foreign languages quickly and to speak them without accent, each in several dialects.

He had been a loner before coming to Canada, not by choice like Morton, but by force of circumstance. Drifting from boarding school to boarding school in a war-ravaged Europe is not conducive to making close friends. Since his father had been Hungarian and his mother Austrian, Lonsdale had ended up more or less on the losing side after World War Two. Not the best of backgrounds for the only foreigner at an English public school where his classmates believed that all Austro-Hungarians were Nazis. Lonsdale had taken it on the chin for three years and had then prevailed on his parents to send him to Montreal.

In Canada things had been better and he would have enjoyed life at the university had he known how to make friends. Unfortunately, he had not. The British had drilled into him that showing emotion, showing ambition, and, especially, showing off, were not proper things to do. Since Lonsdale had been born a gregarious show-off he could only change his personality by adopting an arrogantly aloof attitude. This, coupled with the painful shyness he felt as a result of always being the outsider, made it difficult for him to build relationships. As a consequence, he had continued to be a loner in Montreal.

He'd studied hard and had also worked hard at making money because his expensive tastes had required extra cash beyond his modest allowance. He persuaded the personnel people at the university's teaching hospital to give him a part-time clerical job, which he then kept during four years of undergraduate work, not knowing that the hospital's psychiatric department derived most of its funding from the CIA.

Fate would have it that Lonsdale be put in charge of accounting for special funds for mental health research. This left no choice for the CIA spotters; they had to look him over. The rest had been inevitable. The psychiatrists at Langley developed his psychological profile and identified his principal weakness—he needed to feel that he belonged—and turned him into a viable "asset": an agent programmed to act intelligently and independently, yet with absolute loyalty.

In spite of the excellent food and the friendly service, dinner at Le Béarn, a French restaurant where he and his wife used to dine, unsettled Lonsdale.

As soon as Marie-Claude, the owner, a romantic and Micheline's friend, laid eyes on them she decided to go out of her way to "make nice." She showed them to her special table, which stood in the alcove in the rear of the restaurant and was usually reserved for family and very good friends. She insisted on ordering for them and then came to sit with them while they had their dessert. Obviously fond of Micheline, Marie-Claude began to cross-examine Lonsdale, and, mellowed by the vodkas he had drunk in Micheline's apartment, and the bottle of Brouilly he had shared with her during their meal, he found it increasingly hard to resist her probing.

"It is quite amazing, *cheri*, how much you remind me of another one of my customers," she said as she poured them each a complimentary *Sambucca* to go with their coffee. "He and his wife used to come often for dinner. And then they were killed by terrorists. It seems he was some sort of a secret agent, and they wanted him dead. All the papers wrote about it for days." She took a sip of her liqueur. "It was very sad. They were a lovely couple, very much in love. I liked them."

Lonsdale felt intensely awkward and looked to Micheline for guidance, but she looked away.

It was becoming more and more difficult for Lonsdale to cope with the cumulative effect of Micheline, Marie-Claude, and Montreal. To his amazement, he found himself near tears with frustration. The urge to take Micheline home and to hold her close—to be forgiven and to forget—became so strong as to be almost irresistible.

Sensing that something was wrong, Micheline tried to make amends while driving Lonsdale back to his hotel. "I'm sorry Marie-

Claude jumped at you the way she did, but you should be flattered, not upset. She's only that talkative when she likes someone and wants to get to know them quickly—"

"So you think she liked me?"

"What is there not to like? You're a good-looking, sophisticated man with an air of mystery about you. I can only guess how attentive she would have been if she knew you speak several languages. You're quite a change from the Schwartzes of this world."

Lonsdale was taken aback. "What do you mean by that?"

"Let's face it. There aren't many available men of your age around. Most of them are boring, and some of them are quite crude. Mr. Schwartz is a darling, but much older than me. Besides, he never talks about anything except his business. And I suppose Marie-Claude was glad to see me with someone interesting, someone—"

"Go on."

Micheline threw her head back and laughed heartily. "I was going to say, someone worthwhile, but that would have made your head swell, and you're already too conceited as is." In spite of her bantering tone, she sounded serious.

"What I regret the most about Marie-Claude acting the way she did," Lonsdale said, "was that I never got to ask you about yourself. Come to think of it, neither of us got to tell our stories. Marie-Claude was too present."

Honest and spontaneous, Micheline reacted without hesitation. "You're right, so here's what we'll do. I'm busy with Mr. Schwartz tomorrow, but on Sunday I'll pick you up and we'll go for a drive in the country. Would eleven o'clock suit you?" She stopped the car. They were at his hotel.

"It's a deal," he said and, before she could move, he leaned over and kissed her on the mouth, then got out of the car as quickly as he could.

Tossing and turning in her bed that night, Micheline reviewed over and over the events of the past two weeks and came to the conclusion that, of late, there had been just too many coincidences in her life for them to be just coincidences. Her thoughts shifted to Lonsdale. Oh, how she had loved the man who was Bernard Lands, how she would have given her worldly possessions for being with him for the rest of their lives. She had tried everything to make him happy, but the more she tried the more insensitive, withdrawn, and secretive he became. After three years of frustration she finally left Montreal to preserve her sanity.

And now, this! "As if I didn't have enough troubles already," she whispered into the darkness and got up to make a cup of tea.

Sitting at her kitchen table, staring into the fast-cooling liquid in her cup, she tried to focus on the work-related events that were troubling her.

Ten days earlier, Mr. Siddiqui had given her an internal memo from the bank's regional headquarters addressed to all branch managers advising that the U.S. and Canadian governments were hell-bent on identifying money launderers. They wanted full and enthusiastic cooperation from all banks operating in North America, failing which, the recalcitrant would have their licenses revoked.

And this, Micheline knew, the BCCI could not afford. To survive, it needed every penny of its North American revenues.

Siddiqui, having dumped the problem on Micheline's lap, retreated to the safety of his office, satisfied that he could claim to have done what he had been directed to do. Micheline, on the other hand, found herself in a difficult situation. She had several clients who dealt extensively in cash: two furriers, a chain of food stores, several very successful restaurants and, of course, Mr. Schwartz, the most active of them all. And she knew that, though they were not laundering money, none of her clients could afford close scrutiny by the authorities because they all filed their tax returns in a creative way, especially Mr. Schwartz who consulted her extensively since he depended on her goodwill, his being a very cash-orientated business. Micheline, who took her job very seriously, felt strongly that banks were not supposed to act like policemen. On the contrary, bankers were supposed to respect and protect the privacy of their clients and to keep their affairs confidential. To her, this meant that, unless instructed by the client, or ordered by a court of competent jurisdiction, she would give no information to anyone that she did not have to by law.

How closely dare she cooperate with her former lover? How much information should she give him? What then should her attitude be toward her former lover?

Too many coincidences, too many damned coincidences. The government inspectors' visit a month back, looking for money launderers, then Mr. Schwartz's need for extra cash, and now Bernard's visit.

She washed out the cup and began drying it absentmindedly as she wondered what she should do about Bernard? *I should politely tell him to get lost, that's what!*

She got back into bed and began to play what ifs. *What if the man is an undercover agent? Then he is here to entrap us because he knows all about our big-cash customers and is using Schwartz as a test case. What if he is a real internal auditor? Then he is entitled to the information he is seeking, and I should speak with Mr. Schwartz about the seven hundred thousand dollars he's withdrawn in the last ten days.*

Micheline had to arrange for an overdraft facility for him to be able to take out the money. She had needed additional security before she could give him the last hundred thousand he said he needed, so he came back with five kilos of gold coins called Maria Theresia Thalers. Thirty-five one-ounce coins in each kilo meant there were one hundred and seventy-five coins. With gold at around five hundred dollars an ounce, no matter how many times she did the math, she always came up with about ninety thousand dollars. In the end, she had exceeded her authority by giving him the hundred thousand.

The math was making her sleepy and there was no more need to play "what if" except that Bernard was back in her life and she wanted to cooperate with him. Besides, she was beginning to realize she missed him terribly even after these many years.

CHAPTER ELEVEN

Saturday Morning
Langley, Virginia

Lawrence Smythe, Acting Director of Central Intelligence, squinted across his immense desk at a patently uncomfortable Morton.

"Stop fidgeting," he snapped, and continued to peruse the document Morton had handed him on arrival.

"Your group sure messed things up for me," he finally said, and slid the report across the desk to Morton. "Not that it's your fault mind you. This system of circulating information on a 'need-to-know' basis only often bites you in the ass when you least expect it."

Morton was mystified. "You've lost me, Director. Do you mean to say that my division has inadvertently interfered with someone else's operation?"

"That, in a nutshell, is what I'm saying." Smythe seemed to rouse himself from some sort of reverie as he added, "And what's worse, the operation is mine."

"Yours, Sir?" Morton was getting more confused by the minute. "How can that be? I thought the DCI never ran operations himself."

"As a rule, he doesn't."

"Has it got to do with the Fernandez thing?" Morton was beginning to catch on.

"Yes it does. That's why I asked you for a report. From what I've read I can see that, unless I include you in the 'need-to-know' loop, your man—what's his name again?"

"Lonsdale."

"This Lonsdale is likely to screw things up but good unless we muzzle him pdq."

"But he's already in the field, Sir."

"Can you contact him?"

"No. But he will contact me, maybe even today."

"Tell me about this man, Morton. Tell me about the way his mind works."

"That's a tall order." Morton could not see what Smythe was trying to get at. "Lonsdale is my deputy. He is an opinionated contrarian with a very tough attitude."

"You mean he's a loose cannon?"

"Not really. He's just an independent operator–type." Morton smiled. "As a matter of fact, that's his strength."

"But a loose canon nevertheless."

"Why don't you just tell me what's going on, and I'll see to it that Lonsdale is no threat to your operation."

Smythe poured himself two fingers of bourbon from the bottle on his desk and then offered Morton a drink, which he declined. Sipping his liquor pensively the director leaned back in his chair and gazed at a point on the ceiling above his subordinate's head. After what seemed an eternity to Morton, Smythe appeared to come to some sort of a decision. "I wish it were as simple as that," he said. "You see, I am prepared to tell you about Operation Adios, but only if you give me your word that you will not tell Lonsdale."

"But how do you expect me to tell him not to interfere if he doesn't know what he's not to interfere with?"

Smythe let out a sharp cackle. "That's precisely the point. But, having read your personnel file and that of your deputy, I'm sure you'll figure out a way to make Lonsdale do what we want him to do without actually telling him what to do."

"You mean exploit his contrarian attitude, don't you?"

Smythe nodded as he continued. "Your file says you're a great motivator and manipulator, Morton. Well, here's your chance to live up to your formidable reputation and manipulate your man into doing my bidding."

"And what may that be?"

"Lonsdale will soon find out that the man in the photograph he is showing around in Montreal is General Casas, and that's good for us. Now comes the tricky part. I want your man to contact General Casas, but only after he leaves Cuba, which he is about to do. However, instead of turning him to work for us, or encouraging him to defect, I want him to chase Casas back to Cuba without telling him anything."

Morton was nonplussed. "What on earth for?"

"So the general can obtain indisputable proof that the Castro regime is fully aware of the drug smuggling operation and is solidly behind it."

"You mean to tell me, Sir, that it isn't?"

"No Morton, it isn't. We are."

CHAPTER TWELVE

Saturday Afternoon
Montreal, Canada

Things began to go wrong for Lonsdale on Saturday after lunch. He had ordered breakfast in his room and had spent a couple of hours reviewing his position. His gut told him he was on track and that Schwartz, with his African business connections, had somehow become involved with General Casas and was supplying the Cuban with money, in return for African coins perhaps. But supposing was not enough. He needed proof. He'd learned long ago not to jump to conclusions.

The weather was sunny, but still cool. From the room's window, Lonsdale watched the pedestrians on Dorchester Boulevard for a few minutes before deciding to join them. He put on his overcoat then walked down to Old Montreal, the historic part of the city, to dawdle away an hour, roaming the cobble-stoned streets.

At half past one he called Miami from a public telephone in the lobby of the Grand Hotel on Victoria Square. He asked for Quesada.

"Who's calling?"

Lonsdale was taken aback. He had dialed the supersecret Miami CIA hotline and had expected a professional reaction.

"Never mind that," he snapped. "Just get me Quesada."

"Just a moment, Sir," the voice said and put him on hold. Three minutes and forty-two seconds later the voice returned. "I'm sorry, Sir, but Mr. Quesada is not here."

"Then please find him." Lonsdale was getting upset.

"It might take some time. Can anyone else help?"

"Are you the duty officer?"

"No, Sir. Shall I get him for you?"

"Please do." Lonsdale was beginning to wonder why he was being given the runaround. It was usually the duty officer who answered the hotline.

Another four minutes went by, an unpardonable delay under the circumstances. Obviously, they were trying to establish where he was calling from—not standard operating procedure at the start of a hotline conversation. Were Quesada's calls subject to special watch? If so, why?

"Duty officer here." The voice was different. It sounded firm, but friendly. "How can I help?"

"I wanted to talk to Quesada, but he's not to be found. I need access to one of the people he's holding for me."

"Where?"

"At Miami Airport's Immigration Detention Center."

"And who are you?"

"This is a code one-oh-three-three call. My name is Vector. Your computer will match the name with the number."

"That is affirmative. Whom do you wish to access?"

"A detainee by the name of Fernandez."

"Hold on."

A couple of minutes later a new voice came on the line. "Your party cannot be accessed just now. He's in transit."

"Can you tell me when I can talk to him?"

"Not exactly, but give us half an hour and we'll call you back. Let me have your number."

Lonsdale glanced at his wristwatch. He had been on the line to Miami for about a quarter of an hour, plenty of time for the call to have been traced. "No sweat." He, too, made himself sound super friendly. "Area five one four, seven oh one, seven oh seven,"

"Is that a safe line?"

"It's a public telephone."

"All right, then. I make it thirteen hundred and seventeen hours. Shall we say fourteen hundred and thirty hours, to give us time to get organized?"

Lonsdale looked around and saw that the phone he was using suited his purposes. One of six, it was shielded from the main pedestrian traffic since it was located in an alcove to the side of the busy lobby.

"That's a go," he answered. "Talk to you soon." He hung up and, mind reeling, walked away.

What the hell was going on? Why were they treating him as if he were the opposition? To take fifteen minutes over a routine call on the hotline was very strange. Nothing made sense.

He walked across to the Stock Exchange Tower, a building connected to the Grand Hotel by a common shopping arcade, and called Morton. He let the phone ring ten times. It was unusual for Morton, a man of predictable habits not to have his answering machine turned on. Very frustrated, Lonsdale telephoned his Washington office.

Mrs. Weisskopf, the administrator, answered on the first ring, which surprised him since it was a Saturday afternoon. She recognized his voice right off the bat. "I'm glad you called. Jim Morton is looking for you."

"And I am looking for him." Lonsdale was testy. "Is he there?"

"No. He was summoned to Langley, but we expect him back within the hour."

"To Langley?" Lonsdale was surprised. "Whom is he seeing there?"

"Director Smythe."

"On a Saturday afternoon?"

"It's strange, but then we live in a strange world. Can Jim call you back?"

Lonsdale checked the time. It was a quarter to three. "No, he can't. I'm in and out, so it's best if I call him. Tell him I'll catch him at the office in an hour from now or, if I miss him, I'll call him at home tonight."

"Will do," said Mrs. Weisskopf. "Take care of yourself," she added, seemingly as an afterthought. "I hear you're sailing in troubled waters."

Lonsdale became concerned. "It's as bad as that, is it?"

"The last twenty-four hours have been . . . how shall I put it discreetly . . . most interesting."

"Really? Tell me what's up."

"I had better let Jim do that." Mrs. Weisskopf hung up, leaving Lonsdale confused and insecure. *Why is she holding back?* he wondered.

The telephone in the Grand Hotel lobby was already ringing when he got there.

Lonsdale answered, "This is Vector. Let me speak with Fernandez."

"I'm sorry, but that's not possible. We have no access." It was the second voice that had come on the line during the previous call. The speaker was still friendly, but very firm.

"Come off it. I need to talk either to Fernandez or to Quesada, and I need to do that right now. That's what you were supposed to organize for me."

"As I said, it's not possible. But, I do have a message for you."

"What is it?"

"Call the Liquor Merchant at home tonight."

"Fuck you very much," said Lonsdale and banged down the receiver. It seemed Morton was trying to cut him off from information. But why? And what the hell was Morton doing with Smythe?

Lonsdale called the office again. Weisskopf was still there. "Is Jim around?"

"No, he hasn't come back yet. But he did call in and tell me to ask you to call him tonight."

"Thanks, Weissköpfchen. Keep the faith and have a nice weekend." He slammed down the receiver and headed for the main door.

To fill the rest of the day, he went to an early movie, which helped him to stop thinking about Micheline and Mr. Schwartz. He then had a quick dinner at the Maritime Bar of the Ritz Carlton Hotel on Sherbrooke Street. At ten sharp, he called Morton, the Liquor Merchant, from his table.

"What are you doing with Fernandez?" Lonsdale asked without preamble.

"We're holding him in one of our safe houses in Miami." Morton was equally abrupt.

"Can you find him for me? I need to talk to him."

"No, I can't. Besides, there's more bad news. The Wise Men got wind of our little operation and, after careful analysis, decided that we were barking up the wrong tree."

"So?"

"They have ordered me to shut this thing down."

"As of when?"

"They weren't specific about it, but I think they'd like to see you back in the office on Monday, Tuesday at the latest."

"Jim, none of this makes sense to me. We don't even know which way is up, so how could the Wise Men? Don't you think it's too early to throw in the towel?"

"Listen, my friend. Like you, I only carry out orders. They told me to fold our tents, so I'm folding our tents. And that includes you. Be back at the office on Tuesday morning." Morton did not sound his usual serene self.

Lonsdale was beginning to sweat. "Am I hearing what I think I'm hearing?"

"Hear whatever you want to hear. Just be back in the office on Tuesday morning."

"Is that an order?"

"I'm afraid it is."

"Then good night, Jim, and thanks for nothing."

"Good night. See you Tuesday."

CHAPTER THIRTEEN

Sunday
Montreal, Canada

On Sunday, Micheline picked up Lonsdale at eleven sharp. He was eager to ask her about Mr. Schwartz, but curbed his impatience and made small talk while she maneuvered them out of the city.

"Where are we headed?"

"I thought we'd drive into the Laurentian hills, have a leisurely lunch, then go antiquing."

Lonsdale looked out the window. "Do you think the weather will hold?"

"They say it will be sunny with cloudy periods."

"Let her rip then, and let's see if we can find a real antique or two."

"What do you mean?"

"If the Laurentians are as picked over as the vicinity of Washington, I doubt we'll find anything worth buying."

"So you live in Washington now?"

"I commute between Washington and the Caymans. To be more accurate, I commute from the Cayman Islands to Washington and back. I guess you could say the Islands are my home since the BCCI's head office is there."

"Funny. I somehow thought you would settle in New York. You don't look like someone who lives in the islands."

"I don't?"

"No, especially not in the Cayman Islands."

"Oh, how come? What do you know about the Cayman Islands anyway?" But, of course, he knew the answer ahead of time. He had just forgotten.

"Plenty. As you very well know, for a while I lived in Nassau and my husband and I had friends in Cayman whom we visited often. They were always tanned, not like you. The sun is very strong there." She gave him a strange look.

He shrugged, annoyed with himself for having been careless. "I spend most of my time indoors, in the office. When I'm there, that is. But I travel a lot."

"On assignments like the one you're on now, I suppose."

"That's right." He decided it was time to change the subject. "Now tell me what's new in the Laurentians."

Micheline drove him to Les Galleries des Monts, a quaint little shopping center in the town of St. Sauveur, and proudly showed him around the elegant boutiques, the handicraft shops, and Zen's workshop, renowned for glass blowing. By the time they left the workshop, it was time for lunch.

"You should be ashamed at the way you ogled Zen's female assistants," Micheline joked as they finished their beers at Moe's, St. Sauveur's best deli.

Lonsdale ignored the remark. "How about anything else to eat or drink?"

"No thanks."

"Then let me get the bill." He paid the waiter, and they walked to her car without speaking.

"Where to?" she asked.

"I'm at your command, and if I might add, I'm having a wonderful day, so I know wherever you take me will be just fine."

She turned toward Mont Habitant. Lonsdale closed his eyes and immediately dozed off. He woke with a start when they came to a stop in the driveway of a log cabin overlooking a lake.

"Whose house is this?"

"My son's."

"Your son's? Is he expecting us?"

She was watching him intently. "No. He and his wife have gone to New York City for the week. By the way, the house is my house too."

"What do you mean?"

"When Rudi, my husband, and I lived in Nassau he owned a very successful restaurant, and we had a good life together. Then I got pregnant, and he wanted our child to be born and brought up in Switzerland, so we sold the restaurant and moved back to Pfeffikon, near Zurich. That's where Rudi's parents were from. My son, Karl, was born there, and we lived happily ever after." There was bitterness in Micheline's voice.

"Forever after? Then what are you doing in Canada working for BCCI?"

Her eyes were moist with tears. "When Karl was sixteen Rudi had a terrible car accident. He was in a coma for two years. Then he died, and I moved back here."

"Why?"

"I'd spent most of the money we had saved on trying to make Rudi healthy again. By the time he died, there was very little left."

"And?"

"I brought Karl back here, moved in with my widowed mother, got a job, and put Karl through college."

"He's your only child."

"Yes. He graduated first in his class. He's a brilliant engineer and works for Oerlikon, the Swiss weapons manufacturer, here in Quebec."

They got out of the car. "And with what I inherited from my mother when she died, plus what I saved, plus what Karl had put aside, we bought this house. Karl and his wife live here all year round, I visit on weekends." She turned the key in the lock, pushed the door open, and disappeared into the house.

The furniture in the dining room to the left of the entrance was French Canadian. The refectory table with custom-made "habitant" chairs around it was long enough to accommodate twelve people comfortably. There was an antique sideboard along the wall and in the corner, a wedge-shaped étagère.

"I'm in the den," he heard Micheline call out. "Hang your coat in the closet, take off your shoes, and come sit by me."

Micheline patted the pillow next to her on the flowery sofa. "Sit down here." She smiled as she watched him obey awkwardly. "Tell me, what troubles you about this place? You turned pale when you entered."

He flushed and almost wilted under her gaze. "I don't really know," he said sheepishly, fighting hard to cover up. The house reminded him very much of the one he used to own in the Laurentians. "I suppose this situation is just too strange, too unusual for me." He bit his lip and looked away. "Could we talk about Mr. Schwartz a little? Maybe that'll relax me a bit." He made himself laugh, trying hard to turn on the charm again.

"I suppose you want me to believe," Micheline said, "that you have no idea about this friend of yours, this man in the photograph, bringing gold coins and small ivory statues into Canada and selling them to Mr. Schwartz for cash. He called them figurines," she added inconsequentially.

"What did he call figurines?" At the mention of the word "ivory" Lonsdale had turned ice cold inside. Ivory came from Africa and general Casas was commanding troops there. "And what has all this got to do with the man in the photograph?"

"Bernard, why are you doing this?" Micheline asked. "You meddle in honest people's legitimate businesses, but you overlook the crooks, the really big crooks that run our bank, or I should say your bank, because you're part of it also." She was becoming agitated.

Lonsdale made an attempt to calm her down. "Come on Miche, take it easy and don't blame me. I'm just another small cog on the big wheel, like you."

"Don't patronize me Bernard, please. If you, just like the others, don't want to tell me what is really going on at the BCCI, that's all right, but don't take me for a simpleton." She stood up. "Get your hat and coat. There really is no reason for us to stay here any longer. On our way back to Montreal I'll tell you about Mr. Schwartz and all the things I have found out for you. Then I'll drop you off at your hotel and we'll say goodbye." Her hopes for a romantic reconciliation shattered, she ran upstairs. Lonsdale went to collect his belongings.

For the first twenty minutes the silence in the car was frigid. Past St. Jerome, Micheline began to speak. "At dinner last night Mr. Schwartz told me about one of his clients in the coin business. Actually, the man is his supplier and has been for about a year." She looked at Lonsdale who chose to say nothing, afraid to stop the flow of words.

"This supplier lives in Angola and can lay his hands on gold and silver coins and medals at very low prices. He also has ivory for sale, which, I am told, is a very rare thing because it's no longer legal to hunt elephants for their tusks. Did you know that?"

Lonsdale had the sense to look totally relaxed. "Yes, I did." he replied. Most of his important questions had just been answered.

Casas's army was headquartered in Angola, so he would have easy access to coins, medals, and ivory figurines there. He'd smuggle these artifacts into Canada without difficulty since he'd be traveling on a diplomatic passport. He'd sell them for cash to Mr. Schwartz and could then do with the untraceable money whatever he wanted. There would be no direct banking involvement and, thus, no record of any transaction. It had been careless of Casas to overlook removing the bundling strips when he deposited the money in Cayman, but he had, perhaps, needed them to prove the legitimacy of the source of the money. Had it not been for this oversight Lonsdale would never have been able to connect Casas with the Cayman deposit.

But how did Casas get to Schwartz and where was he getting the money to pay for the coins and the ivory in Africa? And, most intriguing of all, how come Micheline was sure Schwartz's supplier was the man in the photograph?

"—nothing illegal, so I don't understand why you're after him," Lonsdale heard the question in Micheline's tone and forced himself to pay attention to her.

"I'm sorry, what did you say?"

"I said that neither Mr. Schwartz nor his supplier has done anything illegal, and that I don't understand why you have to persecute them, especially since the whole thing was arranged by the bank."

"What was?"

"Are you going to tell me that you didn't know Mr. Schwartz was introduced to your man in the photograph by Mr. Siddiqui?"

"But Mr. Siddiqui said he'd never seen the man in the photograph."

"That's true, he never did."

"I don't understand."

"I didn't either at the beginning, but I was slowly able to get it all out of Mr. Schwartz. Frankly, I don't know why I bothered." Lonsdale could see that Micheline was becoming more agitated. He sighed. "Do believe me when I say I'm very grateful for your help. Take it as the gospel truth that I didn't know anything about the bank introducing the man to Mr. Schwartz."

"Pretty strange words from someone who told us at the bank on Friday that he came to Montreal to make life easier for one of his colleagues who needed help in his complicated job."

"I said 'delicate' job, not complicated."

"Fine." She made a face. "I've told you this much, so I might as well tell you everything I know." She wanted so badly to reach out and comfort him, but instinct told her now was not the time. He was hiding something from her, what and why she couldn't even guess at. "Mr. Siddiqui never met the man in the photograph. What happened was that the BCCI branch manager in Luanda wrote my manager asking for the name of a reputable coin dealer who could handle large transactions. He said he needed it for a good client. Mr. Siddiqui gave him Mr. Schwartz's name and address and then told Mr. Schwartz about the referral. Eventually your man came to Montreal, went directly to Mr. Schwartz and started doing business with him."

"And Mr. Schwartz took him at face value."

"He had a letter of introduction from a BCCI manager."

"Then tell me this. How do you know the coin supplier and the man in my photograph are one and the same?"

"To tell you the truth I'm not sure, I'm just guessing. But Mr. Schwartz did say the man had gray, close-cropped hair and wore glasses."

"So does half the male population over fifty."

"But they don't have introductions to coin dealers from BCCI managers to help them cover up large cash transactions. Maybe this is all part of a big international money laundering operation, something that perhaps the bank knows more about than it would care to admit." Micheline gave him a sidelong glance. "You did say that this man in the photograph is a colleague."

Lonsdale knew that to continue questioning Micheline would trap him in a web of half-truths and outright lies from which he'd never be able to extricate himself, so he said nothing.

He needed to talk to Siddiqui.

After Micheline dropped him off in front of his hotel, Lonsdale raced across the lobby, down the stairs, and through the underground corridor to Central Station where he grabbed the nearest public telephone. Siddiqui's daughter answered and told him that her parents were at dinner and wouldn't be back until after ten.

Disappointed, Lonsdale decided to wait it out in the comfort of a movie theater on St. Catherine Street.

At ten-thirty he called Siddiqui again, this time from the theater's lobby.

"Sorry I wasn't here to take your call earlier." As always, the banker was his polite self. "My daughter did tell me though that you'd call back, so I suppose there's no harm done."

Lonsdale was quick to reassure the man. "None at all, none at all."

"What then can I do for you?"

"I'd like to meet again, preferably outside the office, and as soon as possible. Are you free for breakfast tomorrow morning?"

"Unfortunately not. And after breakfast I have to visit one of our larger clients in Laval, the north end of the city."

"How about lunch? You will be my guest of course."

"Lunch would be fine."

"Where shall we meet?"

"Tell you what. I'll be driving south, so why don't I pick you up somewhere and we'll have a leisurely lunch at my favorite restaurant."

"What's it called and where is it?"

"La Saulaie and it's quite a bit outside the downtown core, on the South Shore. Do you know the general area?"

"I'm afraid not," Lonsdale lied. He had offered to treat Siddiqui to lunch and the banker had called him on it. La Saulaie was one of Montreal's finest—and priciest—restaurants. The man wanted to be taken for a long and expensive lunch. "What do you propose?" he asked the wily banker.

Siddiqui thought for a moment. "I presume you're staying at the Ritz, so I'll pick you up on the corner of Peel and Sherbrooke streets at noon if that's convenient. The intersection is right next to your hotel."

"That should work out quite well."

"I'll be coming down the hill from the north and I'll pick you up on the north-west corner."

"What kind of a car do you drive?"

"It's a bottle-green Aston-Martin Lagonda. You can't miss it my dear fellow; it is the only one of its kind in Montreal. By the way, is there anything in particular that you wish to speak to me about? Should I have my secretary brief me on any specific file?"

"You could, perhaps, ask her for the telephone and fax numbers of your colleague in Luanda." It was an indiscreet remark to make over the telephone, but Lonsdale reasoned that, sooner or later, Siddiqui would have to be told.

Siddiqui chuckled. "Ah, so you are aware of the recent inquiry I had from Rahman."

"Rahman?"

"Yes, Nazir Rahman. My colleague in Angola. We'll talk about him over lunch."

"Very well, Mr. Siddiqui. Forgive me for having disturbed you at home on a Sunday evening."

"My dear fellow, don't mention it. We're here to serve our good customers twenty-four hours a day, seven days a week. That's the BCCI way."

"Then I won't keep you any longer and *'à demain'*."

"À demain." Siddiqui hung up.

CHAPTER FOURTEEN

Monday
Montreal, Canada

Lonsdale was cold; of late he was always cold, but this time he really did feel rotten. His teeth chattered as he stood at the agreed-upon intersection waiting for Siddiqui. He had forgotten how cold and wet and windy Montreal could be in late October on days when the sun refused to come out of hiding.

Finally, he saw the Aston Martin gliding down the hill, and with the biting wind driving the rain into his face, he started across the street, jumping the gutter water and dodging the puddles, trying to time his arrival so that the lights would change just as he got to the other side. "Piece of cake," he muttered as he watched the driver ease over to the right to make things even simpler for him.

He noted the change with a sort of abstract fascination, a subconscious matter-of-factness rather than shock. All of a sudden the car's windshield was no longer clear and smooth and shiny. Instead, it resembled a spider's web in the center of which, however, there was no spider, but a hole—the kind high-velocity bullets made.

The dying driver's foot jerked down convulsively on the accelerator. The car picked up speed and careened into the intersection where, with a glass-shattering crash, a bus ploughed into it.

Nerves screaming, Lonsdale fought the urge to look up toward from where his training told him the bullet had come. Looking would give him away, helping the shooter find the right target this time: him. He had to get away fast, but unobtrusively.

He pretended to gawk at the smashed vehicles and made sympathetic noises while he watched the crowd around him and waited. After a decent interval he walked away with purposeful strides without a glance upward—a man going about his business, on his way to an important appointment. He hoped he'd succeeded in fooling them, but deep down he knew the game was up. Someone, he had no idea who, was stalking him, and would eventually hunt him down and kill him.

Lonsdale figured the assassin shot Siddiqui to stop him from talking to the man the banker had spoken with on the telephone the night before and whose identity the shooter could not be sure of until Lonsdale reached Siddiqui's car. By then it had been too late to kill both men. The second shot to kill Lonsdale, moving in a crowd, had probably become too difficult.

Having lost his anonymity Lonsdale was thus no longer safe. But who was hunting him and why?

He was aware that there was any number of people wanting him dead for a flood of reasons. Thirty years of cheating, lying, and killing certainly did not make him a candidate for Mister Popularity. Nonetheless, the little voice inside him, the one that had been so right so many times in the past and to which he listened very carefully, kept insisting that his troubles were directly connected with his present assignment. And that probably meant that the problem lay within the Agency. Very few people knew that Lonsdale had been given the Casas assignment and even that only a few days ago.

Walking towards his hotel Lonsdale hunkered down into his trench coat, allowing his mind to wander and his instincts to stand guard.

A young, bearded man in a black leather jacket walked by and disappeared into the crowd ahead. It was the same fellow he had noticed at the scene of the shooting: solidly built, with catlike movements, and a sharp face. Was Lonsdale being followed already?

He crossed Sherbrooke Street and headed down Mansfield toward Ben's Deli. The hostess showed him to a table next to a pillar. After looking around, he sat down with his back to the street, the embodiment of innocence.

"Vous attendez quelqu'un?" The smiling hostess wanted to know if he were waiting for someone.

"Non, non, je suis seul." Wryly, he caught his own joke: he was alone all right!

"Your waiter will be with you in a moment monsieur." The hostess smiled again. "Bon appétit."

She headed for the entrance where two student types—an acne-faced youth and his girl—stood waiting to be seated. Lonsdale watched them carefully from the corner of his eye in the long, horizontal mirror running along the wall behind the deli counter. When the girl spotted him she said something to her companion who nodded. They cut in front of the hostess and took their place at a table with an unimpeded view of both Lonsdale and the door.

"Ready to order?" The waiter was at Lonsdale's elbow.

"Sure! Might as well have lunch. A double-smoked meat, one lean, one fat, with fries and pickles."

"Anything to drink?"

"A chocolate milkshake."

The waiter shook his head in resignation and left. *Another idiot who wants to die young from high cholesterol*, he thought. Lonsdale sat back to watch his watchers.

They were young and inexperienced. The real opposition, the people who meant business, was probably waiting for him outside, or worse, at his hotel.

The waiter came back with the steaming sandwiches, and in spite of his preoccupation, Lonsdale managed a contented sigh. Smoked meat, what the Americans call pastrami, at Ben's was the best Montreal had to offer. As he bit into the fresh rye bread, the sandwich oozing with mustard and the fat drippings of the meat, he tried to estimate the number of times he must have eaten the same food in this restaurant. He'd been a regular during his four undergraduate years at McGill University, visiting this pinnacle of the smoked-meat circuit at least twice a week, every week. Why, it was here that the Agency had recruited him thirty years ago; just a few feet from where he was sitting now.

He took a long sip of his milkshake and peered down at the forlorn-looking half sandwich on his plate. He had liked the food, very much, and he was tempted to finish what was on his plate, but he didn't. There was no sense in taking unnecessary risks, not even with amateur lamplighters. Isn't that what the Brits called people who followed people?

He got up and, leaving his coat behind, headed for the washroom. He knew he was taking a risk, but he had few alternatives.

The place was just as he remembered it from his college days, perhaps a little shabbier, except that they had fixed the latch on the window leading to the alley behind the restaurant. He'd have to break the pane to make his getaway, but what was a broken window among friends anyway. He went into one of the stalls, smashed through the glass with his elbow, wrapped toilet paper around his fingers and picked out the shards. He had to stand on the trash can to get through the window, but he made it and landed, slightly winded, in the alley behind the restaurant. It was windy and miserably cold, and Lonsdale cursed the Montreal weather once more. Mercifully, the rain had stopped.

He sprinted back to De Maisonneuve Boulevard, hailed a taxi, and told the driver to take him to Alexis Nihon Plaza, the shopping mall opposite the Forum, home of the Montreal Canadiens hockey team. In the cab he took inventory of his possessions: two passports, his own and a Canadian one in the name of Donald Jackson; his wallet, which held various cards; about four hundred Canadian dollars; and a thousand U.S. dollar emergency "wad," consisting of ten one hundred dollar bills he always carried in his wallet when on a mission.

An hour later, with four more thousand dollars in his wallet, a wide-brimmed hat on his head, and a badly fitting lined trench coat over his expensive blazer, Lonsdale was ready to start thinking again.

To get the money, he had used three of his many credit cards provided by the Agency. No matter. He knew they would not pull his credit immediately; they would wait to see where he'd use the cards. So he obliged by withdrawing the cash, buying some clothes and paying for a first class return ticket to London at a travel agency, all with credit cards.

He took the metro to Place Bonaventure, walked up University Street, bluffed his way into the private St. James Club through his reciprocal membership in the New York Athletic Club, and with a grateful sigh, sank into a comfortable armchair in the second-floor lounge with its large windows overlooking the branch of the BCCI where the late Akhtar Siddiqui had labored so hard.

It was three in the afternoon and Lonsdale wanted to know the extent of the surveillance his opponents had mounted against the branch in general and Micheline in particular.

Surveillance is not easy to spot, but to a trained eye it is usually obvious. In the parking lot on the side street opposite the BCCI two men kept getting in and out of a car strategically located so that its rear view mirror allowed an unobstructed view of the branch's main entrance. They took turns to walk past the branch, peering inside casually during each pass. One had a hat and a jacket both of which he took off from time to time to look different; the other had two hats and a pipe. The backup team, which the fellow with the two hats visited every fifteen minutes or so, was in a panel truck parked a block away. To Lonsdale, the operation looked very professional.

He evaluated his position while watching the action. It wasn't clear whether it was the Cubans who were after him, or his own colleagues who did not want him sticking his nose into places where it didn't belong. Why else would they first deny him access to Fernandez and then have Morton order him to return to base? What was the reason for stopping him from ferreting out whether Fidel was dealing in drugs? Unless, of course, they knew something he didn't know.

Perhaps Fernandez was a plant and his story a hoax, a reverse sting. But if that were the case why wouldn't Morton have told him? Maybe Morton didn't know. Or was he just pretending not to know? Lonsdale doubted that. He and Morton were too close for that—or were they?

The killing of Siddiqui troubled him deeply. Was it intended to be a warning or was it a genuine miss, the gunman aiming at him, but hitting Siddiqui instead. Unlikely. The banker was killed to shut him up.

He decided the only logical answer was that the Agency was cutting him off from information. This meant that the Agency knew about the BCCI in Angola looking for a reliable coin dealer in Canada. And how did they find out? They couldn't have. *But the Cubans knew*!

Lonsdale cursed himself for his stupidity. It was his own remark to Siddiqui on the telephone that had tipped them off. And that's also how whoever killed Siddiqui knew about the pickup on the corner of Peel and Sherbrooke Streets. Hell, he had given them over twelve hours to get their gunman into position, and the man had not failed them.

If they knew about BCCI Luanda, did they know about Mr. Schwartz? If so, Schwartz was as good as dead or perhaps dead already.

What about Micheline? As far as he could remember he had not called her from anywhere, and nobody knew that he had seen her on Friday night and again on Sunday. Unless, of course, she had told someone.

He left his vantage point at four-thirty, walked over to Avis at Dominion Square, rented a Taurus using a credit card, and drove to Montreal's "other" airport, Mirabel, about thirty miles north of the city. He left the car in the fifteen-minute parking zone at the departures level and took the shuttle bus to Dorval Airport from the arrivals level. A twenty-minute cab ride got him to within a block of where Micheline lived.

He walked up the street in the pelting rain, head buried in the collar of his ill-fitting coat, his new hat almost completely hiding his face. He checked for surveillance, but could see none. To make sure, he went past the building for two full blocks and doubled back, checking continuously. He was going to pass the building again, but as he drew level with the door he saw a boy in the lobby, struggling with a large black dog, trying to get it through the half-open door. Boy and dog were dripping wet from the freezing rain and hopelessly enmeshed in the animal's leash. Lonsdale gave the lad a hand and the three slipped through the open door like butter, for all intents and purposes a happy, laughing, joshing father-son-and-dog team.

He got out of the elevator on the fifteenth floor and walked down three flights to Micheline's level. He used the fire escape to get to the outside passageway running along the rear of the building and carefully tiptoed past Micheline's apartment. He couldn't see into the kitchen, but, through the drawn blinds, the TV flickered. Was she alone?

Lonsdale was cold, miserable, and very angry. The bastards in Washington were in the process of betraying him again. To them, loyalty was, as always, a one-way street.

He rang the bell. "*Qui est là?*"

"It's me, Micheline. Bernard."

The door flew open. "For God's sake come in out of the rain. What are you doing on the back balcony anyway?" Micheline was in her dressing gown, a cup of tea in her hand, her eyes bloodshot from crying.

"I'm freezing," Lonsdale replied with teeth chattering, shaking the water off his hat and messing up the kitchen floor in the process. "I'm also hungry, thirsty, out-of-sorts, and in need of information."

Micheline gave him a questioning look. "What's going on, Bernard? They were going crazy at the bank this afternoon." Her voice broke. She sounded agitated and very concerned. "The police came after lunch and said Mr. Siddiqui had been murdered. They sealed his office and then questioned the senior staff. After a while they went away, and we were allowed to leave. I only got home an hour ago." She shuddered. "Has all this got something to do with you?"

Shivering, Lonsdale looked at his watch. It was ten to ten. "I'm very sorry about your boss, Micheline, believe me. I know he was murdered. I don't know why or by whom, but I intend to find out." He made an effort to stop his teeth from chattering. Micheline noticed.

She put down her cup and reached for his hat and coat. "Let me help you out of your wet clothes before you catch cold. Come, I'll make you a cup of hot chocolate. If you want, I'll make you something to eat, too."

"I want—"

"Keep me company while I get everything ready." She hung his hat and coat on the hook on the back of the kitchen door. "Start explaining yourself. Why didn't you call first, anyway?"

Lonsdale took a deep breath. "I didn't call because I didn't want anyone to know that I was coming to see you." He watched her closely. "I need to ask you some questions."

"Before I answer any questions you had better explain your strange behavior yesterday." She pulled her dressing gown tight around her shoulders in a defensive gesture.

"That's not easy." He sat down at the kitchen table. How much could he tell her about what was going on? He decided to play for time. "You're right, there is something very strange going on at the BCCI," he began, trying as gently as he could to ease her into the nightmare he knew was bound to follow. "Mr. Schwartz's friend is part of it."

Micheline's shoulders tensed, but she continued to assemble the makings of an omelet. "Continue. I'm listening."

"Did you see Mr. Schwartz today?" He held his breath.

"He came in around four to make a deposit and waved to me. We didn't get a chance to talk. I was busy with the police." She deftly cracked two eggs and poured them into the sizzling pan.

"Did the police question him, too?"

"I don't know. Certainly not in the bank. Why?"

"Just wondering. Do you think you could get in touch with him tonight?"

"I suppose I could, but why should I?"

Lonsdale looked at Micheline, standing with her back to him, concentrating on getting his omelet done just right—liquidy, the way he liked it—and an immense sense of self-pity engulfed him.

He was cold, wet, tired, alone, and feeling very insecure—he was weary of being betrayed by his own people. He longed for the days before he had become Lonsdale, days when he belonged somewhere and to someone, when he had someone he could trust.

He wondered how close her relationship with Schwartz really was. *Should I confide in her or leave Schwartz to the wolves, whoever they were?* he asked himself. The little voice in his head helped him make up his mind. *You need Schwartz, you idiot. Besides, it's wrong to let an innocent man die.*

Choosing his words very carefully, he said, "You should, because I don't want to be responsible for yet another person's death," he whispered.

She spun around to face him, incomprehension in her eyes. "What on earth are you talking about?"

He stood up and held out his arms to her. "Help me, Miche. I need someone in whom I can confide. Problem is I've forgotten how." Shaking his head, he sat down and covered his face with his hands.

CHAPTER FIFTEEN

Monday through Wednesday
Montreal, Canada

A decade of self-imposed psychological privation is hard to overcome, especially for a loner laboring in an environment of fear and constant deception. Lonsdale knew that if he started to talk it would be hard for him to stop. He would probably say too much and jeopardize not only his own, but other people's lives as well.

After the millisecond it took for this to flash through his mind he concluded that he didn't give a damn about his own life and that he was deathly weary of running from his past. It came to him that he would find peace only by unburdening himself of the guilt that gnawed at him with relentless consistency.

There was yet another factor prompting him to break his rule of absolute discretion. He felt very bitter about having apparently been abandoned by his friend and colleague, Jim Morton. How could Morton do such a thing after Lonsdale had volunteered to shoulder the responsibility of the mission alone?

Lonsdale needed an ally to help him stay alive and to assist him in completing his mission. Micheline qualified as a candidate on both counts.

But was Micheline trustworthy? Was she discrete? Was there a chance she was working or at least in contact with the opposition. And who was the opposition, the Cubans, the Cartel, his "friends" at the Agency? Most likely the Cubans. There was no way to know.

Lonsdale opted to take the risk. He began to talk.

He told her how, having been recruited by the Agency in Montreal, he had spent years undercover in Cuba; how later he had roamed Latin America on behalf of the Agency; how in the early eighties he had managed to "turn" a Cuban intelligence officer operating out of Montreal, who was doubling as the paymaster of a group of Arab terrorists for the USSR. Through him, Lonsdale told her, he had become involved in anti-terrorist work, which ultimately created a situation that lead to his wife's death.

Micheline broke into tears when she found out about how Lonsdale's wife had died. She was horror stricken when he told her about his life in the "wet" end of the business. They talked late into the night, their limbs entwined in her huge widow's bed.

"I knew that you'd come back to me somehow," she kept repeating until, completely drained emotionally and physically exhausted, they fell asleep around three. Surprisingly, they awoke early next morning, well rested and strangely exhilarated, anxiously turning to see if the other were real, and still there. They made love again, this time far more passionately than the night before, reliving the glory days of their youth, making up for lost time, for lost opportunities.

At breakfast, Lonsdale broached the subject of Schwartz once more. "I've got to talk to him, Miche. He's my only link with Casas, and I've got to get to Casas fast."

She came over to give him a tender kiss. "I'll talk to Mr. Schwartz for you. What do you want me to say?"

"That I need to see him, and soon."

"You know he won't do it. He must be quite shaken up. He was very friendly with Mr. Siddiqui."

"Miche, you've got to convince him. It's for his own good, too. Talking to me is sort of like life insurance. They'll leave him alone if they know he's already told someone else what he knows."

"Tell me exactly what you want me to tell him." She was getting ready to leave for the office; he had told her earlier to continue her daily routine so as not to arouse suspicion.

"Get him to take you to lunch. Then explain the connection between Siddiqui's death and his ivory-dealing friend. Tell him Siddiqui was killed by a rival gang member trying to get in on the ivory trade."

"And what do I tell him about you?"

"Tell him I'm an undercover agent for the bank, someone whom you've known for years. Also tell him not to mention coming to meet me to anyone." Lonsdale was improvising on the fly.

"When do you want to see him?"

"Tonight would be best, but if it's a no-go, tomorrow will do." Lonsdale knew that every hour's delay exponentially increased Schwartz's chances of dying, but he did not want to alarm Micheline too much.

"Anything else?" She was at the door.

"Yes, a couple of things. You know me as Bernard Lands, which is my real name, but, officially, Bernard Lands is dead. In Washington I live under the name of Robert Lonsdale, and when in the field, I use whatever name fits the circumstances."

"Like Don Jackson?"

He nodded.

"What's the other thing?"

"Don't call me here, whatever you do. They may have the phone bugged."

"That's great, just great."

He got up and put his arms around her. "Don't worry, Miche. Things will work out, you'll see. All we need is a few days, a week at the most."

"Will you be all right here? What'll you do all day?"

He let go of her. "Wait for you to come home, of course." He gave her a hug and a kiss. "Let me give you some money while you call a cab."

She was incensed. "We're in this together, so put your money away. I'm quite capable of carrying my weight."

He wouldn't hear of it. "Miche, you don't know how expensive it can get when you're on the run. Take the money—here's a thousand bucks—and keep it for me. I might need to borrow it back from you." He stuck the money into her coat pocket and pushed her out the door.

He spent the day cooped up in her apartment, alternately resting and watching TV, letting his subconscious worry about the mess he was in. By not thinking about the Schwartzes and Casases of this world he was able to get real rest, rest he knew he had to accumulate so he could face the chaos he'd have to cope with in the days to come.

Micheline returned home for a few minutes after six.

"I couldn't get to Mr. Schwartz till five, but I've got a dinner date with him tonight at seven," she reported, out of breath. "Come, talk to me while I have a quick bath, and tell me what you want me to do tonight."

He sat on the toilette seat while she bathed, and together they developed a rendezvous procedure that would allow Lonsdale to meet Schwartz under secure conditions.

On Wednesday, just before noon, Lonsdale took Micheline's car and drifted down Cote-des-Neiges toward Sherbrooke Street, cut the corner at St. Matthew, and turned into the parking lot next to the police station on De Maisonneuve Boulevard. Her car was a comfortable Audi 200 that he would have really enjoyed driving had he not been so preoccupied.

The lot was half-empty, just as Micheline said it would be, and he had no difficulty finding a spot alongside the lane running past the back of the building.

He smiled wryly at the incongruity of leaving his car next to a police cruiser while presumably being sought by his adopted country's secret police. He checked his watch. It showed twelve twenty-eight, two minutes to go, if Schwartz was good at keeping his word.

He walked over to the attendant and paid for the parking space, and then with a great show of having forgotten something, walked back toward his car. Schwartz's Mercedes pulled up behind a parked police cruiser just as Lonsdale got there. He slid into the seat beside the coin dealer who accelerated away smoothly.

"Mr. Gould?"

"That's me Mr. Schwartz. Where shall we go for lunch?"

"I was told to drive you out to the West Island."

"Just checking, Mr. Schwartz, just checking. Please do drive out to the West Island and take Highway 20 so I can see if we're being followed."

"Are we being followed?"

"I don't think so."

"What kind of a name is Gould?"

Lonsdale knew perfectly well what the old man was driving at, but pretended ignorance. "What do you mean?"

The coin dealer gave him a quick sideways look. "You Jewish?" He was refreshingly direct.

"Half," replied Lonsdale, lying without hesitation, while congratulating himself on his foresight. He had anticipated the question and had prepared Micheline for it. He would say he was partly Jewish to gain Schwartz's confidence.

"Which half?" Schwartz questioned. "What I want to know is, was it your father or your mother who was Jewish?"

Lonsdale judged the time ripe to take the lead. "Mr. Schwartz we're not here to discuss my ancestry or, for that matter, yours. I'm here to try to protect you, and I need your help if I'm to succeed."

"And why would you want to protect me? I'm not your client."

"But you are the bank's client, one of its good clients, and the bank is my employer. Quite frankly, we don't want any more accidents."

"Accidents?"

"Yes, accidents. Like the one that happened to Mr. Siddiqui."

"That was no accident. That was murder." Schwartz sounded both indignant and worried.

"You're right." Lonsdale folded down the sun visor and, using the vanity mirror, surveyed the cars behind them. They were on the expressway, leading to Dorval Airport and the traffic, though heavy, was moving steadily. It wasn't sparse enough to allow him to draw conclusions. "At the airport traffic circle turn left, and go down toward the river. I know a little Swiss restaurant, Trudi's it's called, on Lakeshore Drive. Let's try our luck there."

In the restaurant's parking lot Schwartz opened the door to get out. Lonsdale pulled him back. "Hold on my friend," he said firmly, but kindly. "First we talk then we eat."

"In the parking lot you want to talk? Are you *meshugah*?"

"No, Mr. Schwartz, I'm not crazy. It's safer here than in the restaurant, so let's not waste time. How long have you known that your friend the ivory dealer is Cuban?"

The old man was taken aback. "Who said I knew?"

"I said you knew. I need information, and I need it in a hurry, so stop answering questions with questions."

"And if I don't?"

"Then I'll leave you here, call a cab, and go home."

"So go ahead!"

With his hand on the door latch Lonsdale turned toward the coin dealer and gave him a big, honest smile. "You're a stubborn soon-to-be-dead old man, my friend. I'll ask you once more, will you help me save your life or do you insist on being stubborn and dying before your time?" He opened the car door slightly.

Schwartz put his hand on Lonsdale's arm. "What's your hurry?"

Lonsdale pulled the door shut. "That's better. Now, please Mr. Schwartz, tell me. How long have you known that your ivory supplier was Cuban?"

"It's a long story—"

"We have all afternoon." Lonsdale sighed and tilted his seat back.

"So where do you want me to begin?"

"At the very beginning."

Schwartz had met General Casas through the good offices of Akhtar Siddiqui and his colleague, Nazir Rahman, the BCCI manager in Luanda. Rahman had asked Siddiqui to identify a Canadian coin dealer of repute, able to handle substantial transactions involving rare coins, medals, and ivory figurines originating in Western Africa. Siddiqui was eager to help. He wanted to demonstrate to Schwartz, an important client, that the BCCI was able to reciprocate business with business.

Siddiqui asked his colleague to provide a letter of introduction for Casas addressed to Schwartz, which the general was to present to the coin dealer at a meeting Siddiqui would set up. Siddiqui would not be present since he had no desire to know the details of Schwartz's business.

The first meeting had taken place two years earlier and turned out to be a resounding success. Schwartz was enthralled by the samples Casas had brought him, and the general was eager to sell.

"Then what happened?" Lonsdale asked.

"Nothing special." Schwartz was getting edgy. "The general—he told me straightaway who he was—General Casas kept bringing me goods, mainly ivory and gold and silver coins, which I resold in the normal course of business."

"At a fair profit, I presume."

Schwartz spread his hands. "I can't complain. Can we go and eat now? I'm hungry and thirsty."

"We're almost there. Hold on for a few more minutes." Lonsdale decided it was time to ask the crucial question. He turned and looked Schwartz straight in the eyes. "Why did you give Casas a million dollars in cash two weeks ago?"

"It was his money, that's why. He asked me for it and I gave it to him."

"His money?" Lonsdale didn't follow.

"Sure. He told me he was entitled to keep a quarter of the money I paid for the goods he sold me. So three-quarters I sent to the Cuban government in Havana by wire transfer and one quarter I kept for the general in the bank here."

"In Mr. Siddiqui's bank?"

"That's right. In the late Akhtar Siddiqui's bank—*aleva sholem*— may he rest in peace."

"Amen," said Lonsdale, greatly relieved. His theory had just been proven. "Come on, my friend, let's go. I'm buying you lunch."

They both ordered wiener schnitzel with mashed potatoes, cucumber salad, a glass of red wine, and Perrier water. His mouth full of veal, Schwartz pointed his fork at his inquisitor. "All right, Mr. Detective, it's my turn to ask a question."

"Go ahead."

"All the money is accounted for, right?"

"Right."

"General Casas has been very correct and precise in his business dealings, right?"

"Right."

"Then, since Mr. Siddiqui was only our banker and not a part of the deal, who would want to kill him and why?"

"That, my friend, is the sixty-four thousand dollar question, a question I cannot answer just yet." Lonsdale was temporizing as he went, along lines carefully thought out the night before. "My theory is, and I repeat, it's only a theory, that General Casas may have competitors in Angola who want to horn in on his coin and ivory business. Obviously, they can't use you, so they must have gone to poor Siddiqui to help them get started. He must have said no, so they killed him."

Schwartz was silent for a while. "But why did they not come to me directly? I could have handled their business and the general's too!"

"For two reasons, Mr. Schwartz. First, you're not a banker and cannot help these people, who are very likely big-time crooks, to launder money. Second, they will probably contact you too, and sooner than you think. Since I'm sure that once you've met them you will not want to do business with them, you will tell them so and they will then threaten you."

"Threaten me? With what?"

"To start with, they'll try to blackmail you." Lonsdale glanced at Schwartz who wasn't looking too happy. "None of us is as pure as the driven snow, so I'm sure they could come up with something, like incomplete tax returns, that would get you all fussed and bothered."

The old man was beginning to sweat, but Lonsdale was relentless. "Having met you, though, I don't think you'd allow them to blackmail you."

"Damn right I wouldn't! I haven't done anything wrong, and they can go to hell."

"I'm sure that's true, and they would soon realize that they were barking up the wrong tree."

"So?"

"They would switch tactics. They would threaten you physically if you didn't play along."

"You mean, kill me?" All of a sudden the old man lost his appetite.

"Mr. Schwartz, I don't have all the answers. I'm just guessing, but I'm afraid you may be right."

"So what do you think I should do?"

"Get hold of General Casas. Arrange a meeting among the three of us and have him help us get to the bottom of this thing!"

Schwartz took a hefty gulp of his spritzer, red wine mixed with Perrier water. "You may have something there, Mr. Detective," he finally said. "Will you help me set it up?"

"Of course I will."

"OK, so where do we meet him?"

"No idea. Here perhaps?" He looked at Schwartz.

"No, no, that won't work. He was just here. He won't be able to get away for longer than a weekend."

"Where is he now?"

"I think he is heading back to Angola."

"Where do you suggest then? London?"

"No, Budapest."

"Why Budapest?"

"He can fly from Luanda to Prague, and from Prague to Budapest on Czechoslovak Airlines, cheaply and at no risk. I can get in and out of Hungary easily also."

Lonsdale raised his glass. "Budapest it is then."

They clinked glasses, then got down to the nitty-gritty of planning the trip.

CHAPTER SIXTEEN

Wednesday
Montreal, Canada and Havana, Cuba

Schwartz dropped Lonsdale off near Micheline's car. Lonsdale walked east for a dozen blocks to make sure no one was following him. Then he visited the Montreal Museum of Fine Arts and, around five, retraced his steps, timing his arrival so as to get to the parking lot at the height of the rush hour. Forfeiting his deposit, he drove off unceremoniously, his destination the CN garage behind the Queen Elizabeth Hotel.

Obsessed by the thought that Micheline might lead the opposition to him by being trailed, Lonsdale had painstakingly explained to her how to make sure she was not being followed: "When you leave the bank after work, go downstairs to the Promenade of Boutiques in Place Ville Marie. Take your time, pretend you're shopping. Even better, buy yourself something nice."

"Like what?"

"Why not a Dior or a Chanel night gown?" He'd loved it that she blushed.

"You're right. Why not?"

"I'm serious. Do buy yourself something and while you're shopping retrace your steps. Zigzag among the stores. If there's someone following, you're bound to spot him. He'll have to let you pass by him at least twice, maybe three times."

"And if someone *is* following me?"

"Whether there is someone or not, here's what you do. Head for the Queen Elizabeth Hotel and take the elevator to the sixth floor. The person following you will have two options. He can either stay downstairs watching the elevator banks and the main lobby so he can spot you when you come down again, which sooner or later you will have to do. Right?"

Micheline had nodded.

"Or, he can get into the elevator with you to find out where you get off. But he can't leave the elevator on the same floor so he'll go up one floor and then run downstairs to the lobby, call for backup and start asking questions at the reception about the people registered on the floor where you had gotten off."

Micheline had smiled. It all sounded like a game.

"As soon as you get out of the elevator, slide into the housekeeper's locker room just left of the elevators. It's always open. Stay there for five minutes then use the stairwell farthest from the elevators to make your way down to the banquet halls on the second floor. Listen for someone going down the stairs ahead of you."

"And if there is someone?"

"Go back and use the other stairwell. On the second floor, go back to the kitchens. At the rear of the hotel take the staff elevator to street level and cross over into the CN parking building behind the hotel."

"How will I find you?"

"Take the elevator up to the third floor. I'll be waiting at the door. If I'm not there, stop to touch up your lipstick for three minutes, and if I'm still not there, start looking for your car. It will be parked as near to the elevators as possible. The keys will be taped under the right front fender. Get in and drive home." He had looked at her dubiously. "Have you got all this?"

She had laughed. "Sure. It sounds challenging."

"Don't laugh. This is a deadly game. If you make a mistake and you lead them to me, we both could die."

Her face had clouded, and he felt he had to give her a reassuring hug.

"What about you?" she had asked.

"Don't worry about me. I'll contact you later." He had kissed her lightly on the lips and added silently 'If I'm still alive.'

Lonsdale got to the CN Building at a quarter past five and parked Micheline's car two lanes away from the elevators. Then he found a strategically located car in the lane leading to the elevators with a hood that he could open. This allowed him to hide behind the raised hood while watching Micheline fix her lipstick and start searching for her Audi.

When he was sure that she had not grown a tail he sprinted over to her car and waited for her to find it.

"Any trouble?" Lonsdale asked as they got in.

"No, not really."

Lonsdale was anxious. He had been waiting for her for over two hours. "What do you mean by 'not really'?"

Micheline gave him an angelic look. "It took me a long time to find something suitable to buy."

He grinned, relieved. "There was no pursuit then?" he asked, just to be sure.

"None that I could spot. But if there was I lost him at the hotel."

"It may have been a her, rather than a him."

She shrugged. "*Peut-être*. But no one came down the stairs before me or after me, I am sure. And when I left the hotel through the back door I crossed the street and stood behind the cashier's booth here, watching if someone came out after me. No one did." She blew him a kiss.

Glancing into the rearview mirror he made a sharp turn onto Route 20, in the direction of Micheline's country house.

By the time they stopped for groceries in Saint Sauveur his mood had changed from elation to apprehension. He was getting very worried about his situation.

"Nothing is ever what it seems," he muttered.

Micheline looked at him questioningly, but he just shook his head and kept on driving. It seemed fairly obvious that General Casas was involved in drug dealing. The amounts of money flowing through Cayman were too large to have any other explanation and, clearly, Casas wanted the United States to know about it. Why else would he have tried to chase Fernandez into the CIA's not-so-open arms?

And why would Morton suddenly want to call off the operation? Who ordered him to do so? What did someone higher up than Morton know that Morton did not know? Or did Morton know?

It was pitch-black when they arrived at Micheline's house, but a spotlight turned on automatically when she approached the door so they didn't have to fumble around in the dark with the parcels.

The house had a magic effect on him; it calmed his fears and soothed his spirit and made him lay his preoccupations aside.

"Why don't you start a fire, Bernard," she called over her shoulder after dinner as she walked toward the kitchen to leave their dirty dishes by the sink. "I want to go upstairs and freshen up."

He smiled at the promise in her voice as he fetched dry logs from the back porch. He built a good bed of kindling that caught quickly, and soon he had a roaring fire going. After putting on a sultry piano blues CD, he closed the shutters, and then went to tidy up the kitchen.

Because of the running water he didn't hear Micheline come downstairs until she was right behind him. "Turn around, my darling," her voice was low and husky, "and see what you've bought for me." Surprised, he spun around and saw she was wearing her new negligee, a striking classic black satin sheath with thin spaghetti straps, decidedly sexy and utterly female. As he reached for her she backed away, drawing him into the living room where she'd spread a thick white eiderdown in front of the crackling fire. He bent to kiss her hungrily. Her response to him was immediate and totally trusting as he opened his arms to envelop her and pull her down gently on top of him where, fumbling blindly with desire, she helped him shed his shirt, his pants, his shorts. "I love you for not giving up on me," he murmured hesitantly, as if testing the words he hadn't spoken for a long time. He watched her glistening eyes in the fire's flickering light. "I'm grateful," he whispered and laid his face on one breast, his hand tenderly lifting the other to cup the satisfying weight in his palm.

For a while she held him close, stroking his face silently while his thumb idly traced the deep tan aureola surrounding her nipple. The steady motion was almost hypnotic. Slowly her nipples became tighter and longer, his hand rougher and more demanding until she couldn't stand it another second and she locked his head in place for him to suck one elongated wickedly alert nipple and pull it deep into his needy lips.

Sinking into her spilling wetness to begin that urgent slippery climb through building heat, faster and faster, he brought her to the very brink of immortality before he rode them both over the edge to the achingly long, hot streaming release they each desperately sought. She arched her back as the aftershocks went on and on.

When at last his pulse had slowed and his respiration was partially restored to its normal state, he rolled over on his back, grinning hugely. "Oh, sweet woman, I'm so happy I'm me!" And Micheline, stretching her glorious body wantonly in the glow of the dying fire, simply smiled in that mysterious way that truly satiated women who are deeply in love smile.

On Wednesday night Oscar De la Fuente could barely restrain himself from shouting at his petulant wife. She was taking forever with her makeup and had changed her jewelry three times. Finally, a totally disgusted De la Fuente could stand waiting no longer. "Tere, if you're not ready to go within five minutes, we're not going." He looked at his watch. "It's just not worth going anymore. Everyone will have eaten." He let his voice trail off. He didn't feel like talking; he felt like screaming.

"Come on Oscar, cool it." His wife wasn't fussed at all. "You like us to get there late. You get off on all the men gawking me as much as I do." She gave him a wink, got up and rubbed herself against him. "Especially since you know that you can get what they want so badly anytime you want it." She fingered his crotch then twisted away from him smoothly. "Come on, big boy, let's go. And, do me a favor today. Drive faster than usual."

In a hurry to see Spiegel again, he surprised her by getting to the Marina Hemmingway in twenty minutes. He was so busy thinking, he didn't say a word during the trip.

The opportunity to speak with Spiegel presented itself only after dinner when, as usual, his wife went off with her friends to gossip and touch up her makeup. Spiegel rose and De la Fuente followed him to the men's room. They sat down in adjacent stalls. The Englishman slid a slip of paper under the partition between them. His note was brief and to the point: "F. has been neutralized. The soldier is under 24-hour surveillance by our people."

De la Fuente used the facilities, then carefully flushed the note down the pan with the toilet paper and went to wash his hands. Spiegel stood at the sink next to his, and started to tell him an elaborate joke. When he stopped talking the Cuban laughed and opened the water taps wide: "Maybe we should neutralize the soldier too." He spoke so softly that Spiegel could barely hear him above the noise of the rushing water. They headed for the towel machines.

"Too risky," the Englishman said, almost to himself, "and too early. We'll just watch him closely."

"Have your people snatch him. I'd feel safer."

"No, that would arouse suspicion, and we need more time."

"If he opens his mouth to the wrong people our goose is cooked." Oscar was pleading.

"Don't you worry, he won't—just yet."

They returned to the dining room, where the band was playing a rumba. De la Fuente asked his wife to dance.

CHAPTER SEVENTEEN

Wednesday
Luanda, Angola

Brigadier General Casas's private air force was based in Angola, but the general, who hated waste, returned to duty from vacation, as was his custom, via commercial airliner. His superior, Raul Castro, appreciated the gesture, and to help make traveling easier for the general, provided him with a diplomatic passport in the name of Carlos Casares.

To get back to Angola, Casas had to fly to Prague first and catch the connecting flight, a real rattler—a Tupolev—to Luanda. By the time he got there on Wednesday night he was tired and out of sorts. To make matters worse, the air-conditioning was failing at the Hotel Presidente, headquarters of Cuba's forces in Angola just around the corner from the head office of the National Bank and two blocks from the beach.

The sweltering heat did nothing to improve Casas's temper. But he was used to physical hardship and had disciplined himself to be in control even when fatigue made him irritable.

Colonel Font, his chief of staff in Angola, was still at his desk when Casas reached the hotel.

"Welcome back, general," the colonel, a tanned and savvy soldier in his mid-fifties, extended a muscular arm in greeting. "Glad to have someone with whom to share the fuck-up that's going on around here."

Casas resented the remark, but didn't show it. "Why? What's up?"

"The usual shit. I guess organizing an orderly troop withdrawal is more difficult than mounting an attack."

"Or perhaps we are not used to withdrawing," mused Casas dryly.

"Maybe, but if they'd let us get on with it without interference we'd do a better job of it."

"And just what do you mean by that?"

"Hell, General, we keep getting these directives from Department Z to do what they call odd jobs for them, jobs that require lots of energy, time, and specialized knowledge, when they know we're stretched to the limit here as is."

"We always were." Casas was beginning to suspect what Font was driving at.

"They want us to organize another ivory hunt, as if we had nothing better to do."

Casas's gut constricted at the news. "On whose orders?" he asked, but knew the answer in advance.

"Deputy Minister De la Fuente. He was on the scrambler earlier asking if you had arrived."

"And?"

"He said he'll call back tomorrow sometime."

"He must have gotten back from lunch early." Both men laughed and Casas went into his office. He glanced at the pile of messages on his desk, sighed, and went out on the balcony.

The view was, as always at night, magnificent. In the full moonlight he could see the horseshoe-shape bay stretch out below him, bathed in the fluorescence of a calm sea gently lapping at the sand. The lights along the road running parallel to the sea hinted at a cosmopolitan city nearby, not unlike Rio de Janeiro, or Havana for that matter. This, Casas knew was an illusion. Luanda resembled Havana perhaps, but not Rio, for the night was kind, hiding the decaying city, softening the harshness of reality.

Cuba's soldiers had first come to Angola in 1975, shortly after the country became independent of Portugal. The new government needed help to stop the South Africans who did not want a sovereign black country as their neighbor. Angola, with the yoke of colonialism removed, was definitely headed for the socialist camp, looking to the Soviet Union for economic assistance. But the Russians themselves were having a hard time; they were pouring eight million dollars into Cuba every day, and they wanted something in return. So Fidel Castro was told to provide military aid to the Angolans and not to look to the USSR for payment of its soldiers' upkeep. The troops, well trained and equipped with the latest Soviet weaponry, were duly transported to Luanda by ships of Cuba's modern merchant fleet and told to make do with their meager wages, paid to them in military scrip.

The pillage of Angola's middle class that followed was remarkable even by modern standards. Boatloads of furniture, household, office and factory equipment, plumbing fixtures torn out of walls, doors and windows removed from private homes, cars, trucks, motorcycles, and bicycles, left Porto Amboin for Cuba en masse, courtesy of Castro's underpaid soldiers who quickly realized that the homes of those well-to-do Portuguese who had quit Angola because they did not wish to live in a socialist country had been left behind unguarded.

Portugal was outraged, but powerless to help its citizens alone. In return for certain military concessions in the Indian Ocean, Portugal enlisted Uncle Sam's help. The States, no friend of Fidel, was glad to be of assistance. One fine day a Cuban merchant ship, loaded to the gunnels with toilet bowls, sinks, and bathtubs was discreetly intercepted by a U.S. submarine and escorted to Puerto Rico. The cargo was unloaded and the ship sent on its way.

No one complained. Publicity would have been too painful for all parties concerned. So the pilfering stopped.

Casas returned to his office, leaving the balcony doors open behind him, grabbed a handful of papers off the pile marked "urgent," flopped into an easy chair, and began to read. It was around one in the morning when he came across what, to the uninitiated, appeared to be a routine request for payment from the Hungarian Ministry of National Defense. Addressed to Casas personally, it said that the Cubans owed the equivalent of seven hundred and fifty thousand U.S. dollars and suggested a meeting in Budapest to settle the matter. Casas was taken aback. From the wording, Casas saw that the request was from Schwartz, the coin dealer, and not the Ministry.

Why did the Montrealer want to see him so urgently?

"It must be serious if he's asking for help," Casas muttered as he reread the fax. Schwartz wanted to see him on Sunday, so Casas would have to leave Luanda on Saturday morning at the latest, which wouldn't be a problem. He'd go via CESA to Prague, and then to Budapest. He had made the trip a number of times.

For the next hour Casas kept at it, reducing the pile by half before he quit and, fully clothed, fell asleep on the couch opposite his desk.

CHAPTER EIGHTEEN

Thursday
Montreal, Canada

Micheline and Lonsdale got up while it was still dark.

"I told Schwartz," Lonsdale said between mouthfuls of yogurt and cornflakes, "to get a message to Casas asking him for a meeting in Budapest."

"Why Budapest?"

"It's easy for both of them to access. Schwartz deals in coins there with the government and so does Casas."

"Deals in coins?" Micheline was no slouch.

"No, my darling. Casas buys ammunition from the Hungarians. They are the designated manufacturers of small arms ammo for the Soviet Bloc."

"I see." Micheline took a sip of her coffee. "And I suppose you'll go along with Mr. Schwartz for the ride."

"Not quite. He'll make his way to Hungary via London. I'll go via Amsterdam. The object of the exercise is for Schwartz to arrange a meeting between Casas and me."

Micheline pursed her lips. "Do you think Casas will cooperate?"

"It seems the two meet often in Budapest, whenever Casas has stuff to sell."

Micheline was puzzled. "I thought Casas brought the stuff to Canada for Mr. Schwartz. At least that's what he told me."

"That too, but only the finer pieces. The bulk stuff they transact in Hungary."

"Why?"

"For many reasons, one of which I suspect is tax driven."

"And I suppose it somehow involves the BCCI."

"Maybe, but that doesn't concern us." Lonsdale collected the breakfast dishes and placed them in the dishwasher. "What does concern us is that Schwartz should not chicken out at the last minute."

"And how will we know that?"

"He's supposed to come to see you in the bank late today to confirm he's going."

Micheline shook her head. "He usually comes in around lunchtime, so he can try to talk me into going to eat with him."

"He won't this time."

"Why?"

"He'll wait until he has General Casas's reply to the message he was supposed to have sent him yesterday."

He helped her on with her coat, then kissed and held her for a while before gently cautioning her: "Drive carefully and come home safe and sound. These country roads are slippery." He watched her drive away.

As he jogged along a country road, Lonsdale breathed deeply, enjoying the crisp, cold air. Although the trees had lost their foliage to winter, making them look sad and spiny, there were plenty of magnificent evergreens to lend color to the landscape. The lake, a metallic gray under the fall sky, glittered harshly in the light of a pale, rising sun.

"It'll freeze over soon," he murmured as he ran up the hill and turned onto the main road. He forced himself to think positively and to feel good about his body, which he was keeping in good shape, about his mind, which seemed to be sharpening with the improvement in his physical condition, and about his relationship with Micheline. He was beginning to think things might just work out somehow.

As he ran, he tried to figure out what was happening. He thought that the Cubans had probably shot Siddiqui, because they did not want anyone with knowledge of Casas's affairs to talk to the CIA.

Lonsdale wondered if it was the Cubans who were following him? Maybe they wanted to see if Lonsdale would try to make contact with Schwartz and through Schwartz with Casas. So then, the next victim would have to be Schwartz—to shut him up permanently.

What about Micheline? The Cubans were bound to wipe her out *en passant*, as the chess players say. As a friend of his *and* Schwartz's, she was a risk.

But this presupposed that it was the Cubans, and that they had been watching Siddiqui for some time and had been tapping his phone, thereby overhearing his conversation with Lonsdale. Why not? Lonsdale was aware of how extensive the Cubans' intelligence operations were. Montreal was the headquarters of Cuba's spying activities in the West, and Florida was crawling with Fidel's agents.

If they had been watching Schwartz they would know about Micheline. But they were unlikely to touch her. It was reasonable for them to hope to get away with one murder, Siddiqui's, but killing Schwartz and Micheline—three murders—would be tempting providence.

No, Micheline was safe, but they would follow her around to see whom she met up with, how often she would run to Schwartz to comfort him and be comforted by him, and, above all, whether she would lead them to Lonsdale, someone they had to slow down somehow.

Micheline got back from town a few minutes past eight. "I did what you told me, mon amour, and I didn't have any trouble," she reported. "Mr. Schwartz came in just before five and confirmed that he was leaving for London tonight. He wants to do some business there tomorrow. He will fly to Budapest on Saturday."

"Has he got his ticket?"

"Only to London. He will buy the portion to Budapest there."

Lonsdale was pleased. The old man was following instructions. "What about you?" he asked. "Did anybody try to follow you?"

"I don't think so. I left the car at the De La Savane Metro Station when I went to work this morning and took the Metro the rest of the way. I bitched to everybody about the garage where my car was being fixed. I must have been convincing because I got two offers of lifts home."

"Both from men, I bet."

"What's the matter, cheri? Jealous?"

Lonsdale smiled "Maybe just a little."

"Well you're wrong. They were from my assistant, Lucille, and from a secretary in the credit department." She went upstairs to change, and Lonsdale followed.

At dinner he asked her to go over what she had done to avoid pursuit.

"I took the Metro to Cote-des-Neiges Station, you know, the one near where I live. I got out, then, at the last minute I jumped back in again."

"And?"

"And nothing. Nobody jumped back in after me. So I went to De la Savane, picked up my car, drove toward Dorval Airport and then cut off to come north. Nobody followed me as far as I could see."

"What about in the village up here?"

"I went to the convenience store, like you said I should, and bought groceries. I watched if anybody pulled up to wait for me and I couldn't spot anybody, so I'm pretty sure there was nobody after me. From the store you can see up and down the highway for a mile each way."

Lonsdale took three thousand dollars from his pocket and handed the money to Micheline. "Tomorrow I want you to buy me a return ticket to Amsterdam via KLM. I looked up the address, they're on Greene Avenue." He gave her a piece of paper. "Make the reservation in the name of Linsdahl. Make sure you spell the name carefully."

"Linsdahl?"

"Yes. The name resembles my own close enough to get me past passport control, but will not cause the computers to sound the alarm and alert the authorities. I am assuming, of course, that my colleagues are searching for me."

"Passport control in Canada?"

"Not really passport control, but control at the check-in counter to make sure the airline doesn't have to fly me back if I'm denied entry at destination."

"And why a return ticket? Don't tell me you're coming back here." Micheline tried to sound flippant, but was making a poor job of it.

Lonsdale was expecting the question. "Miche, once I've finished this mission I will apply for my pension. With my years of service I'm way past retirement age." He gave her a crooked little smile. "I have no one in the world I care for except you. Of course I'll come back here. I'll even marry you if you'll have me."

"You mean that?"

He laughed delightedly. "I mean it with all my heart."

She began to cry, and he leaned over to kiss away the tears.

CHAPTER NINETEEN

Thursday
Langley, Virginia

Lawrence Smythe took a sip of his drink, then, shifting his arthritis-riddled body painfully, turned toward Morton. "Have you heard from him?"

"No, Sir. I haven't for a few days now. He's either gone to ground, afraid they'll try to take him out or they have already taken him out."

"Is there anything you can do?"

Morton sighed wearily. He hated amateurs, especially amateurs with clout, and Smythe had plenty of that. "Sir, if you remember," he explained for the umpteenth time, "you told me that this operation was set up on orders from the president on a need-to-know basis. Therefore, only those who needed to know were told about it. This did not include our embassy or our stations in Canada. My asset is operating on a need-to-know basis as well. He's soloing."

"Soloing?"

"Yes, Sir. He's on his own and reports directly to me when he feels he has something to say."

"And what do we do about him if he gets into trouble?"

"Nothing."

"Nothing?"

"We just let him be. He either comes home or he doesn't."

"And if he doesn't?"

"Then we write him off and your Operation Adios goes ahead as planned."

"And the fur will fly."

"And," Morton got up and headed away from the man, "as you say, the fur will fly." He was at the door, ready to open it.

"*Morton*!" Smythe's voice sounded like a whiplash. Startled, Morton turned around. In the dusk the director's wasted body was almost invisible. But the huge, penetrating blue eyes in the heavily lined face were blazing at him with such intensity that, momentarily, Morton felt fear. "Morton," Smythe said more softly, but very firmly. "Don't fuck with me! I'm not going to let that bastard in Cuba continue to give our nation grief for very much longer!"

"But, Sir—"

"But nothing. Get Lonsdale sorted out and quick, or else."

"Or else what?"

"You got the message. Now leave."

Smarting from the insult, Morton left, slamming the door behind him as hard as he dared.

CHAPTER TWENTY

Friday and Saturday
Budapest, Hungary

As expected, Lonsdale had no difficulty with passport control at Mirabel Airport, and he passed the security check with flying colors.

His seat was in the upstairs cabin of the 747. He had charmed the passenger agent supervisor into blocking off the seat next to his, so he felt free to remove the inside arm rest. As soon as they were airborne, he stretched out across the two seats, tucked a pillow under his head, pulled the blinkers provided by the airline over his eyes, wrapped himself in a blanket, and was asleep within minutes.

Seven hours later he exited the plane in the Amsterdam airport. He checked the departure console and saw there that an Austrian Airlines flight departed to Vienna at eight thirty. He bought a one-way business-class ticket for cash in the name of Donald Jackson, got two bottles of liquor at the Duty Free Shop, a bottle of Grecian Formula in the drugstore, and hurried on board with ten minutes to spare.

He was in Vienna by noon. He mentally complimented Austrian Airlines for its service: the flight had left on time, breakfast had been ample, and the seats had been comfortable.

He took the bus from Schwechat to the downtown railway station and bought, again for cash, a one-way, first-class ticket to Budapest on the express leaving at ten past five.

He had plenty of money and four hours to spare, so he took a cab to the Hilton, got a day-room, once more for cash, showered and shaved, had a couple of hours' sleep and was in his seat on the train fifteen minutes before departure time, rested, but tense.

He thought he had the compartment to himself until a Hungarian family of three barged in huffing, puffing, and fussing. The father, Lonsdale gathered, was some sort of senior banking official, the son a precocious high-school student. The mother, a Hungarian housewife, was a stay-at-home type.

The thought brought Lonsdale up short. How did he know all this? Then it dawned on him. He had been reading a magazine, yet he had been following the conversation subconsciously and had understood just about everything that had been said, even though his travel companions were speaking Hungarian. This, of course, pleased him immensely. Though born in Budapest he had spoken no Hungarian since changing identity almost two decades ago. Quietly he gave thanks for the exceptional language skills with which he'd been endowed and went back to reading his magazine.

But he couldn't concentrate. With the language came a flood of memories—of his youth, of the war, of his parents and his brother, all dead long ago.

His brother, Anthony, three years older than Lonsdale, had been killed by shrapnel during the siege of Budapest in 1944. Anthony, whom Lonsdale had idolized, had always been a curious kid who wouldn't listen. He had disregarded his mother's orders one Boxing Day when, he had ventured into the street to see what was happening. He had barely stepped outside when a tiny piece of shrapnel from an exploding mortar shell pierced his brain.

Lonsdale had gone looking for his brother when Anthony failed to return for lunch, and he had found him less than ten yards from the entrance of their apartment building, sitting on the curb, facing the street, his back against the base of a street lamp which shielded him from view. To Lonsdale, he had appeared to be asleep, so he had given him a playful shove to wake him up. The sliver of metal that had killed him had been so small that the entry wound could not be seen for the hair that was covering it.

The three months following Anthony's death had been a blur of mental and physical pain that had seared Lonsdale's psyche indelibly.

He'd had to cope with a hysterical, then deeply depressed and guilt-ridden mother, forever blaming herself for having let Anthony out of her sight. There was no privacy in the overcrowded basement where twenty-four families had taken refuge while the city above them was being shelled to pieces and fought over by the German, Hungarian, and Russian armies. There was hardly any food, it was freezing cold, and the Russians came by regularly to rape the women.

In March his dad came home from the Russian front. He'd been taken prisoner near Kiev, some two thousand kilometers from Budapest, but had escaped to walk home disguised as an old peasant woman.

A year later, having sold everything they owned in Hungary, Lonsdale and his family left Budapest to stay in his paternal grandmother's home in Vienna. Lonsdale was sent to boarding school, first in Switzerland then in England. By the time he got to Canada five years later, his mental wounds had healed, at least on the surface.

Lonsdale's reverie was interrupted by the arrival of the Austrian border police. Their attitude was perfunctory. They couldn't care less about who was leaving their country, especially not for places behind the Iron Curtain.

On the other hand, the Hungarian border guards, who clambered aboard at Hegyeshalom in pairs, were thorough and focused, especially on what they could confiscate from returning citizens on the pretext of having uncovered "restricted" merchandise.

Lonsdale watched them work over the banker and his family, who really did have an extraordinary number of suitcases. When it became apparent that the guards were not about to leave without their pound of flesh, Lonsdale gave them the bottle of Scotch he had purchased at Schipohl, Amsterdam's airport. The guards disappeared and the train was soon on its way again.

All members of the banker's family spoke English. They had lived in London and New York where the banker had represented the Hungarian National Bank. Profuse in their thanks for his kindness, they asked Lonsdale whether he had somewhere to stay in Budapest. When he sheepishly admitted that he had no specific destination, they supplied half a dozen hotel names and listed their pros and cons. He listened carefully and made note of a couple that sounded low-key enough for his purposes.

Lonsdale planned to arrive in Budapest around half past nine at night and to bribe his way into a second-class hotel. He would debrief Schwartz on Sunday morning and go over the details of the upcoming meeting with Casas.

Morton had ordered him to be back at the office on Tuesday. He had no reason to think Lonsdale would not follow orders, yet Siddiqui had been murdered on Monday. The murderers, while bugging Siddiqui's phone, must have overheard Lonsdale making arrangements to meet the banker on Monday and wanted to prevent the meeting at all cost. This meant that either Siddiqui or Lonsdale, or both, had to die. The opposition had acted with skill and quickly, which meant they must have had agents nearby.

Canadians? Unlikely.

Cubans? Maybe. They had the manpower in Montreal.

Did Morton ask for surveillance on Siddiqui? Lonsdale concluded that he had no reason to do so since he was not even aware of Siddiqui's existence. There had been no time for Lonsdale to brief Morton on him.

The Agency, the Agency, the Agency, the little voice inside Lonsdale's head kept on repeating. *The left hand never knows what the right hand is doing. Everything is based on need-to-know.* He stared out the window. It was dark. The train's wheels kept clicking: "Need to know, need to know, need to know."

In Budapest, he headed for the nearest taxi. "Hotel Taverna," he said, hoping it would be enough to get him where he wanted to go.

It was.

The Taverna Hotel turned out to be exactly what he was looking for and he was able to get the last available room, a single. In spite of being located on Váci Utca, Budapest's upscale shopping street, it was far from a five-star hotel. Lonsdale took it gratefully and paid cash in advance for three nights. Although the lobby was narrow and dingy and the staff surly, Lonsdale fell in love with the place at first sight. The reason: you could get out of the building four different ways; one was through the garage, without having to pass the front desk.

By half past eleven he was walking up and down Váci Utca, wearing his newly acquired hat and horn-rimmed glasses, ostensibly window-shopping, but in reality watching the parade of whores, and checking for signs of surveillance, as always.

After several entertaining and salacious discussions with several *belles de nuit*, he decided that he was not being followed and picked out the woman he wanted: a no-nonsense brassy, buxom streetwalker.

"So you got tired of walking up and down," she challenged him, "or did you finally make up your mind about getting laid?"

He nodded and said nothing.

"You picked me because of my great-looking body."

He nodded again.

"Ha, you like the big package?"

He nodded for the third time, then asked "What's your name?"

"Berta."

"And how much is the package for the night?"

She named a number, which, by Western standards, seemed extremely reasonable.

"There's only one little problem," he said. "I don't have anywhere to take you."

"Don't worry about it big boy. We'll go to a hotel I know. Just follow me." She turned on her heels and headed for the nearest cabstand.

"Not so fast," Lonsdale called after her. "How much will the hotel cost me, and besides, I want to know which hotel you're proposing to take me to."

"The Citadella, on Citadel Hill in Buda, and it's only twenty-five American dollars."

Lonsdale pretended to hesitate. "Listen, that's just too much for me in total." He made himself sound rueful. "I guess I had better just say good night and ask for a rain check. I don't have the money."

"Suit yourself," the woman shrugged, visibly peeved, and walked away. Lonsdale was pleased. All he had wanted was the name of a *hotel de passage* where he would probably not have to show identification.

The Citadella is an impressive fort-like building strategically located on St. Gellért's Mountain and overlooking the City of Pest toward the east and the Royal Castle of the Kings of Hungary to the north. The castle was built on the ruins of fortifications that had withstood the onslaught of the Turks for over a hundred years, thus becoming Hungary's symbol of resistance against all oppressors. The Citadella, on the other hand, had been built by the Austrians after the Hungarian War of Independence in 1848 to serve as a garrison for the troops charged with keeping an eye on the rebellious Hungarians.

Lonsdale flagged down a cab on Rákoczy Boulevard and directed it to this massive edifice, now ignominiously converted into a combination YMCA and *hotel de passage*.

In the dark, the "fort" appeared ominously menacing and singularly uncomfortable. Three-feet-thick walls, pierced by gun ports that now served as windows, a narrow circular parapet, and sentry posts every fifty feet, all made for an uninviting and inappropriate-looking site for a so-called romantic interlude.

No matter. All Lonsdale wanted was a secret refuge, a backup venue where he could hole up in case he had to disappear from the Hotel Taverna in a hurry.

In contrast to its stark exterior, the Citadella's interior was warm and friendly. The clean, well-lit, and whitewashed lobby was large, the furniture comfortable. Despite the hour, the receptionist greeted him with a welcoming smile.

"Can I have a double room for the night please," Lonsdale said in English and handed the clerk a ten-dollar bill. "Preferably upstairs."

"For the night? No sweat." The clerk was falling all over himself trying to be helpful. He took Lonsdale's money and then asked, "What is your name, Sir?"

Lonsdale handed him another ten-dollar bill and the clerk gave him a slip of paper. "Mark down your name and address for me, will you?" Lonsdale obliged and then paid for the room.

"Can I see some ID please?"

"Berta will give it to you when she gets here," Lonsdale replied and headed for the stairs.

The clerk did not call after him.

CHAPTER TWENTY-ONE

Sunday Morning
Budapest, Hungary

Lonsdale had slept deeply and had awakened rested and refreshed. After a quick shower and a shave with the foam and razor he had stashed in his coat pocket before leaving the Hotel Taverna, he had headed for the reception area. It was early, half past seven, and the same clerk was still on duty.

"Where can I get something to eat?"

"Have breakfast in our cafeteria. We bake our own bread, and it's good."

"And where's that?"

"On the mezzanine floor."

Lonsdale made as if to leave then turned back. "Say, can I have my room for another night?"

"Sure."

"Let me pay you in advance." Lonsdale gave the man fifty bucks, double what the room cost.

"No sweat. I've got you covered." The clerk yawned. "Keep your key and have fun. As for me I can hardly wait to get off."

While pretending to read the Sunday *Magyar Nemzet*, Lonsdale contemplated what he had to do next.

Contact with Casas was the objective, but this could only be achieved through Schwartz. And, by now, Schwartz must either be under American surveillance or actively cooperating with the Agency, of this Lonsdale was almost certain. After all, the CIA had almost a week to identify Siddiqui's client as the Angolan contact.

Whether Schwartz was working with Lonsdale's tormentors was immaterial. It was best to assume that he was being followed in hopes he would lead to Lonsdale or to Casas, or both.

"I'll have to take the appropriate precautions," he murmured and sighed because he knew these would slow him down. "Don't let's take chances," he admonished himself, finished his breakfast, put on his hat and coat and left the hotel.

He took a cab to the Inter-Continental Hotel and walked around the lobby, locating the service elevator by watching how arriving luggage was being handled. Then he put a blank sheet of paper into an envelope, addressed it to Schwartz, and asked the clerk at the front desk to have it delivered to the old man. As expected, the clerk put the envelope into Schwartz's key slot, thereby giving the room number away. Lonsdale headed for the toilets, but, at the last moment, ducked into the service bay and took the elevator to the seventh floor. He walked down two flights and knocked five times on the door of room 512. It was exactly nine-thirty.

Schwartz was glad to see him. He had news. But before he could say a word, Lonsdale led him into the bathroom and turned on the taps. Admittedly, this was not much of a defense against sophisticated concealed microphones, but it was better than nothing.

"Keep your voice down," he cautioned.

"Casas contacted me last night," the old man reported breathlessly. "He wants me to meet him during the twelve o'clock mass, between twelve and twelve thirty, to be more precise, in St. Stephen's Basilica. It's not far from here."

Lonsdale laughed. *What irony*, he thought.

A Jew was meeting an atheist during a Roman Catholic mass celebrated in a supposedly godless, communist country, ostensibly for the purpose of betraying his people. He put up his hands. "Slow down my friend, slow down. First, fill me in on how things went for you since we last met."

"I followed your instructions and from Montreal I booked to London only. Then I went about my business as always—"

"And were you followed?"

"I think so."

"By whom?"

"I should know?"

"What did they look like?"

"Like two Italians."

"So what did you do?"

"What you told me to do. On Friday night I went to the Highgate Synagogue in North London, the one I told you about, the one with the two entrances. It was Shabes so the place was full, but you know that too, so why should I be telling you this?"

"Keep on talking." Lonsdale was curt.

"All right, already, Mr. Spy." Schwartz was imperturbable. "I went in at the front and they came in after me. It was funny. They weren't Jewish and didn't know enough to put on a *kepah* to cover their heads. So the *shames* got after them and they had to go out to get a couple of yarmulkes. I waited for them to come back, playing the innocent, just as you told me. Then I went to the men's room downstairs, and one of them came after me, but when he saw the sign at the head of the stairs, he figured I just went to pee."

"And he didn't follow you down?"

"No, he didn't. So I went through the exit on the subway level, the 'Tube' they call it, and took the subway to Waterloo Station where I booked a sleeper on the boat train to Paris. From there, I flew here."

"What about your luggage?"

"I left it at my hotel in London like you said I should. I'll call them from Montreal and they'll send it home. Here I only have my sample case with two shirts, two pairs of socks, and my necessaries."

"Your what?"

"My 'necessaries.' You know: razor, toothbrush, toothpaste, that kind of thing." The old man sat down on the toilet seat. He was visibly tired. The excitement and the traveling were getting to him.

Lonsdale was impressed. "You did well my friend, really well. Just hang in there for a little while longer, and we'll all be going home, happy and safe." He was trying to sound reassuring, but in his heart of hearts, he knew it was wishful thinking. "Now tell me about Casas."

"Casas sent me a note. It said 'Bon Voyage, Daddy.' It was signed 'Dorothy,' which is my daughter's name, and had one big *X* and two small *x*'s—you know for kisses—before the signature. The *x*'s did not have a circle around them."

"And what does that mean?"

"Don't you remember, Mr. Hotshot? He and I have a simple code. *X*'s with no circles are St. Stephen's Basilica in Pest, *x*'s with circles, St. Mathias Church in Buda. Circles mixed with no circles means the Catholic Church in Óbuda, a suburb of Budapest on the Buda side. So the message means that I have to meet him during the twelve o'clock mass at the Basilica."

"How do you know it's the twelve o'clock mass?"

"Simple. After the signature, big *X* means ten, little *x*'s mean one each. One big and two small *x*'s mean twelve o'clock."

"Have you and Casas met in Budapest often?"

"Sure. It's convenient. I'm known in numismatic circles the world over and the Hungarians are great coin collectors and dealers. I can come and go here as I please, more so now that Canadians don't need visas any more. The authorities leave me alone. I deal with the National Museum, and they know it. I mean money to them."

"And Casas?"

"For him it's convenient too. The Cubans and Hungarians are officially political friends. There is cultural exchange, you should pardon the expression, between the two countries." Schwartz winked at Lonsdale.

"What kind of cultural exchange?"

"On St. Margaret's Island, the island which is in the middle of the Danube, there is a nightclub in the Thermal Hotel that they call the Havana Club."

"So?"

Schwartz looked toward heaven for assistance. " 'So,' he asks me." He faced Lonsdale. "Are you sure you're half Jewish?"

Lonsdale laughed. "Yes, I told you I was."

"For a half-Jew you're dumb."

"What do you mean?"

Schwartz was shaking his head in disbelief. "Oy, have we got an innocent here." He was laughing, too. "What do you think they do in a night club already, dance the ballet? Maybe perform Swan Lake?"

"Meaning?"

"I mean they have a nice, old-fashioned Cuban burlesque show there every night except Sunday. And you should see the girls. They're *zoftig*."

"What's 'zoftig'?"

"Rubenesque, ample, big." Schwartz used both his hands to outline the shapes.

Lonsdale looked at his watch. It was only ten in the morning. "It's always a pleasure to listen to you, Mr. Schwartz, but I don't think it's a good idea for me to hang around here for the next couple of hours. It's too risky." He dampened a facecloth and wiped his face. "Let me sneak out of here and meet you later in the Basilica. By the way, any particular area?"

"In the back of the left nave there is a chapel. You can see it as you—" The door buzzer cut him off, and Lonsdale's gut tightened.

"Are you expecting someone?"

Schwartz dismissed the question with the wave of a hand. "Just the room-service waiter," he said and switched off the water. "I ordered something to eat."

He left the bathroom. Lonsdale closed the door, grabbed his hat and coat, switched off the light, stepped into the bathtub and drew the shower curtain.

"Who is it?" he heard Schwartz call out.

"Room service," a muffled female voice answered, and Lonsdale heard Schwartz open the door. There was a clatter of dishes and cutlery as the waitress pushed the table through the door. "Good morning, Mr. Schwartz," she called out.

"Here, let me help you," Schwartz said. The door slammed shut and the clatter receded toward the window.

"Where would you like me to set up the table?" the female voice asked in remarkably good, slightly accented, English.

"By the window please," more clatter, then Schwartz's voice "This will do just—" The familiar plop-hiss-plop-hiss, the kind of noise a silencer-equipped automatic makes, cut Schwartz off in mid-sentence and jolted Lonsdale as hard as if he had been the one to be hit.

Rigid with fear, he stood unarmed and dead still in the bathtub, straining to hear what the assassin was doing next door and cursing himself for having been careless, for having allowed Schwartz to answer the door even though Schwartz did say he'd ordered food.

Damn, damn, damn!

He heard nothing for about a minute, which, to him, seemed an eternity. Suddenly, the bathroom door flung open, the light came on and the woman marched past him to the toilet. She lifted the top and swept the food on the plate she was holding into the bowl. Then she left, but was back a few seconds later with a second plate to repeat what she had done before.

When she returned for the third time Lonsdale thought that, for him, the end had surely come.

He sensed that the woman was standing in the middle of the room, examining something. Was she facing him, or was her back to him? Did she have her weapon with her or was she unarmed? Had she seen or heard something suspicious or was she just following routine?

Lonsdale's mind raced. *What to do, what to do?* He was unarmed and at a total disadvantage. There was still hope, though. Had the woman suspected that there was someone in the bathroom she wouldn't have come by twice with the plates. She would have shot first and done the dishes later.

Why the hell is she so still. Why doesn't she do something?

It suddenly dawned on Lonsdale that the assassin must be looking at herself in the mirror, perhaps even fixing her hair or her makeup. As if to confirm his thoughts he heard her put something on the counter, a comb or brush perhaps. The hiss of a vaporizer followed, and Lonsdale could smell perfume.

It's now or never!

Lonsdale burst from behind the shower curtain and drove his shoulder into the woman's kidney in a flying tackle. She doubled over and sank to one knee, but she was a seasoned veteran and somehow rolled away from him in spite of the intense pain. He went after her and she aimed a kick at his groin that Lonsdale managed to parry with a last-second half turn.

She scrambled to her feet while he struggled to regain his balance and reached for her automatic lying next to the sink. Lonsdale hammered down on her wrist with his right fist and the weapon slithered along the counter toward the toilette bowl. They both reached for it and the woman got there first. But by then Lonsdale had his arm around her neck so she drove her elbow into his ribs. Lonsdale hung on and when she tried to make the pistol bear he broke her neck with an instinctive, savage tug, just as he had been taught to do during basic training on the Farm.

Lonsdale laid the woman's body out on the floor. Well-endowed, she appeared to be in her mid-thirties, dark haired, latina-looking, dressed in a maid's uniform. He searched the body and found no identification. He lifted it into the bathtub, drew the shower curtain, and allowed himself the luxury of leaning against the wall. Legs trembling from relief, he thanked the Fates for his good fortune, for sparing his life once more. "So you do care after all, you burntout old man," he whispered. "All it takes is a close call to make you want to go on living. Not that you deserve to, you heartless, conniving bastard."

He let a minute go by, and then sat down on the toilet to rub his legs vigorously to ease the cramps and stop the trembling. When he stood up, he caught a glimpse of his ashen face in the mirror, and it nauseated him. He threw up in the washbasin.

It took him another couple of minutes of deep breathing to pull himself together, to clean up, and confront what he had to do.

He walked into Schwartz's room and looked around. The place looked like a typical hotel room. The bed was made, and the drapes were half drawn. Schwartz's large sample case was on top of the desk, his alarm clock on the night table. A paperback lay in one of the armchairs near the window. Schwartz had apparently dropped it when he had gone to open the door for Lonsdale. Nothing out of the ordinary could be seen anywhere, certainly not to the casual observer, such as a room supervisor who might look in to ensure that everything was in order.

But Lonsdale was not a casual observer. He knew what had happened and where Schwartz's body would likely be. He double-bolted the door and went to check. As expected, the assassin had maneuvered Schwartz into the space between the bed and the wall near the window by pushing the table gently, but firmly toward the old man who kept backing up to accommodate.

When she had him where she'd wanted him—against the wall— she shot him twice through the heart.

Schwartz, mortally wounded, had slid down into a sitting position. The assassin had doubled him over so that the bed would hide his body from view. The poor old man's body lay in a twisted heap, mostly on his side, shirt soaked with blood, eyes wide open in surprise, hands clutching his chest where the bullets had hit. There was no exit wound in his back. The bullets that killed him were low velocity, high impact, very efficient, and highly destructive. *A real pro job* Lonsdale concluded as he carefully searched the body.

Schwartz's jacket yielded a mercifully undamaged Canadian passport and a bloodied, bullet-riddled but beautiful crocodile wallet containing pictures of a somewhat overweight woman and her two children. "Dorothy," Lonsdale whispered. He kept the passport and replaced the wallet. In Schwartz's left trouser pocket he found a thick wad of hundred dollar bills and Hungarian paper money. He took most of the money except for a couple of thousand Forints and three hundred dollars.

Searching further he also found a small key in the same pocket, which, he correctly guessed, opened the coin dealer's sample case. This contained some laundry, which Lonsdale removed and placed in a drawer, and six coin demo albums, each with spaces for twenty-four coins of various sizes. Lonsdale estimated that about half of the slots were filled.

He went back to the body, removed Schwartz's glasses and tried them on. Surprisingly, not only did they fit, but he could also actually see with them. He decided to keep them. Schwartz's black cashmere overcoat was in the closet. It, too, fit Lonsdale. But Schwartz's hat, a distinguished looking Homburg, was too big. Lonsdale fixed the problem by stuffing toilet paper behind the headband.

He retrieved his own hat and coat from the bathtub and stuffed them into the sample case, used a damp washcloth to wipe all surfaces he remembered touching, put on Schwartz's hat and coat, then with washcloth and sample case in hand, left the room after pushing the breakfast trolley out the door and aligning it against the wall. He carefully wiped the doorknob behind him and hung the Do Not Disturb sign on it.

No need for room service to go looking for the table in Schwartz's room.

Lonsdale turned up his coat collar and boldly took the elevator down. He hurried through the lobby with his head down, and stepped out into the cool, late October sunshine.

The doorman saluted. "Have a nice day, Mr. Schwartz," he said and waved. Lonsdale half-turned and waved back. The disguise had worked.

CHAPTER TWENTY-TWO

Sunday Noon
Budapest, Hungary

Lonsdale walked along the Danube's embankment toward the Forum Hotel. As he approached the building, he began to feel weak. His teeth started to chatter, and his vision blurred. He was sliding into shock again; the morning's events were catching up with him.

He almost missed the Café Vienna sign before it registered. Hot chocolate, his favorite, was what he needed.

The café was on the mezzanine floor. Lonsdale blinked, took a second look and shook his head to force his rapidly numbing brain cells to believe what he was seeing. *I've fallen through the looking glass, and I'm living in the thirties*, he thought then pulled himself together and strode purposefully toward the newspaper rack. He unhooked a Hungarian language daily and barely beat a smartly dressed matron to the last available table.

The Café Vienna was bustling with life. Elderly ladies and gentlemen dressed in their Sunday best were enjoying their elevenses: a cup of powerful espresso with something sweet such as a brioche or a piece of Viennese pastry. Women in tweed suits with fox-fur boas clutched matching muffs. Though nothing fancy, almost every woman wore pearls. The men, way outnumbered by their female companions, squirmed uncomfortably in stiff, starched shirts and ill-fitting, heavy suits.

The café itself was essential art deco: all chrome, glass, mirrors, and *fer forgé*. It seemed everyone was smoking. Lonsdale took in the scene at a glance through the thick haze, then, placing the paper on the table, turned toward the counter, which displayed an amazing variety of pastries. He half raised his arm to attract a waitress's attention, and when she came over he ordered a double hot chocolate. He took off his hat and coat, placed the sample case on the floor beside him, and legs trembling, carefully lowered his body into a chair.

The daily was strung onto a wicker reading rack to make turning the pages easier. It allowed him to hide behind the spread-out newspaper while waiting for his drink to arrive. Mercifully, the girl brought him his hot chocolate within minutes. He gave her a tired smile and he watched her leave. Slowly, very carefully, willing his trembling fingers to hold steady, he took a gulp of the hot, sweet liquid, and then another, and another.

After a while he felt better, well enough to stick his head between his legs, pretending to be looking for his sample case. This improved the blood flow to his brain noticeably, relieving the weakness and dizziness he had felt since entering the café. He felt he was ready to carry on.

The clock on the wall showed eleven twenty. He paid his bill and on the way out ducked into the men's room to splash cold water on his face. He took the coins out of the sample case and put them in his coat pocket then checked the case with the wardrobe lady and left for the Basilica at a quick pace, partly to keep his blood flowing, but mainly because he wanted to get to the church before mass started.

St. Stephen's Basilica, on the west side of Bajcsy Zsilinsky Boulevard near where it intersects Andrassy Ut, has a checkered history. Commissioned in the mid–eighteen fifties, it was not finished until the turn of the century. In 1868 the dome collapsed due to "building defects," meaning the builder had used substandard materials to make extra money on the contract.

When Lonsdale got to St. Stephen's and took in the massive neo-Renaissance structure before him, he found the inscription above the main entrance very apt: EGO SUM VIA VERITAS ET VITA. It was exactly what he needed: the way to truth and life.

Only the right panel of the entrance to the building was in use; both the left and center panels of the door were locked. Lonsdale dipped his fingers in holy water, crossed himself, genuflected as he traversed the aisle in front of the altar, and kept on walking until he reached the left nave. He strolled up and down it then knelt before

St. Joseph's statue located behind a solid supporting pillar at the very rear of the church.

He had not been in a church since his wife's death over two decades ago; the rage within him would not allow for such an act of faith. Rage had given way to fury and fury to cold, calculating, murderous hatred, but, mercifully, even that had faded as the years had clicked by. However, old habits die hard, and to his surprise, Lonsdale found he still knew how to behave correctly in a church.

He had worried about there not being enough people around to make his meeting with the Cuban general an unremarkable event. He need not have. In addition to the faithful there were at least two busloads of German tourists wandering about.

Casas's choice of the Basilica as a meeting place had been excellent.

With his back to St. Adalbert's Chapel, the one he guessed Schwartz had meant, Lonsdale looked around slowly. He was sure Casas was not in the church yet, not in the left nave area anyway. But then Lonsdale had not expected him to be. He would probably arrive during mid-mass, attempt to make contact with Schwartz in front of the little chapel, and then, after mass, leave via the exit to the left of the main altar. A neat plan, Lonsdale had to admit. Far away from the main altar and separated from the principal body of worshippers and their prying eyes, the general would have plenty of time to talk and exchange written messages or coins, and money for that matter.

Lonsdale strolled back toward the main entrance and stopped to the right of it, pretending to admire the architecture, the statues, the carved marble columns, and the beautiful ceiling of a truly great church. Every now and then he'd refer to a guidebook he had bought on the way in and which he held conspicuously chest high.

To his surprise, General Casas crossed his field of vision ten minutes before mass was to begin. Lonsdale remained motionless, trying to melt into the stonework, waiting for pursuit of Casas to materialize. He was not disappointed. First came the decoy, a somewhat overweight, middle-aged man, probably a local police detective moonlighting for the Cubans or the Agency, dressed in casual wear, a brownish-orange leather jacket of all things, a dead give-away. But then, he was meant to be noticed.

The policeman watched dutifully from a distance while the Cuban walked up and down the same nave Lonsdale had inspected earlier.

Casas then stopped in front of St. Adalbert's chapel, hesitated for a few seconds, and seeing that mass was about to begin, knelt down. The policeman sauntered back toward the rear of the church, passed Lonsdale by now surrounded by a group of tourists, and headed for the right exit door. On his way he managed to bump into a tourist couple to whom he seemed to mumble a few words of apology, whereupon the couple split up. The man crossed the church and sat down near the main altar from where he could see the exit at the end of the left nave. The woman went past Lonsdale to kneel before St. Joseph's statue, which enabled her to watch Casas from up close.

Lonsdale noted that both the man and the woman were carrying bulky camcorder bags, large enough to conceal a walkie-talkie or a pistol or both. *He has the radio and she the weapon*, Lonsdale's inner voice announced. He took out his pen. On the inside of the guidebook cover he wrote in Spanish: "Schwartz is dead. You are under surveillance by a fat policeman in a light brown leather jacket and a tourist couple with bulky camcorders concealing a weapon and communications equipment. Backup car with radio must also be in vicinity. Slip away and meet me in Room 218, Citadella Hotel, Buda side between three and four this p.m. We will talk about Captain Fernandez. Come alone. Knock five times. Destroy this note. B, Your friendly CIA contact."

While waiting for the credo, the recital of Catholic Dogma, Lonsdale, playing the art-loving tourist, slowly edged toward Casas. By the time the faithful began the common recital, Lonsdale, with his back to the tourist woman and his body shielding his activities from her, was standing behind and slightly to the right of the general. He waited for a bunch of tourists to come alongside him, then dropped his guidebook on the floor, and kicked it over to the Cuban. "General Casas," he said in Spanish, "don't turn around. Just pick up the guidebook and read page one." He joined in the recital of the credo, and slowly walked past the kneeling woman as if on his way to communion.

But the woman must have sensed something. She reached for her camcorder, but was too slow. By the time she got it going Lonsdale had his back to her, well on his way toward the exit. He appreciated the woman's predicament—stay with Casas or follow Lonsdale? He bet on that she would stay with Casas and send her companion after Lonsdale. Her choice mattered little. What did matter was to entice one of the two into following Lonsdale, thereby making Casas's getaway easier.

CHAPTER TWENTY-THREE

Sunday Afternoon
Budapest, Hungary

In his room at the Citadella Hotel, praying that he had judged his man correctly, Lonsdale sat sweating, waiting for General Casas to show. He had gone over the events of the afternoon a dozen times, analyzing how he could have handled matters differently, trying to identify areas of weakness in his game plan.

He had left the church through the exit at the end of the nave without looking back and had crossed Bajcsy Zsilinszky Boulevard to walk quickly up the street opposite to the Basilica. At the first corner he had taken a sharp right and a right again, which brought him to one of the entrances of the Revai triangular building.

He had been lucky. There had been no need to ring the doorbell; a shabbily dressed woman was just letting herself in and Lonsdale slipped in behind her. She eyed him suspiciously. He gave her an engaging smile and bent down to stroke her little terrier, which was yapping at Lonsdale with determination. The dog quieted down and the woman was mollified.

"What do you want here?" she asked, but her tone was not unfriendly.

He told her about how as a child his boy scout troop had lined up mornings in the building's courtyard before marching into the Basilica to attend ten o'clock mass.

"I live in Canada now and came back here for a visit. I wanted to see the courtyard again. It brings back memories."

She watched him as he began to look around.

He turned to her and pointed at the little fountain in the middle of the courtyard. "Just as I remember it. Thank you for letting me re-live my youth a bit." He made as if to leave.

She smiled. "Take your time, there's no rush." She pointed to her dog. "Toto likes the fresh air."

"No, no. I must go. I'm late as is. There's another way out of here in the back, isn't there?"

"Yes there is. Come, I'll show you."

He followed her across the courtyard and opened the door for him. This allowed Lonsdale to look up and down the street. There wasn't a soul in sight.

He gave the surprised woman a peck on the cheek, walked to the nearest major intersection, hailed a cab, and had himself driven to the Western Railway Station where he bought two first-class tickets on the express to Vienna, one for Sunday evening at half past seven, and one for Monday at ten minutes past nine a.m.

His problem was Schwartz, or more precisely, Schwartz's corpse. The maid coming to turn down the old man's bed was bound to stumble on it unless the Do Not Disturb sign stopped her from going in before morning. But that would be stretching it. Best to play it safe and leave the city somehow by Sunday night.

He took another cab, this one to Gerbeaud, the famous pastry shop, on Váci Street. From there he walked two blocks to the Taverna Hotel. He used the basement garage entrance to avoid the front desk and took the elevator to the fourth floor. He raced up the stairs to the next floor and opened the stairwell door. All clear. Six strides got him to his room.

He checked his tell-tales, matchsticks and bits of paper he had placed in and on his bag before leaving the room the night before. They were still in place; no one had tried to look through his things. Within two minutes he had his toiletries packed and was on his way down the stairs to the garage. He walked back to the Forum Hotel to retrieve his sample case, and a cab got him back to the Citadella Hotel by ten minutes to three.

Since Casas was not likely to show much before three thirty Lonsdale had too much time to fret and to second-guess while rubbing Instant Gray Grecian Formula into his hair to enable him to use the Schwartz passport in case he had to flee.

Was Casas going to come or would he send a Cuban goon squad to exterminate Lonsdale? Would the Agency's local thugs find him before he and Casas could exchange confidences? Would the Hungarian police come looking for him for the murder of old man Schwartz? Worst of all, would Casas simply not show and withdraw beyond Lonsdale's reach forever, thereby making his efforts an exercise in futility, which thus far, had cost the lives of Siddiqui, Schwartz, and the female assassin and—soon perhaps—Lonsdale.

So he waited and worried, sweating with fear, wanting very much to leave the room, but not daring to take the chance of missing Casas. No, that would spook the Cuban for good. The only way to play the game was to sit and wait, thereby showing the general that Lonsdale was willing to put his own safety at risk for the opportunity to meet and talk. He tried reading the magazine he had picked up in the lobby, but his brain refused to cooperate. It kept thinking that he was a ridiculously easy target for the opposition, whoever the opposition might be.

He wondered how many times he had put himself in harm's way, and for what? They had operated on his face and had put him in the employees' protection program only to return him to active duty under another name so that he could continue to fight the good fight for freedom. This had meant the end to his "first" life. *Better than being dead*, he reasoned, but not by much. Alone and without any background in his new world in Washington, he had to make new friends somehow. But that had taken an agonizingly long time because of the lingering, bitter ache in his heart.

He had watched his parents grow old and frail from afar and had not been able to attend their funerals. His new friends, all with Agency backgrounds, viewed him with mistrust, jealous of this mysterious parvenu who had appeared so suddenly in their midst from nowhere and who had then been appointed to a senior position to rule over them.

He couldn't blame them for not trusting him because he did not trust *them*.

"So where does that leave you, asshole?" he muttered. "Alone as ever," he answered his own question. But maybe, just maybe, from now on things might be different. There was Micheline, someone from the past, someone to whom he could reveal himself, someone he could perhaps even trust.

Five sharp raps on the door—they sounded like pistol shots—snapped Lonsdale out of his reverie and brought him to his feet. His watch said three fifteen: his gut announced the end of the world. Bracing himself he called out, "Come in, it's open."

Briefcase in hand, Casas stormed into the room, slamming the door behind him, and headed for the bathroom. Then he checked the cupboard and looked out the narrow window. Dispensing with preliminaries he bluntly turned on his host.

"Who killed Schwartz, and who's following me?" he asked in Spanish.

"Is or was?"

"Was. It took me an hour, but I managed to shake them."

"Frankly, General, I don't know. It may be your own people; it may be the Colombians or even the CIA."

Casas was taken aback. "The CIA? I thought you were the CIA."

"I am, General, but I work for the drug-liaison division, the one that ensures that the FBI, the DEA, and the CIA coordinate their activities and that they don't get into each other's way." Lonsdale tried to sound helpful and friendly.

"Are you telling me they sent a glorified narcotics agent to contact me?" Casas was furious. "I provide you with information you can use to bury Fidel Castro and the Cuban Revolutionary Movement, and the CIA sends a . . . a lowly administrator to interview Cuba's most-decorated and popular soldier-general and a member of the Cuban Communist Party's Central Committee. You arrogant, insensitive bastards." Casas was working himself into a fit. "Is this what I'm risking my life for? Are you the people who are going to help me expose Fidel?" He took a deep breath, fighting for control. He advanced menacingly toward Lonsdale, who stood his ground in silence. "Answer me," he hissed through clenched teeth.

"Calm down, General." Lonsdale's voice was sharp, "And listen up. I know you're under pressure, but so am I, so don't raise your voice, and above all, don't threaten me. We're in this together, and we need to help each other, not fight. My simulated rank is colonel, one grade below yours, which is brigadier general, and I am the deputy head of my department. You claim you're risking your life for us. This is precisely why I'm here. I want to find out the reason you're conducting this little charade." He added the last sentence to provoke the Cuban.

Casas could not believe his ears. "Claim to be risking my life? Playing at charades? Go back to America, CIA man, or whoever you are." He moved toward the bed to retrieve his briefcase. Lonsdale, who had just about had enough, positioned himself between the exit and the Cuban. "Stop acting like an asshole, Casas," he commanded. "You're not leaving this room without telling me why you sent Captain Fernandez to Miami." Casas turned to face him and Lonsdale let his shoulders sag after a resigned little shrug and changed the timber of his voice. "But, on second thought, why bother. The whole thing is such a blatant ambush, such an obvious scheme to entrap the CIA that we'd be foolish to take any of it seriously."

That's when Casas lost it. The lack of sleep, the stress of the last ten days, Lonsdale's insults and apparent indifference, and being called a liar by a stranger were just too much for his Latino blood. He charged Lonsdale who seemed to stumble as he got out of the way, forcing Casas to make a last-second correction in his attempt to grab him and crush the daylight out of him with his well-publicized bear hug.

The Cuban extended his hand to reach Lonsdale, who took it slowly, almost gently. Then he let the man's hand slide partially out of his until he was holding on to the ring and little fingers only. Casas tried to draw Lonsdale to him and Lonsdale allowed his body to fall toward Casas, taking the hand he was holding behind the general's back.

Casas tried to follow with his body, but too late. With a vicious tug Lonsdale broke the two fingers he was holding. Casas screamed with pain and fell to his knees. Lonsdale kicked him in the gut, and Casas doubled over.

Lonsdale turned the softly moaning man on his back, patted him down, and separated him from his service automatic. He flicked off the safety and cocked the pistol by pulling the barrel back. He felt the first round slam into the breach. It felt good.

He flipped the safety back on and stuck the pistol in his belt. Carefully, he helped Casas off the floor and onto the bed.

"We'll give you a few minutes to get your strength back, General," he said in a conversational tone. "Then we'll get your car, and I'll drive you to a clinic to have your fingers looked at. We'll talk on the way."

Casas was massaging his groins with his good hand. The other lay inert on his chest. He was in a daze from the pain, the shock of defeat, and the realization of the enormity of his own stupidity. He was especially devastated when he realized that he had deluded himself into believing the Americans would appreciate what he was trying to do and would know how to assist him.

Schwartz was dead, probably killed by De la Fuente's Montreal-based goons, Fernandez was next. De la Fuente was no ally. Casas was no longer sure that the drug operation had the blessings of the Cuban government, that the deputy minister had not organized the entire operation for his own and his MININT cronies' benefit.

In which event he, Casas, was an unwitting dupe of an international drug dealer.

He was trapped and had no one to turn to for help except this violent, insolent, and inept typically *yanqui* deputy head of some probably insignificant department of the DEA.

"How did you know I had a car?"

"You threw the keys on the table when you came in," Lonsdale replied.

"Why should I cooperate with you after all this?"

"Because if you don't, I won't drive you to the clinic."

"I can always take a taxi."

"Yeah, but I'd make you leave your briefcase with all those little secrets in it behind."

"What do you know about those secrets?"

"Nothing, but I'm sure you'll tell me all about them on the way to the doctor."

After that there was nothing much left to say, and Casas decided to play along because he had no alternative. He urgently needed his fingers fixed and time to think.

CHAPTER TWENTY-FOUR

Sunday Afternoon
Budapest, Hungary

They were headed for the Hilton by a quarter to four, where Lonsdale got the name of a private clinic from the concierge. By the time they arrived at the clinic, the doctor on duty, alerted by the concierge and spurred on by the prospect of many U.S. dollars, had everything ready. In exchange for five hundred dollars payable in advance, he gave Casas a local anesthetic, X-rayed the hand, set the fingers, applied the splints and the bandages, provided a sling for the arm, supplied a bunch of painkillers in a little vial, and saw Casas and Lonsdale on their way, all within the hour.

"I'll drive to the train station and take leave of you there," Lonsdale said to the visibly suffering Casas as they got into the car, a nondescript, reddish Lada. "I'm sorry things turned out this way, because I hoped you and I could work together. I guess that'll never happen now." He started the engine. "Unless," he gave Casas a thoughtful, sideways glance, "unless, of course, what Fernandez told me in Miami is true, in which case I think you're one of Cuba's greatest patriots."

Casas shifted painfully in the cramped passenger seat so that he could face Lonsdale. "Of course it's true," he said matter-of-factly. The painkillers had subdued him. "It never occurred to me that the CIA would not believe me. I chased Fernandez to Miami because I could think of no other way of getting your government's attention."

"What do you mean *chased?*"

"I had to frighten him, so he would think he had made a serious mistake involving money. I also had to tempt him with a lot of money. I succeeded in doing both." He gave Lonsdale a crooked grin. "I even succeeded in helping you find a way to get in touch with me without Fernandez's help."

"How's that?"

"Tell me, how did you locate me?"

"Through our late friend, Schwartz."

"And how did you get to him?"

"I traced the Cayman money to him."

"And how did you do that?"

"I suppose you'll be telling me soon that you helped me find you."

" 'Help' is perhaps the wrong word. 'Providing hints' is the way I would phrase it."

"Meaning?"

"Depositing money in bundles, with the bundling intact, for example."

Lonsdale's head snapped back as it struck him that he had grossly underestimated Casas. His mind went into overdrive. Was Casas trying to capitalize on a mistake of which he had become aware only subsequently or was he for real? Hard question to answer. Lonsdale said nothing for a while, concentrating on driving.

"Help me make sure we're not being followed," he finally said, playing for time. "Watch the rearview mirror on your side while I make a couple of quick turns." Lonsdale accelerated down Palota Boulevard and took a sharp left on Váralja towards the tunnel leading to the Chain Bridge. Another sharp left through the traffic lights got him into the tunnel. He drove as fast as the sparse Sunday night traffic would allow and soon emerged onto the Adam Clark roundabout that connects the tunnel with the bridge. He raced around it at speed, making a full circle and went back into the tunnel. He cast a questioning glance at Casas as they carefully surveyed the cars coming from the opposite direction.

"There seems to be no one following us." Casas sounded very positive and more alert. "What do you think?"

Ignoring the question, Lonsdale made up his mind. "I have come to the conclusion that, maybe, just maybe, Fernandez was telling the truth, at least the way he understood the truth to be. Suppose you tell me your version, and then we'll do a little analyzing."

"And then?"

"Then we'll see."

"How do I know you're CIA?"

"You don't, but to show good faith I'll tell you the highlights of what I know and you'll judge for yourself. Is that a fair deal?" He held out his hand and Casas took it awkwardly. Lonsdale began to talk, just as they were reentering the tunnel on their way toward the Chain Bridge and Pest for the second time.

It took an hour to tell Casas about Fernandez's flight to freedom, Lonsdale's trip to the BCCI in Cayman, his subsequent visit to Montreal, Siddiqui's death, Lonsdale's talks with Schwartz, and the way the old man had died. He was careful to present a coherent and logical story without mentioning Micheline or the strange attitude of his own colleagues toward him. He wanted to hear Casas's unbiased take on the situation.

"Hold on, hold on." The Cuban held up his good hand to stop Lonsdale. "Do I understand correctly that you thought the shot that killed Siddiqui was meant for you?"

"Not really, because at the time the assassin, unless he was working for the Agency, which I doubt, did not know my identity."

"Who then would have arranged for you to be followed?"

"Whoever the shooter was working for—the Cubans or the drug cartel. After eliminating Siddiqui to shut him up they needed to stop me from continuing my investigation."

"That's fair," Casas bit his lower lip, "but you also said that before Siddiqui got killed your colleagues wouldn't let you speak to Fernandez again."

"Right."

"And they had ordered you to stop working on the investigation and report back to your head office."

"Right again."

"They know something you don't know, and they don't want you to find out what it is."

Lonsdale, who had been driving around the city aimlessly, now headed for the Eastern Railway Station. "You might be right, but I'm damned if I know what it is. What do you think the reason is for holding back information? Why don't they let me have the full picture?"

"Maybe the man to whom you report does not have the full picture."

"That's possible."

Neither of them said anything for a while. It was Casas who broke the silence. "You've told me little that I didn't know, except the Schwartz and Siddiqui assassinations of course. These events reinforce my theory that they don't want you to get to know certain things. I'm beginning to attribute more significance to something that has been bothering me only slightly up to now."

"What's that?"

Deep in thought, Casas did not reply. Lonsdale pulled over to the sidewalk and stopped the car. They were alongside the railway station. He knew better than to say anything. He understood that Casas needed a few moments to marshal his thoughts.

As the minutes ticked by, Lonsdale's chances of catching the Sunday evening express to Vienna were fast evaporating, but the general had to be given the opportunity to conclude on his own that he required help from Uncle Sam, so Lonsdale stuck with him. He started the car again and drove back toward the downtown area.

Finally, Casas bestirred himself. "Listen to this, Mr.—"

"Call me Roberto."

"OK, Roberto. Before I left Cuba, Oscar De la Fuente and I had a violent argument. That was about ten days ago. We were discussing the Fernandez situation, and he said we'd have to volunteer to go on trial and swear in public that Oscar and I were the highest-ranking Cubans who knew about the drug operation and that the government and Fidel were not aware of anything. He said we needed to do this to save Cuba's reputation because of what Fernandez was telling the CIA."

Casas began to stroke his injured fingers. "Oscar also said he would have to involve more of his own people in the drug operation to make it look as though it were a bunch of MININT—pardon me, Ministry of the Interior—people who thought up the whole scheme.

Then he went on to say that Fernandez, being the only person who heard me talk to Raul Castro about the drug operation, had to be killed to erase any possible connection with the government."

"Sounds logical to me, but go on." Lonsdale tried to sound encouraging.

"But by killing Fernandez we would be committing suicide, don't you see? We'd be found guilty at our trial, condemned to death, and shot. I told De la Fuente that our life insurance was Fernandez, that if he was dead we were dead."

"And what did he say to that?"

"That Fernandez was not enough, that we needed to manufacture more proof that Fidel knew, so that we could threaten to expose his complicity if he allowed us to be condemned to death."

"Instead of?"

"Instead of, say, being sent into exile, like Fidel had been after he had attacked the Moncada barracks."

"What about world opinion?"

"As long as there was no proof that Castro or the government knew, the world would have to assume that they were innocent and we were the guilty parties."

"And your life insurance, as you call it, would have been Fernandez?"

"Or someone like Fernandez, or several Fernandezes, or documents, such as minutes that would attest to knowledge at the highest levels."

Lonsdale felt sick with apprehension. "You mean to tell me we're holding Fernandez, the only proof to what you're saying being true, and we're not aware of this?"

"That's exactly what I'm saying." Casas was shaking his head, unwilling to believe what he was about to say. "And he doesn't know, so he couldn't have told you, and you're probably not guarding him closely enough."

"You mean because Fidel's or Raul's assassins could get to him—"

"And Oscar and I would be dead men."

"And Fidel and Raul would get off scot-free."

"Yes."

Lonsdale seized his opportunity. "But not if you come to the States with me."

Casas looked stunned. "I would never do that!"

"Why not?"

"I could never live with myself thinking I've saved my neck and abandoned my family."

"But you wouldn't." Lonsdale made himself sound as persuasive as he could, but within, he felt unconvinced. "You could present what you know to the world and explain how you made Fernandez flee to alert the United States of what was going on."

"No good, not even with Fernandez corroborating what I was saying." Casas shook his head. "People would simply say Fernandez and I were either in the pay of the United States or guilty as hell."

"And De la Fuente?"

"What about him?"

"Would he not be sufficient to corroborate?" As soon as Lonsdale had uttered the phrase he knew his cause was lost.

"Whether Oscar corroborated what I said would make no difference," Casas said softly. "Don't you see, Roberto, I've painted myself into a corner. Fidel would put Oscar on trial, Oscar would take all the blame, and he would be shot. Fernandez and I would come off as the cowardly drug dealers who ran for their lives, abandoning their coconspirators to certain death."

"They would have to get to them first."

"I'm sure that would not be difficult."

"There is another 'unless.' " Lonsdale made himself sound optimistic and smiled at Casas, trying to convey hope. "Suppose we enrolled both you and Fernandez in our witness protection program. You could disappear and start afresh with new identities."

"Now there's a stupid idea if I ever heard one," Casas retorted, sounding disgusted. "I don't know about Fernandez, but I wouldn't want to find myself in a position of never again being able to see my mother, my two daughters, and my friends—assuming I'd have any left after all this." He shook his head sadly. "No, Roberto. Without intending to, I've dealt Fidel a winning hand, and all because I didn't watch my back."

"What do you mean by that?"

"What I mean is . . . what's bothering me is that I have begun to suspect the worst." He was having difficulty saying what he had to say. "I have begun to suspect that this entire drug operation is a private-enterprise deal, cooked up between De la Fuente and Raul, or De la Fuente and his father-in-law, or maybe De la Fuente alone."

"You mean for their personal enrichment?"

"That's exactly what I mean."

"Yet involving a number of people in the MININT and the army."

"All of whom are following orders convinced they are working for Department Z on a legitimate highly secret, government-authorized smuggling operation, designed to break the U.S. embargo and to generate much-needed hard currency, while at the same time undermining the morale of the people of the U.S."

"With drugs."

"Yes, with drugs, habit-forming drugs, the use of which kills directly and indirectly." Casas stared straight ahead, not daring to look at Lonsdale. "Just think of all those infected needles spreading AIDS." He shuddered.

"Let me understand this, Patricio." Lonsdale said quickly, choosing his words very carefully. "You have begun to suspect that, without Fidel's or the government's knowledge, Oscar alone or Oscar and Raul are smuggling drugs for profit, using the facilities of the Cuban Army and the Ministry of the Interior."

Casas nodded without looking at Lonsdale. "Yes, that's it in a nutshell."

"Let's get to basics, Patricio." Lonsdale needed to get to the core of Casas's knowledge. "Who first approached you about the drug operation and when?"

"Oscar, in Africa, about a year and a half ago."

"In Africa?"

"Yes, Angola." Casas thought for a bit. "You see, we were conducting these foreign exchange operations on behalf of the Ministry of the Interior's Department Z, and Oscar was in charge in Africa."

"What kind of operations?"

"Ivory and gold coins. Diamonds also. Oscar handled the diamonds, but needed help with the ivory and the coins, first to find them, then to collect them, and, most importantly, to sell them for hard currency, preferably dollars. He needed a reliable partner with army connections and a diplomatic passport. I filled the bill."

"So you worked for Oscar, your troops gathering the ivory and coins, and you, yourself, transporting the stuff?"

"That's right. For about six months before he started talking about drugs."

Lonsdale held up his hand. "Wait. Who set up the banking arrangements?"

"Oscar."

"With the BCCI?"

"Yes, with the BCCI in Luanda."

"And in Montreal?"

"The Luanda BCCI manager."

"What about the Cayman Islands? Who set up the account there?"

"The Colombians did at Fernandez's request. But the account was controlled by him and me jointly. As you know, it was just a transfer account. As soon as the money came in from Colombia it would be transferred to Panama into a Department Z account."

"And the drugs?"

"I guess Oscar set that up. I've known Oscar since the days of the fighting in the Sierra Maestra." Casas let out a bitter little laugh, "I trusted him implicitly as an old comrade in arms. Oscar knew that I knew how to follow orders."

"And did he give the order?"

"He did, indeed. In Havana, at a special meeting in his office, in the Ministry of the Interior's building on Calle 23, convened for that purpose."

"Is that where Department Z now operates from?"

"No, not quite." Casas's hand had begun to hurt again. "Oscar is an organizational genius. He compartmentalized Department Z to maximize security. Headquarters were at his own office in the Ministry of the Interior, where he set policy, but each of the department's subdepartments had its own separate place."

"In the same building?"

"No. Spread around Havana in various buildings."

Lonsdale was impressed. "And who ran the money?"

"You mean who had final authority over its disposal?"

"Yes."

"I'm not sure at all about that."

"Did any other official, higher in grade than you or Oscar, ever discuss the drug operation with you?"

"Only once. Raul, in the presence of Fernandez."

"In detail?"

"No, only in general terms." Casas was sweating; he recognized how exposed, how precarious his position was, and how lame he sounded. Lonsdale, on the other hand, felt that the general had been naive to say the least, or perhaps, he hadn't wanted to know what was going on so as to be able to claim, when the day of reckoning came, that he was just following orders. Why then the change of heart now?

"Let's get back to the money. Who has ultimate control of it?"

"I don't know."

"Well then, we have a way out for you from this mess."

"We do? How?"

"Simple. Let's find out who has final control over the money."

Casas whipped around to face Lonsdale. "That's the reason why I can't go with you to Washington. Only I, working from the inside, can find out who manipulates the money. If it is the government, I'll get proof and let you have it. If it is by private persons, then I'll go public with the information in Cuba."

"Why?"

"Because, under this scenario, the principles of the Revolution would not have been betrayed by the government, only by some high-up individuals."

"For their own personal benefit."

"As you say, for their own personal benefit."

Lonsdale thought for a while. Then he said softly, "In any event, Patricio, whatever the answers to your questions turn out to be, we must work together. You must allow me to help you. You cannot succeed alone."

"I agree!" Casas answered without hesitation. "Now explain how you propose to go about helping me."

"Fair deal." Lonsdale was all business. "Before I tell you what we'll do I want you to realize that we're about to undertake something that will be very dangerous for both of us." He parked the car alongside the Hyatt Hotel and began to brief Casas in detail about how to keep in touch and how to flee if that became a necessary option.

When they parted almost an hour later Casas asked for his weapon back. Lonsdale obliged without delay and apologized for having hurt him. He then grabbed his bag from the trunk of the Cuban's car and went over to the group of limousine drivers huddled in front of the Hyatt Casino to find one willing to drive him to Vienna.

CHAPTER TWENTY-FIVE

Sunday Evening
Budapest, Hungary

General Casas extracted his hand from the sling gingerly and tried to use it. Although his broken fingers were throbbing, the pain was manageable. He attempted to shift gears and found that if he used a combination of the palm of his hand with his thumb, index, and middle fingers, he could get by.

Not that he had much choice. He had to get to Conchita's apartment somehow.

Without Conchita Borrego, life in Budapest would have been very complicated. She allowed him to stay in her apartment, lent him her car, did his laundry, and provided him with background information he needed to be effective while doing business in Hungary's capital city.

She was a tall, exceptionally attractive woman with a beautiful face and a statuesque figure. These attributes, and the fact that she was politically reliable because of her campesino background, had earned her the job of lead dancer at the Tropicana, the Caribbean's most spectacular nightclub. Since she was also intelligent, the powers-that-be put her in charge of the little troop of nightclub performers Cuba maintained in Budapest. She had accepted the job with enthusiasm, said a tearful good-bye to her boyfriend in Havana, and off she had gone to dance for the Hungarians.

Conchita and her troupe performed in the Havana Club on St. Margaret Island, Budapest's only "respectable" nightclub, where, although human flesh was generously displayed, the emphasis was on dancing. Hungarians loved the tropical beat and the club soon became a favorite of tourists and locals alike.

Mr. Schwartz, a regular visitor to the Havana Club, had taken Casas there for dinner during one of the general's early visits to Budapest. Schwartz knew Conchita, and when she came around to say hello he had introduced her to Casas. One thing lead to another and Casas became the dancer's semi-regular boyfriend. Although he had never told her his real name, she, and all the Cubans in Budapest, knew very well who he was. But she went along with the charade and pretended that he was a civilian businessman visiting Hungary on important government business.

Their relationship had started as one of convenience based on the need for mutual protection and regular sexual encounters, which both enjoyed a great deal. Then it blossomed with the realization of how much they enjoyed each other's company. They loved dancing and music and laughed a lot when they were together.

Casas sighed, put the Lada in gear, and drove out of the Hyatt's parking lot toward Conchita's apartment near the Margaret Bridge. Tonight, he was in no mood for laughing; the man from the CIA had seen to that. He reflected on his position as he steered the car as best he could along Akademia Utca, passed the parliament buildings, and fetched up in Jaszai Mari Square. He was very much aware of being in a lose-lose situation, unlikely to succeed in his self-appointed mission. Either the Castro government was aware of what was going on, in which event, when unmasked, it would claim it had done nothing except attempt to generate much needed foreign exchange for its Department Z. That this action also weakened the moral fiber of its sworn enemy, the United States, was a bonus. Or, the whole thing was a free-enterprise deal for the personal benefit of certain individuals.

But who were these individuals? Oscar De la Fuente? Oscar's boss and father-in-law, the minister of the Interior? Or was it Raul Castro, the minister of the Revolutionary Armed Forces? Or was it all three? For sure not for the benefit and personal gain of one beleaguered, hurting, and more than slightly confused Patricio Casas.

Where did his duty lie? The answer seemed clear: to safeguard the ideals of the Revolution and, if necessary, to help topple the Castro regime if it was behind the drug scheme.

Why are you changing your attitude, Patricio, he asked himself. *You were dead sure the government was behind the operation. Now you're ambivalent. Why?*

He answered his own question. *It's that damned CIA man Roberto. He's highlighted the lack of proof. And what little proof there was, I've unwittingly destroyed by sending Fernandez over to the Americans.*

He had to get to Oscar to find out if the little bastard had set this thing up for himself or for the state. "Good thinking, but how about the people who are following me around? Do they know something I don't know? And are they the ones who killed Siddiqui and Schwartz?"

He went rigid as a new thought struck him. Suppose they were following him looking for an opening to kill him?

No, that couldn't be. They've had plenty of opportunities for that.

He parked opposite Conchita's apartment and looked up and down the street.

He spotted the two cars right away. The Volvo was up the street, with the man and the woman from the Basilica in it. The decoy, a Trabant, driven by the pudgy policeman, was parked at the opposite corner.

He got out of the car and locked it. Then he put his arm into the sling, and with his left hand gripping the pistol in his coat pocket, he walked across the street and rang Conchita's bell.

She was going to be annoyed with him for sure. He had taken shameless advantage of her all weekend, spending almost no time with her by day and making only perfunctory love to her at night.

He stole a glance at the Volvo's occupants. They could have shot him or kidnapped him right then and there, yet they made no move. They just sat there, watching. But who were they and who did the work for?

"Who is it?" Through the speaker, Conchita's voice sounded hostile to say the least.

"It's me. I know it's late and I'm sorry."

"You son-of-a-bitch," Conchita exploded. "I'm of half a mind to let you freeze down there for the rest of the night. Do you realize what time it is? Do you realize you've kept me waiting all evening? You were supposed to take me to dinner at seven. Sunday is my only night off, and you've ruined it for me."

"Calm yourself," Casas said firmly "and please come down to open the door. I'll explain everything."

Conchita hung up and Casas prayed she would not make him wait too long. He felt exposed standing in the doorway with his back to his enemies. But he had to pretend he didn't know they were there.

With a raincoat over her nightgown Conchita clattered down three flights of stairs to open the door. The descent did not improve her disposition, but one look at the sling around Casas's neck changed all that.

"*Ay, mi amor*, you've been in an accident," she whispered. "Come in, come in and let me help you."

Casas climbed the stairs, pretending to feel worse than he really did, and allowed her to help him off with his coat.

"Have you had anything to eat?" she asked after he had spun a yarn about having been attacked by hooligans in the Castle District after a long meeting with his contacts in the Ministry of Defense.

"I've had lunch," he lied, "but I had to wait at the clinic a long time and, frankly, after the painkillers they gave me I felt like puking rather than eating. But I'm famished now," he added.

"Would you like me to whip up an omelet with some chorizo?"

"How about you, *mi vida*?" he answered her question with a question "Have *you* eaten?"

"No. I waited and waited for you, and then I began to worry." She turned and headed for the kitchenette. She did not want him to see the tears of relief in her eyes.

He followed her and watched while she prepared a light meal for two. He devoured his portion and washed it down with a couple of bottles of weak Dreher beer.

She had never seen him eat that way and wondered what had gotten into him. She tried as gently as she could to make him confide in her, but he wouldn't even admit that there was anything wrong. In the end he asked her to fetch his briefcase from which he extracted a small oblong box and handed it to her.

"*Corazon*, soul of my life, I want to thank you for all you've done for me these past months. You've given me shelter, you've given me food, you've provided me with transportation, you've given me love. I'm deeply grateful." He got up with difficulty and went around to her side of the table to kiss her tenderly on the lips. "I love you and ask you to forgive me for having made you worry. I also ask you to forgive me for any trouble our relationship might create for you in the future."

She held him to her chest. "I know who you really are, Patricio," she whispered into his ear, "and I know, everybody knows, that you are having trouble putting up with some of the things that are going on in Havana. Believe me, the common people are with you, so please don't give up; it's just a question of time. You'll see. Everything will turn out right in the end."

Gently, he drew away from her, touched by her caring and her insight. "Thank you," he said simply and squeezed her hand. "You are a good woman, and you deserve to be right." He gave her a big smile. "Now open your present and tell me if you like what I brought you."

She opened the box and let out a squeal of delight. "Oh, Patricio, what a surprise. Where on earth did you find such a beautiful necklace?"

"I had it specially made for you in Africa."

"Will you help me put it on?"

He stepped behind her, and, as he bent over to take the necklace from her, she stood up slipped out of her nightgown and thrust her beautifully formed, firm breasts forward. Aroused, he fumbled with the clasp awkwardly and the necklace slipped from his fingers. But instead of falling to the floor, it slid down her breasts and came to rest against her erect nipples. He turned her toward him slowly, tenderly, lovingly. "Kiss me," she whispered, and he did, first her mouth, then each of her nipples, then, lowering himself onto his knees, her stomach.

On Monday, after eight hours' sleep, Casas felt much better physically. His broken fingers, though tender, were not hurting thanks to the painkillers he had swallowed with his morning orange juice.

Emotionally, though, Casas was not doing well. A sense of foreboding had come over him. He felt he was, like Don Quixote, tilting at windmills, that there was no way he could bring the Castro regime down, proof or no proof of drug smuggling, even with the CIA's help. He was being drawn into a vortex of frenzied activity, irreversibly leading to his death by firing squad.

Then there was Conchita to worry about. She would have made him a wonderful wife, but with things as they stood now, he was unlikely to see her again. Hopefully he would not involve her in his downfall, but God only knew what would happen to her once the authorities moved against him. Guilt by association was very much in fashion in Havana these days. He felt futile and very sad.

At the window, without disturbing the drapes, he looked out into the street. The Volvo was gone but the Trabant, with its lone occupant, was still there.

He made up his mind. He would not return to Havana just yet. Oscar was coming to Angola next week anyway, and he would have it out with him then. By that time, Casas would know what fate had befallen Fernandez, whether or not De la Fuente had him killed.

CHAPTER TWENTY-SIX

Sunday Night
Langley, Virginia

Morton was apprehensive. Lonsdale was six days overdue, and he had no idea where his deputy was or what he was doing. To make matters worse, Smythe, who never seemed to sleep, had asked Morton to be briefed about the file on Sunday night, which meant Morton had to cut his weekend short. He got to Langley after an enervating hour's drive in heavy traffic through a rainstorm. His mood did not improve when he found himself subjected to a spot security check, which meant emptying his pockets and turning over the contents of his briefcase for scrutiny. Another fifteen minutes wasted for nothing.

He was shown into Smythe's inner office without having to put up with the usual twenty-minute wait, which signaled bad news. It was clear the man was very anxious to see him.

Smythe, irascible at the best of times, was particularly irritable. He had a cold and considered it unnecessary to offer a greeting. "Your man has disobeyed orders and should be disciplined." His weak, reedy voice barely carried across the immense desk to Morton.

"In theory you are correct, Sir," Morton acquiesced. "But he is doing what we want him to be doing."

"Meaning?"

"Meaning that he is probably in contact with our Cuban soldier, trying to convince him to defect and give us proof of Fidel's improprieties."

Smythe bristled. "You said 'probably.' Does that mean you don't know for sure where your boy is and what he is doing?"

"I'm afraid so, Sir."

"You aren't up to speed Morton, are you? We're trying to make sure there's evidence leading to Castro himself, and you're sitting here hypothesizin' and supposin' without a shred of hard information from your man."

"True, but I do know that we've confused and frightened him enough for him to take the initiative, just as we planned." Morton was indignant. He had fought against the order to keep Lonsdale in the dark. Now, with the order carried out and the scheme he had developed working as planned, he was being harassed by an amateur, however high-ranking, with no patience for waiting out the results of the end-game of a double-reverse operation.

Morton's problem was that he could offer only circumstantial evidence of Lonsdale doing what he was expected to be doing.

"And supposin' he does convince our Cuban soldier boy to defect?" Smythe sounded menacing.

"Then, Sir," Morton smiled wanly and stood up. He was dog tired and sick to death of dealing with this idiot. "I will have failed as a psychologist, just as I have already failed as a friend and loyal colleague." He headed for the door.

"And where the hell do you think you're going?" Smythe's voice was no longer reedy or weak. "I have not dismissed you."

Morton turned around slowly "Director, you are way out of line! You are a man with few loyalties and even fewer scruples. Your single-mindedness about Castro has blinded you to the need for rewarding dedication, loyalty, and long service. Without men like Lonsdale, the Central Intelligence Agency could not function at all. And, God knows, it has trouble enough functioning as it is." Morton was having difficulty controlling himself. "You say we should discipline him. What for? For doing what we set him up to do? For sensing that something is not quite right, does not quite add up?" He took a deep breath. "Well, Senator, one thing is for sure. We can't discipline him without first finding him, can we?"

Smythe, though offended, was enjoying himself. He gave Morton a derisory smile, "If this thing turns out right, I'll disregard your insults."

"And if I fail?"

"Then I will not only have your boy scout's balls, but yours as well."

The last remark was too much for Morton. He stormed back to Smythe's desk and leaned over it as far as he could. "You insulting, miserable old man! This operation will turn out to be a great success, you'll see, and you'll then claim full credit for it mainly to make points with your right-wing Cuban constituents in Florida. You'll go on sucking up to everyone who might help you even in the remotest way to get confirmed as Director of Central Intelligence. I don't care a damn about myself, but I will not have you talk this way about a senior officer of the Agency, a man who has proven his loyalty and worth many, many times. Nor will I stand by idly to watch you trying to work your way into a job for which you are totally unqualified and temperamentally unsuited."

Morton knew there was no turning back and that he might as well let Smythe have it with both barrels. "Who do you think you're threatening? I come from a respectable and wealthy family, old money if you will. I am not some impoverished parvenu, a bankrupt farmer, like you!"

Smythe looked up at him unfazed and took a sip from the glass of bourbon he was holding. "Why, I do believe your feelings have gotten the better of you." His beady eyes had a malicious glint. "But then I prefer men with feelings, strong feelings . . . and strong opinions . . . real men. I don't like dealing with cold fish, not even New England cold fish. As for being a parvenu, I sure am a parvenu."

Smythe put his glass down. "You see? I know the meaning of the word, having been married to a Parisienne whom I had met at the Sorbonne, which I attended on a scholarship that I won at the University of Southern Florida. Lived in Paris for two years. And my farm did surely go bankrupt. I tried hard, but couldn't keep it going. Had no time; too busy politicking. Then my wife got killed."

The old man smiled bitterly, remembering. "So you see, you can't buffalo me with highfalutin' words like 'parvenu.' I parley-voo pretty damn fluently."

Morton had his emotions under control again. "I'm sorry for having expressed myself rudely, but I did mean what I said about your being prematurely judgmental about my colleague."

"Cut the crap, Morton, and don't pull another cold fish act on me. You hate my guts, you mistrust my motives, and you are offended by my crude behavior. Well, I don't give a flyin' fuck, d'ya hear? You've got one week to produce your man." He took another sip of his drink. "If he's not here next Sunday to report to me personally, I'll have Q Division deal with him."

Morton could not believe his ears. "Q Division? Are you serious??"

Smythe struggled to his feet and stared at Morton unblinkingly. "Yes, Q Division. I want no loose cannon getting in our way, no bleedin' heart liberal to be pulling heroic stunts. I want Operation Adios to succeed."

His mind churning, Morton tried to play for time. "Who came up with the code name Operation Adios and what is the connection?"

"I came up with it, Morton, and it is short for 'Adios Motherfucker.' " Smythe fell back into his chair. "You've got till next Sunday. Otherwise you'll be drawing your pension, and your man will be history."

"Not even you can do that."

"Just watch me. Just watch me." The old man grimaced deprecatingly. "Why, the way I see it, your boy ain't even a proper U.S. citizen."

Morton looked at the man with disbelief. "You mean you'd blow his cover? After all these years?"

"The Cold War is over in case you haven't noticed, and your boy is getting on in years. Time for him to quit." A sudden thought struck him. "Come to think of it, he doesn't really exist anyway, does he?"

The enormity of what he had done to Lonsdale suddenly dawned on Morton with such force that he almost became physically ill. "I should have known better," he whispered, more to himself than to his tormentor.

"Known what, Morton?"

"To take your word, Sir."

CHAPTER TWENTY-SEVEN

Monday
Vienna, Austria and Montreal, Canada

Air Canada has flights leaving Vienna for Toronto every Monday and Friday at forty-five minutes past noon. Lonsdale made sure to be at the airport by eleven to have time to make his final travel arrangements.

He held two reservations made via telephone: one in business class under the name of Schwartz, the other under the name of Jackson in hospitality class. He would decide at the last possible moment which of the two to activate, depending first, on how he read the security arrangements at Schwechat, and second, on passenger load. Having purchased in cash two one-way tickets from two different travel agents, he had no constraints.

In addition to the two tickets, he had three passports, including Schwartz's, which contained a picture of a gray-haired man. But he was sure the Jackson and Lonsdale passports were already on the Interpol "to watch for" list. Since Interpol meant CIA, Lonsdale would be tipping his hand to Washington by using either of them, something he didn't want to do too early.

It was clear that, despite the obvious danger, the Schwartz passport was the safest to use since he'd had no difficulty crossing the Austro-Hungarian border with it at Hegyeshalom the night before.

The old man's body would probably not be found before noon. It would then take about three hours for the Hungarian police to establish Schwartz's identity and passport number from his hotel registration card, to conduct a preliminary investigation, and to report the murder to the Canadian Embassy and Interpol.

Another three to six hours would pass before immigration officers the world over would be notified that the Schwartz passport was no longer valid. That would mean relative safety until about six p.m. Vienna time, noon in Toronto.

He called Air Canada and was told his flight would be half empty. This helped him decide. Schwartz would leave Austria and arrive in Canada as Jackson, a common name that might just slip by undetected. With glasses and wearing the hat he had bought in Montreal covering his gray Schwartz hair, Lonsdale would have no trouble passport-picture-wise. As for the "watch-for" issue, he'd cross that bridge when he came to it. He could always elude surveillance and disappear.

At eleven thirty sharp he presented himself at the Air Canada Maple Leaf Lounge and asked to be checked in. The attendant smiled as she took his ticket and asked for his passport. He fumbled around. "Sorry about this, but I seem to be more tired than usual," he said in English.

"Too much wine last night in Grinzig?" she grinned, teasing him. Lonsdale laughed. "At my age even a little wine is too much." He bent down, fumbled some more, opened and closed his sample case, let out an exaggerated groan as he straightened up and clutched at his waist. "Don't ever get old," he said. "My arthritis is killing me." He extracted the Schwartz passport from his breast pocket and opened it on the picture page. Instead of handing it over he waved it at her. "Will this do?" he blinked at her over Schwartz's bifocals.

She checked him in, gave him an aisle seat and, as a bonus, blocked off the seat next to him.

"You're sure I won't have trouble with my bags at security?" he asked her, pointing to his large sample case.

The attendant rose slightly and looked over her computer. "No, not at all. You should see the monsters some passengers get away with. But here," she said sweetly and handed him a special tag, "put this on your bag and you'll sail through security with ease."

He thanked her profusely and went to get himself a cup of tea.

Hurdle number one out of the way.

Hurdle number two was another matter. The Austrian border policeman he got was grouchy. His attitude was hostile. "Passport and boarding card please."

Lonsdale obliged. The policeman began to sift through his documents.

"Schwartz. What kind of a name is that for a Canadian?" *A racist*, Lonsdale thought, *and I had to have the misfortune of getting involved with him.* "Jewish," he replied.

The man smiled. "You Jewish?"

"Yes."

"Good for you, so am I." He stamped Schwartz's passport and waved Lonsdale on.

He had no trouble at the boarding gate. To his surprise, they were not checking passports there, and as for the X-ray machine, the only metal he was carrying was a collection of old coins.

He was safely in his seat ten minutes before take-off, but dared not breathe a sigh of relief until half past two: the time he estimated they exited Austrian air space.

He asked for a double vodka and Perrier, gulped it down, made his seat go as far back as it would, closed his eyes and set his mind on replay. The things Casas and he had discussed in Budapest were all jumbled up in his mind and needed sorting out.

Casas had told Lonsdale that he had flown from Prague to Budapest via Czechoslovak Airlines, just as Schwartz had said. He was traveling on a diplomatic passport, which made his luggage exempt from search of any kind. He always traveled with a maximum of two small bags, like Lonsdale's, and everyone assumed his briefcase, resembling Schwartz's sample case, was full of important papers, when actually, Casas was steadily smuggling rare coins and priceless ivory figurines from Africa to Hungary. Schwartz then took over, exporting these items to Canada under a license from the Hungarian National Museum.

The general was scrupulous in his affairs. Cuban soldiers were allowed a bounty of twenty-five per cent of everything they "liberated" in Angola. Casas followed the rules carefully and had arranged for Schwartz to remit from BCCI Montreal to the Cuban Ministry of the Interior's account at the Banco Nacional de Cuba in Havana, three-quarters of what Schwartz paid for the coins and figurines.

The balance Schwartz kept for Casas in Montreal. Thus, technically, Casas was absolutely on side. The Cuban government got paid its due and the general, though his funds were being kept for him by Schwartz in U.S. dollars, was not in possession of foreign currency, a criminal act punishable in Cuba by deprivation of personal liberty, in other words, prison.

Lonsdale and Casas had tried to estimate how much money was involved. They calculated that, during his thirteen-odd trips to Hungary in the last year and a half, Casas had sold Schwartz about four million dollars' worth of coins and carved ivory figurines of which a quarter was Casas'. All this he had sacrificed to spook Fernandez!

How much money old man Schwartz made on the deal they could only guess at.

The entire operation, except the arrangement with Schwartz, was known to the Cuban government and had its wholehearted support. It was brilliant in its simplicity because it depended on only two men.

As for the drug thing, that was a highly complex and entirely different matter. It required close coordination between the Cuban Ministry of the Interior, including Department Z, and the army, and the cooperation of more than two hundred people, of whom no more than twenty were in the know.

Casas had spent a good hour explaining to Lonsdale the rationale behind Cuba becoming mixed up in drug trafficking and the complicated logistics involved. He had then pulled a three-ring binder with a fluorescent orange cover from his briefcase. It was the complete operations manual of "Golden Gate," the code name for Cuba's drug-running operation. "Only ten copies of this are *known* to exist," he had said, sounding exhausted from the pain and the tension. "I'm giving you my copy, which I always carry with me in case I need to look up some detail. Guard it with your life."

In return, Lonsdale had given his newfound friend the addresses of a series of dead-letter drops throughout the Republic of Cuba regularly serviced by the CIA. He also provided Casas with recognition codes and escape routes that he had developed specifically for the general prior to his departure from the Bethesda office.

Lonsdale began to enumerate the escape routes in his mind, but didn't make it beyond number three. He fell asleep.

The stewardess's gentle touch on his shoulder startled him. "I didn't mean to disturb you, Sir, but would you care for some lunch?"

Lonsdale realized that he was famished. During the last thirty hours he had only eaten twice—a light breakfast at the Hotel Citadella and another at the Vienna Hilton, where he had spent the previous night.

"I'd love some lunch," he answered eagerly.

"We have chicken or beef."

"Beef it is. And some red wine, please."

He wolfed down his meal, had a cognac with his coffee, and was fast asleep by the time the cabin was darkened for the movie.

He awoke to the sound of the cabin crew clattering the dishes used for serving afternoon tea. He felt refreshed, but agitated. He figured his subconscious must have been reminding him of the problems he was going to have to face in very short order. He waved off the proffered tray of Viennese pastries and hunkered down to some serious decision making.

At Toronto he would have two choices: go on to Montreal and see Micheline, or rent a car and drive to Washington. There was also a third obvious choice, that of calling Morton and demanding to be brought up-to-date, which his inner voice vehemently opposed. Under the circumstances he felt that, discretion being the better part of valor, he would follow his instincts rather than logic.

Since he had no more than a couple of hundred dollars left—and, foremost, because he was desperate to see Micheline again—he opted for Montreal.

At most major airports of the world there are designated lines for returning citizens to facilitate their reentry into their own country. Not so in Canada where those "coming home" must line up with the rest of the travelers. Lonsdale assumed this was due to the essentially self-effacing nature of the country's citizens.

The immigration hall at Toronto's Pearson International Airport was a zoo. There were more than a thousand people milling about.

Sporting Schwartz's hat, he lined up behind a five-member African family, obviously about to take up residence in Canada. Their turn at seeing the immigration officer came about forty minutes after Lonsdale had gotten into line behind them. The harassed official applied himself to the paperwork, which took him ten minutes to complete.

Lonsdale was next. He handed the man his Jackson passport. The officer, relieved to be dealing with a simple case, hardly looked at it. "Sorry to have kept you waiting," he mumbled then looked at the customs declaration Lonsdale had meticulously completed. "Anything to declare?"

"Nothing."

"How long will you be staying in Canada?"

"About an hour; long enough to rent a car and drive to Buffalo."

The man handed him his papers. "Good luck." And that was that.

So much for the Interpol "to-be-watched-for" list, thought Lonsdale as he waited for the shuttle to take him to the Bristol Hotel, just around the corner. "Here we go again," he murmured. "I had better start worrying about surveillance again." Being cut off from head office, and out of favor, he had no way of finding out who may be looking for him: the CIA for not turning up at the office as ordered, the Cubans because he was messing with Casas, or the Colombians who must, by now, be wondering what Fernandez, their contact with Cuba, was up to.

The bus arrived and he got on. Off it went from Terminal 2 to Terminal 1, with Lonsdale standing in the rear door watching for pursuit. Although there didn't seem to be any, he wanted to be sure, so he waited until the passengers embarking at Terminal 1 were all on board, then got off at the very last second. Nobody followed, and Lonsdale melted into the crowd.

He took the escalator to the departure level, bought himself a ticket to Montreal on a Québecair flight leaving within forty minutes, and repaired to the washrooms to change underwear and freshen up. His instincts were insisting that time was running out on him.

At Montreal's Dorval Airport he exchanged Schwartz's elegant cashmere overcoat for the ill-fitting but warm and water-resistant coat he'd bought in Montreal. Details, details, but he knew that this garment, rather than Schwartz's, would be the one to keep him dry should he have to walk in the rain.

By half past eight he was in a cab on his way to Micheline's apartment reasonably certain he was not being followed. Again, to be sure, he made the driver drop him two blocks from her apartment.

Before reaching the building he circled the little park oppo-site it then cut across, striding purposefully, sample case in hand, just another working stiff on his way home after staying late at the office. He didn't even glance at Le Sanctuaire's main entrance as he rounded the corner and headed down the street leading away from the building. He continued for one bloc, turned right for two blocs, then right again, to fetch up against the rear of Le Sanctuaire, oppo-site the garage entrance.

He sprinted across the street, down the ramp leading to the garage door, slammed the access card Micheline had given him into its slot and prayed for the heavy overhead door to open. It did.

Lonsdale was through in a flash and, turning immediately to his left, took refuge behind a fat pillar. He waited, listening intently for footsteps, but heard none. After thirty seconds, the door began to close and Lonsdale took off toward the elevators, hoping the noise of the closing door would mask the clatter of his footsteps. About ten yards from the elevator door he hid behind a pillar once more and willed himself to remain stock-still. He listened intently for a full minute, but could hear no one.

He strode over to the elevator door and tried to open it. It was locked!

"Shit!" He'd forgotten that a special key was needed to get in. "It's the details that will kill you every time," he cursed silently and fished through the keys Micheline had given him. "Good girl," he murmured when he spotted the funny-looking Abloy key he needed. "You're better at this than me."

She lived on the twelfth floor, but he took the elevator only to floor number ten and used the stairs for the rest. Although he felt ridicu-lous about doing it, he tiptoed up the remaining two flights with great caution, still watching out for pursuit. He continued on tiptoes until he reached her kitchen door. Like the last time, he listened to what was going on in the apartment. There was no one in the kitchen even though the lights were on. He tried the door. It was locked.

Using her key, he entered, closing the door softly behind him. He put his sample case down, took a quick step forward, and shed his hat and coat. Then, by pure instinct, he picked up a large knife from the kitchen counter and tiptoed into the unlit dining room.

The area was separated from the living room by sliding doors, which Micheline liked to keep open to make *le salon* seem more spacious. Lonsdale could clearly hear what was going on.

"—his own safety," he heard a familiar-sounding male voice say.

Micheline answered: "But I've told you a dozen times already that I have no idea where he is. I have not seen him or heard from him for two weeks."

"Yes, you did tell me that, but can you remember what day that was?"

"I think it was a Thursday, but I'm not sure."

"Was it the Thursday before Mr. Siddiqui was killed?"

"Definitely before."

"You sure?"

Lonsdale stepped into the living room. "Leave the poor woman alone," he said "or risk having yourself killed dead with a kitchen knife." Turning to the startled man sitting in an armchair in front of him, he held the object in his hand high. "What the hell are you doing here, James Morton, and how did you find out about Micheline?"

Try as he would, Morton could not stop himself from laughing. All was well with the world. Lonsdale had come in from the cold in more ways than one.

The man seemed to be in love again.

PREPARACIÓN

CHAPTER TWENTY-EIGHT

Tuesday
Washington, DC

Lonsdale had barely had time to give Micheline a peck on the cheek before Morton had him back at St. Hubert Airport and on their way to Washington in the Agency's plane. During the flight Morton had been uncharacteristically reserved, insisting that he hold his questions until they met Smythe the next day.

Lonsdale got to bed at three a.m., nine in the morning in Budapest. He had managed five hours' restless sleep before having to drag himself to the great man's office.

"Sit down, Lonsdale, and listen. I owe you an explanation and an apology." Smythe was not in character. He was being gracious to the point where he even offered glasses of his favorite branch water to Morton and Lonsdale. "I hate that bearded bastard in Havana with a passion, and I want him the hell outta there. I'm doing my darndest to accelerate his political demise short of killin', him and I'm having a devil of a time."

Lonsdale bristled, but a glance from Morton made him hold his tongue. "About two years ago the then-director of Central Intelligence asked for my support for a highly imaginative, but extremely risky plan to dislodge Dr. Castro. Risky for the agent running the operation in Havana, risky for the government of these United States because of the possibility of the scheme backfiring on us if it were discovered by Dr. Castro's intelligence apparatus prematurely, risky for the CIA because, if improperly implemented, it would make the Agency a laughingstock worldwide."

Director Smythe leaned back in his chair and paused for effect. "Most importantly, the plan represented a risk for me because the operation would never have been authorized by the president without my backing, and its failure he would surely lay at my feet." He glanced at Lonsdale. "Now don't get all itchy and uppity. I know what you're thinkin'."

"And what may that be, Sir?"

"That success, on the other hand, would guarantee my confirmation as director of Central Intelligence. And you're right." Smythe went so far as to wink at Lonsdale. "So I was on the horns of a dilemma. Should I trust you two with details, or should I keep things strictly on a need-to-know basis?" He sighed. "Manpower-wise, apart from the communications boys at Langley, there were originally only five people involved: the agent on the ground and his control, plus the DCI, of course, me, and the president. The agent—let's call him Charley—had warned us that it would take about two years to get things goin' and he was right." Warming to his subject, the senator began to pace about.

"Charley was really cookin', and we only needed another three to four months before we could pull the trigger and kiss Dr. Castro adios. And then—" He turned to Morton, "Why don't you take it from here and tell your man what happened then." Smythe rounded his desk and sank heavily into his chair.

"And then," Morton picked up effortlessly from where the old man had left off. "Fernandez happened. He bolted, and the CIA contact at the INS in Miami got us involved before anybody could stop him from doing so." Morton looked very uncomfortable. "Director Smythe didn't find out about our being in the picture until the day you left for Montreal, chomping at the bit to get at General Casas. By then the INS man had done what he had been trained to do."

"And called you." Lonsdale made himself sound matter-of-fact, but inside, he was seething. *Yet another cluster fuck*, he thought, *due to the left hand not knowing what the right hand was doing.*

"That is correct."

"And asked you to suggest a way to turn to the director's advantage my unwelcome intrusion into an operation about which I still know nothing."

"Bingo," interrupted Smythe, chortling with self-satisfaction. "Your boss then came up with a doozer." He winked at Lonsdale again. "I've got to hand it to him. He's a genius at manipulating folks. You have a reputation of being the original eager beaver, someone who, once he gets his teeth into something never lets go. So, Morton here came up with the idea of using psychology on you."

The senator squinted at his two agents then swung his swivel chair around, turning his back to them. Seemingly addressing the window, he continued: "He figured the less information he gave you the more you'd give chase; the more he ordered you to come home, the less likely you'd be to obey; the less secure you felt, the more determined you'd be to succeed."

"But to what end?" Lonsdale interrupted "What was I supposed to do differently from what I originally set out to do? How did the plan you had in mind differ from the one Jim and I had worked out? Was the objective not always to get to Casas?"

"Not quite. Almost, but not quite." Morton's voice was soft. "You see, getting to Casas was only step one."

"I know, I know." Lonsdale was no longer bothering to hide his impatience. "First I was to contact Casas, which I did. Next, I was to bring him back here, which I failed to do. I'm sorry—"

"Don't be." Director Smythe swung around to face them again. "You did good. You did exactly what we wanted you to do. You chased that Cuban soldier right back to mama."

"I did? Is that what you wanted?"

"Exactly."

"But what on earth for?"

"Because he's going to help you find the proof we need to show the world what a bad bastard Dr. Castro really is: a drug dealer, money launderer, and cheat!"

"He could have done that easier from here, but I failed to convince him of that."

"No, he sure as hell could not have. Could he, Morton?"

"No, surely not."

Exasperated, Lonsdale turned on Morton. "What are you talking about? I thought you and I were clear on this thing from the word go. Either Casas was telling the truth, in which event we had Castro by the balls, or it was a put-up job by the Cubans to suck us in and make us look really stupid. My job was to find out whether Casas was on the level, and if in the affirmative, to turn him."

The director cut in swiftly. "And what did you manage to find out?"

"That, in my opinion, he is on the level."

"Is that so?"

"Yes, Sir. I'm convinced that the man is sincere, but very concerned about lack of proof linking the drug operation undeniably with the Cuban government."

"You think there exists any such proof?" Smythe was staring at Lonsdale intently.

"Some, but tenuous."

"Such as?"

"There was a meeting between the general and his minister at which the drug operation was briefly discussed."

"Really. That's very interesting. Were there any witnesses?"

"Yes, one. Captain Fernandez, the fellow who bolted and whom we're supposed to be holding in protective custody here, but, whom for some reason, I'm not being allowed to access." Lonsdale's look at Morton was accusatory.

"Well now, things ain't necessarily always the way they appear to be. Are they, Morton?"

"For sure not, Sir."

"You did good, Lonsdale, don't you fret," the senator repeated and allowed himself a fleeting smile. "But I wouldn't want you to rely on this story of a meeting with the minister too much. Would you, Morton?"

"No, Sir."

"And why the hell not, for Christ's sake?" Lonsdale's temper was getting the better of him. "Let's pull in Fernandez and Casas. Let Casas reveal the details of the drug operation on television and let Fernandez corroborate what Casas says, then let's watch Dr. Castro squirm."

"Atta boy, Lonsdale." The old man's voice was firm. "Full o' piss and vinegar, eager to get on with the job, as always. There is only one small problem."

"What's that, Sir?"

"Remember Charley, the agent in situ?"

"What about him?"

Smythe was grinning. He reminded Lonsdale of the Grim Reaper, gleefully waiting for his next victim.

"It so happens that it was Charley who organized this entire drug operation. The Cuban government had nothing to do with it. Castro happens to be innocent for once. In this particular case, he is the designated fall guy."

Lonsdale felt as if somebody had kicked him in the solar plexus. He felt winded, nauseated, and dizzy. "Charley . . . the agent in situ . . . the snake in the grass?" he whispered. "Oh my God, it's Oscar De la Fuente." What a mess. The naive, idealistic general tricked into participating in an unauthorized drug smuggling operation; Fernandez the trusted factotum, unknowingly running errands for the CIA, the killing of the girl in Cayman, of Siddiqui and Schwartz—because they were witnesses to what?

Lonsdale needed time. He needed to get away from Smythe and Morton, into the fresh air, to think, analyze, absorb, and digest this dreadful avalanche of gut-wrenching information. The Agency didn't trust him. Again, it had made him cause the death of at least two innocent people. It had also tricked him into sending yet another man, an honorable soldier, to his certain death. His superiors, cold-blooded, manipulating bastards, felt no loyalty toward the man, and, this time, the group included his lifelong friend Morton.

After a few seconds he regained his composure and allowed the cold, ruthless, and scheming Lonsdale of years gone by to take over once more.

He closed his eyes to listen to his inner voice. It was clear as a bell. *The story you're being fed doesn't make sense*, it was warning. *It's not logical. They're not the ones in control. Follow the money trail, follow Fernandez.*

"—count on your help." He heard Smythe through the fog of fury that had enveloped him for a while, but that had now begun to lift.

"I'm sorry, Sir, but would you mind repeating what you've just said," he requested, sounding sincere, respectful, and eager to help. Yes, "eager" was the key word here, he reminded himself. *Keep sounding eager—that will fool them.*

"What's the matter? Can't keep up?" Smythe was his malevolent self again.

"It's just that I have a lot of information to absorb and sort out in short order, information, I might add, that you, Sir, and Jim have been privy to for some time, but which is new and a bit of a shocker to me, so please bear with me." He gave them the warmest smile he could muster.

"What I said was that I'm sure General Casas can be relied upon to produce the proof we need to link this drug operation to the Castro regime, especially now that he can count on your help."

"My help, Director?"

"Yes, your help. There's no one more qualified than you to act as the general's control, no one more familiar with the file, more involved in the details."

"Except Oscar De la Fuente—"

"Yes, that sure is so, but he can't afford to come out of the tall grass. Not just yet."

"Very well, Sir." Lonsdale made a big show of thinking about what to do next, although he knew precisely where he was headed. "You may count on me to do my best, but I ask you to remember that we face serious problems here. Should even a whisper of what's going on reach the upper echelons in Havana they'll blow the whistle faster than you can say 'adios.' "

"Why would they want to blow the whistle? I would have thought they would want to cover the whole thing up."

"Not if the highest echelons are really not involved and can prove it. In such an event it would be in their interest to put Casas and De la Fuente on trial and have them confess to initiating the operation without authorization and for their own personal financial advantage to boot."

"They would never do that!"

"What, Sir?" Lonsdale was playing stupid on purpose. "Put them on trial or have them confess."

"Casas and De la Fuente would never confess."

"Casas certainly would. He is basically an honorable man, naive and idealistic. He would confess for sure if he thought it would save his precious Cuban Revolutionary government from international censure."

"He wouldn't have to." Smythe sounded too smug for Lonsdale's liking. "There's no proof of General Casas's complicity except De la Fuente—"

"And Fernandez."

"Don't you fret about Fernandez. He's being looked after."

"What about De la Fuente?"

"De la Fuente will certainly not fess up. He'll keep on saying he was told to initiate the operation by the highest echelons in Cuba."

"But, Sir, all of us in this room know that without proof of some kind of a link, his story will not stand up."

Smythe gave in. "I take your point." He leaned back in his armchair and contemplated the ceiling for a while. Then he snapped forward and fixed Lonsdale with a baleful eye. "What do you propose we do?"

"Follow the money trail and make sure it cannot be shown we're the ones who have ultimate control over it."

"We've started working on that."

"Then, Director," Lonsdale was greatly relieved, "you don't really need me to intervene, do you?"

"Yes I do." Smythe had no intention of letting Lonsdale off the hook. "I want insurance. I want you to provide watertight proof that the link to the Revolutionary government is clearly, visibly, and indisputably there."

"In other words, Sir," Lonsdale met the old man's gaze unflinchingly, "You, the acting director of Central Intelligence, ex-chairman of the Senate Intelligence Oversight Committee, and a close confidant of the president of the United States, are requesting that a lowly civil servant, an employee of the Central Intelligence Agency, fabricate proof of wrongdoing by the Castro government when you know full well that no such wrongdoing has taken place?"

"I know no such thing," Smythe snapped. "Although we did start it, for all I know, Casas's minister is the one behind this drug thing now, and," he paused to catch his breath, "as for asking an employee of the CIA to do a naughty thing or two, that's what you fellers get paid for: to do naughty things. In your particular case, you're not an employee of anyone, you're believably deniable, because not only are you not a citizen of these United States, you don't even exist, having died a long time ago!"

Lonsdale would not be baited. He laughed. "So, if I'm dead you cannot really harm me, or tell me what to do, can you?"

"That's so, but since you aren't physically dead it would help your chances of physical survival if you cooperated with me."

Lonsdale stood up. "I understand perfectly, Senator, and although I can certainly not guarantee success, you may rest assured that I will do my best." He made as if to leave. From the corner of his eye he saw Morton getting ready to accompany him, so he stopped and turned back to face the old man once more. "Before I leave here, and in the light of what you have just said I require two things. One, that you here and now verbally instruct my immediate superior, James Morton, to give me written orders specifying what I am to do. Two," he held up two fingers, "that you hereby authorize Mr. Morton and me to mount a full-scale rescue operation to extract Casas and De la Fuente from Cuba should, in our sole opinion, this become necessary to save their lives."

Smythe thought for a while. "Your request seems reasonable. Morton, you have my authority to proceed with cutting written orders for your assistant here and to mount a rescue operation to extract the general and Charley, if necessary." He scratched his nose. "Come to think of it, such a rescue operation can only have a beneficial effect. It will make great copy and it will also show that the United States means business and looks after its own."

In a pig's eye, thought Lonsdale as he followed Morton out of the room.

On leaving the senator's office, Morton tried to reestablish the old camaraderie with Lonsdale by inviting him to lunch, but his deputy begged off politely.

"I've invited Micheline for a few days."

"Micheline in Washington?" Morton was surprised and glad. "Hey, that's wonderful. How long is she staying?"

"About ten days." Lonsdale grinned. "So if you don't mind, I'll take some of my accumulated sick leave and spend it with her."

Morton's heart sank. "When are you thinking of coming back to the office then?"

"I'll be in on Friday to pick up my expense check and to visit with you for an hour. Then I'll be gone until a week from Monday. Give you time to organize the paperwork for our next project." A quick smile, and Lonsdale was gone.

CHAPTER TWENTY-NINE

Tuesday through Friday
Washington, DC

Morton looked at his watch. It was ten to ten on Friday morning and no sign of the famous insomniac. Either Micheline was still in town or Lonsdale had changed his habits drastically. Half an hour later, just as Morton was about to call his wayward deputy, Mrs. Weisskopf stuck her head through the door: "He's here," she announced, "and he looks like hell."

"Stop worrying about him, Mrs. W." Morton glowered at her. "He's tired because he just spent an athletic week with a rediscovered old girlfriend."

"How about that," she beamed. "Is this thing serious?"

"Don't know yet. Might become serious though. The man is vulnerable."

Mrs. Weisskopf bristled. "As for vulnerable, look who's talking." She withdrew in a huff, her motherly instincts ruffled. She almost bumped into Lonsdale in the doorway. Everybody laughed, and for a millisecond Morton thought things were improving. But he was wrong. Without sitting down Lonsdale came straight to the point. "Have you got the paperwork ready, Jim?" He asked politely.

"Yes, I do." Morton was disappointed and allowed it to show in his tone of voice. "It's in the form of a minute of a meeting of the Wise Men, but I think you'll like it."

Lonsdale speed-read through the text that Morton had handed him. "Pretty vague, this," he said, chewing his lower lip. "They seem to acknowledge the existence of an ongoing operation the aim of which is to topple the Castro regime."

He paused. "They even go so far as to approve its continuation for the next twelve months. But although they refer to our department as the lead horse of the team the language is vague enough to allow them to twist the action away from us if it suited them."

Morton spread his hands in resignation. "You're right, but that's all I could get. I confess I didn't even expect this much; not after the hard time they gave me when I asked them for it."

Lonsdale gave Morton a noncommittal look. "What does it matter anyway? I'll go along with the gig as long as you write me a letter that refers to the minutes and is more specific than this garbage." He picked up the document again. "This letter, I hasten to add, I will submit for registered cataloguing in Central Files. I intend to lodge the registration number with my attorneys."

Morton took the offensive. "Aren't we being a bit too formal this morning, old buddy?"

"Senator Smythe is a powerful man, Jim. He made some disturbing and, to me, offensive remarks the other day about my not really belonging anywhere. Now you and I both know that Smythe is an uncouth opportunist and not much more, but I feel time has come to protect myself, just in case."

"Just in case of what?"

"Just in case Smythe gets obsessed with the idea that I am some sort of a threat to him, and that I'm superfluous."

"Aren't you flattering yourself?"

"You mean about being a threat?"

"Yes."

"Well Jim, alone maybe I'm not much of a threat." Lonsdale walked to the window and looked out. The bullet proof, one-way glass distorted the view, just like his own paranoia distorted his relationship with other people. "But you and I together are, indeed, a threat. Furthermore," he continued, "Smythe knows that although you don't like him you will not act against him on impulse or allow yourself to be motivated by personal reasons, while his perception of me is quite different."

"Meaning?"

"He knows I dislike him a lot and that I'm a good hater. He knows he went too far the other day when he said that legally speaking I didn't exist, that I'm believably deniable. So he figures he has reason to fear me."

Morton could see Lonsdale had done some serious thinking, none of it positive, which was worrisome. "So where do we go from here?"

"We'll go by the book. Every wet job our department undertakes will have to be authorized in writing from above. No more veiled verbal instructions, oblique references, and all that kind of shit."

"What else?"

"Every assignment I'm given from now on will have to be backed by the proper paperwork."

"Such as?"

"In the case of Casas and company, a letter from you giving me carte blanche as the agent in situ to handle him as best I can and authorizing me to develop a comprehensive plan for his extraction, if need be."

"You want to act as Casas's exclusive control then?"

"Isn't that what needs to happen if we are to help him fabricate the so-called proof Smythe is after?"

"I suppose in a way it is. But what happens if I refuse to give you the letter you're asking for? Are you going to abandon your new-found Cuban friend?" Morton felt he had to test the depth to which their relationship had sunk.

"My friend, I will not be the one who will have abandoned him. It will have been our organization as a whole and you in particular." Then Lonsdale added sadly, "But then, of late, you've had practice in abandoning friends." He turned his back to the window to face Morton, who looked away.

"I cannot give you the letter you want."

"Then you'll have to face the consequences, Jim."

"Which are?"

"A full board of inquiry hearing about my past, present, and future, lots of bad publicity in the press, not to mention the wrath of Senator Smythe."

"But you have no proof of his involvement."

"Jim, what kind of a jerk do you think I am?"

"What do you mean by that?"

"I was wearing a body wire during the meeting with the old man."

"You what?" Morton was appalled.

"You heard me. I've got the whole meeting on tape. You should hear the quality of the sound. It's excellent."

CHAPTER THIRTY

Sunday
Miami, Florida

Captain Fernandez could not believe his good fortune. The CIA was finished with him and they were going to let him go! Moreover, they were going to enroll him in the witness protection program to enhance his chances of living out his natural life.

At first they'd given him a very hard time. After that obnoxious Mr. Bob or whatever his name was had grilled him all day Sunday they had turned off the air conditioner and left him to rot for four days. Finally, on Friday, Reyes Puma had come to see him. Apparently, he'd had to apply for a writ of habeas corpus before they let him visit.

Fernandez thanked God he'd had the good sense to consult with him before turning himself in. Reyes Puma sure knew the ropes; that they would call in the CIA once they'd heard his story had been a foregone conclusion. And that bastard Mr. Bob and his colleague were CIA for sure, he could smell it. But why hadn't they followed up on his story? Why had they left him to sweat for four days? Maybe to soften him up.

Fernandez couldn't understand what was happening. OK, so they had wanted to lean on him a bit to make him more cooperative, but Mr. Bob never came back, never followed up. Instead, the INS had handed him over to the CIA. The Agency's case officers had then made him write out his life's story in the greatest of detail four times.

This took almost a week during which, he had to admit, the CIA had accommodated him in a luxurious safe house with garden, pool, servants, good food, and video movies at night. He'd then spent another four days answering questions about his career in the military while they tried to poke holes in his story and to confuse him.

Ungrateful bastards. He was handing them the scoop of the century, the lever with which to dislodge Castro from control of Cuba, the story that would discredit the Revolution. And what did they do? They had let him cool his heels for twelve days during which he had to answer questions about just about everything, except about details concerning the drug-running operation.

Then Reyes Puma, who really did seem to have a lot of clout, had managed to get to see him again and the day after, on Friday, they had said they'd let him go. But good old fat and perspiring Reyes Puma wouldn't let them do that without compensation for what he had done to help the United States's cause against Cuba. He had demanded money and adequate arrangements for his physical safety.

Another week had gone by while his lawyer-cousin bargained with the INS. His biggest ace in the hole of course had been the photo Reyes Puma had arranged to have taken of him at the Immigration and Naturalization Office just before he had turned himself in. Nice, sharp picture, with the calendar in the background, a uniformed immigration officer on one side of him and Reyes Puma on the other.

In the end the INS and the CIA had come through. They had given him back his carry-on bag containing his clothes and his million bucks and added a million more to it. The money was no longer in cash. They had given him bankers' drafts in hundred thousand dollar denominations and a nice letter explaining that these were, at his request, in payment for some Canadian stock called INCO he was supposed to have sold on the Toronto Stock Exchange. The letter said the money was net of taxes.

They also gave him a hundred thousand bucks in cash of which he would give his cousin half, for services rendered. But the best part was the way the INS had fixed him up with a complete set of papers: social security card, driver's license, credit cards, even a U.S. passport, all made out in the name of Raul Hernandez (conveniently similar to Fernandez), born in Oaxaka, Mexico, but now a naturalized U.S. citizen.

He was ready to leave. Where the hell was Reyes Puma anyway? Late, as always.

Reyes Puma, who'd fled Cuba a year after Fidel Castro's revolution triumphed and who'd been blackmailed by Castro's agents in Miami into working for them, had good reason to be late. As the most senior member of Cuban Military Intelligence in Florida, he was busy editing and encoding an "eyes only" message to Cuba's Minister of the Revolutionary Armed Forces. The handwritten message had to be ready in time for pickup before noon by one of Compay Secundo's musicians, who thought he was doing Reyes Puma a personal favor by delivering a letter to a mutual friend in Havana. The letter looked innocuous and the addressee happened to be the man in charge of issuing exit visas to musicians planning to travel abroad as part of Cuba's worldwide cultural exchange.

Reyes Puma could never understand how the United States, hell-bent on bringing down the Castro regime, would allow Cuban artists to travel with no restrictions to, from, and within the United States. Did the Americans not realize they were handing the Castro an unparalleled opportunity to spy and subvert?

Reyes Puma found his position very rewarding. The descendant of once wealthy landowners, he had arrived in Miami penniless. He had worked his way through college and within six years become a member of the Florida bar. In the year of his admission he was approached by Cuban Military Intelligence to join up in return for a generous stipend for his aging, widowed mother whom he'd been forced to leave behind in Havana, and who, at the time, was living in very strained circumstances. Reyes Puma accepted without hesitation, and was then told to specialize in immigration law.

It had taken him three full years to develop the contacts and acquire the experience that made him one of the most sought-after practitioners of his specialty in Miami. As his reputation grew and his clients became more numerous and prosperous, so did his usefulness to Cuban Military Intelligence. By the time of Fernandez's defection he was their number one intelligence agent and reporting to the minister directly, which only added to his stress.

Reyes Puma could find only one way to escape the constant pressure—by eating. And the more he ate the more he wanted to eat.

Fernandez's story had not been news to Reyes Puma. He'd heard rumors about the operation before, and from none other than his puppet, Acting Director Smythe, whom he had been blackmailing on behalf of the Castro government for a couple of years now. Under the circumstances Reyes Puma wanted to be certain his report was carefully worded and covered every aspect of the Fernandez situation and the arrangements he had made to keep his cousin in sight after his liberation.

In spite of these elaborate preparations he was only a half-hour late for Fernandez's release hearing at the INS office. The judge, put out by having to work on a Sunday and then made to wait, was mercifully brief. In no time Fernandez was clutching the Stars and Stripes and taking the Oath of Allegiance. He was then handed an envelope with instructions on how to start his new life and told to get out of town for his own safety.

He paid Reyes Puma fifty thousand dollars for his services on the spot and then asked to be dropped off at the nearest car rental agency.

"And then?" his cousin asked.

"Hell, I don't know. I'll drive north or west and take a few days to look around, find a bank, buy clothes—"

"How will you keep in touch with your family?"

"What family, Filberto? I'm an orphan, I'm divorced, my kids are grown up and married. I have no grandchildren and the rest of the family living here in Miami barely remembers me."

"Still, your kids ought to be able to contact you." Reyes Puma kept pressing. He wanted to double check on what Smythe had told him about Fernandez's new identity. "In case of an emergency for example."

"I thought about that quite a bit." Fernandez gazed out the car window pensively. "I'm almost fifty, and I have been granted a reprieve, a new beginning. I have money, I'm free of my past and I can do whatever I please. I don't want to fuck this up."

"What do you mean by that?"

"I just want to disappear. Go somewhere and start fresh. Travel a little perhaps, maybe find a new wife." He let his voice trail off.

"OK, so where do you want me to drop you off?" It was clear that his cousin would confide in Reyes Puma no further.

"Right here will do." Fernandez pointed at the hotel they were just passing. "I'll grab a cab and be on my way." He turned to his cousin, obviously moved. "Thank you for everything you've done for me."

Reyes Puma stopped the car, and they got out. "Don't mention it, *mi primo*, it's all right. I did no more than my duty to a client." He gave a short, bitter laugh. "And a damned well-paying client at that, whom I'm at the point of losing forever." They embraced warmly and, out of breath, Reyes Puma climbed back into his SUV specially built to accommodate his bulk. "Take care of yourself Paco, d'you hear," he yelled through the open window, "and remember; if you need something, all you need do is call."

"You take care of yourself too, and watch that weight of yours." Fernandez shouted back. "Eat less and get some exercise."

Almost in tears, Reyes Puma waved good-bye and drove off.

He had been forced to choose between saving his mother's life and that of his cousin.

He couldn't stop shaking.

Fernandez walked to the hotel's main entrance and took the first cab in line. "Take me to Alamo Car Rentals," he said to the driver.

"There's no need for that," the man replied. "They have a desk right here in the hotel."

In less than twenty minutes he was at the wheel of a comfortable car, on his way to Bertram Yachts in Coconut Grove.

It never occurred to him to check for pursuit. He felt safe: safe from Casas and the army, safe from De la Fuente and his gang at the Cuban Ministry of the Interior, safe from Castro, and safe from the most dangerous of them all, the minister of the Revolutionary Armed Forces.

After all Fernandez was now a citizen of the United States of America.

CHAPTER THIRTY-ONE

Monday and Tuesday
Naples, Florida

Having spent a pleasant afternoon looking at boats, checking prices and evaluating bargains at the yacht broker, Fernandez booked into the Coconut Grove Hotel and got laid by a high-class hooker who'd picked him up at the bar downstairs.

The next day he drove across the Florida peninsula, arriving at the Ritz in Naples a few minutes before noon, and took immediate possession of his very comfortable cabana, which he'd reserved in advance. He spent part of the afternoon organizing his finances at a branch of the Florida Federal Savings Bank after which he went for a twenty-lap swim in the hotel's Olympic-size pool to get the kinks out of his body. Feeling better than he had for weeks, he took a nap and, after a lavish gourmet meal at the hotel's elegant dining room, retired to his room to relax and start planning his future.

It was one of those fragrant and lush nights for which Southern Florida is justly famous: waves quietly lapping at the sandy shore, the sea like a mirror from afar, reflecting the silver dish of a full moon frolicking in the water.

Fernandez felt almost at home. The beaches along Florida's west coast were similar in texture, smell, sound, and atmosphere to the beaches of his youth along Cuba's Costa Habanera, las Playas del Este. Sitting on the veranda of his rented cabana, he looked out over the sparkling, velvety sea, and allowed the tensions of the last two years to ebb out of him.

Then he shuddered, remembering how he had murdered the clerk in Grand Cayman. He went back into the cabana to fix himself another stiff Cuba Libre with real *ron añejo* and real Coca-Cola.

Yes, the girl had definitely been the key to moving the money. Because the Cubans were charging a thousand dollars per kilo for drugs passing through their territorial waters, the Colombians could get a ton of the stuff into the States in exchange for the up front payment of a million bucks. They would transfer the money to one of the Cayman bank accounts a few days after a ship, laden with the drugs, left their country and would then wait for word from the ship's captain advising that he was approaching Cuba. The Cuban Coast Guard would allow the ship to enter Cuban territorial waters, but would not allow unloading or departure without permission from the army's liaison officer.

This officer, who was also the army's liaison officer with the Ministry of the Interior, was none other than Fernandez, who coordinated operations from a special communications unit.

Once the drugs were in Cuban waters the Colombians would telephone the girl in the stationery store and give her a series of numbers—the relevant bank account and passport numbers—which meant nothing to her, but which she would inscribe under the front dust cover flap of a copy of *A Businessman's Guide to the Cayman Islands*. She would then wait for someone with the right password to show up and ask for the book.

The Cubans, advised of the ship's name via shortwave radio, would watch for it and dispatch a courier to Grand Cayman on the day before it entered Cuban waters. Thus, on the day the ship entered Cuban "territory," Castro's people would be in a position to take control of the money in the Cayman bank. If the Cuban side would then refuse to let the drug ship discharge its cargo into the cigarette boats that came blasting out of Florida to meet it, the Colombians could take retaliatory measures in Grand Cayman against the Cuban courier. But since the schedule called for two drug shipments per month neither side wished to see the operation discontinued. There was just too much money at stake.

Fernandez figured that, by now, the balance in Department Z's Panamanian bank account must exceed thirty million dollars.

Remembering, Fernandez shook his head in disbelief and took another sip of his drink. *Twenty four million dollars a year or more they could have made for years and years if someone hadn't gotten greedy. Why could the big shots not sort things out amongst themselves? Why did they have to involve me, a lowly captain?*

The trouble had started about three months after he'd taken over running the logistics of the show. They had successfully completed eight transactions without major problems and everything seemed to be pointing toward a long and profitable business relationship with the Colombians when the shit hit the fan and the minister had sent for him.

He had gone to the top floor of the Ministry of the Revolutionary Armed Forces with trepidation, but with a clear conscience. Proud of his work, he had been certain the minister wanted at best to commend him for his efforts, at worst to get more detailed information about what was going on.

Before allowing him to enter the minister's office, they had frisked him, taken his sidearm away, and X-rayed him to make sure he had nothing on him that he could use to harm Cuba's second most powerful man. They had then escorted him into the great man's office. The minister did not greet him, which emphasized the difference in rank between them.

"I see you've been working for General Casas for over three years," the minister had said, flipping through Fernandez's personnel file on his desk. "He has given you four citations during those years: two for bravery and two for exceptional service to the nation."

"That is correct, Comandante," Fernandez had replied, looking squarely into the eyes of the short, pockmark-faced man sitting opposite him. The minister had nodded at Fernandez's escorts who withdrew.

The minister's demeanor had immediately changed. He became affable. "Sit down, Captain. Make yourself comfortable. Would you like a cup of coffee? Or a soft drink?"

"No thank you, Comandante. Nothing." All Fernandez had wanted was to get through the meeting quickly and to get the hell as far away as possible from this dangerous little man who was being too solicitous by half.

"Very well then. I hear you've continued the good work by concentrating your logistical talents on reorganizing a new operation in Department Z."

"That is also correct, Comandante."

"I don't want to know any details, so stop fretting," the Minister had then said, thereby adding to Fernandez's discomfiture. "All I want to know, Captain, and without a hint of a doubt, that the money, all of the money, generated by this little caper finds its way into the coffers of the government and nowhere else. Am I making myself clear?"

"Yes, Comandante," said Fernandez automatically though not sure what his superior was hinting at.

The minister continued as though he had read Fernandez's thoughts. "I want you to work with me on this directly, Captain. I repeat, I need to know how the money flow is being handled and that there's no hanky-panky."

Fernandez had been mystified. "But surely, Comandante, the comrades at the Ministry of the Interior are already doing this. They have the setup, the checks and balances, to make sure everything is as it should be."

"Do you think I have not taken this into consideration?" The minister had looked at Fernandez over his half-moon glasses. "Do you think you'd be sitting here if I was sure these people were doing their job properly?"

"Do you mean to say, Comandante, that the Ministry of the Interior—"

"Captain, do not speculate. That's an order." The voice had no longer been solicitous, not even friendly. "Here is what I want. First, a detailed written report about the money flow, and second, a rough calculation of how much money has been generated so far. Get your report done within the month and submit it to me directly. Keep your mouth shut about this meeting, and remember, it is possible in our army to skip a rank when being promoted." The minister had allowed himself a fleeting smile. "Do you take my meaning?"

Fernandez stood up. "I do, absolutely, Comandante. I will, as always, do my best." He took the minister's meaning only too well. There was a power struggle between the army and the Ministry of the Interior. They both wanted control over the drug money. He saluted, and was about to leave when the minister, bending over his desk, handed him a slip of paper.

"When you're ready, Captain, call this number and ask to see me. A meeting will then be arranged."

Fernandez had resolved then and there to bolt at the earliest opportunity. Hell, he was being asked to spy on his comrades at the Ministry as well as in the army. To boot, he was also being set up as the fall guy if anything went wrong.

"I did absolutely the right thing," he murmured as he finished his drink and stretched luxuriously. *I didn't take their money, only the extra amount, which the Colombians or General Casas or whoever had stuck into the account. I even went to the trouble before giving myself up in Miami to telephone the code word to Havana so that the operation could proceed as planned.*

As for the other million bucks in the bank account, that money belonged to *La Patria*, so he had told the BCCI to transfer it to the Panamanian bank account, which presumably belonged to or was controlled by the Ministry of the Interior.

Fernandez went deep-sea fishing the next day, something he'd always wanted to do, but could never afford before. By five he was back at his hotel and, having swum his obligatory twenty laps in the pool, was beginning to feel hungry. He planned to drive to Naples soon, have a few drinks at a singles bar, and see what female company he could rustle up for the evening. Then he'd think about dinner, and who knows what else.

He was in no hurry about anything. Back in his room, he fixed himself a drink, sat down to rest for a few minutes, and let his mind drift.

By now he was sure that the extra money in the account had been deposited by the general himself, not only because of what the girl in the bookstore had said, but also because of Casas's curious insistence four weeks earlier that Fernandez take a turn at being the so-called "Cayman Courier." This had been very unlike Casas. If at all avoidable, no commander would expose to capture a key man privy to important secrets.

When Fernandez saw the extra money in the bank account he took it as proof positive that his superior officer, as much against dealing in drugs as Fernandez, was trying to send a signal to the outside world through Fernandez about what was going on in Cuba. OK, so Fernandez had done just that, but the sixty-four thousand dollar question was this: how much of the money was he supposed to have taken?

A knock on the door brought him back to the present. "House-keeping," the maid called out and tried to open the door with her passkey, but the safety latch was on. "Sorry," she said through the partially open door, "I'll come back later to turn down the bed and bring you fresh towels." She sounded Hispanic.

"No, no it's all right." Fernandez went to the door and opened it. The woman, in her late thirties, was petite, good-looking, and friendly. "Where are you from?" he asked her in Spanish.

"Cuba, Señor," she answered and came through the door, a bunch of towels draped over her arm.

"Oh really? Where in Cuba?" he asked as she closed the door behind her and headed for the bathroom from which she reemerged a few seconds later.

"I'm sorry Señor" she said as she came toward him. "I didn't hear what you said. The door—"

Fernandez, seated in front of the TV, waved his drink at her. "I asked where you were from in Cuba." He gave her a big smile. The woman smiled back and took a step toward him. "From Matanzas like you, you treacherous bastard," she said in an even voice and, as he was scrambling to get to his feet, shot Fernandez through the heart twice with the silencer-equipped Walther PPK she held hidden under the towels.

CHAPTER THIRTY-TWO

Thursday
Cozumel, Mexico

Lonsdale and Micheline were vacationing at the Hotel El Presidente, in Cozumel, Mexico, and having a fabulous time. Their room was right on the beach, the food was great, the weather beautiful. They ate, drank, danced, swam, and made sensuous love for four days.

On Wednesday they joined a group of Americans who had chartered a plane for a day-trip to Chichen Itza to view the magnificent ruins there.

Thursday was yet another marvelous day in paradise. They were watching the sunset on their little veranda when a bellboy interrupted them apologetically. "*Señor*, there is an urgent telephone call for you. Please come with me to the lobby and I will show you where you can take the call in private." There were no phones in the rooms, one of the reasons why Lonsdale had chosen the Hotel El Presidente in the first place.

Lonsdale excused himself and followed the young Mexican. "Hello?"

"It's me," the all-too-familiar voice of Jim Morton said by way of greeting. "I've got news you won't like."

"Never mind that. How did you get this number?"

"Micheline left it with her son in case of an emergency, and this is an emergency." Morton was all business. "Uncle Sam is still paying your bills; so he has preemptive rights to your time."

"Cut the crap, Jim." Lonsdale was annoyed. "I'm on vacation and just about to go out to dinner. I'm sure whatever you have to say will wait till Monday."

"It won't." Morton's voice betrayed his agitation. "Our friend the captain is dead." He didn't sound happy.

Lonsdale cut in swiftly. "This is not a secure line, so I won't comment further. Besides, I need details."

"There's a plane on its way for you as we speak. When you get to Miami call me at home from our office there."

"When will the plane get here?"

"Within the hour."

"I can't make that timetable Jim. It's physically impossible."

"I'm not asking you to come to Washington, just to Miami, so we can talk."

"What do you mean?" Damn Morton. The bugger had a way of reeling him in every time.

"Listen. You're due back at the office on Monday, so go to the Doral Golf and Country Club in Miami and stay there on company expense for three days. On your way to the Doral, stop by the office to talk to me."

Lonsdale looked at his watch; it was getting on toward seven. "Tell the pilot we'll be at the airport at nine, Cozumel time."

"That'll put you into Miami at eleven thirty."

"Arrange for us not to have to go through the usual immigration hassle and have chilled champagne and a sumptuous meal waiting for us in an extraordinarily beautiful suite at the Doral."

A pause. Then Morton was back on the line. "I'll go one better, sport. There will be a scrambler phone in the limo that will pick you up at the airport. You won't have to leave the lovely Micheline for even a moment. You won't have to pass by the office." It was evident Morton was trying to do his best to be accommodating.

"Deal." Lonsdale hung up and returned to the room to break the news.

They were driving toward the Doral by eleven thirty that night. The limo that met them was one used by the Secret Service to accompany the motorcades of VIPs, such as the president of the United States. It was referred to as a "battle wagon" because, in addition to being fully armored, it contained super-sophisticated communications equipment and, when on "patrol," a veritable arsenal of weapons. Lonsdale sat in the back and Micheline up front, the soundproof glass divider separating them.

He picked up the phone. Morton was already on the line. "Can you hear me clearly?" he asked.

"You sound as if you were surrounded by cotton wool."

"That I'm certainly not; it's the scrambler."

"All right then. Tell me what happened, step by step."

"Fernandez was enrolled in the witness protection program last Sunday. He was given a brand new identity and a million one hundred thousand dollar bonus for the information he gave us."

"You mean on top of the million bucks he brought with him?"

"That's right."

"Who negotiated the deal for him?"

"His cousin, the lawyer Filberto Reyes Puma. He specializes in immigration work."

Lonsdale was shocked. "Hang on for a moment. You did say Fernandez was enrolled in the program only last Sunday. Where was he being held until then, and why wasn't I given access to him?"

"At one of our safe houses in the Miami area. You were denied access to him on Director Smythe's specific instructions."

"So what did that stupid bastard mean by 'he's being looked after' when I last spoke with him?"

"A fair question, which I'm afraid you'll have to ask him."

"Continue."

"Fernandez was given the money in negotiable bank drafts. He was also given a full set of identity papers: passport, social security card, credit cards, and so on, so he took off."

"How?"

"Reyes Puma picked him up and drove off with him."

"Has anyone interviewed Reyes Puma?"

"Yes, we did. He dropped Fernandez off at the Doral Beach Hotel, the place you'll be staying at. That was the last time Puma saw him."

"When was that?"

"Sunday afternoon."

"Do we know what happened next?"

"Fernandez rented a car from Alamo, spent the night in Miami then drove to Naples on the West Coast of Florida."

"And?"

"He checked into the Ritz on Monday, spent the afternoon organizing his affairs. He opened a bank account at the Florida Federal Savings Bank, deposited most of his money there, went deep-sea fishing with a Canadian couple on Tuesday and returned to the Ritz around two p.m."

"Next?"

"He was shot to death in his room between six and ten p.m. while watching TV."

Lonsdale went rigid. "Back up Jim and give me details."

"Like what?"

"You said he was shot while watching TV in his room."

"That is in the affirmative."

"Standing up, sitting down, or lying on his bed?"

"Sitting in an armchair, having a drink in front of the TV set in his cabana."

"And nobody saw or heard anything, right?"

"Right."

"Who found him and when?"

"The assistant manager of Housekeeping the day after he was shot, on Wednesday, around six in the evening."

"And it took that long to find him because the Do Not Disturb sign was on his door and nobody wanted to disturb him. Right?"

"Yes, but how did you know?"

"Never mind that. I'll tell you later." Lonsdale began to see things clearly. "I suppose he was shot to death at close range with a silencer-equipped pistol and the assassin used low-velocity high-impact bullets, leaving no exit wound."

"Right again. Are you onto something?"

"Has ballistics analyzed the bullets?"

"Yes, they have. They were fired from a Walther PPK model semiautomatic 42-caliber pistol."

"How many bullets?"

"Two."

"Did Fernandez call room service before getting himself killed?"

"We thought about that and checked, but the answer is no."

"How do you think the assassin gained access to him?" Lonsdale asked.

"We don't know for sure, but we think, based on what the Ritz people told the police, that a woman impersonating a member of the housekeeping staff knocked on his door and offered to turn down his bed. He opened the door and let her in. She went to the bathroom with some towels; he returned to his chair and his drink. She came out of the bathroom, shot him, wiped all surfaces she touched with the towel under which she was holding the weapon, then left the room, and hung the Do Not Disturb sign on his door."

"How do you know all this?"

"One: the housekeeping staff doing the turn-down service at the Ritz is exclusively female. Two: the police found the towel with powder burns in the laundry chute. Three: one of the maids reported her uniform missing from her locker—which, by the way, she always locked after changing into her uniform and going on duty, never before," Morton replied.

"When was that?"

"What?"

"What day and at what time did the maid report her uniform missing?"

"On Tuesday afternoon, around two thirty, just before going on duty. The maids' shifts start at three and they finish at eleven."

"I suppose it's no use asking why the head housekeeper did not immediately investigate the case of the missing uniform."

"Missing uniforms are a frequent occurrence. The maids leave their uniforms in their unlocked lockers after going off duty so that the Housekeeping department can check to see if they need cleaning. In the case of the maid in question the head housekeeper figured the uniform had been sent to the cleaners and the person in charge had forgotten to provide a replacement."

"Did you follow up on this?"

"We did, but there are over sixty maids at the Ritz: two to each floor of the building, plus two for the cabanas. The head housekeeper says such mistakes happen all the time." Morton was getting impatient. "In any event, what difference does all this make? Fernandez is dead and we're in trouble."

"You're absolutely right. One last question. Why was Fernandez not being kept under surveillance by us in spite of the fact that we knew we may need him as a material witness?"

"He was, but the surveillance was passive in the sense that it was nonintrusive. Nobody got excited when he didn't show before noon on Wednesday. His car was in the parking lot, the lights in his cabana were turned off, as was the TV by the way. Everybody figured he had decided to sleep in." Morton let out a deep sigh. "Under the circumstances, I can't fault anybody."

"I agree."

"In any event, we would never have been able to amass this much detail on such short notice had we not had a surveillance team in place."

"The Naples police seem to have been of help too." Lonsdale was thinking out loud. "Tell me. Did you, yourself, interview the cousin personally?"

"No, not yet. But the Miami police who know him well, respect him. He has an excellent reputation. Why?"

"He was the last person known to have seen Fernandez alive. Maybe he even knew his new identity. For sure, he is the key to how the Cubans or the Colombians found Fernandez so soon after his release."

"What makes you think it was the Cubans or the Colombians?"

"Who else but they—and perhaps one of us—would have an interest in shutting him up?"

"One of us? You mean you or me?" Morton's voice had a cold edge to it.

"Or Smythe." Lonsdale was trying to set the cat among the pigeons. *Divide and conquer, divide and conquer, divide and conquer.* His inner voice kept insisting.

"That's a thought." Morton sounded troubled.

"Isn't it just?" Lonsdale was pleased. His strategy to rattle Morton seemed to be working. "By the way, while you're at it, get in touch with the Budapest police and get a copy of the ballistic report on the bullets they dug out of poor Mr. Schwartz."

"Why?" By now Morton was really puzzled.

"I'll explain when I see you Monday. Meanwhile, get the necessary paperwork authorizing Casas's and De la Fuente's extraction ready by the time I get in." He hung up. They had arrived at the Doral.

CHAPTER THIRTY-THREE

Thursday through Sunday
Prague, Checkoslovakia and Luanda, Angola

Oscar De la Fuente hated everything that had to do with airplanes, especially flying in them. By the time he landed in Prague on Friday morning, he was irritable and sick to his stomach. Knowing he would have to take another flight within eight hours didn't help his disposition or his stomach for that matter.

When he got to the Forum, definitely not a five star hotel, all he wanted was a cup of hot tea and a few hours' sleep.

He had left Havana on Thursday late afternoon, planning to arrive in Angola twenty-four hours later. Altogether too long a trip, he decided. Since he was going to stay only three days in Angola it hardly seemed worthwhile spending two full days getting there and back.

Plus, it was quite impossible for him to concentrate on anything while flying. He was far too nervous for a book or a movie to hold his interest. All he could do was to obsess over the consequences of Fernandez's defection and its effect on his own relationship with Patricio Casas Rojo.

It had been a bad moment when, during their meeting at Casas's house, Patricio had demanded to know how compartmentalized the drug operation really was. His own offhand reply seemed adequate then, but now he wasn't sure. The seed of doubt had somehow taken root in Casas's mind and De la Fuente feared it would soon grow into a plant of dangerous proportions.

And without Casas, Operation Adios would be just that—"adios."

The past month had been absolute hell for De la Fuente. In damage control mode ever since Fernandez's unfortunate departure, he'd been too busy to maintain a balanced overview of what was happening. He'd gotten Fernandez's second-in-command to confirm that all the money that was supposed to be in the BCCI account in Cayman was properly accounted for. It turned out that Fernandez had carried out his tasks with scrupulous precision to the very end. As a result, the Colombians' last shipment had reached its destination without incident and they had no reason to suspect that anything was amiss.

This enabled De la Fuente to arrange for the shipment scheduled for the second weekend after Fernandez's departure to be postponed, but time was running out and the Colombians' supply line was backing up. Customers in the States were getting restless and turning to alternative sources of supply as their regular dealers began to run dry.

The problem reached crisis proportions when De la Fuente attempted to postpone the shipment scheduled for the very day he intended to meet with Casas in Luanda. The Colombians told him in no uncertain terms that unless two catch-up shipments were processed within the next two weeks they would come to Havana to take the matter up with representatives at the highest levels of the Cuban government, not a mere deputy minister.

De la Fuente was caught between a rock and a hard thing: he had yet to inform the Colombians that their contact in George Town was dead and that their banking operation in the Cayman Islands was blown. As if he didn't have enough troubles already.

Meanwhile, where was his buddy, his ally, his comrade in crime? Seeing his buxom girlfriend in Budapest, that's where. He looked at his watch. Another two hours and he would have to leave for the airport. Then there would be six more hours of agony on that bone-rattler to Africa.

Casas met him at Luanda airport; the staff car pulled right up to the plane's steps as soon as the aircraft's engines were switched off.

"Welcome, Oscar," the general extended his hand in greeting. "What's the matter? You look like hell."

"I wouldn't talk if I were you." De La Fuente was in a foul mood. "Have you looked in the mirror lately? Whatever happened with your hand?"

Colonel Font, General Casas's second-in-command, coughed discreetly. "Gentlemen, if you've finished sniping at each other we could perhaps get back to headquarters in time for the briefing."

"What about my luggage?" De la Fuente wanted to know.

"Already in the car, comrade. It was the first piece off the plane."

"What time is the briefing?"

"Every Friday night at ten p.m."

"What a strange hour."

Font laughed. "Cuts down on the time our officers have to get themselves into trouble during the weekend."

"Things are that boring around here then?"

"Strategic withdrawals are never fun—all work and no play. Besides, this isn't Havana, you know."

It was midnight by the time the meeting broke up and De la Fuente could barely stay awake. Casas, equally tired, tried to put things off until the morning, but De la Fuente would have none of it. "Get some coffee up here, and let's talk for a couple of hours. We have a lot of ground to cover." They were in Casas's office on the top floor of the Hotel Presidente. "By the way Patricio, is this office a secure place?"

"What do you mean?"

"Is it bugged or is it safe to talk here?"

"I don't know, but I don't much give a care," the general said, then indicated the ceiling with an upward nod of his head and pointed to the balcony. "There's nothing we have to discuss that is illegal, improper, or even immoral. To tell the truth, we're so busy here we don't have time to sweep the offices for bugs."

"What if the locals were to snoop?"

"They need no bugs. They have other ways of finding out what we're up to."

"Such as?" De la Fuente asked, but just then the coffee arrived, saving Casas from having to elaborate.

The general poured them two generous cups, which they took with them to the balcony and leaned out over the railing.

"You first Oscar," Casas whispered. "What's up?"

"The Fernandez defection really threw a spanner in the works. His second-in-command is not as swift as the captain was, so I had to do part of his job for him. As a result, I had to reschedule a couple of shipments and the Colombians are very upset."

"Because?"

"Their dealers in the States are running out of merchandise."

"So relieve the guy. Put one in charge who knows what to do."

Easy for you to say that, Patricio, you self-righteous bastard, De la Fuente thought, *because you're under the impression our operation is legit.* Out loud, he protested testily. "Easier said than done. Remember when you first approached Fernandez, how reluctant he was to go along? Well, guess what. He's not the only one objecting to doing drugs."

"Don't tell me you can't find a competent replacement."

"Patricio, my friend," De la Fuente had had enough, "aren't you forgetting something? Military liaison with the Ministry of the Interior is your responsibility, not mine. I was only pinch-hitting for you in Havana while you were in Hungary."

Casas had to fight hard to retain his cool. "Come off it, Oscar. You know very well I had to go to Budapest on business. There was a problem with the Hungarian Ministry of Defense that I had to clear up. Besides," he added, almost as an afterthought, "I also had a message from Schwartz asking me to meet him in Hungary."

"Oh?" De la Fuente pretended surprise. "How is Schwartz?"

"No idea." Casas lied smoothly. "Never got to see him. He didn't show."

De la Fuente was taken aback. "He never showed up?"

"That's correct. I left him a note as always, giving him the time and place of the meeting. I went to the rendezvous, but the old man didn't turn up."

"Did he get as far as Budapest?"

"I verified that he had checked into his hotel all right, that he'd been given my message all right, but something must have happened to him."

"What?"

"I was hoping you might be able to tell me that, Oscar."

"Me? How do I come to figure in this situation all of a sudden?"

"Come off it, Oscar." Casas was barely able to control his anger. "Your people have been following me around for weeks now—in Budapest, in Prague, even here. Do you think I'm stupid or blind? Ever since Fernandez defected you and your people have been hounding me."

De la Fuente's mind went blank with panic. He knew damn well that it wasn't his people who were following Casas around. The candidates were the CIA and Cuban Military Intelligence. But the CIA was unlikely to be keeping Casas under surveillance in Luanda. So it must be Raul Castro's men.

He had to marshal his thoughts fast and control his fear. "I have no idea what you're talking about. To the best of my knowledge nobody at the Ministry of the Interior is keeping you under surveillance. You must either be imagining things or you are being followed around by Military Intelligence."

"That's impossible. First, I would know about it from my friends, and second they have no reason. I've done nothing wrong." *Except spook Fernandez*, he said to himself.

De la Fuente seemed to read his mind. "Except that *your* man is spilling his guts to the Americans as we speak."

"He's a defector, pure and simple." Casas couldn't think of anything else to say. "And these things happen in the best of families. I have over two hundred officers under my command."

De la Fuente decided to put in the needle. "But very few in the drug business," he said. "And tell me Patricio, has anyone questioned you about Fernandez's disappearance?"

"Not yet, but that's no surprise. If anyone should have been questioned, it should have been you. The man was seconded to you, remember?"

De la Fuente bit his lip. Casas was right. "Of course you know I've covered for us by passing the word that Fernandez was on a special mission." His stomach began to churn, a prelude to an attack of diarrhea caused by the sudden realization that things were unraveling faster than he'd expected. He and Casas were on the brink and there was no safety net below.

"Oscar!" Casas pretended to be running out of patience. "First, Fernandez, working under your orders, goes missing. Then you tell me you want him killed to save our necks. Now you inform me I'm probably subject to investigation by M.I. There is only one explanation for all of this. The drug thing is not a legitimately authorized government operation."

"What is it then?"

"It is an exercise in free enterprise." Casas, his eyes wide with the shock of discovery, looked at De la Fuente, with distaste. "And it looks to me as if the chief free enterpriser in this venture is you."

De la Fuente saw that allowing Casas more room for guessing-games could mean the end of Operation Adios and serious, indeed deadly, danger for himself. "Patricio, listen up." He was exhausted and worried sick, but, somehow, had to keep up appearances so as to extricate himself from immediate peril. "It no longer matters who did what to whom and for what reason. I told you in Havana we needed proof of the government's involvement in the drug operation to save ourselves. I got on with obtaining such proof, but you did not. Instead, you ran off to Budapest to see your precious Conchita."

Casas was furious. "You leave her out of this," he shouted.

"Don't raise your voice, Patricio," De la Fuente cut in. "It won't do for people to think we're quarreling."

Casas backed down. "So what proof have you found?"

"My wife has been giving me little tidbits of information about my wonderful father-in-law. Apparently, he's been on the take for a long time. She has gotten quite interested in his activities because she wants him to buy her . . . buy us . . . a beach house in Varadero."

"What has that got to do with the drug business?"

"Don't be impatient, Patricio." Although dying to go to the bathroom De la Fuente sat down in one of the armchairs on the balcony and motioned Casas to pull his over next to him. "Although I doubt that her father knows about the operation, we could say he did and then provide the old man's bank account numbers to the investigators. I'm sure the money they'd find there would be substantial enough to make them believe the minister was one of the free enterprisers."

Casas was stunned. "Are you now confirming that the operation is not a properly authorized one?"

"I'm confirming nothing. I'm just lining up our defenses."

"Why this brotherly concern all of a sudden? You know very well I'm not guilty of any wrongdoing. You're the one who told me about the operation and that it was legit. It was you who provided the contacts with the Colombians, and, finally, it was you who kept on and still keeps on, about involving more and more innocent people in this dirty business to make it look as if our Revolutionary government were involved in drugs, which I now see it is not!" Casas could barely keep his voice down. Gripping his visitor's upper arm he pulled the man toward him and whispered fiercely into his ear. "You have set this whole thing up for your own benefit, haven't you, Oscar? And you have now painted yourself into a corner."

"And you with it," De la Fuente cut in before Casas could go on.

"What do you mean by that you . . . you . . . you son-of-a-bitch?"

De la Fuente shook off Casas's grip and got up. "Patricio, I'm tired of your insults. Can't you get it through you head that we're in this thing together, that we are, through our own acts, so deeply compromised that no amount of righteous protestation will get either of us off the hook. Besides, there are documents . . ." He let his voice trail off.

"What documents?"

"We'll talk again tomorrow, Patricio." Oscar headed back into the room. "I'm going to bed before I faint of fatigue." *And fear*, he added to himself. Tomorrow he would have to tell Patricio the truth about Operation Adios and face the consequences, but just now he needed to get to a bathroom before he burst.

CHAPTER THIRTY-FOUR

Sunday
Luanda, Angola

To De la Fuente the facts were clear, as were his own and Casas's fate. Casas was under surveillance by Cuban Military Intelligence, which was bound to tumble onto the drug-smuggling operation within days, perhaps even hours. His own involvement would be discovered within a week and Casas and he would be arrested by the end of November at the latest. That they would have a speedy trial was beyond question. To stem international criticism Castro would have to demonstrate as soon as possible that his government was not involved. The verdict at such a trial was a foregone conclusion. With De la Fuente claiming that Casas had been the instigator Casas would be shot for treason and De la Fuente imprisoned for life.

He would have to serve about five years of his sentence before the United States would arrange to have him exchanged.

Casas on the other hand, was bewildered and desperate. He had played "what if" until dawn then had gone to the pool for a long swim to calm his screaming nerves. The realization that he had totally misread the situation and that he had made the wrong moves was almost more than he could bear. He was trapped and could not escape. All the money he'd squirreled away with Schwartz was gone, taken by Fernandez when he had defected. Irony of ironies: Casas had used the means of his salvation to engineer his own downfall. Spooking Fernandez had been a horrible mistake. By making him run away,

Casas had not only tipped off the CIA, but the Cuban government's Intelligence Services as well.

What to do next? Getting in touch with the CIA man and defecting was one option. This would be an act of admission of guilt and not even the Americans would believe his story. They'd use him anyway. His going over to the other side would just muddy the waters, making it that much more difficult for Fidel to prove that the government was not involved. But with De la Fuente also pointing the accusatory finger at Casas, Castro would have a fair chance of escaping unsullied.

No. He had to go back to Havana and explain to Fidel personally what had really happened. He would then have to bear witness at trial against De la Fuente and, if necessary, shoulder all the blame. How else could he protect his mother and daughters? In the meantime, he'd have to keep close watch over Oscar and prevent him from leaving for Cuba before he, himself, did.

Having made the necessary arrangements to ensure De la Fuente's presence in Luanda until Tuesday, the day Casas intended to return to Havana, Casas took De la Fuente for a plane ride early Sunday morning, using the excuse of looking at troop deployments. They landed in Lubango, about four hundred and twenty miles south of Luanda on the Huila Plateau.

From there they took Casas's reinforced all-terrain vehicle to visit the troops dug in south of the highway leading from Mocamedes to Lubango and to Menongue. This line of defense would protect Lobito, Angola's most important port, about two hundred and fifty miles south of Luand, from the South Africans long enough to allow the Cubans to evacuate through Lobito in an orderly fashion.

The inspection tour was not easy to organize. Men of their rank had to be protected. By the time they got underway they had become part of a convoy consisting of a communications/scout car leading the way, followed by Casas's vehicle, and a half-track troop carrier filled with bodyguards bringing up the rear.

Casas was ready to have a showdown with De la Fuente at the earliest opportunity, but the deputy minister surprised him. "Before you get on your high horse again and lose your temper, allow me to explain how I see our respective situations," De la Fuente said and made himself sound reasonable and conciliatory. "We're both in big trouble and, to tell the truth, neither of us will escape unharmed, let alone unsullied. I'm sure we both spent the night trying to figure out what to do next. You, unlike I, are an idealist who thinks it is immoral, but, at least, amoral, to deal in drugs. I suspect it was you who somehow, frankly I have no idea how, put Fernandez up to defecting."

Casas began to protest, but his companion stopped him. "Please Patricio, hear me out. Keep driving while I say what I have to say, then park the vehicle somewhere and I promise I will give you all the time in the world to rebut my arguments."

"Go on, then."

"Allow me to assume it was you who put Fernandez up to defecting. Your reason: you wanted to alert the Americans to what was going on in Cuba and how low the Cuban government has sunk, running drugs, smuggling ivory, and looting. You might even have entertained the idea of helping the CIA bring the Castro regime down by publicizing these immoral activities and getting public opinion on the side of proponents of a U.S. invasion of Cuba." De la Fuente took a deep breath and watched Casas carefully as he continued. "As far as I'm concerned, it no longer matters what we think. What matters is to determine how to limit the damage we've done to ourselves, for whatever reason."

Casas signaled the convoy to pull over. His heart was racing, and he was nauseated with fear. "What do you propose we do next?"

"We have to go back to Havana and continue implicating people. We must also find proof that the government is involved."

Casas shook his head "Come off it, Oscar. We both know there is no such proof."

"There can be."

"There can? What?" Casas sounded doubtful. It was only ten in the morning, but he was already exhausted. He took a few deep breaths to calm himself then gave the order for the convoy to resume moving. They were approaching the Mocamedes Desert. These hot, arid plains used to team with wild life—elephant, rhinoceros, antelope—but, with the advent of modern transport, such as the tough jeep for example, the region was opened to extensive hunting and many fine species, like the mountain zebra, became extinct. The Cubans' presence did not help. They hunted for ivory shamelessly.

"What's the matter with you Patricio, don't you ever listen?" De la Fuente, who could barely wait to get back at his father-in-law for always siding with his daughter against him, pretended to be exasperated. "Don't you remember me telling you about my father-in-law's secret bank account?"

"Of course I do, Oscar." Casas was also fed up. "But, to tell the truth, I think you're dreaming. Once Fidel gets to know about that little bit of corruption he will simply jail your father-in-law with us and, ultimately, we'll all be shot."

"Not if I can implement my plan."

"What plan?"

"A plan whereby I would involve my father-in-law in the drug deal by showing that the drug money in the Panamanian bank account is slowly being transferred to my father-in-law's Swiss bank account." De la Fuente put his hand on Casas's arm. "Hang in there for a few more weeks Patricio and have confidence. In the end all will come right, you'll see."

CHAPTER THIRTY-FIVE

Monday
Washington, DC

On Sunday night, Lonsdale flew home from Miami, and, by Monday morning at seven, he was going over the reports on Fernandez's murder. Unfortunately, the ballistics report the Agency had requested from the Budapest police through Interpol had not yet been received. Lonsdale wasn't surprised. Replies to such requests took weeks rather than days.

Another matter of concern was the lack of detailed information about the interview with Reyes Puma. Lonsdale gathered that the lawyer was very much respected by the police and the INS alike. "Did Fernandez tell him about his new identity?" Lonsdale muttered just as Morton walked through the door, hand outstretched. "Talking to yourself, I see." He shook his colleague's hand warmly. "Welcome back. You look tanned and rested. How's Micheline?"

"Fine thanks. She's back in Montreal." Lonsdale decided to cut Morton some slack, figuring he would need all the help he could get to pull Casas out of the mess he was in. "But you don't seem too happy."

"I am very concerned about Casas." Morton's face was pasty from lack of sleep.

"Then let's do something about it."

"But what?"

"Sooner, than later, we'll have to extract him." Lonsdale looked at Morton. "Have you fixed up the paperwork, authorizing us to save his scrawny neck?"

"Yes and no."

"What does that mean?"

"When I told Smythe that Fernandez was dead, he wasn't pleased, nor was he surprised, which surprised *me*. In any event, when I finished giving him the details he just sat there for a while, mumbling and cursing, with his mind obviously in high gear. Then he said something that surprised me even more."

"And what was that?"

"He said—and listen to this—'Tell Lonsdale that his prayers have been answered. He better get his ass in here to see me pronto, but in any event, not later than noon on Monday,' which is today."

Lonsdale looked at his watch. "Plenty of time. It's not ten yet. Do you have any idea what he wants from me?"

"I certainly do. He's going to propose a deal to you that you will find very hard to refuse."

"What kind of a deal?"

"I'd rather he told you himself." Morton felt at a loss for words. He feared that laying out Smythe's plan there and then would lose him his deputy's friendship forever.

"That bad, eh?"

Morton shook his head. "You'll find out soon enough. That's all I'm permitted to say." He squared his shoulders. "Let's get on with the rest of it. Are there any questions with regard to those?" He pointed to the pile on Lonsdale's desk.

"Just a few hundred."

"Like?"

"Like, why was Fernandez not kept in protective custody in the first place? Why was he released to his cousin? Why wasn't the cousin interviewed in depth? Who else beside the cousin knew Fernandez's identity and the time of his release? Does Fernandez have family beside his cousin?"

Morton held up his hands. "Hold on. He was released because the cousin, Reyes Puma, is the most high-profile civil liberties lawyer in Florida and an influential member of the Miami Cuban community. Puma pressured the INS to release Fernandez and negotiated the witness protection deal for him. He volunteered to pick up Fernandez on his release, which the captain welcomed, and off they went. As for the cousin, I can think of no one better to interview him than you."

"No Jim, I think not."

"Why on earth not?"

What Lonsdale said next surprised him as much as it surprised Morton. "I don't want to meet the man because I don't want him to know what I look like. I have something else in mind for him."

"Such as?"

"I want you to interview him. Wear a body wire and transmitter and we'll camcord you from afar. I'll watch and listen in. Then we'll replay the interview, do some voice analysis, and see where it gets us."

Morton gave in. "OK, we'll do it your way. But first, we had better get over to Smythe's office."

"Operation Adios may be in trouble," the Smythe said without preamble.

"How so, Sir?"

"With Fernandez dead we urgently need Casas to produce evidence of the Cuban government's involvement in the drug trade."

"I haven't heard from him recently."

"I know. You were on vacation. But you're back now, so get busy. Go to Cuba if need be, but get things going before it's too late."

"Too late for what?"

"Nobody killed Fernandez or this fella' Siddiqui, or the coin dealer Schwartz just for the fun of it. They had a pressing reason. Question is, who?" He looked at Lonsdale.

"There are a number of people who may want him dead."

"Such as?"

"The Colombians, for betraying their banking and other procedures, or for absconding with what they may perceive as being their money."

"Unlikely."

"The Cuban government, to eliminate the only witness who can tie Casas and De la Fuente to the second-highest-ranking Cuban government official, namely the minister of defense."

"You've got somethin' there."

"Then there is the minister himself, God bless him, acting as an independent free enterpriser."

"Any more?"

"As a matter of fact, yes." Lonsdale gave Smythe a warm smile. "General Casas himself, in a noble gesture of self-sacrifice, to save the Revolution embarrassment, which would, incidentally, drag our friendly agent, Charley De la Fuente, down with him. In this scenario, Casas would go on trial with De la Fuente and Casas would take the blame . . . by confessing."

"You're really digging deep." Smythe was not happy. "Of course that last scenario we wouldn't want to see unfold, unless absolutely unavoidable."

"No, I guess not."

"Well then, what do you propose we do?"

"Director Smythe, I came here under the impression you had some sort of a suggestion that would make both of us feel comfortable with this operation. Am I to understand that you are now asking me to develop a plan?"

The old man nodded. "You've almost got it right. I have a suggestion that would make me feel comfortable."

"Tell me what you want, and I'll tell you if I can live with it."

Smythe turned to Morton "Set things up for us, will you please."

Morton obliged. "Our analysts believe the Cuban government is behind the killings. I say killings in the plural, because they believe Siddiqui, Schwartz, and Fernandez were killed by the same people. There can be only one reason for these killings." Morton was adamant. "The Cuban government found out about the drug operation and although it is convinced that the operation is a free-enterprise deal created by De la Fuente and Casas—in other words not one inspired by us—it cannot take the risk of allowing the Cuban government to be linked to drugs, even remotely."

"That's a bit of a stretch, don't you think?" Lonsdale interrupted.

"Remember, Casas had instructed Schwartz to pay the Ministry of the Interior its share of the so-called bounty money from Angola. This must have alerted the Cuban G2 investigators to both Schwartz's and Siddiqui's existence and since they were involved in the deal, however indirectly, they had to be terminated with extreme prejudice."

"What about the BCCI manager in Luanda? He was involved too."

"He was also killed over the weekend in a suspicious car accident. The Cuban government has now isolated Casas and De la Fuente. It can prove that the two are up to their necks in drug dealing. They, in turn, have no way of proving that there is a connection between the operation and the government."

It was obvious that Morton was pretty fed up. "On the contrary, the Cuban government will soon stumble onto the fact that the money in Panama is not controlled by either the Ministry of the Interior or by Casas and De la Fuente, and they will guess the rest."

"You mean that the operation is ours?"

"Correct."

"Unless we distance ourselves from the money in Panama."

"You've got it." Smythe and Morton were looking at Lonsdale expectantly for suggestions.

"And you want me to help you do this?" Lonsdale could not believe his ears.

"No." the Director cut in coldly.

Morton carried on, avoiding eye contact with Lonsdale. "We consider Operation Adios blown and are in damage control mode. When the Agency started Adios, it arranged for the Panama bank account to be owned by an untraceable Panamanian sub-subsidiary of the Agency."

Morton squared his shoulders. "But then, De la Fuente recruited the unwitting General Casas and someone—probably De la Fuente's control, Spiegel—came up with the idea of having papers cut to show that the owners of the Panamanian company were Casas and De la Fuente. Of course, neither Casas nor De la Fuente were told about this, the idea being that, if the fur flew, the Agency would not appear to be involved."

"Which means that De la Fuente and Casas are on their own," Lonsdale finished the story for Morton, "unless Casas can give us proof of complicity by the Cuban government, which we all know does not exist."

"I'm afraid that just about sums it up," Morton agreed.

"And you say you think Casas is under intense surveillance?"

"Yes."

"And that time is running out fast because Casas and Charley are going to be arrested, and soon."

"Yes."

A feeling of weariness overcame Lonsdale. "I did my best to get Casas out, not realizing that Charley De la Fuente was the designated man of the moment. How could I have known since you bastards never told me anything, never cooperated with me, never supported me, and did nothing except try to confuse the issue." He felt like beating up Morton and strangling Smythe. "There's no way I'm going to Cuba to help fabricate evidence thereby getting Casas, who is already in deep shit, into even deeper shit. There's no way I'm going to risk my life for you." He pointed at Smythe.

"And I suppose," Smythe added almost gently, "the hell with our loyal and trusted agent Charley De la Fuente and his naive and innocent buddy, who, by the way, is your buddy too: General de Brigada Patricio Casas Rojo, whom you are now proposing to abandon."

"I'm not abandoning them, Director. You and the Agency are."

To Lonsdale's surprise, Smythe smiled. "That's quite correct. But that does not make it right and that certainly does not mean that you also have to. Here is what I propose. The Agency will grant you a leave-of-absence stretching well into the New Year, as long as you need. You will, on your own, as a private citizen, organize and execute an operation involving the extraction of De la Fuente and Casas." Smythe leaned forward over his desk for emphasis. "You will be given full logistical support by the Agency for this operation, with the usual cutout procedures, of course. Should you fail or be captured or whatever, the Agency will deny ever having had anything to do with you, and you will be strictly on your own."

"No exchange in case of capture?"

"None."

"What happens if I succeed?"

"You get your old job back and may even get promoted, but for sure you'll get a medal."

Lonsdale thought hard for a minute. Then in a flash of inspiration he perceived how he could get even. "It's a deal, subject to one condition."

"What's that?"

"A bonus."

"How much?"

"Three million dollars in Switzerland."

"What? You're a paid employee of the Agency. You get a salary, that's all."

"Director," Lonsdale addressed Smythe with great dignity. "You and I have disagreed on a number of issues, but we have never disagreed that both of us are intelligent and motivated men." Smythe nodded. "You have just told me that if there is to be a rescue mission of not only my man, Casas, but, more to the point, also of your deep asset, De la Fuente, you're only willing to authorize such a mission if it is undertaken by me as a believably deniable individual."

"Go on." Smythe looked at his watch.

"Here's how I see the situation. On the one hand, you will deeply embarrass the president if it gets out that the operation he authorized on your recommendation is going down the drain, and with it one of the Agency's best assets in Cuba."

Lonsdale could tell that Smythe was listening intensely. "On the other hand, if I go to Cuba and succeed in getting both your man and mine out you will have redeemed yourself at least partially by having mounted an operation that got Fidel nervous."

Lonsdale took a deep breath. "If I fail and the CIA is accused of being behind the setup, you can save the Agency from international censure by denying all connection between me and the CIA on the basis of the old rogue-agent-risen-from-the-dead ploy." He waved his hand in a gesture of dismissal. "Come to think of it, the worst case scenario would be that two men would die for being traitors, and I also would die. Although not smelling of roses, both you and the Agency would get off almost unscathed."

"So if you think you will die what do you need the money for?"

Lonsdale made his answer sound as amicable as he could. "I need the money in case I fail, but go on living and you then cut off my pension, my livelihood, my access to my friends, my job; you know, that sort of thing—"

"You know very well I couldn't do what you're asking." Smythe replied.

"For me to be entirely deniable I must be on unpaid leave. Then, I can hire myself out as an independent consultant. Right?" Lonsdale asked.

"Right."

"OK, so my fee for two months' work as an independent consultant is three million dollars, payable in advance."

"One million."

"One million seven hundred and fifty thousand dollars, plus my regular salary."

"One million five hundred thousand in unmarked bills, plus your salary, the latter fully taxable."

"Done, provided I get your and Morton's full—and I mean full—cooperation, and access to Charley's control."

Smythe sat back in his chair and thought for a while. Then he came around to Lonsdale's side of the desk.

"It's a deal," he said and held out his hand. Lonsdale shook it, then got up and left.

Morton was the first to speak. "That was easier and less expensive than I thought it would be." He too got up, but Smythe motioned him to stay.

"I haven't finished with your man. He's too dangerous, too much of a loose cannon by half." Smythe swiveled and looked out the window for a while. "We've got to get him under control somehow," he murmured, almost as if to himself. Then he turned to face Morton again. "Any ideas?"

"We could always make him one of the owners of the Panamanian company."

Smythe was very pleased. "Brilliant. Do it, Morton. Do it!"

CHAPTER THIRTY-SIX

Monday and Tuesday
Washington, DC

Lonsdale's three-bedroom, double-decker penthouse was spacious and very comfortable. The walls, the fabric covering the furniture, the table linen he used, the drapes, even the dishes reflected his love for the colors of Provence: marvelous golden yellow and a refreshing light blue. The apartment's western exposure guaranteed that in the evening a bright sunset would illuminate the entire place and make it glow. In the spring and summer Lonsdale would get home early enough from work to see this spectacle and enjoy its magic.

To analyze his new project in comfort he poured himself half a glass of red wine, a decent Brunello di Montalcino, and then settled into his favorite armchair facing the high floor-to ceiling glass doors leading to the large balcony. He used the remote to turn on the stereo and pressed Play. The elegant sounds of Django Reinhardt playing "Nuages" filled the room.

Lonsdale loved guitar music, both classical and jazz, and he still played the instrument on occasion, but only when he was alone. *Too irregularly*, he reflected, but that could not be helped in his line of business.

He could foresee three scenarios. In the first, he would succeed in extracting both, or at least one, of Casas and De La Fuente from Cuba and survive in the process. In the second, he would extract neither of them, but survive. In the third, and worst-case scenario, he would get neither of the Cubans out and die trying. He resolved to acquire the best technology, the best equipment, and the best people money could buy to ensure that he had the best chance to survive.

Lonsdale figured he needed about two dozen men: two teams of four in the field, plus two in logistics, two to four in communications, two helicopter personnel and six sailors, plus the command staff, of course.

These people would have to be found, assembled, trained for three weeks, then infiltrated into Cuba, which would take another two weeks, and given time to acclimatize. Hell, he was looking at two months before he could even think about trying to extract two heavily guarded men from Fidel's fiefdom.

He didn't have two months. He had a maximum of six weeks!

He grabbed pen and paper and began to scribble furiously. Within an hour he had the outlines of a plan with a fifty-fifty chance of success, a plan worth trying.

He emptied his glass, picked up the phone, and dialed Delta Airlines. He needed to be in Zurich by the weekend. Then he phoned Morton and made an appointment with him for the next day. His final call was to Micheline. He told her he'd be absent for a while and that he'd call her as soon as he got back. And no, he couldn't say when.

Even at five thirty in the morning it took Lonsdale half an hour to drive from where he lived in Georgetown to his office in Bethesda.

He pulled into the building's underground garage and used his card to gain access to the section watched over by three security guards on duty twenty-four hours a day, seven days a week.

He got to his office a few minutes before six and was in the process of organizing a couple of cups of fresh, hot coffee when Morton walked through the door.

"I suppose you have a to-do list as long as your arm." Morton entered talking.

Lonsdale laughed. Although he had gotten very little sleep, he was so energized by being back in the game that he felt no fatigue. "Longer than both my arms."

Morton looked at his watch. "It's six fifteen. The banks open at nine. Where do you want your money?"

"You mean you're ready to disburse?" Lonsdale had not expected the Agency to be so speedy.

"Smythe wants to have you fully funded by the end of this week."

"What's his hurry?"

"Believe it or not he wants you to have time to succeed."

"This can mean only one thing: Operation Adios is in bigger trouble than I think it is. Did he make any suggestions?"

"He wants you to meet Oscar De la Fuente's control."

"When?"

"He'll give you thirty-six hours' notice."

"If he can find me."

"What is that supposed to mean?"

"Didn't you say Smythe wanted me off the premises by the end of the week?"

"Yeah, but you'll be required to keep in touch."

"That won't be easy without leaving a trail."

"No it won't, so let's get to sweating the details."

"Not before I get my money."

It took Lonsdale four hours to explain what he wanted to do and how.

To comply with Smythe's directive that the operation be believably deniable, Lonsdale intended to revert to his original identity. It would be Bernard Lands, the rogue agent, risen from the dead, who would hire the people, procure the equipment, arrange the transport, and direct the extraction of Casas and De la Fuente. Thus, funds for the operation—fifteen million dollars is what he estimated he'd need—would have to be transferred into an account traceable to Bernard Lands.

He would have to fly to Zurich as Lands, and instruct his lawyers there to open an operating bank account, perhaps in Panama, the ultimate beneficiary of which would appear to be Bernard Lands.

As for his "consulting" fee, it would have to end up in an account controlled by Robert Lonsdale. This Lonsdale hoped to arrange through a lawyer friend who lived in the Channel Islands.

Personnel-wise, Lonsdale would recruit a deputy who would help him identify the squad leaders and communications technicians. The rest would be hired by the deputy, acting independently. Although it was still early days, Lonsdale estimated that, to succeed, he would need at least seven well-trained, key men to mount an extraction operation.

"Whom do you intend to pick as your deputy?"

"Reuven Gal. I've worked with him before."

"I remember Gal. He was with the Mossad till five years ago." Realization suddenly dawned on Morton. "Wasn't he with you when—"

"The Arabs first tried to kill me?" Lonsdale finished the sentence for him.

"Do you know where to contact him?"

"He lives in Palm Beach and is a security consultant to the rich."

"What kind of personnel, ordnance, and equipment do you think you'll need?"

"A couple of dozen people all told and two cars, a van, a helicopter, and the *Barbara*."

"What is the *Barbara*?"

"The *Barbara* is a freighter that the Colombians use to smuggle drugs into the States through Cuba. It was in Quesada's notes of his initial interview with Fernandez."

Morton said nothing.

Lonsdale tried to sound conciliatory. "Here's the list of what I need. Let me know what dealer I should buy weapons from. Once I know his name we'll work on the cutout procedures to keep the Agency out of the picture. Leave the vehicles and the helicopter to me. I'll purchase them myself."

Morton glanced at the list Lonsdale had handed him. "I see you picked the Galil as your assault weapon."

"Yeah. It's a bit heavy, but more reliable than most such weapons."

"OK. Now give me an outline of what you're planning."

They spent another four hours refining Lonsdale's plan, developing cutout and communications procedures and administrative details. Finally, they addressed the money issue again.

"Jim, I'll call you from Zurich. No, even better, I'll fax you the name of the Guernsey and Vaduz lawyers and their bank account numbers. The fax will be your authority to transfer the money to them, for me in trust. I'll look after my end."

"What do you mean?"

"I'll tell them where and how to send my money so that I can have final use of it."

"That means that once I've disbursed, you'll have control, and since I will be disbursing in advance, the Agency will have no leverage on you to ensure you keep your end of the bargain and carry through with the extraction plan."

"That's true, but it will have my word that I will. I believe the saying is 'as an officer and a gentleman.' "

"And where does all this leave us?"

"At a Mexican standoff, that's where."

Neither of them spoke for a while. It was Morton who finally broke the silence. "There is only one way out of this impasse. I'll have to vouch for you personally, on pain of losing my job and pension."

Lonsdale was amazed. "You mean Smythe actually asked you to do such a thing?"

"That he did."

"And would you?"

"Yes, I would."

"Why?"

"Because, contrary to what you believe, I do trust you and feel I have to make amends for having been less than forthright with you during this past month." *Besides, I've got you by the shorts, my friend,* Morton added silently to himself. *If it ever came to light that you were a part-owner of the Panamanian company you'd look like a drug dealer and you'd be toast.*

"Is this an apology?" Lonsdale asked.

"Yes, it is. I'm very sorry."

Lonsdale felt vindicated. "Your apology is accepted." *As for your being more forthright in future, we'll see,* he thought, not at all sure he would ever trust Morton again.

Morton left for an early lunch and Lonsdale called the FBI liaison office on the special secure line. Having provided the proper credentials, he asked for the duty officer.

"How can I help?" the man asked.

"Get your file on a Reuven Gal, Israeli citizen, I think, residing in Palm Beach, Florida, and tell me if he has an e-mail address."

After ninety seconds he had his answer.

"Your man has two e-mail addresses. One he uses for his business, the other—the personal one—he uses via a so-called blind readdresser."

"You mean a rerouter who keeps his customers' identities secret from the people who receive e-mails from him?"

"Something like that, but more secure. Your man has not one, but two buffers, so working back up the line is almost impossible from far away."

"But your guys traced him back."

"Not quite. We had help from the source."

"From Gal?" Lonsdale couldn't keep the surprise out of his voice.

The FBI man laughed. "That would have been too easy. No. Let's just say we looked at his computer when he wasn't looking."

Lonsdale jotted down Gal's particulars, including address, both unlisted home numbers, the car cellular number, the portable cellular number, and the two e-mail addresses.

"Do you want his bank account details?"

"Might as well."

The FBI man sighed. "How about if I sent you a fax on this?"

"No. Send me a memo by messenger."

"OK. How fast do you need it?"

"Before three p.m."

"Can do. Anything else?"

"Well now, seeing that you will be writing me, why don't you give me some details about the man's marital status, girlfriend status, and business dealings. Nothing too in-depth on the business thing, just a general outline."

"Is the guy a philanderer?"

"One of the greatest."

"What else?"

"That's it, except for one rather difficult request. Try to find out if the guy will be home this afternoon or evening."

"I'll try."

Lonsdale hung up and switched on his computer. Having gained access to the Internet, he activated his own blind re-addresser system, a system far more sophisticated than Gal's, one that not even an Internet encryption specialist could break into. He then sent a message to Gal's personal e-mail address that would bypass the man's readdressers and hit his e-mail address directly. Lonsdale chuckled. He could see Gal going squirrelly trying to figure out what had happened. Such a breach of his defenses would drive any security consultant crazy.

Lonsdale was equally proud of the message itself: "Reuven. Some years back, when the Arabs were after my proverbials you were kind to me, and I have not forgotten. Meet me at the Bice Bar tonight at ten. Ask for Meisner. It's payback time. L."

CHAPTER THIRTY-SEVEN

Tuesday
Gander, Canada

On the trip back to Havana, Casas and De la Fuente barely spoke to each-other. The uncomfortable trip on board their Tupolev 18-passenger jet that had seen better days was in no way alleviated by the abominable food they were served. Only the Stolychnaya vodka was any good.

A half-hour before the Gander refueling stop in Newfoundland, Canada, De la Fuente excused himself and went to the bathroom. There he extracted an Executive Dictaphone from his pocket and delivered himself of a to-the-point memo, intended for Spiegel. Then he pocketed the small cassette and put a fresh one in the machine.

In Gander, while Casas visited the washroom, De la Fuente went to the gift shop to browse through the merchandise, or so he told Casas, who was to meet him there later. He wandered around the store for a minute or two then went to look for a sales clerk called Harry or Henry or Harold or Horace. These were the names Spiegel had given him when they set up De la Fuente's escape route in case he had to get out of Cuba in a hurry. The gift shop, ostensibly a partnership owned by the four H's who worked around the clock, seven days a week and met every international flight landing in Gander was a joint RCMP-CIA listening and assistance post for the likes of De la Fuente.

He spotted Harold near the newsstand. "Excuse me, but can you tell me where I can find some Christmas Holiday music?"

"This way, please." Harold led him to a rack in the corner. "Do you have anything specific in mind?"

" 'White Christmas,' with Bing Crosby."

"A very popular tune," Harold said and pointed to the top shelf of the rack. De la Fuente extracted the cassette, pretended to examine it, and then, while shaking Harold's hand to thank him, palmed off the minicassette he had fished out of his pocket previously. He looked at his watch. "When does the plane for Cuba depart?" he asked.

"No idea, Sir. You had best check with the Cubana desk." Harold reached for the "White Christmas" recording De La Fuente was holding. "Shall I wrap this for you?"

"No, I've changed my mind," said De la Fuente. He handed the cassette back to the clerk and left him to join Casas whom he had spotted entering the shop.

CHAPTER THIRTY-EIGHT

Tuesday and Wednesday
Palm Beach and Miami, Florida

Lonsdale got into West Palm a few minutes past nine at night and drove to Bice's in exclusive Palm Beach as fast as he dared, well aware of the local police's unforgiving attitude toward speeders.

The FBI had confirmed shortly after lunch that Gal was indeed in Palm Beach. By late afternoon their voluminous report on the Israeli had also landed on Lonsdale's desk. He had reviewed it in detail during the flight from Washington.

Gal was a confirmed bachelor, very fond of the ladies, who regularly managed to latch onto attractive, wealthy women with whom he would cohabitate for a year or two and then move on.

At present he seemed to be "on standby," in between women, and living alone in a million-dollar home on the Inter-coastal Waterway. His consulting business seemed to be doing well. He had money in the bank, drove a bottle-green Jaguar and had a backup car, an expensive Cherokee Chief four-by-four. He also owned an eighteen-foot Mercury Outboard Cruiser, which he used as a runabout, mainly for short, daylong fishing trips.

Lonsdale smiled. Four years earlier, Gal, who had left the Mossad at age fifty with nothing but a modest pension, had seemed an unlikely candidate for riches and fame. But then Lonsdale remembered what his late mother always said. "Make sure to associate with people who are richer than you. Some of their wealth is bound to rub off." Gal, who was handsome, athletic, and a great dancer, seemed to have learned this lesson well.

The valet took Lonsdale's car keys and gave him a tag. Lonsdale thanked him and went through Bice's elegant, etched-glass doors.

The maitre d' met him at the door. "Do you have a reservation, Sir?"

"No, I've just come in for a drink. By the way, my name is Meisner. I expect someone to be asking for me." He gave the man ten dollars.

"What time do you expect your party?"

Lonsdale looked at his watch. It was ten. "In about ten to fifteen minutes."

"And does your friend know you?"

"I'm afraid not."

The maitre d' pocketed the money. "Please have your drink at this end of the bar if you can, Sir, so I can spot you. As you see we're awfully busy."

A glance over Lonsdale's shoulder confirmed the statement; the customers were lined up three deep. Lonsdale ordered a double pisco sour—Bice's bartender was one of the few men in Southern Florida who knew how to make a proper one.

The maitre d' came over at five past ten and handed him the cordless phone. "Call for you, Sir."

"Hello."

"Mr. Meisner?"

"Yes."

"Do me the honor of walking out into the street so I can have a look at you."

Lonsdale grinned. "Still as formal as ever, are we Reuven?" he observed. "What do I do once I'm outside?"

"Turn right and walk up the street. I'll look after the rest." The line went dead.

Lonsdale paid, waved at the maitre d', and left the restaurant.

He spotted the Jaguar as soon as he stepped outside. It was double parked up the street a block and a half away. He began to walk at a leisurely pace, passed it without glancing at it, and sensed rather than heard that the car was following. He kept going until the Jaguar accelerated past him and, tires screeching, turned right at the next corner.

Lonsdale continued walking without looking back. Within minutes the car was behind him again, but, this time, it slowly drew even and a window opened.

"You're fat," Reuven Gal shouted out at him from the driver's side.

"And you're ugly," Lonsdale replied laughing.

Gal pulled over and stopped the car. "Get in Bernard before you catch cold." Lonsdale slid in without a word. Gal accelerated away from the curb.

Lonsdale waited for a minute out of respect for having put his erstwhile colleague to so much trouble on such short notice and then, half-turning toward the Israeli, inquired with some delicacy. "How pissed off are you?"

"Me? Pissed off, no; intrigued, yes."

"Intrigued?"

"Yes, intrigued. I thought you were dead. Where the fuck have you been all these years?"

"How do you know I'm me and not an impostor?"

"Come on Bernard, give me a break." Gal sounded hurt. "Nobody waddles the way you do."

"You mean you identified me by my walk?"

"Why else do you think I followed you for two blocs?"

Lonsdale grinned. "All right, all right, you win. Now tell me where you're taking me."

"To eat, of course. I presume you're hungry."

Lonsdale remembered that he had not had time to have lunch. "Starving."

Gal was pleased. "I'm glad. I booked us a table at Cafe Europa. How I got us in on such short notice I'll never know."

"Come off it you big show-off. Everybody in Palm Beach knows that you know everybody and that your connections in high places and low are better than ever."

Gal was ready to give as fast as he got. "Is that why you called me? For my connections?"

"Partly. But I'll tell you all about it after we've eaten." The car slowed, and Lonsdale started to open the door. Gal put a hand on his shoulder. "Not so fast my friend, not so fast. I want to tell you something before we go in."

Lonsdale closed the door and faced Gal.

"I'm glad you're not dead," said Gal deadpan. "I liked working with you and hope to work with you again, but on one condition."

"And what would that be?"

"That you don't hold out on me."

"You mean information-wise?"

"That too."

"I won't, I promise"

"Then let's go get 'em."

During the meal they revisited old times. Although Gal tried to be delicate, it soon became apparent that, to get Gal's cooperation, Lonsdale had to give a plausible explanation of where he had been during the last two decades.

Having spun a yarn about residing in Argentina and making a living as a security consultant, thereby implying he and Gal were colleagues Lonsdale steered the conversation around to the present.

"You're listed as a security consultant too," he said, stirring his coffee. "How's business?"

"Can't complain. And you?"

"Just a little too good," Lonsdale allowed, testing the waters. "And that's why I'm here."

"Really?" Gal leaned back in his chair laughing, "I can't wait to hear what you're in the process of cooking up."

Lonsdale shook his head. "Not here, Reuven. Let's find a more private place somewhere."

"OK, but first: where are you staying?"

"I have a guaranteed reservation at the Breakers."

"Can you afford to lose the guarantee?"

"What do you have in mind?"

"Be my guest for the night. I've plenty of room, and we can talk in complete privacy at my place."

Lonsdale reasoned that the advantage of seeing Gal's headquarters from the inside and, perhaps, getting a glimpse of his operation, outweighed the strong likelihood of Gal recording every word that would be said at his place.

"What about your wife?"

"I'm not married."

"You live alone?" Lonsdale pretended surprise. "I don't believe it. A leopard doesn't change its spots."

"I live in a large, well-located and well-protected house. There's a maid comes in every day to do for me, so don't worry about putting me out. She'll look after both of us. Makes a damn fine breakfast."

Lonsdale gave in. "Sold. Drive me back to Bice's to pick up my car, and I'll follow you to where you live."

It was past midnight by the time they got to Gal's house on Ibis Crescent located on the Inter-coastal Waterway and shielded from the street by a solid brick wall. Lonsdale dumped his bag in the bedroom next to the office and joined his host for a short nightcap on the screened part of the pool patio between the house and the sea.

Gal poured them a small brandy each. Raising his glass he said, "Nice to see you alive and well and healthy."

"*L'Chaim.*" Lonsdale countered with the traditional Jewish toast: "To life."

They settled into comfortable armchairs facing the waterway and neither spoke for a while. It was Lonsdale who broke the silence. "How secure is this place?"

"Quite. Once the gates on the outer wall are electronically locked no one can get through them. There are infrared motion sensors on top of the wall, and above the flower beds along the two sides of the property. The rhododendron bushes separating me from my neighbors are, as you can see, very thick, but when you'll look at them from close up tomorrow you'll discover I didn't rely on nature. There is razor wire strung through them to a height of nine feet."

"So you can be penetrated only over the wall or from the waterway."

"True, but I have twenty-four hour regular and infrared surveillance from four TV cameras through monitors in my bedroom. They display the entire area at all times and keep a taped record of all goings-on."

"Wouldn't like to be your gardener, or pool boy." Lonsdale mused.

Gal laughed. "Right." His English was near perfect and sometimes very Englishy since he had been educated in the UK. "I view the tapes daily, of course, and about a year ago had the pleasure of watching the pool boy making it with the maid at the poolside."

"In broad daylight?"

"Yeah, on the chaise this side of the pool."

"What did you do—fire them?"

Gal was taken aback. "Why should I want to interfere with the civil liberties of two consenting adults? Besides, they're both Cubans and good at that sort of thing."

"Which brings me to my reason for visiting you."

Gal emptied his glass. "At last. But first, let me neutralize any eavesdroppers who might be around." He got up and flicked one of the light switches upward. Nothing visible happened.

"What does that do?" asked Lonsdale.

"See the mosquito screen around us? It's a bit heavier gauge than normal. I've just electrified it thereby creating a magnetic field around the patio, which knocks out all electronic listening devices in the vicinity."

"What about the rest of the house?"

"Only the office is safe. It's always locked, and I have the only key. Of course, I sweep it for bugs daily, but we both know that, although conversations inside the office can be protected, the wires, telephone, fax, computers, and so on are all open to interception at the other end."

Lonsdale leaned forward in his chair and put his glass on the table. "Let's get down to business."

"About time."

"We have to extract two heavily guarded men from a Latin American country."

"Who's the client?"

"I don't know because the job was contracted to me through an intermediary."

"Do you have a plan?"

"A rough one. It involves a total of twenty men in the field and four backup."

"Does that include the diversionary team?"

Lonsdale was pleased. Gal had not lost the touch. "Yes, it does."

"How many vehicles?"

"A panel truck, two taxis, a helicopter, and a cargo ship."

Gal looked at him perplexed. "You're not crazy enough to be thinking of mounting an amphibious operation?"

"In a way, I suppose I am."

"Explain."

It took Lonsdale until three a.m. to put Gal into the picture. He had to be careful not to give away his targets' identities or the specific area where the action would take place. When he finished, Gal poured them both a last drink. "What's our budget?" he asked.

"About twelve million bucks, I estimate." Lonsdale decided to keep three million dollars in reserve.

"How much of it is mine?"

"One million guaranteed, half up front, the other half at the end. You get another quarter million for each target we bring out alive."

"In other words, about 10 percent of the total is mine. How much are you taking?"

"I'm being paid separately."

"So we have about ten million dollars for the operation itself."

"About."

"Twenty men in the field at a quarter of a million dollars each is five million. Your support people are another half million, so total payroll is five to six million. The helicopter with fuel and maintenance is another million, as is the cargo ship. This leaves about two million dollars for weapons, uniforms, protective gear, and three motor vehicles." Gal closed his eyes for a few seconds. "What kind of artillery are we thinking about?"

Lonsdale was glad Gal had said "we" for a second time. "Galil assault rifles, side arms, tear gas, stun grenades, and perhaps a couple of rocket launchers."

Gal closed his eyes again, this time for a full minute. Then he got up and stretched. "My preliminary impression is that our budget is somewhat tight, but let me redo the sums, and I'll let you know tomorrow morning." He yawned and held out his hand. "Sleep tight, Bernard. I'll see you at nine thirty for breakfast."

Lonsdale was pleased. The bargaining had begun. He bade his host goodnight and headed for his room.

"How do you propose to smuggle all those men and their equipment into Cuba?"

Lonsdale almost choked on his orange juice. "Who said anything about Cuba?" he managed to croak.

Gal grabbed a piece of toast from the rack in the middle of the table and wiped the remains of the egg yolk off his plate. "Come off it, Bernard! What kind of a schmuck do you think I am?" He stuffed the soaked toast into his mouth and washed it down with a gigantic gulp of hot coffee. Then he burped discreetly and sat back in his chair with a contented smile. "I worked it all out last night. Your clients are the Colombian drug cartel and the people whose necks you're to save must be some high-up Cuban officials whom Fidel has sent to the pokey for helping the cartel smuggle drugs through Cuban waters. What I don't understand is why anyone would want to spend upward of ten million dollars to spring two has-beens from jail once their usefulness has come to an end."

"Maybe it's the men themselves who're putting up the money for their own liberation."

"Then why don't they just offer the money to Fidel and be done with it? For fifteen million dollars Fidel could buy a lot of much-needed agricultural equipment for his people."

Lonsdale helped himself to a tangerine, peeled it, and stuffed the skin into his coffee cup. He looked past Gal and beyond the pool. The houses across the Inter-coastal Waterway shimmered tantalizingly in the morning sunshine, their windowpanes glittering like huge diamonds.

"Reuven, I don't deny that the Colombians might be my ultimate clients, but I don't know for sure. I've been retained by a Panamanian, and he's the one who's paying. As for the extraction targets, I have no clue about their identity, nor about the place from which we're supposed to extract them. What I do know, because I've checked, is that there've been no recent arrests of senior Cuban government officials on drug-related charges, nor are there any such individuals being held in jail in Cuba."

He reached across the table for a glass of water. "My instructions are to train a team of about twenty commandos and have them and their equipment ready to move out at a moment's notice three weeks from today. Everybody, and that includes you and me, gets paid half their basic pay in advance and the other half at the conclusion of the mission, whether successful or not. Bonuses will be paid only if the mission is successful. And this we'll only know at the end."

Gal was skeptical. "This whole thing sounds to me like a fairy tale."

"Would a half million dollar transfer into your bank account make you into a believer?"

Gal was delighted. "It would certainly help; in fact it would go a long way—"

"Give me a bank account number, and I'll arrange for the money to be in it within ten days."

"And what's my job to be?"

"Field commander. You are to recruit and supervise the training of the seventeen-man field force that will carry out the diversionary and extraction operations."

"I thought you said twenty men."

Lonsdale nodded. "I did, but two will be flyers, copter pilots to be more precise, and I will recruit them."

"You'll look after transport and ordnance?"

"Yes to transport, no to ordnance. You'll have to do that, but I'll give you a supplier. And you are to secure a mixed bag of Argentinean, Venezuelan, and Italian passports, just in case."

"Why?"

"I want Latino-looking, preferably Spanish- or Italian-speaking men who won't stick out like a sore thumb in a South American environment."

"You don't want much, do you?"

Lonsdale gave the Israeli a friendly grin. "Hey, I'm paying top dollar, ain't I? I deserve top-quality service." He became serious. "Kidding aside, it shouldn't be too difficult to find seventeen reliable and trained Israelis, Italians, and Cubans thirsting for action and needing money."

"You keep on saying seventeen."

"Yeah. You're number eighteen."

"You mean I'm to go into the field?"

Lonsdale looked at Gal hard. "For a million and a half U.S. dollars, yes!"

"But I'm not fit."

"You've got three weeks to get fit."

"I don't really need the money."

"But you want the excitement, don't you, Reuven?" Lonsdale was at his persuasive best. "You're bored, you're soft, and you're in a rut. You make nicey-nicey to rich people whom you don't like; you play up to wealthy women you don't really love; you're indolent, slothful, and purposeless. In other words, you're no longer the Ben Gal Tiger."

"How did you find out my Mossad cover name?"

"You'd be surprised how much more I know about you." Lonsdale shrugged. "But never mind—just tell me: are you in or not?"

"For two million guaranteed, plus bonus, I'm in."

"I'll give you a million now, five hundred thousand when we finish, in whatever way we finish, plus a bonus of a quarter of a million bucks for each target extracted alive—that's a possible total of two million bucks."

Gal held out his hand. "It's a deal, provided you deliver the million within ten days."

Lonsdale took his host's hand and shook it. "I will." he said simply. "And I thank you, Reuven. I know you're doing this as much for old times' sake as for the money. By the way, why do you need your money precisely within ten days? I know your business is doing well so why the hurry?"

"You said we only have three weeks. Finding and recruiting men properly qualified for this thing is the hardest part of my job, so I'll need to get on it right away. Once I've found them I can lead them on for a week, but no more. Otherwise it'll affect my reputation. If you produce the first million in ten days I'll know you're well connected and that your clients are serious. That's when I'll bring the men down here for training because you're bound to pay them."

"You trust no one, do you?"

It was Gal's turn to look hard at Lonsdale. "Do you?"

"Touché." Lonsdale looked at his watch. "I've got to get going. Give me your banking particulars."

Gal wrote them down on a paper serviette. "How do we communicate?" he asked.

"I'll e-mail your instructions."

They gave each other a bear hug, pats on the back, and then shook hands.

CHAPTER THIRTY-NINE

Wednesday Morning
Coral Gables, Florida

The streets intersecting Ponce-de-Leon Boulevard in Coral Gables have elegant Spanish names reflecting the background of the area's predominantly Hispanic residents at the turn of the century, when the community was built. Even today the tradition continues. Coral Gables is home to upper-middle-class Cubans, Argentineans, Venezuelans, and Colombians who, although they work and reside in Florida, maintain close ties with their countries of origin.

On Valencia Street, between Ponce-de-Leon and South West Thirty-Seventh Avenue, stands an elegant, expensive-looking house. The plaque on the gate pillar, somewhat obscured by the branches of a magnificent bougainvillea, is of subdued burnished brass. It reads: F. Raymond Rodriguez, Certified Public Accountant, Business Hours: Monday to Friday 10 a.m. to 4 p.m. Very few people know that the F. stood for Felix and that Rodriguez used to be Ramirez. But Lonsdale did.

He and Rodriguez, then known as Felix Ramirez, had spent six months working together in South America during the bad old days of the Tupamaro crisis in Uruguay. Then, out of the blue, Ramirez was recalled, leaving Lonsdale to fend for himself as best he could. He'd regretted the Cuban's departure. The two had made a good team.

It was likely that Rodriguez's house was under periodic photo surveillance by the FBI, but that did not concern Lonsdale. Nevertheless, he decided to proceed with caution.

He parked his car in front of the office complex on Ponce-de-Leon, at the corner of Sevilla, put on a wide-brimmed straw hat he had bought for the occasion, and walked east on Sevilla to Galiano. There he turned left for two blocs until he reached Valencia where he turned right then put his head down and quick-marched—almost ran—the couple of hundred feet that brought him to Rodriguez's garden gate.

He pressed the bell, and after being buzzed through, followed the arrows to the entrance at the side of the house. The CPA office was downstairs, where he was confronted by an attractive, determined-looking woman.

The sign on her desk said she was Sylvia Gonzalez.

"You have an appointment?" she inquired, sounding formal and noncommittal. "Mr. Rodriguez is very busy."

"I'm afraid I don't." Lonsdale was appropriately contrite. "But I'm sure that if you told him that Mr. Jackson from Langley Disposals is here to see him he'll fit me into his busy schedule somehow." Anyone with a name starting with the letter *j* and claiming to be from Langley Disposals, the Agency's clean-up squad, was a senior CIA officer. The woman gave him a piercing look and picked up the phone.

Rodriguez appeared within seconds. He was wearing dark glasses. "Mr. Jackson please come this way." He led Lonsdale into his inner sanctum and indicated a comfortable-looking couch. "Take a seat, and tell me how I can be of help."

"Come off, it Felix. It's me, Bernard Lands," Lonsdale said in Spanish. Ramirez's surprise was total. He began to grope around in an attempt at getting out of his chair and that's when Lonsdale realized that the man was blind. He wanted to bite his tongue in half.

It took him a few minutes to calm down Ramirez, who at first thought he was in the presence of a ghost. Then Ramirez asked Sylvia for a couple of Cafe Cubanos.

Lonsdale spun Ramirez the same yarn he had told Gal and quickly came to the point. "Felix, I need a paymaster for my operation. Will you handle it?"

"How much are we talking about? What's the budget?"

"Fifteen million."

"Over what period of time?"

"About a month."

"I'll charge 1 percent of all disbursements."

"You mean a hundred and fifty thousand bucks?"

"Yes, but that includes all bank charges and so forth."

"Nice return on your time."

"True, but who else would go near the shit you'll be throwing at me?"

"I guess you have a point there."

"So tell me what you want done first."

"No. First you tell me about your eyes."

"Thanks for being discreet and not bringing up the subject right away." Ramirez smiled sadly. "There's nothing much to tell. You might remember that the Shah of Iran went to Panama for a while after he was thrown out of power."

"In the mid-seventies."

Ramirez nodded. "Yes, around that time." He sighed. "Anyway, he was holed up in this luxury hotel on an off-shore island with his Savak people guarding him. As you know, I was pulled out of the field in South America very hush-hush and sent to Panama by the Agency to advise the Shah." He took a cigar from the humidor on his desk and offered one to Lonsdale who declined. "The poor bastard didn't need an advisor; he needed a doctor. He was dying of cancer." He held out his cigar for a light.

Lonsdale obliged. "But what has all this to do with your eyes?" He lit Ramirez's cigar, "Oh that." Ramirez dismissed the question with the wave of his hand. "I was inspecting the disposition of the Shah's guards around the hotel and one of them threw a phosphorous flare at me by mistake, which burnt my eyes out." The story sounded unlikely, but Lonsdale got the message: Ramirez lost his eyesight during a politically very sensitive and secret mission for the Agency that was still classified.

"Is that when you changed your name?"

"No. About a year later when I married the nurse who put me back together again."

"What do you mean?"

"Being blinded is a terrible trauma, especially for an active man like I used to be." Puffing away at his cigar Ramirez said nothing for a while and Lonsdale knew better than to push. "Anyway," his host finally got going again, "there's one damn good thing that came out of this. I settled down." He chuckled. "Remember how I used to play the field?"

Lonsdale nodded. "I sure do."

The Cuban shook his head as if to chase away the past. "Let's get on with the job. By the way, what's your operational cover name?"

"Bernard Lands, and it's not a cover name. I was baptized Bernard Lands when I was a week old. And, in case you're wondering, I'm no longer with the Agency."

"OK, by me *socio*, my old buddy. Where do we go from here?"

Lonsdale sighed. This session was going to be a long one, and he'd have to spend the night in Miami, which was not what he had planned.

"I have a list of requirements I want you to order from the suppliers I have marked against each item." He laid a three-page list on the man's desk.

"In whose name do I purchase?"

"A Panamanian company, the name of which I'll fax you next Wednesday."

"What do I use for money?"

"You'll have a Panamanian bank account with ten million bucks in it by next Wednesday for a start."

"Who'll have disbursing authority?"

"You and you alone."

"And what if I don't play it straight?"

"Neither you nor Sylvia will reach old age," said Lonsdale softly, but firmly.

"What do you know about Sylvia?"

"You mean apart from her being your eyes, your assistant, and probably your business partner?"

"That's exactly what I mean."

"That she is your wife whom you love very much; that she is the best thing that has happened to you in your life, and, finally, that she is probably almost as discreet as you are, Felix."

Ramirez smiled "Almost."

"Yes, almost. Nobody is as discreet as you are."

They worked all afternoon and well into the night with Sylvia, who sat in on most of their deliberations, making sandwiches and coffee to keep them going. Lonsdale left the Ramirez house a few minutes past three a.m. and was duly photographed by both the FBI and the CIA, but then that was part of the overall plan.

CHAPTER FORTY

Thursday through Saturday
Washington, DC and London, England

Lonsdale got back to his Georgetown apartment at eight thirty on Thursday morning. His message light was flashing so he dialed his answering service. "Happy Birthday," the recorded voice said. Lonsdale hung up and retrieved the *Washington Post* from the kitchen garbage bin where he had just thrown it.

It took him a little while to spot the small notice camouflaged within the Births, Deaths, and Marriages section. It read, "Meet D. contact at Stafford Hotel London Saturday three p.m. Ask for Harold Dee."

Lonsdale walked over to the shops near Georgetown Park and called an unlisted telephone number from a public telephone. When Morton answered, he said quickly, "London's OK. I will be back mid-next week and will contact you at this number." He hung up and got on with the paperwork he needed to complete before he could leave Washington for London on Friday evening.

By the time Lonsdale booked into the Stafford in London's Piccadilly district it was almost nine o'clock Saturday morning. Luckily, his room was ready.

He had hoped to get some sleep on the way over, but his mind had refused to cooperate. The pace he'd set himself had begun to take its toll, and he couldn't switch off. After a fast shower and shave he swallowed half a 300 mg Melatonin pill, set the alarm on his watch for two thirty, stuck the Do Not Disturb sign on his door and slept. He awoke a few minutes before the alarm went off, refreshed and alert.

At three p.m. on the dot he was at the front desk.

"Is there a Mr. Dee in the house?"

"Sir, he has booked one of the conference rooms and is waiting for you there," the concierge replied. "Please follow me."

Seated in a comfortable armchair, Spiegel was reading the *Daily Mail*, his spectacles perched on the very tip of his generous nose. "Would you like some tea?" He held up a paper-thin porcelain cup by way of greeting.

"Tea would be nice."

"Please arrange for fresh, hot tea," Spiegel said to the concierge.

"Right away, Sir" answered the man with the dignity only an English butler can muster.

Spiegel turned to Lonsdale "What's your name?"

"John."

Spiegel's nostril twitched in disdain. "John it is then. My name is Jim."

"Jim it is then, Ivan," retorted Lonsdale. Spiegel did not look pleased and Lonsdale was glad. Smythe seemed not to have divulged his identity to Spiegel.

"I'm relieved to have this opportunity of meeting you." Spiegel tried to sound friendly.

"Relieved?"

"Yes. Things are not going well." He took a piece of paper and a small tape recorder equipped with a plug-type earphone from his pocket and handed them to Lonsdale. "Listen while you read."

Lonsdale sat down opposite to Spiegel, plugged himself in, and pushed the appropriate button.

"Greetings, you old woman chaser," said a heavily accented, unmistakably Cuban, male voice. "I'm sending this message through

Harry Dee. We won't be able to complete the deal we're working on because, as you know, my partner's employee was sent on an unauthorized trip, which complicated things. I think my partner and I will receive official termination notices in a few days. There may be one way out. If we could organize the paperwork to come from Switzerland to Panama we could connect Terry's father with the deal and negotiate ourselves out of our difficulties. If we cannot do this, you will have to ask for help from my partner's friends. You will have to speak to my partner's mother about this. I hope to see you soon." Lonsdale closed his eyes. All of a sudden he was very tired again.

There was a knock on the door. Tea had arrived.

When they were alone again Spiegel turned to Lonsdale. "Do you understand what he is saying?"

"I think so."

"Then tell me."

"De la Fuente thinks Operation Adios is compromised because of Fernandez's defection and expects that he and Casas are going to be arrested within days. He feels that if the paperwork could connect De la Fuente's father-in-law to the Panamanian bank account with the drug money in it, we could ask him to intervene and negotiate a light sentence, perhaps limited to deportation, for Casas and De la Fuente. Failing this we need to speak with Casas's mother to get the names of close friends of the general, presumably in the military, with whom we could organize some sort of an extraction operation." Lonsdale leaned back in his chair and closed his eyes. "I should've set up a sting against the minister with the help of Casas. This would have delayed the general's and Charley's arrest and given me more time."

Spiegel did not follow. "Who's Charley?"

Lonsdale caught himself. "Sorry. Charley is my name for Oscar De la Fuente."

Spiegel smiled. "It's still not too late, you know," he said softly.

"For what?"

"For stinging the minister."

"Are you kidding? I wouldn't even know where to start."

Spiegel smile widened to an almost obscene grin. "But I do."

"Oh yeah? I bet!"

"Listen up, Lonsdale!" Spiegel's mild-mannered behavior disappeared in a flash, shattering Lonsdale's composure in the process. "Let me tell you a story, which, by the way, I only heard recently, about what happened in Zurich one fine day, a dozen years or so ago."

Jesus Montalba, Cuba's minister of the Interior, was very happy. The sun was shining, the birds were singing, and the jewels in the display window of the shops along Zurich's Bahnhofstrasse glittered invitingly. It was May and warm. He and his beautiful daughter, Tere, were out for an afternoon's window-shopping, which was all he could afford. Ministers of the Castro Regime did not have the means to buy even the least expensive item of jewelry on the world's most expensive street.

Never mind. They were having a great time anyway.

His invitation to the Internal Security and Human Rights Conference in Gstaad, which he had received months ago, had been for two persons, all expenses paid. Since he was divorced and had no current steady girlfriend, it occurred to him that his twenty-five-year-old daughter, herself recently divorced and down-in-the-dumps, might just be the ideal companion for the five-day trip.

She'd been thrilled and eagerly accepted the invitation. Neither of them had ever been to Switzerland.

Montalba and Tere flew to Prague via Cubana Air Lines, and the conference organizers had picked up their tab from there onward. They were as anxious to hear his comments about human rights violations in Cuba as he was to make them. Since the Gstaad trip was costing Cuba nothing, Montalba decided to tack an inexpensive three-day sightseeing tour of Zurich and the surrounding area onto it. He had arranged to stay at the Hotel Eden, a modest three-star hotel, where he shared a room with his daughter, thereby keeping costs to the absolute minimum.

By scrimping and saving and exaggerating his expenses on previous trips he had taken on behalf of *La Patria*, Montalba had managed to assemble a stash of one thousand American dollars in cash, something that was totally illegal in Cuba and punishable by five years' labor on a *granja*, or farm. Whenever he went abroad he would take the money with him (ten one hundred dollar bills carefully hidden in his wallet) hoping to find a small, worthwhile investment of some kind: jewelry, art, or silver. Thus far, he had found nothing that had tickled his fancy.

"What are you thinking about, Papa?"

He covered up instinctively. "I was thinking about where to take my beautiful daughter for lunch."

She looked at her watch. "No wonder I feel hungry. It's past noon." They were standing on the southeast corner of the Bahn-hofstrasse where it met the Parade Platz. "Look," she pointed at the building behind them. "Lind und Sprüngli, the chocolate people who make those fine sweets that we ate on the plane from Prague."

"Let's buy you some chocolates," he said and, hand in hand, they approached the display window. "Even better. I'll buy you lunch in the restaurant upstairs."

"What restaurant?"

"See what it says over there?" He pointed to the sign next to the door.

"I don't speak German."

"It's in English too, Tere," he admonished her gently. He had been paying for English lessons for her ever since she was born.

She shrugged. "Anyway Papa, what does it say?"

"It says they have a restaurant upstairs."

They studied the menu and selected their food in a way to make every Swiss Frank count and managed to enjoy a very decent meal at the end of which Tere ordered a chocolate soufflé. It would take twenty minutes their waitress said, but Tere insisted and, as always, her doting father relented. Then an idea struck him. "Darling, while you wait for your dessert why don't I complete a little errand. I just remembered I promised to buy one of my colleagues a stamp collector's album."

He ignored her pout and stood up. "I'll be back by the time you finish your soufflé, and we'll have our coffee together." Before she could reply he was gone.

"Nice story, but what has it got to do with me?" Lonsdale asked.

"De la Fuente's wife has been after her father to buy her a house in Varadero," Spiegel went on. "He keeps putting her off, says he has no money, but she's convinced he has plenty stashed away in Switzerland. She's now told Oscar that she thinks she knows where the money is and would he please do something to get his hands on some of it."

"How do you know all this?"

"I met Oscar in Havana before he left for Angola to see Casas."

"OK. Then tell me: where does Teresa Montalba think her old man's money is and how much of it is there?"

"She thinks there are millions of dollars in a Swiss bank account her father opened when he left her to eat her soufflé alone at Lindt und Sprüngli's."

Lonsdale roared with laughter. "Hell hath no fury like a woman scorned—not even when she is your daughter. Just because he left her alone for a few minutes."

"Stop it." Spiegel held up his hand. "I felt the same way you do when De la Fuente told me the story. But guess what! Bodner & Cie, Banquiers, one of Switzerland's finest boutique banks catering to an exclusive clientele, has its offices in the Lindt und Sprüngli building's third floor. It is quite possible Montalba saw the firm's nameplate on his way to the restaurant and took advantage of the opportunity. At least, that's what Señora De la Fuente thinks."

Lonsdale thought he got the picture. "Let me guess the rest." He leaned back, smiling. "You want me to go to Zurich, see Mr. Bodner of Bodner & Cie, and persuade him to reveal whether or not his bank does business with a Señor Montalba, who also just happens to be the Cuban minister of the Interior. Knowing the Swiss, Ivan, I would say my chances of success are slim to none." He pursed his lips and then added as an afterthought: "Especially now that I'm a rogue agent."

Spiegel was not bothered. "You may be right. That's why I brought you some ammunition."

He extracted a large manila envelope from the briefcase at his feet and handed it to Lonsdale. "I explained to my contacts at MI6 that I needed help and they were kind enough to provide me with this. Have a look at the pictures inside."

Lonsdale did. The six glossy, high-resolution, 9 x 12 photographs of a balding, surprisingly fit-looking middle-aged man cavorting with a number of naked pre-teen boys disgusted him and made him very sad.

"Those are Herr Bodner's pictures you're looking at," Spiegel said quietly. "I'm sure you'll put them to good use."

CHAPTER FORTY-ONE

Monday
Zurich, Switzerland

"Bernard Lands" had to appear to be respectable and high profile. So, on Sunday night Lonsdale, using the Lands alias, checked into Zurich's most prestigious hotel.

The Baur-au-Lac enjoyed institutional status among the rich and famous. Its elegant garden pavilion is a favorite of the world's beautiful people who meet and mingle there during the summer season's afternoon *Thés Dansants*. Unfortunately so do the world's jewel thieves who religiously attend the antique jewelry auction held annually in the hotel's magnificent salons.

Early Monday morning Lonsdale called the Liechtenstein law firm that had been recommended to him. Mario Dreyfuss, the man he had been told to contact, was not expected before eight thirty, but would call Mr. Lands at his hotel at that time.

His phone rang just after room service had delivered his newspaper with his breakfast: coffee and bread rolls. Lonsdale checked his watch. Eight thirty sharp.

Mr. Dreyfuss was initially very polite and cool, but warmed to "Mr. Lands" considerably when he discovered the identity of his sponsor, Reuven Gal. Although it was short notice, he said he could accommodate Mr. Lands after lunch and asked if four o'clock would be convenient. Lonsdale figured this would give Dreyfuss time to verify his bona fides with Gal.

Lonsdale was glad to have the morning to himself. He had work to do. He called Bodner & Cie after breakfast, asked for Mr. Bodner and was put through to his secretary, Mrs. Fischer.

"Frau Fischer, I would like to see Mr. Bodner this morning about an urgent personal matter."

"What is your name, please?" Her voice was ice cold but polite.

"Cherriex, Jean Cherriex, with an *x*."

"Does he know you?" Still ice cold.

"No, but please tell him I am from Belgium and we share a common interest. I'm sure he will want to speak with me."

"Mr. Bodner is very busy, but please hold."

Mrs. Fischer was back in less than a minute, somewhat flustered. "Mr. Bodner can see you at ten o'clock if that is convenient." She tried to make amends. "Do you know where our offices are?"

"Yes, thank you. I'll be there at ten." Lonsdale hung up.

Manila envelope in hand Lonsdale walked up Tal Strasse at a leisurely pace, inspecting the buildings, the shops, even the traffic lights. There was no doubt about it; in their ponderous way the Swiss over-engineered everything. If there was a way to provide redundant equipment, the Swiss found it: an extra traffic light for buses only, a plethora of white lines painted on the pavement ahead of every inter-section, street lights backing up street lights in case they failed—the list was endless.

When he reached Lind und Sprüngli, Lonsdale scanned the nameplates and found Bodner & Cie's with ease. While taking the stairs to the third floor, he noticed that there was indeed a restaurant on the first floor and that it took less than a minute to walk up from the restaurant to the bank.

He rang the bell, the door clicked open, and he found himself in an antechamber decorated with original masterpieces: two Picasso inks, a Leger, and a Braque. The receptionist gave him a friendly smile. "Are you Monsieur Cherriex?" she inquired in French. Lons-dale nodded and she phoned Frau Fischer who appeared within sec-onds to escort him to the Herr General Direktor.

Bodner's office was understated elegance. The Persian rug cover-ing most of the glittering parquet floor felt as if it were three inches deep. Bodner's desk, a large Empire escritoire, was a genuine Napo-leonic antique, the client armchairs original Louis XVI. In the corner opposite the door of the large room yet another beautiful antique, a full-length Empire sofa.

Above the sofa and the first item a visitor would notice when entering this handsome room, was a discretely illuminated Renoir. Further along the wall toward the window, a Restauration vitrine housed a number of exquisite pewter pieces—a remarkable collection. An immense bookshelf along the wall on the other side of the room overflowed with rare, leather-bound and gold stamped books.

Bodner rose from his carved Belgian armchair and, with outstretched arms, met Lonsdale halfway. He spoke French with a typically Swiss accent. "Come in, come in, Monsieur Cherriex." He pointed to the armchair nearest him next to the coffee table. "Why don't you sit here and take coffee with me?"

Lonsdale sized up his host: about fifty-five, five-ten, weighing about a hundred and seventy pounds, and athletic. Bodner was eyeing the manila envelope in his visitor's hand.

"No, thank you, Mr. Bodner, no coffee for me."

"Nor for me then either," Bodner said to Frau Fischer. "Please make sure we're not disturbed," he added. She withdrew. "Shall we sit?"

Lonsdale took the armchair nearest the wall then watched the banker arrange himself in the armchair opposite. He was wearing a beautifully tailored charcoal-gray three-piece suit and a pearl gray tie over a flawlessly ironed, blinding-white shirt. Bodner took off his glasses and put them on the table, rubbed the bridge of his nose with index finger and thumb, adjusted the matching *pochette* in his breast pocket, then leaned back and linked his hands over his midriff, thumbs pointing upward. "Now then Monsieur Cherriex" he smiled pleasantly. "How can we be useful to each other?"

"I don't know how I can be of use to you, Herr Bodner," Lonsdale said in English, "but you can certainly be of use to me."

Taken aback, Bodner did not quite know what to say. "I'm sorry, but I do not understand. Did you not say your name was Cherriex and that you were from Brussels?"

"No, I did not. I said my name was Cherriex and that I was from Belgium."

"Brussels, Belgium, what's the difference? Let us not split hairs."

Lonsdale took the plunge. "Herr Bodner, I came to see you because I need some information. I hope you'll give it to me."

"What kind of information?"

"About ten years ago a man opened an account with your bank. I want details relating to that bank account."

"We don't give out this sort of information."

"I think you might if I gave you the man's name."

"What is his name?" Bodner snapped, visibly put out.

Watching intently, Lonsdale told him. Although the banker had steeled himself against giving anything away he couldn't help but blink at the mention of Montalba's name. "How can I know about such a thing?" Bodner was becoming annoyed. "We have thousands of clients. You don't expect me to remember one in particular who may have opened an account with us ten years ago, do you? Besides, what has all this to do with our common interests in Brussels?"

"Nothing." Lonsdale reached for the manila envelope on the table in front of him. "I was afraid you might say you couldn't remember, so I brought you something to jog your memory, and galvanize you into action."

"What kind of action?" The banker's anger rose.

"Like checking your records, getting a printout of the account . . . that kind of a thing."

"How dare you come in here on false pretenses and then ask me brazenly to break the bank secrecy law?" Bodner shouted and reached for the telephone on the end table beside him. "I am calling security to have you escorted out of here."

Lonsdale held up his hand. "You don't want to do that before you look at these." He handed Bodner the envelope and watched as the man extracted the pictures in it.

He glanced at them and then grabbed a lead-glass ashtray and hurled it at Lonsdale, who ducked in the nick of time. The heavy object struck a painting of Napoleon on horseback behind Lonsdale, splitting it. The picture clattered to the floor as Lonsdale scrambled out of his chair to subdue his attacker.

Bodner was waiting for him. He grabbed a bronze lamp off the end table and came swinging at Lonsdale, who sidestepped, but not before the shade scored his left cheek. The momentum of his swing made the banker spin around and he got entangled in the electric cord. Lonsdale kicked his legs from under him and the two tumbled into a heap on the floor. Lonsdale tried to roll away, but Bodner would not let go of his left trouser leg, ripping the fabric as he pulled at it. Lonsdale, on his back, kicked him in the head with his right foot, but the kick was badly aimed, and hardly slowed Bodner who scurried away and stood up somehow as Lonsdale got to his knees. Bodner, stronger than Losndale had expected, threw himself at Lonsdale who brought his right elbow up and hit the Swiss just above the temple.

The man went down like a stunned ox, out cold.

Lonsdale staggered to his feet and surveyed the damage. Other than the painting, the lamp, and his trouser leg, nothing seemed to have been damaged, not even the ashtray, which had ended up on the seat of the armchair on which Lonsdale had been sitting.

Lonsdale felt his face. No blood, probably only a nasty scratch. He looked at Bodner who was not doing well. He was unconscious. His breathing was shallow, and he was probably suffering from a concussion.

Got to get some water to revive the bugger, Lonsdale said to himself. He needed to find the door to the private bathroom without which no self-respecting Swiss chief executive could exist. He went to Bodner's desk and carefully inspected the walls to the left and right of it. Sure enough, between the end of the bookshelf and the window there were almost imperceptible parallel breaks in the brocade about three feet apart. He tried pressing on the wall. There was a click and a door swung open. Lonsdale went into the bathroom, soaked two hand towels in cold water and returned to Bodner.

The banker came to slowly, moaning softly, his head moving from side to side. There was a lump the size of a small egg above his left temple and a nasty welt on his right cheek where Lonsdale's shoe had grazed it. His waistcoat had a couple of buttons missing, as did his jacket. His once beautiful white shirt was a mess. "Time to wake up sweetheart," Lonsdale told him and dropped one of the towels on the banker's face. Bodner spluttered, then reached for the towel and wiped his face. Lonsdale helped him to an armchair and, fetching a pillow from the sofa, made him comfortable. Then he knelt down and held up his index finger.

"Look at my finger Bodner and try to follow it with your eyes," he said. Instead, Bodner kicked him in the stomach. Lonsdale fell back, winded—the kick had been well aimed and strong. Bodner staggered to his feet. Lonsdale, fighting nausea, somehow managed to kick the man's legs from under him once more. This time Bodner fell between the armchair and the coffee table, banging his head on the way down. Lonsdale left him there and sat down in the armchair opposite. His stomach was in spasm and he attempted to ease the pain by taking a few deep breaths. Bodner tried to get up, but Lonsdale gave the coffee table a vicious push and jammed the banker against the armchair.

"Listen you disgusting man. You try one more stunt like this and I'll beat you within an inch of your life." He got up with difficulty and leaned over the Swiss. "You saw the pictures and you know what would happen if they got into the wrong hands."

Bodner nodded dumbly.

"Well then, cooperate. Don't make me go to the police and the press with them."

"Who . . . who are you?"

"Never mind all that. Just get me a copy of the account."

Bodner shook his head. "I don't give in to blackmailers, ever. There is no end to it." He tried to get up, but Lonsdale knelt on the coffee table to keep it pressed against the banker's body.

"I'm no ordinary blackmailer, Bodner. Actually, I'm not a black-mailer at all."

Bodner snorted "Why are you here then?"

Lonsdale thought fast. "To put money in your client's bank account."

"What?"

"To put money in your client's bank account" Lonsdale repeated and got off the table. Bodner twisted himself upright and Lonsdale handed him the other wet towel. The man wiped his face again then looked around and spotted the photographs on the table, where he had dropped them. He collapsed into the armchair.

"Where did you get these? I demand to know if it was Pierre who gave them to you."

"Pierre? Who's Pierre?"

"Your brother, you lying bastard." Bodner was working himself into a rage again.

"Take it easy Bodner. You're way off base." Lonsdale made him-self sound as conciliatory as possible. "I chose the name Cherriex because in one of the pictures, in the background there is a delicatessen and caterer's shop called Cherriex. Now that you mention it, it does say Cherriex and Frères. I guess you know Pierre Cherriex, who must have a brother called Jean."

"So what is your name?"

"Bernard Lands."

"And where are you from?" Lonsdale saw that Bodner was feeling better and that he did not have a concussion. His questions were too sharp for that.

"Miami, Florida."

"And what do you want from Mr. Montalba?" Lonsdale was pleased with the question. He sensed Bodner wanted to negotiate, to save face, to feel he was not betraying his client.

"I want to put a million U.S. dollars into his account."

"Well then, do so." Bodner sounded imperial. "Send it to us and we will credit his account."

Lonsdale took a menacing step toward his host who backed away.

"Nice try, Bodner, but it won't work. I am not sending you money until you let me see a copy of the account."

"That is out of the question."

"Very well then, listen. Your client, who opened the account ten years ago and who, as you know, is Cuba's minister of the Interior, desperately needs the money I am prepared to send him. His life may depend on it. As you see, my group has ways of finding out and documenting things. We are careful and discreet, and we don't bail out our business associates when they say they are in trouble without checking out their story. Montalba told us he has, to use his words, 'relatively little money' and that he urgently needed a million dollars more. We are ready to help, but we want to be sure we are not being led by the nose."

"A likely story." Bodner was holding his head. It was aching and the pain was getting worse by the minute.

"Fine, don't believe me. But remember this. If, because of your stubbornness, Montalba gets into trouble it will affect me and my people. Whether his goons get you or not, we will make these photographs public, just to hurt you, to punish you, so to speak, for hurting one of us."

"How do I know your name is really Bernard Lands and that you are telling the truth?"

Lonsdale took a deep breath. "Call the Hotel Baur-au-Lac and ask for me. If I am registered there they must have my passport and credit card numbers. N'est-ce pas?"

Bodner got to his feet with a groan and staggered over to his desk. He pressed the intercom and asked Frau Fischer to call Bernard Lands at his hotel. In no time Frau Fischer reported that Mr. Lands, who was indeed registered, was out. Was there any message?

"Never mind." Bodner hung up and turned to his visitor. "You've scored a point, but how do I know you didn't just borrow the name, which you could have overheard in the hotel's lobby?"

He's thinking clearly again, Lonsdale said to himself and answered brazenly. "You don't, but think carefully. If I were an ordinary kind of blackmailer would I go to all this trouble?"

Bodner seemed to hesitate, and Lonsdale was sure he was going to cooperate. It was only a question of time.

The banker sat down and remained motionless for a while. Depressed, he stared at a fixed point above Lonsdale's head. Then he turned on his computer and keyed in some numbers. Within thirty seconds his printer spewed out Montalba's account activity since inception: three sheets of paper. After glancing at them the banker handed them to Lonsdale. "Your friend has about three hundred and fifty thousand dollars in his account, which he deposited over a twelve-year period. There have been no withdrawals. The account is not in his name, but in that of his daughter, Maria Teresa. Montalba remains the sole signatory as long as he's alive."

Lonsdale glanced at the sheet. Bodner's summary was dead on. Montalba was putting aside money for his only child, his daughter. But where did the money come from? Lonsdale looked at the papers in his hand again. All deposits, except the first thousand dollars, were wire transfers from the National Bank of Mexico.

"You've got what you wanted," Bodner ordered, still dazed. "Now get out."

Lonsdale turned on his heel and left, straightening his tie as he passed Mrs. Fischer on the way out.

Back in his room he cleaned up then booked himself an appointment with the hotel's *masseur* in the steam room and on his way down in his bath-robe, bought a new shirt and pair of pants in the Baur-au-

Lac's haberdashery. By the time he got to the sauna his muscles were beginning to stiffen up and his bruises were seriously hurting.

Bodner had been a far more effective physical adversary than Lonsdale had expected.

Lonsdale spent a half hour in the steam room and another forty minutes with the *massseur* under whose capable and soothing fingers the kinks and knots in Lonsdale's muscles soon dissolved. Thus, by late lunchtime he could move his body almost without pain.

Almost. There was still pain, but it was bearable.

Lonsdale had a double vodka and San Pelegrino in the grill, followed by a roast beef sandwich washed down with strong espresso. At three he called for a limousine to drive him to Vaduz, Liechtenstein's capital city.

Then he checked out.

CHAPTER FORTY-TWO

Tuesday and Wednesday
Jethou, The Islands of Jersey

Built on a bluff, Antony Benedict's magnificent house on the Island of Jethou offered spectacular views of the ocean from every window, but none more dramatic than the one from the living room, cantilevered out over the sea.

Sipping a double Absolut with San Pelegrino, Lonsdale told his host about the purpose of his visit while, a hundred feet beneath him, the sea boiled as it exploded against the rock then retracted, only to come racing back to crash again into the mass of the island.

A corporate lawyer, Benedict practiced his profession from his spacious home office, and specialized in forming and administering offshore corporations around the world. A graduate of Trinity College, Cambridge, he'd been a University rowing "blue." Although years of easy living had made him overweight you could still see the power in his shoulders and barrel chest that had caused his teammates to elect him with one voice their scull's "stroke," or lead rower.

The lawyer had bought Jethou, an island in the English Channel between Jersey and Guernsey, after living twelve years in the Caribbean, where he had acquired firsthand knowledge of the chicanery and double-dealings of members of the international jet set. During these years—his years in the monkey house he called them—he had also learned that the super rich showed one common concern: how to protect their assets from confiscation triggered by sudden and violent political upheaval.

"What I need is for you to incorporate an offshore company in Switzerland and to open a bank account for it," Lonsdale told Bendict, whom he had known for years and who had assisted him very effectively in the past. "After that, I want this company to appear to be owned by you, but its shares, which will all be bearer shares, will be in my possession. Once this is done, I'll have someone wire a million and a half U.S. dollars into your trust account in Cayman." Lonsdale looked up at his host. "I assume the account is still at Barclay's Bank?"

Benedict nodded and Lonsdale continued. "The money will arrive with instructions saying to be called for by *X*." He looked at Benedict again and asked "What would you like *X* to be?"

"You mean what name we are to use?"

"Precisely."

Benedict pursed his lips. "How about some sort of a difficultish code name?"

"Like . . . ?"

Benedict closed his eyes for a few seconds then said: "Let's try D91N."

"All right with me, but why?"

Benedict laughed. "Think about it for a bit. I'm sure you'll stumble onto the reason sooner or later."

Lonsdale made a face and continued: "As soon as the money arrives transfer it to the Swiss company's bank account."

"Who will have signing authority over the account?"

"For the time being, you will, Anton, and if you die, your partner Caldwell in Cayman will, but Caldwell is not to know who the beneficial owner of the Swiss company is."

"I have to tell him *something*."

"Then tell him the company is owned by whoever turns up with the bearer shares."

"Which you will have in your possession."

"Which I, or, if I die, my legal heirs will have possession of to do with as they please."

Benedict nodded. "I see what you're trying to achieve. Now tell me, what's her name?"

"What the hell are you talking about?"

"Come off it, Lonsdale." The lawyer's light-blue eyes twinkled with merriment. "I have known you for fifteen years during which I never once saw you concern yourself with your death, or its effect on your assets." Benedict rose and, drink in hand, walked over to the large window. He watched the sunset for a while then turned to face his guest.

Lonsdale laughed and told him about Micheline.

"You will be careful, won't you?" said Benedict.

"What do you mean?"

"Look old chap, I'm not trying to pry, but I've been watching your comings and goings during the past decade and a half and I've a general idea of how remarkably well-informed you are. After what you've just asked of me I'm more convinced than ever that your many varied responsibilities, of which, I confess, I know precious little, include the directing of substantial operations one of which seems to be in the process of making its debut, and a well-financed debut at that, I might add." Benedict took a contemplative puff on his cigar and continued. "I'm rather fond of you, you know that, and I don't want any harm to befall you. That's all."

Lonsdale was touched. "I promise I'll be careful."

"You should be at your age, old chap, you should be. I'll look after everything you've asked for first thing tomorrow morning. I'll sell you one of my shell companies and I'll have your bearer shares for you by Monday next. Your company's bank account will also be open by then. You may thus inform your people that they should be prepared to wire the funds next Monday. I'll provide the details when I send you your share certificates. Where do you want them sent?"

"To Micheline, via messenger."

"You must then give me her address."

Without a word Lonsdale handed the lawyer a sheet of paper with all the particulars then got up to leave. Benedict waved his cigar in Lonsdale's general direction. "Good-bye old chap and good luck."

"Good-bye Anton and thank you."

"For what?"

"For your hospitality, for your advice and for caring."

At three a.m. that night Lonsdale sat up in his bed. His subconscious had worked out that D91N stood for NSD, as in LoNSDale.

CHAPTER FORTY-THREE

Thursday
Palm Beach, Florida

Lonsdale felt great. He was perfectly on schedule. While driving from Miami to Palm Beach he mentally ticked off the principal accomplishments of the past few days: debriefing Spiegel; obtaining copies of Montalba's Swiss bank account; forming a Panamanian company through the attorneys in Vaduz and opening a bank account for it; forming a Swiss company for his own purposes through Benedict; and opening a bank account for it in Zurich. He'd also recruited a field commander, Gal, whom he was on his way to visit, and he'd likewise secured the services of a paymaster, Ramirez, who was standing by for instructions.

What remained to be done?

Getting the account numbers from Vaduz and Benedict and passing them along to Morton so he could fund the operation was priority one. Then there was the recruiting, the training, the purchase of weaponry, the *Barbara*, the helicopter . . . lots to do still. And he had a month left at best during which he also had to somehow squeeze in a trip to Cuba. Lonsdale needed help big time. He could hardly wait to see Gal.

As it turned out Gal was just as anxious to get on with the job. He had identified two team leaders, both on leave from the Mossad, robust and Spanish-speaking, each with a "following," two in one case and three in the other. That made a total of eight with Gal.

"I have my eyes on two Cuban drivers. They know Havana and are handy with weapons. If we can secure their services we have half the field force we need and can start training." They were sitting on Gal's porch in the dark, sipping Diet Cokes. "What about the money?" Gal asked. "It's due tomorrow."

Lonsdale was embarrassed. "I know I haven't kept my promise, but the problem is technical, not financial." He then explained that the Panama account would not be open before late Friday so that funds could not be transferred to it before Monday. "But I fully expect to be in funds by Monday at the latest. As I told you, Ramirez is the paymaster and sole signatory on the account. Deal with him."

"What will be the effective date of employment of my men?" The delay was making Gal nervous.

"Monday."

"And when can I start ordering material?"

"Also on Monday. Ramirez has the list of suppliers." Lonsdale had an idea. "Reuven, why don't I turn the purchase program over to you? That'll leave me free to look after chartering the *Barbara*, buying the helicopter, and hiring the pilots and the communications guys." He looked at his host. "Would that be OK with you?"

Gal seemed relieved. "Sure. Too many cooks spoil the broth." He took a gulp of his drink. "The new starting date, Monday, gives me a chance to honor my previous commitments."

"Such as?"

Gal laughed. "I'm involved in politics a little."

"How deeply?"

"Oh, just some light fund-raising for the Republicans here in Florida." He got up and stretched. "I have a lunch to attend tomorrow—five hundred dollars a plate—to help finance the campaign of the new Republican candidate for the Senate."

Lonsdale was surprised. "How did you get involved in that?"

Gal shrugged. "You know how it is. They have a professionals-to-professionals campaign and they cold-call you. In my case a lawyer who had sent me some business put the bite on me about two years ago. He's not a bad guy; keeps sending me business. He's quite well-known in the Miami area. Practices immigration law."

Lonsdale went rigid. "He must have been working for the previous Senate incumbent then." He tried to sound calm, casual.

"Yeah." Gal yawned and picked up his glass. "He and Acting CIA Director Smythe, the previous incumbent, are still close friends. Smythe will be at the luncheon tomorrow."

Lonsdale forced himself to tread with care. "Your guy must be making a killing here with the hundreds of thousands of Cubans and other Latinos around."

"You're right. Especially with the Cubans, since Ray is Cuban himself."

"Ray?"

"Yeah. Ray Puma, all around good guy."

Lonsdale felt as if someone had kicked him in the solar plexus.

Gal stood up and began walking toward his room. "Let's start work early tomorrow. Would seven o'clock suit you?"

"Fine by me."

"Goodnight then." Gal left Lonsdale to face his newfound demons alone.

There is no greater agony than uncertainty. Lonsdale couldn't sleep. Ray Puma was a close friend of Smythe! Ray Puma may have had access to information about Fernandez's new identity. Smythe certainly had. Did Puma betray his cousin? Was Puma working for the Cuban Intelligence Services? How much did Reyes Puma know about what was going on? Lonsdale had to find out. But how with so little time left?

CHAPTER FORTY-FOUR

Friday
Miami, Florida

Morton was very worried. Lonsdale had called him on the special line at six a.m., declaring a Grade 1 emergency and asking for a meeting in Miami at lunchtime. This, in spite of their having agreed to keep communications between them to an absolute minimum and to declare emergencies only in extreme circumstances.

Morton had not expected complications this early in the mission.

"What's going on?" he asked as soon as Lonsdale sat down. They were having lunch at The Office, a small restaurant on LeJeune Boulevard near Miami's International Airport.

"Jim, I think it's very bad." Lonsdale gulped down some water.

"What's up?"

"I've been up all night chewing on what I stumbled into by pure chance yesterday evening. Our operation may be compromised; it may even be in the process of being turned against us."

"Suppose you start from the beginning."

Lonsdale drained his glass then told Morton about his conversation with Reuven Gal. "Fernandez," he ended up, "must have told Reyes Puma everything about the Cuban drug operation prior to surrendering to the INS. Reyes Puma could have asked the director about Fernandez. Since Reyes Puma was representing Fernandez and already in the know, Smythe may have told Reyes Puma about his cousin's new identity."

"You're assuming Smythe knew it."

"Yes. It's the first point we have to clear up."

"But even if he did, why do you assume he would be so indiscreet as to reveal it to Reyes Puma?" Lonsdale's hypothesis did not make sense to Morton.

"Because Smythe may have assumed that, as Fernandez's attorney and cousin, Fernandez was entitled to the information."

"That's unlikely. Smythe wants to bring Fidel down at any cost so why would he blab? But let's assume Smythe *was* indiscreet. How does this tie in with your theory of a reverse sting?"

"Let us now assume," Lonsdale was trying to sound calm, but, within, he was anything but, "that Reyes Puma is working for the Cubans, either as a freelancer or as a regular informer. He passes the information along to Cuban G2 and this enables the Cubans to kill Fernandez."

Morton was skeptical. "But even if you're right it still wouldn't explain why we may be looking at a reverse sting."

Lonsdale rushed on. "Fernandez is the third person to die, after Siddiqui and Schwartz."

"The fourth." Morton corrected him.

"You mean counting the girl in Cayman?"

"No. I mean the BCCI manager in Luanda."

Lonsdale nodded. "Tell me, Jim, what do all these people have in common?"

"What do you mean?"

"What knowledge did these four people share?"

"What?"

"They were all in a position to testify that Cuba was participating in questionable activities."

"Such as?"

"Plundering in Angola, smuggling gold and silver coins, ivory, and God knows what else. What's more, Fernandez knew that Raul Castro knew about the drug operation."

Morton was still skeptical. "You know as well as I do that it was the Agency, and not Castro who started Operation Adios."

"It's for this very reason that I'm convinced we're facing a reverse sting."

"I don't follow you."

"Listen to this. According to both Casas and Fernandez, Raul seemed to know about the drug operation before Fernandez defected. If so, he also knew that he and Fidel had authorized no such thing. So why then did he not intervene to stop the operation and have Casas and De la Fuente arrested?"

"You tell me."

"One: to get his hands on the drug money; and two: to harm the CIA by showing that the operation was CIA inspired."

Morton saw what Lonsdale was driving at. "So you think Raul started killing off the people who could testify to Cuba being involved in questionable operations."

"Yes."

"And you think he is trying to isolate De la Fuente to force him to confess to CIA involvement in exchange for his life."

"Yes."

"And you think Reyes Puma is working for Raul?"

"Yes, absolutely."

Morton allowed himself a bitter smile. "You may be right."

Lonsdale was taken aback. "How come all of a sudden you agree with me?"

"Because of something I know that you don't."

"What's that?"

"We completed our background check on Reyes Puma. He has a seventy-year-old mother in Havana who, for no apparent reason, receives a stipend from the Castro government well in excess of the average pension paid to Cubans over age sixty-five."

Lonsdale's excitement was mounting. "Reyes Puma working for the Cubans explains all the murders. He might even be the guy responsible for setting them up. Maybe he is running a network of Cuban undercover agents in the States. And maybe he is trying to send us a message."

"What message?"

"Simply that the Cubans know we Americans are behind Operation Adios. And that they're a step ahead of us, and that they are eliminating all potential witnesses who could testify to Cuba's involvement in any kind of impropriety. They also want us to note that Cuban Intelligence has a widespread network of agents who can function with lethal effect on at least two continents."

"Sounds hard to believe." Morton, though hesitant, was becoming a convert.

Lonsdale pressed. "We must find out at once what Reyes Puma is up to. Otherwise, I cannot continue our operation. It would be too risky."

Morton was beginning to feel very uncomfortable. "There is also the problem of De la Fuente. If you're right, he is the keystone of Castro's case against the CIA. Therefore, there can be no question of abandoning efforts to extract him."

"Or of killing him before he can hurt us." Lonsdale felt he had to articulate what both of them were thinking. He wanted no subsequent misunderstandings.

"What do you propose we do?"

Lonsdale cut into his steak. "I'll tell you in a minute, but first I want to settle pending money matters."

"Do you have your bank account numbers?"

Lonsdale handed Morton a piece of paper. "It's all there."

Morton glanced at it. "I'll take care of the two transfers as soon as I get back to Washington. Your money should be in your accounts by noon on Monday."

"There's one more thing." Lonsdale extracted another piece of paper from his inside pocket. "As you know, I met with Ivan Spiegel in London—"

"I know all about it. Smythe showed me Spiegel's summary of the meeting."

Lonsdale was aghast "What if Smythe also told Reyes Puma about Ivan Spiegel?"

"Don't be silly. Smythe may be indiscreet, but not stupid."

"Or a traitor?"

"You're becoming paranoid," Morton snapped.

Lonsdale shrugged and handed Morton the piece of paper. "That's a copy of Maria Teresa Montalba's Swiss bank account, which I obtained with Spiegel's help. It shows a balance of over three hundred and fifty thousand U.S. dollars, made up mostly of transfers from the National Bank of Mexico. We need to find out who is originating these transfers in Mexico and why."

Morton nodded. "I'll see what I can do, but frankly, I fail to see how this can be of any use to us. Montalba's daughter is not Montalba."

"Agreed, but the account was opened by Montalba with a thousand dollar cash deposit, and Montalba remains the sole signatory on the account as long as he is alive."

"That's a different story." Morton was impressed.

"Let's get back to Reyes Puma. Here's what I propose we do."

CHAPTER FORTY-FIVE

Monday, November 28
Miami, Florida

Sunday, November 27, was Reyes Puma's fiftieth birthday, which he celebrated at a gigantic barbecue in his own backyard organized by his family and close friends. There was lots to drink, good Cuban music, and, in typical style, mountains of food to consume. But there were no stone crabs. For this delicacy, Reyes Puma's favorite, he had to wait until the following day, on which some of his grateful clients and business contacts had organized a special dinner in his honor at Joe's Stone Crab Restaurant in South Beach.

The event was called for nine, but by half past eight most of the fifty attendees, who'd arrived by car, boat, and motorcycle, were at the bar of the famous crab house. Reyes Puma showed up a few minutes after the hour and was greeted by thunderous applause and boisterous shouts of "Salud" and "Viva."

Dinner got underway an hour later, and Reyes Puma ate as if he'd never eaten before, demolishing more than a dozen fair-size crabs in the process.

The party was in full swing when the guest of honor began to complain about a stomach ache, something he very seldom experienced. By midnight he was seriously ill. One of the guests, Quesada, who had been so helpful with organizing Fernandez's release, arranged for an ambulance to take the ill, semiconscious Cuban to a private clinic nearby. The doctor in the ambulance administered an emetic at once, which caused the three hundred pound attorney to be violently sick. The doctor then injected him with a tranquilizer, which was also an antidote to the stomach irritant Reyes Puma had unknowingly ingested during his marathon meal.

At the clinic he was rushed to the room that the solicitous Quesada had reserved for him, where the doctor, who had never left his side, arranged for intravenous treatment. In addition to the regular rehydrating saline solution, the treatment also contained a generous amount of sodium pentothal. The doctor waited for thirty minutes for the drug to take effect and then administered a stimulant that brought the fat Cuban back into a more or less conscious state.

That's when Lonsdale took over. Dressed in Cuban Army fatigues with the insignia of major on his shoulder tabs, sporting a false beard, his nose and cheeks altered by a master make-up artist to resemble a bit to El Che, and sporting dark glasses, he clattered into the room, followed by Morton, similarly attired, but showing the rank of Lieutenant.

"Good morning, Major Reyes Puma, can you hear me?" he asked in Spanish.

"Yes, I can, but who are you?" whispered the drugged attorney.

"We're from Havana, here to congratulate you on the fine job you're doing for La Patria."

"Then you know I'm not doing this for La Patria, but mamá," replied Reyes Puma, "besides, I'm not a major, only a captain."

"You have been promoted, comrade." Lonsdale turned to Morton, who handed him two shoulder tabs marked with the *galones* of a major in the Cuban Army. He laid them on Reyes Puma's shoulders then saluted smartly. "Congratulations Comrade Major on your promotion," he snapped. "La Patria thanks you for your efforts. Your pay has been increased to correspond with your new rank," Lonsdale improvised, "and will continue to be paid to your mother in Havana."

"Thank you, and thank Comandante Raul for me." Reyes Puma tried to salute, but his arms were tied down, though in his drugged state he had the impression he was actually saluting.

Lonsdale pulled up a chair and sat down beside him. "How is Director Smythe?" he asked. "Is he still providing useful information?"

"Yes, he is."

"I understand he was of help in the Fernandez affair."

"Not really, but then I didn't need any help, anyway."

"How come?" Lonsdale played along. Reyes Puma's answer was not what he had expected.

"Fernandez was being released in my presence. I had him followed."

"And who killed him?" Lonsdale was trying to get back on track.

"Laura."

"Who's Laura?"

"One of Raul's professional hit women. Very discreet."

"Was the woman who killed the jeweler in Budapest one of your people then?"

"No. That plan also came from Havana. It was another female. Laura looked after Fernandez."

"You mean the assassination?"

"Yes, she assassinated Fernandez." Reyes Puma was becoming agitated and the doctor adjusted the flow of intravenous liquid.

"And the other assassinations?"

"Three by shooting, one by accident. Havana made three look alike—to send a message." The Cuban was getting tired. Lonsdale looked at the doctor, who rotated his hand, indicating that Lonsdale should press on quickly.

"What message?"

"To the Americans." Puma whispered. "So they should know we know."

"Know what?"

"Operation Adios. They started it. De la Fuente started it for them. We didn't."

"How did you find out?"

"Smythe. He's a big shot now. They'll confirm him DCI soon and then we'll be all set. If I survive." The Cuban's voice was barely audible.

"Can you not control him?"

"Hard to control the DCI. Too powerful . . ."

"How do you control him?"

"His wife . . . he wanted his wife killed . . . I arranged it . . ." Reyes Puma lost consciousness.

Lonsdale motioned to the doctor, and they stepped outside the room. "Can you wake him up so I can continue asking questions?"

"Not without risking a heart attack."

"What are the chances?"

"Sixty percent in favor of a massive one. He's too fat and out of shape."

Lonsdale looked at Morton who had joined them. "What do you think, Jim?"

"We have enough to follow up on," Morton replied. He was ashen-faced, shaken.

Lonsdale began to pace about, chewing his lower lip. "You're right. And we can't risk killing him."

"Why not?"

"Because we need him to pull a double reverse on the boys in Havana, that's why."

"How's that?"

"We'll start a disinformation campaign through Reyes Puma to obscure the details of the extraction operation. We'll feed Havana false dates, false details, false plans." Lonsdale's mind was far away, working out the details.

Reyes Puma woke up next morning with a blinding headache and totally disoriented. He was mighty glad to see his wife at his bedside.

"*Como te sientes, mi amor?*" She spoke softly, wiping his forehead gently with a moist facecloth. "You gave us all a terrible fright."

"Where am I?"

"At the clinic. Don't you remember? You ate too much and got sick. Had it not been for the quick thinking of your friend, Quesada, things could have gotten far worse." There were tears of relief in her eyes.

"Yes, yes, Quesada. He's a good friend."

"They brought you here by ambulance, pumped your stomach and gave you a sedative to sleep." She pressed the bell at his bedside. "I'm calling the doctor to tell him you're awake."

"Maybe he can give me something for my headache. It's a real screamer."

"I'm sure he will. Just rest easy, *mi amor*."

He turned toward her painfully and smiled "You know Anita, I had the weirdest of dreams." He caught himself just in time and was saved from continuing by the arrival of the doctor.

CHAPTER FORTY-SIX

Tuesday, November 29
Miami, Florida

Sitting on the terrace of their suite at the Sheraton Towers Hotel over-looking Miami Bay, Morton and Lonsdale silently watched darkness descend upon the waters.

The hotel was part of a complex consisting of four spectacular towers rising from reclaimed land bordered by Brickell Boulevard on one side and the sea on the other. Though the view from the fif-teenth floor was breathtaking it was not sufficiently so to distract the two men from their preoccupations.

They were in damage-control mode. Finding out that Smythe was being blackmailed into treason by an agent of the Cuban govern-ment had shaken them both. Neither had slept much during the last thirty-six hours and that hadn't helped either.

"Where's the video tape your people took of Reyes Puma and us at the clinic?" Lonsdale asked.

"It's in my briefcase. I played it back on the monitor a while back and the picture quality is superb."

"What about the sound?"

"Don't worry; it's first class." Morton smiled fleetingly. "Your insistence that we suspend a mike over the bastard's bed paid off."
Lonsdale grunted and said nothing.

"What do we do next?" Morton rubbed his temples.

"We carry on as usual, except that we start feeding Smythe spam."

"We can't do that." Morton wasn't happy.

"Yes we can, Jim. We have to." Lonsdale closed his aching eyes and leaned back in his chair. "A few more days of the status quo are neither here nor there. I'll go to Havana to contact Casas and De la Fuente and tell them to get out immediately, even if it means risking their necks in an open boat."

"We can always have them picked up by our Coast Guard en route."

"As long as we do it outside Cuban territorial waters."

"Twelve miles out."

"At twenty knots that's half an hour."

"If their Coast Guard does not intercept them."

"Whatever." Lonsdale was getting wearier by the minute. "If I can't persuade them to leave I'll try to identify a group of his followers who might be able to help during extraction. With Casas's help of course," he added

"Sounds risky."

"Jim, we have no choice. We've got to get these two out of Cuba, and fast. I just hope I get there before they're arrested."

"Which brings me to Spiegel." Morton shuddered. "I tried to call him in London to stop him from going to Havana."

Lonsdale's eyes snapped open in disbelief. "You mean the man is ready to risk his life by sticking his head into the lion's cage?"

"He doesn't know about Smythe."

"Oh my God. I overlooked that." Lonsdale cupped his hands over his face. "Did you reach him?"

"No. By the time I called this morning his plane had already left for Havana."

"I suppose he wanted to get there the day before his scheduled Wednesday-night meeting with Charley De la Fuente. Makes it look less contrived."

"That was the idea." Morton sighed. "Now that we know the Cubans know everything about Operation Adios, we must assume that Smythe has told them about Spiegel as well. I guess they'll hold off arresting Casas and Oscar until Oscar has met with Spiegel."

"Why?"

"I'm just guessing. The Cubans are meticulous investigators, especially in cases involving foreign citizens. They will try to catch Spiegel and De la Fuente red-handed in the act of exchanging information."

"When did Oscar and Casas get back from Angola?"

"Two weeks ago tomorrow."

"Then their goose is cooked," Lonsdale said with resignation. "They, and Spiegel, will be arrested before the week's out."

"Which brings me back to what I was asking before. What do we do next?"

"Give me fifteen minutes. I have an idea. I just want to think it through." Lonsdale got up and headed for the shower.

CHAPTER FORTY-SEVEN

Wednesday, November 30
Washington, DC, Nassau and Havana

At eight a.m. on Wednesday, Morton met the third secretary of the British Embassy in Washington, who immediately arranged a scrambled telephone conversation with his ambassador in Havana. The ambassador was most gracious and said his sister, visiting Havana for the winter, would be delighted to have drinks and dinner with Mr. Spiegel at the Old Man and the Sea that evening.

Meanwhile, with colored contact lenses to make his eyes look blue, hair dyed blond, and features altered by extensive makeup to look like the actor William Hurt, Lonsdale, using a British diplomatic passport, flew to Nassau to replace the courier on the special diplomatic flight from Nassau to Havana. The flight was operated every Wednesday jointly by the British, Canadian, and Australian embassies.

Ten minutes from Havana, the aircraft, a vintage turboprop, developed engine trouble and limped into Rancho Boyeros Airport after lunch, a half hour behind schedule. While the diplomatic bags were unloaded under Lonsdale's watchful eyes, an inspection of the faulty engine revealed that a blown gasket had been the cause of the trouble. The aircraft could not return to Nassau until a replacement part was properly installed, and the part would have to be flown in on the next available flight from Mexico City, at eleven p.m.

The diplomatic courier and the pilots and cabin crew had to overnight in Havana. The diplomatic duty officer, a single woman, who happened to be the third secretary of the British Embassy, arranged for the crew to be put up at the Hotel Havana Libre while the diplomatic courier was invited to stay at the British ambassador's residence.

What then would be more natural for the diplomatic courier, who claimed he had never been to Havana, than to ask the third secretary to show him the sights?

It didn't take much of an effort to make up a foursome for the evening: the diplomatic courier, the third secretary, the ambassador's sister, and Ivan Spiegel.

When Spiegel arrived to pick up his three guests at the ambassador's residence, he almost had a heart attack when he laid eyes on Lonsdale, but, being a pro, carried on without blinking an eye.

On the way to the Marina Hemmingway the men sat up front and the ladies made polite conversation in the back. Lonsdale turned on the radio and briefed Spiegel about Smythe. "The consensus is that Casas and De la Fuente will be arrested this weekend and so will you."

Spiegel was sweating. "What do I do?"

"Continue to do what you always do. Be the life of the party as always. You'll dance with all the women, you'll make Oscar dance with the ambassador's sister, who has been briefed about what to tell him. But do not dance with the third secretary, and do not, I repeat, do not remain alone with Oscar for one millisecond. No going to the bathroom together, no telling jokes. Friendly, yes, but not too friendly."

"And then?"

"You'll pretend to have had too much to drink and will ask me to drive all of us back to the residence, which I will be delighted to do. We'll help you out of the car, and you will stagger into the residence and stay the night. We will try to get you on board the diplomatic flight tomorrow. If that fails you'll stay at the residence until the Cubans are ready to let you go."

"And if they won't?"

"Don't worry. Several ministers will intercede on your behalf."

"Including the minister of the Interior?" Spiegel was catching Lonsdale's drift.

"You've got it."

Spiegel stopped the car. They had arrived.

CHAPTER FORTY-EIGHT

Friday, December 2
Montreal, Canada

"What do you want for breakfast?" Micheline shouted from the kitchen.

"Bacon and eggs, sunny-side up, toast, marmalade, and coffee," Lonsdale yelled back from the living room. He folded the newspaper he was reading and padded into the kitchen in his bare feet.

"Don't you ever get bored with this diet?" Micheline was laughing. "Your cholesterol must be sky-high."

"I control it with copious quantities of good red wine," Lonsdale replied and kissed her on the cheek. "Did you sleep well?"

She nodded and snuggled against him, happy to have him in her home again, happy to forget the previous night's unpleasantness between them.

She had met his flight from Nassau in the evening, and he had taken her to dinner at Le Toqué. During the meal he'd brought her up-to-date on his activities in general terms and told her he was going to have to go away again soon. She had bristled.

"Why can't I go with you?"

"Because it's too dangerous."

"But I want to be part of your life, like your wife had been. I don't want to be just a sort of bystander. I know I could help."

"Easier said than done."

Micheline had flared up. "Don't patronize me. Although I'm a woman I'm just as good as any man I know."

"Come off it, Miche, you know I'm no male chauvinist. It's just that you're not trained for this sort of thing."

Micheline would have none of it. "Nor was your wife," she had said, feeling bitter. "Yet you made her part of your secret life!"

Deeply wounded by her remark Lonsdale had fought hard not to lose his temper. "And she got herself killed in the process," he had shot back.

The old feeling of guilt was gnawing at him again. He saw the logic of Micheline's argument all right, but, under the circumstances, couldn't bring himself to tempt Providence once more by risking the life of someone he loved. Turning inward, he could not stop the feelings of self-pity and loathing, so deeply rooted in his soul, to surface, although he knew that this process of self-mortification would cause him to spiral into depression again.

Trying to ease his pain he had reached for her hand, but this had angered her even more because she realized she had hurt him much more than she'd intended.

"What's the matter," she had demanded. "Are you still unable to forgive yourself for your past mistakes and be done with them?"

Her harsh words had hit home hard. He saw he would lose her again if he continued to feel sorry for himself, if he refused to dare. His problem was complex. He could not compromise the mission, he dared not put Micheline in harm's way, and he did not want her to leave him—all seemingly irreconcilable goals.

"I can't Miche, I can't," he had whispered.

"Can't what?"

"Can't risk getting you hurt."

"Making me leave you would be better?"

Next day, over breakfast he outlined a plan that absolutely delighted her. He proposed that she accompany him to Cuba for a week as the wife of a member of a Canadian government-sponsored trade mission.

CHAPTER FORTY-NINE

Sunday, December 4
Washington, DC

Discretely inserted into Lonsdale's Sunday *New York Times* was an
unwelcome supplement, an extract from GRANMA, the Cuban Communist Party's official newspaper:

INFORMATION BULLETIN

*"We find ourselves in the unenviable position of hav-
ing to inform the public that Brigadier General Patricio
Casas Rojo and Deputy Minister of the Interior Oscar De
la Fuente y Bravo, both highly decorated revolutionaries who have, in the past, been given important responsibilities by the Party, the Revolutionary Armed Forces, and
the Ministry of the Interior, have been arrested and are
subject to investigation relating to serious acts of corruption and dishonest manipulation of economic resources.*

*Whoever he may be and whatever his previous merits
may have been, the Party, the Revolutionary Armed Forces,
and the Ministry of the Interior will not, in any way, grant
impunity to any person who, deviating from the principles of
the Revolution, gravely violates socialist morality and laws.*

In accordance with the norms governing the conduct of members of the Revolutionary Armed Forces and of the Ministry of the Interior, Brigadier General Patricio Casas and Deputy Minister Oscar De la Fuente are to appear before a Tribunal of Honor, composed of officers equivalent in rank to theirs, which will then recommend the subsequent legal and other measures to be taken in view of the improprieties committed by them.

The recommendations of such a Tribunal of Honor and the reasons for such recommendations will be communicated to the general public at the opportune time."

Ministry of the Revolutionary Armed Forces.
Ministry of the Interior of the Socialist Republic of Cuba.

Lonsdale was relieved that the article did not mention Spiegel.

CHAPTER FIFTY

Monday, December 5
Palm Beach and Miami, Florida

Lonsdale folded the copy of the GRANMA article into thirds and stuck it into his pocket. "I figure we have four weeks left. We must be ready to snatch our people at a moment's notice any time after the trial begins."

"You don't think they'll put on a show trial during the Christmas holidays?" Gal was still trying to recover from the shock of being involved in such a high-profile operation. Lonsdale had only told him about the true purpose of their mission the previous evening.

"Unlikely. They will want the world to focus on the trial and nobody focuses on anything during the week between Christmas and New Year's Day. Since they need at least three weeks for trial preparation and for whipping up a feeding frenzy among the world's paparazzi, I doubt very much that they will start anything before January."

"How is your end coming?"

"The *Barbara* is chartered, the helicopter is bought. I've hired two pilots and got hold of three communications experts who are familiar with satellite imaging. Ramirez has bought the Galils and has had four delivered to Nassau. I have smuggled these into Cuba with the ammo we may need. The rest can go in the false bottoms of the two specially equipped Toyotas, which we're sending to Havana disguised as taxis."

"What do you mean by specially equipped?"

"The radios of all three vehicles have been altered to give them two-way communications capability. Satellite imaging equipment can also be attached to them as can GPS."

Lonsdale was rather proud of his achievements. With Morton's secret assistance he had been able to garner state-of-the-art equipment and top talent to operate it.

"How do you propose to smuggle all that equipment into Cuba?"

"The GPS and satellite stuff are going in via diplomatic pouch, disguised as radios and small TV sets, which, in a way, they are. The stun and smoke grenades will be packed into the false bottoms of the taxis."

"How about sidearms, flak jackets, gas masks, and clothing?"

"They'll go into the false bottom of the command van, which we're shipping to Havana disguised as a maintenance truck for the taxi company."

"Does the taxi company know this?"

"No, but one of the clerks working for it does."

Gal was impressed. "How the hell did you manage that?"

Lonsdale shook his head in disbelief as he recalled the incident. "When I flew down to see you the first time, I sat beside a weeping, deeply distraught woman who turned out to be Cuban. I asked her if I could get her something and she blurted out that what she wanted was her twenty-two-year-old son, trapped in Havana due to an administrative misunderstanding. He was working for the Havana Cab Company as their purchasing supervisor and dying to leave the country. I sent some people I know in Cuba to talk with him and, in return for a special trip to Florida—"

"Via cigarette boat, I presume," Gal cut in.

"Via Cigarette Boat," Lonsdale confirmed. "He agreed to help me."

Lonsdale did not consider it necessary to enlighten Gal about the arrangements having been made through Agency assets operating in Cuba.

Gal stood up, stretched, and then walked over to where Lonsdale was sitting. "When are you shipping the taxis and the van?"

"They'll be in Havana, or Matanzas, the port near Varadero, by Christmas."

"You're that sure nothing will need to get done before then?"

"I'm not sure of anything. I'm making educated guesses and hoping they're the right ones." Lonsdale got up to face Gal. "It's your turn now. How is the training program going?"

"Pretty well. As you know I've got two Mossadniks as squad leaders, and they brought in three other Israelis. I also engaged six Cubans whom some friends found for me here in Florida. With you and me that makes thirteen."

"My lucky number." Lonsdale was pleased: thirteen was indeed his lucky number. He looked at Gal expectantly, waiting for him to continue.

"Three more people, drivers, are reporting for training on Thursday, so by Friday we'll have a total contingent of fifteen."

"Let's see." Lonsdale began to count. "Three people per vehicle, that's nine, plus two ambulance guys—"

"What ambulance, what guys?"

Lonsdale laughed. "I know, I know. I never had the chance to tell you. I came back from Cuba full of new ideas."

Gal was nonplussed. "You've been to Cuba since you last visited me?"

"Just a quickie, in and out, but enough time to have a preliminary look at the presumed target area and to conclude that an ambulance and two jeeps might come in handy."

"Jesus, Bernard. You're scaring me." Gal was not happy. "You're telling me three things: we need more men, we need two more vehicles, and third," he gave Lonsdale a piercing look "we're likely to take serious casualties."

Lonsdale shook his head. "No to the first two of your assumptions. The ambulance is window dressing, and the personnel and the jeeps will be provided by the locals."

"Cubans?"

"Yes, but if you don't mind I'd rather not give you the details yet."

Gal raised his eyebrows, but let it go. "The men are being trained at a range in Georgia, which the Association of Security Consultants maintains for that purpose. The training is general and consists of hostage taking, hostage rescue, defensive and offensive driving, small arms drill, sharp-shooting, explosives handling and physical fitness courses."

"Are you training them with Galils?"

"Affirmative."

"When will they be ready?"

"In less than three weeks. By Christmas for sure."

"Good. Have the best nine, including you, your two Israeli squad leaders, and six Cubans ready for gradual insertion during the Christmas–New Year period. That'll give us a few days to familiarize the team with the extraction site."

"What about the rest of them?"

"We'll need them for the diversionary attack."

"Who will lead them and when do they get inserted?"

"I'm still working out the details, but will have a plan for you the next time we meet."

Gal headed for the door. "And when will that be?"

"I'll call you early next week. In the meantime, get fit."

"Look who's talking," grumbled Gal as he ushered his guest out of the room. He noted with concern that Lonsdale had not addressed his assumption about taking heavy casualties.

Two hours later Lonsdale was at the Churrasceria Argentina Restaurant in Coral Gables. He had a luncheon appointment with José Basulto, the founder of Hermanos al Rescate—Brothers to the Rescue.

Basulto, a courtly man in his late fifties with black hair that was graying at the temples, had founded Brothers to the Rescue in 1991, at the height of the refugee flow from Cuba when thousands risked their lives in sailboats, rowboats, and makeshift rafts to reach the safety of the Florida Coast and freedom from oppression. During their most successful period of activity the Brothers operated six aircraft, which patrolled the Florida straits from dawn to dusk, locating floundering refugee embarkations and radioing their position to the U.S. Coast Guard that would then dispatch a vessel to assist them.

Basulto walked into the restaurant at one o'clock sharp and was shown to Lonsdale's table. Lonsdale came straight to the point.

"As I told you over the telephone, Mr. Basulto, my name is Antonio La Copola and I am from Argentina. I represent a group of wealthy Cubans living in Buenos Aires who were profoundly upset when they learned last year that Castro's fighter jets had shot down two of your unarmed aircraft." The waiter appeared at the table to take their drink orders and Lonsdale said nothing more until the man left.

"My clients would like to do something for the Brothers to the Rescue and sent me to Miami to find out what your organization's needs are."

"A couple of new airplanes would be nice," Basulto said, half-joking.

Lonsdale surprised him. "I don't think my clients could afford two aircraft, but I'm pretty sure they'd spring for one if it did not cost more than half a million dollars."

Basulto could not believe his good fortune. "If you really are serious about this, Señor La Copola, please show me some proof of your bona fides, and I will be delighted to go into details." Basulto's smile was open and earnest. "With half a million dollars we could certainly buy an aircraft, the kind we like to fly: a Cessna, or a Beachcraft. It would not be new, but it would have the avionics that would keep our pilots safe." His voice trailed off.

Lonsdale had anticipated the request and had made arrangements with a Buenos Aires law firm to back up his story. He took a business card from his pocket and handed it to Basulto. "As you can see I am an attorney-at-law and a partner in the firm of Langariza & Scherz. Call Mr. Langariza, and he will confirm that there is half a million dollars in the firm's trust account earmarked for the Brothers." He returned Basulto's smile just as their drinks arrived. "Let's drink to our joint enterprise." He lifted his glass and Basulto followed suit. They ordered lunch then got down to details.

"Let me assume for the time being that your credentials check out, Señor La Copola. What would the next step be?"

"Locate a suitable aircraft, purchase it, equip it, and have it registered in the Brothers' name."

"You're making this sound too easy. Where is the catch?" Basulto was not a great believer in manna from heaven.

"There's no catch. My clients are impressed by the humanitarian aspects of your organization's mission. With the additional aircraft you could increase the frequency and area of coverage of your patrols, thereby saving additional lives, Cuban lives, I might add."

"And what would the timing be?"

"It would be nice if you could locate and equip the aircraft in the next two to three weeks. That way my clients could give it to you as a Christmas present. I may be able to talk them into coming up from Buenos Aires, and we could have a little celebration. Better still," Lonsdale made as if a great idea had just struck him, "we could name the aircraft Argentina and every time it flew you could call the flight the Argentine Patrol to distinguish it from the others."

"I have no problem with that." Basulto cut into his steak. "We might even have an inaugural flight in which all of our aircraft would participate . . . a sort of flight of honor . . . in memory of our fallen comrades."

"That's an excellent idea." Lonsdale pretended to think the matter over. "But we would have to have things squared away by no later than the period between Christmas and New Year's, and the inaugural flight would have to take place during the first week of January."

"Why is that?"

"Time commitments," replied Lonsdale, waving his fork, his mouth full of juicy meat. "My clients are very busy and could not get away after Reyes, January 6. Epiphany."

"I think I could meet such a timetable." Basulto took a sip of wine. "I have been thinking about buying another aircraft to replace one of the planes we lost, and I have been looking at what was available on the market." Basulto pushed his plate away; he was finished eating. "I have my eye on a Cessna, and I have been trying to figure out where to get the money for it. And now you've come along—"

"You mean you could buy the plane right now?"

"This afternoon, if you wish."

"Let's do it!"

"Do you have a way of guaranteeing payment?"

"No, but I can give the seller a ten thousand dollar bankers' draft as a nonrefundable deposit to hold the plane for you for three days. That's about the time it would take to wire the balance of the purchase price from Argentina to the seller's bank account."

Basulto signaled the waiter for the bill. "Let's go. I want to call the seller before someone else snaffles my plane away from under my nose."

On the way to Basulto's office Lonsdale silently thanked Reuven Gal for the excellent information he had provided on the Brothers to the Rescue, especially with regard to the organization's plan to purchase additional airplanes, and to Gloria Estevan, the famous Cuban American singer who, two years previously, had donated an aircraft to the Brothers thereby unwittingly setting a precedent for Lonsdale.

CHAPTER FIFTY-ONE

Wednesday, December 7
Washington, DC and Langley, Virginia

Lonsdale took an early flight to Washington, and was preparing brunch for Morton in his apartment by half past eleven: smoked salmon with onions and capers, delicious Montreal bagels he had kept frozen to preserve their freshness, cream cheese, a few hard-boiled eggs, plenty of fruit, a bottle of chilled white wine, San Pelegrino, and espresso.

He brought his visitor up-to-date while they ate and, over coffee, scanned the documents Morton had brought with him. These consisted of two Canadian passports—for Roger and Micheline Tremblay; a document stamped by External Affairs, Canada, and countersigned by the Third Secretary of the Cuban Embassy in Ottawa, attesting to the Tremblays being members of Canada's Special Trade Delegation to Cuba; two tickets on a VIP chartered flight from Montreal to Havana and back; and a lengthy report compiled by Fisheries Canada on the state of fish stocks and the fishing industry in Eastern Canada.

"Your flight leaves Friday at seven in the morning so you had better get up to Montreal by Thursday night," Morton counseled.

"That's no problem." Lonsdale said, looking worried.

"What's bothering you then?"

"I see we're supposed to be from the Gaspé, in Eastern Quebec. Not too many people up there and most know each other."

Morton held up his hand. "Say no more. You two are the only people who signed up from the area."

"How come?"

"We checked and chose your identities accordingly." Morton allowed himself a brief smile. "Although we do miss you at the office, we haven't fallen apart totally." He got up to leave. "Is there anything else?"

"Just one small but important point. Have you arranged for the escape mechanism for Micheline that I suggested we put in place?"

"I have. A private sailing yacht will be standing by for her at the Marina Hemmingway from Christmas Day onwards. It will be crewed by a couple—very professional, in every sense of the word. They will arrange to bump into you at the Hotel Internacional at Varadero Beach on New Year's Eve." Morton handed Lonsdale an envelope. "Here are their pictures. Her name is Marie and his is Jacques. They speak English, French, and Spanish."

Director Smythe told his secretary to hold all his calls and to ensure that no visitor disturbed him for an hour. He needed time to think so he could figure his way out of the dangerous situation in which he found himself.

Reyes Puma, that snake in the grass, was making his life unbearable and had to be gotten rid of. But how?

Step one was obvious: get confirmed as director of Central Intelligence. Step two would then not be too difficult. He'd have Q Division, the CIA's extermination squad, take care of that despicable man.

How he could ever have allowed himself to fall victim to Reyes Puma's blackmail was, to this very day, incomprehensible. Sheer careless stupidity, that's what it had been. Worse, weakness of character.

It had started with that bitch of a French wife he'd married while at the Sorbonne. Who would have thought she'd turn into the snobbish social climber she had become ten years into their marriage. To be wed to a wealthy farmer wasn't good enough. She had more grandiose ambitions.

She talked him into running for the Senate. Then, while he was stomping the hustings, working his butt off politicking, and spending his own money like water, she lead the life of a grande dame back home in Orlando, sampling just about every Tom's, Dick's and Harry's unzipped cock.

He had literally bet the farm on getting elected Republican senator for the state of Florida, hoping things would change after his victory. But no, the more well-known he became the more hell-bent she was on augmenting her notoriety and humiliating him at every turn. She knew he couldn't divorce her. Not if he wanted to get reelected. She knew too many of his dirty little secrets.

Emboldened, she kept on tormenting him until, a few weeks before the end of his junior term, she pushed him over the edge.

He was campaigning hard for reelection and had to attend a fundraising dinner in Fort Lauderdale one Friday evening. He was going to sleep over and drive to Orlando the next day, but the dinner ended early and one of his wealthy supporters gave him a lift in his private plane.

When he walked into his house a few minutes after one in the morning he found his wife in her dressing gown saying good-bye to one of his young campaign workers who just stood there with his jacket over his arm, no tie, his shirt wide open and an awkward grin on his face. Smythe brushed past them and went upstairs. The bed was unmade.

They had a tremendous row. She claimed the man had brought her home from a party where she had spilled a glass of red wine on her dress. As soon as she got home she changed into her dressing gown so that she could soak the dress in salt water. The bed was unmade, she explained, because she hadn't bothered to make it up that morning, and the maid was off sick.

He had been amazed by her quick-wittedness. She had, under pressure, effortlessly concocted a plausible cover story on the spot. And by the time he got down to the basement to check, there was her dress, soaking in water.

A brazen liar and cheat, she was an intelligent, and dangerous, potential enemy. "Keep your friends close, your enemies even closer," his father had taught him. "Or kill them," he murmured, and left the house.

Next morning he flew to Miami to talk with Reyes Puma, his confidant and campaign manager.

"Filberto, I can't go on living with that woman." Smythe was so upset he couldn't eat his lunch. "Can you imagine, hopping into the sack with one of my own campaign workers! The word is already out that I'm a weak husband. If the kid talks to the press I'll be a proven cuckold and no one will respect me."

"The kid won't talk, Lawrence; be assured of that." Reyes Puma sounded very sure of himself. "Believe me, he won't want to jeopardize his career for a night's salacious adventure."

"What d'ya mean?"

"Simply this." The Cuban got up to clear the plates away; they were having lunch at his house. "If word got around that the boy was indiscreet, none of the other guys would hire him. I know the kid. He wants desperately to break into politics and can't afford to get a reputation for blabbing." Reyes Puma called over his shoulder as he headed toward the kitchen. "Help yourself to some coffee, the pot's on the table, as is the bourbon. I'll be right back."

When the attorney returned he was happy to note that Smythe had helped himself to a couple of bourbon-laced cups of coffee. The level of the liquid in the bottle had dropped by about three fingers.

"Sit down Filberto and let's talk man-to-man." The senator sounded a great deal more relaxed. "Tell me honestly, what would you do in my place?"

Reyes Puma thought hard before replying. "The most important thing is to get reelected. So you have to put up with your wife's shenanigans for a month or so." He smiled at Smythe reassuringly. "After that we'll see."

"What do you mean by that?" The senator was unconvinced.

"I promise to look after the kid for you. Trust me, Lawrence. After I've had a talk with him, he won't dare open his mouth."

"What about my wife?"

"I'll look after her for you as well, but not just yet."

CHAPTER FIFTY-TWO

Friday, December 9
Havana, Cuba

Roger and Micheline Tremblay were a last-minute addition to Canada's Special Trade Delegation to Cuba. Mr. Tremblay called himself a simple fisherman from the Gaspé Peninsula. Mrs. Tremblay said she taught school in Paspebiac, a small town on the shores of La Baie-des-Chaleurs, a cod-fishing and -distribution center. Tremblay seemed to know everything about the Cuban and Quebec fishing industries, constantly spouting boring statistics. Meanwhile his wife, a sweet, unassuming woman, appeared to have no conversation at all.

In other words, the Tremblays seemed to be hardworking, unsophisticated folk with whom the smart business set from Montreal, Quebec City, and the Beauce Region had little in common. This suited the Tremblays fine. They attended every business meeting where they were a great success since the Cubans' favorite delicacy was bacalao salao, salted cod from the Gaspé. They also participated in every social event organized for the delegation, but they kept to themselves and said little. Their great passion seemed to be photography and, when sightseeing, they were forever wandering away from the group to take pictures of everything and everyone in sight. That's how they met Juan, the taxi driver.

They had gotten ahead of the guided tour and were standing in front of La Bodeguita del Medio, a famous hole-in-the-wall restaurant in Old Havana, when Juan came up to them and asked if they would like to have their picture taken in front of this famous landmark. They said yes. Tremblay knew a few words in Spanish and the taxista a few in English. Juan gave them his card. He said he lived next door to the restaurant and earned his living as a dollar-cab driver, which meant that the fare he charged had to be paid in U.S. dollars, in advance. He added that he could be found most mornings at the Copelia cabstand opposite the Hotel Havana Libre, just up the street from the Hotel Nacional where the Canadian Delegation was staying.

The Tremblays thanked him profusely for his help. Next morning, while her husband was meeting officials of Cuba Pesca, the Ministry of Fisheries, Micheline walked up Calle 23, found the Copelia taxi stand, named after the giant ice cream parlor next to it, and engaged the services of Juan to show her the "real" Havana.

Meanwhile her husband, having met with the Cuba Pesca people in the morning, made his way to the Floridita bar near Old Havana for a refreshing pre-lunch daiquiri, a drink Ernest Hemmingway had made famous. There he met a couple of tourists (two Mossad-niks) with whom he went for a walk-around visit of the old part of the city, ending up at La Bodeguita del Medio for a late lunch.

Juan, whose full name was Juan Antonio Montané, duly reported his contact with the *estrangero* to the president of his district's Committee for the Defense of the Revolution, the organization charged with spying on the populace. The president, in turn, passed the report on to the ministry of the Interior. When Mrs. Tremblay returned the next day, accompanied by Mrs. Forget, the wife of another delegate, he took them for a spin to the fortress of La Cabaña, the prison, and to Havana del Este, a building project completed in the early days of the Revolution. That evening he dutifully informed his CDR President of this second contact with Mrs. Tremblay.

Mrs. Tremblay was so impressed by Juan's knowledge of Havana and its surroundings that she persuaded the Forgets to share the cost of engaging him for a full day during which they planned to drive to Pinar del Rio, a town about a hundred miles west of Havana. There they would visit a cigar factory, then have a traditional lunch of *lechon*, Cuban-style roast pig, before returning to Havana.

Montané reported this third contact to his CDR president as well, who could not be bothered to pass the information on to the Ministry of the Interior—it was too routine in nature. A dollar-cab driver was supposed to meet *estrangeros* and the more the better for the economy of La Patria.

What Montané did not report was that the first day he took Mrs. Tremblay for a drive he gave her an envelope he had retrieved that morning from a CIA dead-letter drop. Nor did he report that, on the second day, Mrs. Tremblay slipped him a paperback novel, entitled *Dreaming in Cuban*, which he deposited in the dead-letter drop that evening. And he certainly did not tell his CDR president that the day he drove the Canadians to Pinar del Rio he gave Mrs. Tremblay a second envelope, retrieved from a different CIA dead-letter drop.

The first envelope, encoded by means of a so-called one-time pad, contained the following message: "Your friends are being held in La Cabaña, each in his own cell, their accomplices at Via Viento Prison. Interrogations are continuous. Trial to start Monday, January 2: anniversary of Revolution."

The author was the commander of La Cabaña, Colonel Telmo Bellon, whose life Casas had saved two decades previously when Bellon was left for dead on the battlefield. At great risk to himself, Casas had gone back to get him and had carried him to safety.

The paperback, destined for Colonel Bellon, outlined in code the details of a rescue plan "Tremblay" had worked out after having spent five days inspecting the target area. Colonel Bellon was to analyze and comment on the plan and to provide the names and coordinates of two men, loyal to Casas, who would be willing to help rescue him.

The second envelope contained Colonel Bellon's comments and data on two men.

Colonel Bellon's name had been provided by De la Fuente while dancing with the British ambassador's sister at the Marina Hemmingway. The dead-letter drops were part of the escape route Lonsdale had set up for Casas and about which he had briefed the general in Budapest.

The Canadian trade delegates flew back to Montreal at the end of their five-day visit, reluctant to leave the sunshine, the sparkling sea, and, especially, the warm hospitality of the Cuban people. None seemed more chagrined than the Tremblays, who vowed to return as soon as possible—maybe as soon as Christmas, less than two weeks away.

CHAPTER FIFTY-THREE

Saturday, December 17
Montgomery County, Virginia

Lonsdale was having a busy week. He had spent three days training with his communications team: a satellite imaging specialist, a radio communicator, and a backup technician. By Monday night he felt he knew enough to get by, provided his team, which he proposed to install on board the *Barbara* anchored just outside Cuban territorial waters, would give him a hand now and then.

On Tuesday and Wednesday he took a small arms refresher course, acquainting himself with the Galil assault rifle and the sundry other gear to be used on the mission, such as side arms, tear gas canisters, smoke bombs, stun grenades, and so forth.

Although he had been jogging at least every other day with monotonous regularity he intensified his regime and started every day with a five-mile run, followed by an hour of calisthenics.

On Thursday, feeling confident and in top shape, he met with his boss for a final briefing.

"A routine is beginning to emerge, just as you said it would." Morton, like Lonsdale, was dressed in U.S. Army fatigues, and was wearing a forage cap to shield his head from the blazing Virginia sun. They were sitting behind the firing line at the shooting range and the noise made it impossible for anyone to overhear their conversation.

"You mean the prisoners' routine?"

Morton nodded. "At first, they were being interrogated separately at La Cabaña prison. But lately Casas and De la Fuente are being taken to Havana almost daily, I guess to be questioned by members of the various departments of the army, the coast guard, and the Ministry of the Interior. The routine is always the same. Breakfast at six, in the car by seven. A convoy, consisting of two specially equipped Fiats, one for each prisoner for purposes of security and isolation, and two military jeeps, forms and off it goes to La Plaza de la Revolución, where army headquarters are located, or to Calle 23, to the Ministry of the Interior."

"Do they stay in Havana all day?"

"Quite often." Morton glanced at the notes he was holding. "They are returned to La Cabaña by convoy at four p.m., locked up, and fed dinner at six."

"How many guards?"

"Where?"

"In the convoy."

"Four in each of the jeeps, including the driver, and two in each of the Fiats, plus the driver. The prisoners, handcuffed to the roll bar in the back, are locked in, separated from the driver's compartment by a thick wire mesh."

"Do you have any more details?"

"I'm afraid not."

Lonsdale hid his disappointment. "What about Ivan Spiegel. How are they treating him?"

"They're not. He's living in the British ambassador's residence, sort of under house arrest, but the general feeling is they will let him go once the trial is over."

"Now there's a guy who'll never set foot in Cuba again."

"That's a given." Morton got up and Lonsdale followed. Morton seemed agitated.

"What's bugging you?"

Morton shook his head, as if to clear the cobwebs. "Smythe. What a bastard." He sighed. "A couple of months into his second term in the senate, somebody shot and killed his wife in the parking lot of a bar where she had gone to meet her latest paramour. Of course, Smythe had an airtight alibi . . . he was in Japan that day."

"You think he was behind the killing?"

"The killer was a professional. Shot her in the head at close range with a silencer-equipped Beretta automatic. And get this." Morton was really upset. "Some eyewitnesses thought they saw a young woman near her car at the time of the shooting."

"You mean to tell me that—"

"One of Reyes Puma's contract killers, perhaps even this same Laura he was talking about the other day, did the job. In one word: yes!"

Lonsdale was shocked. "But that was years ago."

"So what. Maybe she started her career as a professional killer in her twenties." Morton's voice trailed off.

"And what kind of proof do you think Reyes Puma has?"

"Probably a tape of Smythe giving him the go-ahead to do the job. We can't question anyone directly since we don't want word to get back to Smythe."

"Or Reyes Puma" Lonsdale added.

"Quite." Morton sighed again. "We'll have to deal with the Smythe situation once De la Fuente and Casas are out of Cuba . . . and it will be a stinker."

"Not necessarily." Lonsdale was speaking so softly Morton had to lean toward him to hear. "Forget the Smythe problem for the time being, and leave it to me. I'll solve it for you discretely once Operation Nameless is over."

Morton smiled. "Is that what we're going to call it."

"Not on the record, just between the two of us."

A canon boomed out somewhere and all firing ceased. Morton looked at his watch. Sixteen hundred hours on the dot, end of the physical part of the training day. Two hours of lectures would now follow. He turned to Lonsdale "Where are you off to now?"

"I'm checking out of here and flying to Montreal to spend Christmas with Micheline."

"You're taking time off?" Morton couldn't hide his disappointment. Every moment from here on was precious.

"Not exactly," said Lonsdale. He turned on his heels and left before Morton could wish him a Merry Christmas.

CHAPTER FIFTY-FOUR

Saturday, December 24
Havana, Cuba

Patricio Casas had reached the lowest point of his life: Christmas Eve in jail, far from family and friends, accused of high treason. He continued pacing up and down his cell. Seven steps from window to steel door and seven steps back. What window? Three ventilating slits, angled so that he couldn't see out, allowed some light and sound to enter the room. He could hear the noise in the courtyard that he couldn't see; he could smell the smoke rising from a cooking fire, probably tended by guards.

His cell measured eighteen feet by six. There was no furniture, aside from a steel-framed wooden bunk that folded down from the wall, held in position by a chain at each end. A wall at the foot of the bunk, and equal in width to it, separated the "bathroom" from the "sleeping area." The toilet was a hole in the ground; above it a tap at the end of a piece of pipe did double duty as shower and toilet flusher.

They had taken his clothes except his underpants and loafers, and had given him beige prison overalls to wear. A toothbrush, a bar of soap, and a towel made up the balance of his possessions. There was no bedding, just a well-used quilt for cover; his shoes served for pillows while he slept on his stomach, arms folded under his chest. He would wake up several times during the night from the pain caused by the lack of blood circulation.

The food was barely adequate: four ounces of bread in the morning, for lunch some sort of pasta, at times with a sprinkling of meat, with the occasional slice of avocado thrown in to prevent scurvy; and three large soda biscuits for dinner.

Casas had always been wiry and fit with not a single ounce of superfluous fat on his bony frame. Because in prison he had continued his disciplined regimen of daily exercise, consisting of thirty minutes' running in place followed by calisthenics and then fifty push-ups, he had begun to lose weight and was starting to look emaciated. Nor were his appearance and mental condition helped by the lack of sleep and the endless and repetitive questioning to which he was subjected almost daily.

He felt alone in the world: in semidarkness when in his cell, isolated between interrogation sessions, and surrounded by guards who would not speak to him. He never saw his fellow inmates even when being taken for questioning. The guard accompanying him would whistle tunelessly and, on hearing the tuneless whistling of another guard-prisoner combination, would push Casas's face into the nearest corner, nose against the wall, while the other prisoner passed behind his back. Because Casas was right-handed, his guards always stood to the left of him, just in case. Nor did they wear side arms. If a prisoner wanted to make a run for it, they would let him. The cell-blocs were sealed by steel grills at each end and there was no way out.

It seemed to Casas that his cell was getting colder as the days went by. Then he realized that this was only an illusion. It only felt that way because he was losing weight, not sleeping, worrying, and afraid of dying—for nothing! Dying would prevent him from defending himself against the accusation that he was working to destroy La Revolucion and La Patria as a CIA agent. Time and again his interrogators asked when, how, and by whom he had been recruited. They said they knew De la Fuente was a CIA agent, and for years at that. They said the drug operation was a CIA plot to discredit Fidel. It seemed they were going to execute him for all the wrong reasons.

He had no idea what was being said about him by the common people in the street. The authorities had allowed him no contact with his family, and the lawyer appointed to defend him had been given permission to speak with him only once, two weeks after his arrest.

The guard rapped on his door. "Prisoner 2704. Step away from the door."

He did, and to his surprise, the door swung open. The guard deposited an open paper box on the floor, just inside the cell.

"It is from your mother. Feliz Navidad." The solid metal door clanged shut.

The box contained a small chocolate Christmas log, his favorite holiday dessert, thinly sliced to ensure it was not being used to smuggle something in to him. There was also a slip of paper, apparently from a letter his mother had written: "*Jesus es tu pastor*" it said. "*El te cuida siempre porque estas inscrito en la palma de su mano, para guiarte y salvar tu alma. Que, al final, es lo más importante. Adios. Tu Madre.*"

"Jesus is your pastor. He watches over you always, for you are inscribed in the palm of his hand, to guide you and to save your soul. Which, in the end, is the most important of all things. Goodbye. Your Mother."

With trembling hands he helped himself to a slice of the wonderful pastry his mother had baked for him. Then he reread her note and had two more pieces of cake.

The jolt of sugar in his system gave him a surge of energy. He got off his bunk and began to pace about again, continuing to eat cake until there was no more left.

He lay down on his bunk, tucked his shoes under his head, pulled the quilt over himself, and stared at the ceiling while fighting the panic caused by the realization that everybody had given up on him—even his own mother!

CHAPTER FIFTY-FIVE

Christmas Week
Havana and Varadero Beach, Cuba

The Tremblays had returned to Cuba. Jose Hernandez, the Cuban consul general in Montreal, who considered them valuable business contacts, somehow got them on board an Air Transat charter flight at the very last minute. They arrived at the Havana Riviera Hotel a few minutes before the Christmas Eve party for tourists was to begin and planned, so they told everybody who would listen, to stay in Havana for a few days with the friends they had made on their previous trip. Of course, they made frequent use of Juan Antonio Montané's taxi, who, in turn, dutifully reported his renewed contact with the Tremblays to his CDR president.

What he failed to report was that the Tremblays spent long hours with their "old" friends, the three Israeli tourists, walking around Havana and eating in restaurants in the La Cabaña—Havana del Este district.

On Wednesday, Juan drove the Tremblays to Varadero Beach and supervised their settling-in at the modest, clean boarding house Hernandez had found for them where they were received as if they were family. The boarding house, only a short block from the beach, was run by the consul's sister and her husband, Emilio Granda.

Meanwhile, Reuven Gal flew from West Palm to Key West in a private plane and boarded a yacht that took him to a place called the Mule Key, an island in the Florida Keys within the boundaries of the

Key West National Wildlife Refuge, an area placed off limits by the U.S. Government. Mule Key is supposedly uninhabited except for two Park Rangers.

In reality, the Agency, using a dozen cigarette boats with special markings to allow easy identification by satellite cameras and anti-drug trafficking surveillance aircraft, has an extensive people-smuggling operation on the island.

Gal loved living on the edge and looked forward to the adrenaline rush that his body would generate when he was in action. But he was also a careful and savvy field commander who knew that clandestine operations usually failed either because an important practical detail was overlooked at the planning stage or because too much reliance was placed on the ability of the participants to improvise—or both.

Determined to make sure this would not happen during Operation Nameless, he chose the final team with extraordinary care.

His squad leaders, the Mossadniks, were already in Cuba pretending to be tourists. That left two drivers and four "foot soldiers"—all Cubans—to be smuggled into Fidelandia via cigarette boat at the rate of two per voyage.

Gal opted to accompany the drivers on their insertion trip, which went off without a hitch. He then returned to Mule Key and repeated the trip twice more, staying in Cuba after the third voyage.

On Thursday, in the port of Matanzas, the purchasing clerk of the Havana Cab Company, accompanied by two drivers, took delivery of a panel truck and two cabs that had arrived a week earlier on board a Greek freighter. It was unusual that the paperwork for such a release should be completed in less than a month, but it was the holiday season and the customs and freight people needed the "bonuses" the cab company clerk was willing to pay for speeding things up.

The three vehicles were driven along the Autopista Nacional toward Havana and met, approximately halfway to the capital, by Juan and two Cubans. The men got into the panel truck and the clerk who had been driving the truck into Juan's taxi.

One of the men, using props he had brought with him in a small suitcase, then "transformed" into a woman in the truck because two men frequenting a "hot-pillow" place in Cuba would look suspicious. The couple then drove the truck to La Posada Monumental, a motel just off the Havana-Varadero highway. They were in luck; they found an empty unit on their first try and, breathing a sigh of relief, drove the truck into this "love nest's" garage.

Meanwhile, the two cabs were driven to a restaurant nearby the motel where their drivers ate a late lunch, while Juan dropped the clerk off at the Caves of Bellamar, a popular tourist spot near Matanzas about forty miles east of Havana. At the entrance to the caves, the clerk was accosted by a local who offered him a room at his modest boarding house. The clerk accepted to stay overnight. At three a.m. he was led to a spot on the beach and rowed to a cigarette boat that took him Mule Key.

La Monumental is a rent-by-the-hour roadhouse for amorous Cubans, a rectangular-shaped building constructed around an inner courtyard situated in the middle of a quarter-acre lot surrounded by a nine-foot wall. It contains units along the four walls of the quadrangle, each consisting of a garage, a small entrance hall, a bedroom, and a bathroom. The bedrooms have mirrors on the walls and ceilings. Discretion is assured.

The routine is to take one's lady friend to La Monumental after a night's dining and dancing, drive into one of the garages, pull down the overhead door and then help the lady into the bedroom. While she showers, her beau would order drinks by telephone then adjust the light and sound systems to his taste and get ready for his paramour. Their lovemaking over, the couple would call for the bill, pay in cash through a small trap door in the wall contiguous with the inner courtyard, and leave the way they had come—without being seen by anyone.

One could stay at La Monumental *para un rato*, which meant a maximum of two hours, or for *una media noche*, six hours.

The couple in the maintenance truck opted for two hours, ordered their drinks, went into the garage, deployed a thick tarpaulin under their vehicle, and got down to work quickly and in absolute silence. First they freed up the two metal plates that constituted the false bottom of the panel truck and folded them back to reveal the space beneath into which ten grenade-launcher-equipped Galil assault rifles, ten SWAT-type commando helmets, fully equipped for two-way hands-free communication and infrared goggles, ten respirators, ten flak jackets, four sets of "dragon's teeth," and some ammunition had been secreted. After checking that the equipment was not damaged, they folded the metal plates down and replaced the bolts that held them in place. Next they covered the false bottom with the thick tarpaulin, carefully precut to fit. Total elapsed time: one hour, forty-nine minutes.

The occupants called for their bill, and left a few minutes past three in the afternoon. They found themselves a "dollar" restaurant and had an ample late lunch. Around six they drove to La Posada Canada Dry, a motel near the Canada Dry bottling plant in the Ayestaran district, this time for six hours' sleep. By that time they were just about all in. They had spent most of the previous night hiding in an abandoned tobacco barn near Ovas in Pinar del Rio Province where their guide, who had smuggled them into Cuba on board a cigarette boat, had left them to wait for Juan.

From La Canada Dry they proceeded to yet another motel just past La Monumental, where they spent six hours cleaning, checking and loading weapons, and verifying that the communication features in the helmets worked. They also inspected the "dragon's teeth" assemblies designed to allow a vehicle to pass over them in one direction, but to cut the vehicle's tires to ribbons if it tried to cross the opposite way.

After breakfast on Friday they responded, as pre-arranged, to a call from Juan who was having mechanical trouble inside the British Embassy's Chancery compound. This required the maintenance truck to enter the compound.

While the mechanics were "repairing" the broken-down vehicle, Juan, helped by one of the embassy guards, transferred a television set, a few radios, and a case containing four Galil assault rifles and some ammunition to the truck. Once the taxi was "repaired," it was driven downtown, with the truck following it.

Meanwhile, the drivers of the two specially equipped cabs were crisscrossing Havana and scouting the target areas.

The vehicles were then parked in predetermined spots and left unattended while their drivers had dinner. After finishing their meal they returned to their respective vehicles in which each found an additional passenger waiting for them, freshly in from Florida via cigarette boat.

The two sets of three men then went through the process of going from motel to motel to extract and store the weapons, ammunition, grenades, and other gear hidden in the false bottoms of the cabs. This process had to be conducted with care because, to look believable, each cab had to appear to be containing two women and one man.

New Year's Eve, Lonsdale had a team of ten fully equipped, highly mobile, and action-craving men in Havana: three Israelis, including Gal, six Cubans, and himself.

For New Year's Eve the Tremblays invited Mr. and Mrs. Granda and Juan, a bachelor, to the party for *estrangeros* at the Hotel Internacional, where the food was delicious, the drinks copious, and the floor show spectacular. During the night Tremblay ran into an old classmate, Marie. She and her husband, a keen yachtsman, had sailed all the way from Montreal to Havana to spend Christmas in Cuba. The couple invited the Tremblays to come sailing with them the following week on their forty-five-foot sailing yacht, the *Vagabundo*.

Everybody had a wonderful time at the party. Juan, who stayed over at the boarding house for the night, woke up on New Year's Day around noon with a tremendous *crudo*, or hangover. It took him until late afternoon to settle his stomach, and Roger Tremblay, worried about Juan's health, insisted on driving him back to Havana and staying with him overnight to make sure he was all right.

Micheline remained in Varadero.

EXECUCIÓN

CHAPTER FIFTY-SIX

Monday, January 2
Havana, Cuba

The Casas-De la Fuente drug trial was a first in Cuban revolutionary history: a public admission that, although the Socialist Revolutionary Movement subscribed to high moral principles, its leaders were no less immoral and corrupt than their counterparts in America.

To the man in the street General Patricio Casas Rojo had been an idol in the past, a brave and highly decorated soldier. But now, public opinion was divided. There were some who felt an innocent Casas was being used as a scapegoat by a government with its hand caught in the cookie jar. There were others who shrugged and said they had known for years that the ideals of the Revolution had been compromised long ago.

And then there were those who were convinced Casas was being framed because he had become too much of a rival of Fidel.

The people were troubled and restive. Childlike graffiti in red chalk of little houses appeared overnight on the walls of public buildings everywhere. Red houses—*casas rojas*: an obvious indication that General Casas Rojo had wide-spread public support.

This concerned the government. Under no circumstances could the trial end without the vindication of the government, the condemnation of the guilty and the unmasking of the true villain, the one pulling the strings behind the scene: the U.S. Central Intelligence Agency.

For the CIA, such an ending would mean acute embarrassment and yet another failed operation; for the Republican president yet another diplomatic fiasco; for Smythe, speedy retirement into oblivion. Unless, of course, Castro failed in his efforts to prove CIA involvement.

Lonsdale concluded that Smythe's best interest lay in the mission succeeding, but only if it succeeded before De la Fuente opened his mouth on the witness stand. With CIA involvement unproven, Castro would look very bad and Smythe's stock within the Agency would rise, perhaps enough to carry him through nomination for DCI. Thus, Smythe needed the mission to succeed and the sooner the better. He would, consequently, keep the operation a secret from Reyes Puma.

Of course, there remained yet another alternative for Smythe: silence Casas and De la Fuente by having them terminated with extreme prejudice by Q Division. Lonsdale thought that such a scenario was unlikely: too many checks and balances would be affected within the Agency, the operation, even if it succeeded, would damage the CIA's public image considerably, and Smythe's image with it.

Juan stuck his head into the bedroom. "I'm back."

Lonsdale looked at his watch: a few minutes past seven a.m. "Where have you been?"

"Had to go to the bakery early this morning."

"What for?"

"For bread, of course. And this." He handed Lonsdale a piece of paper, a coded message from Colonel Bellon from one of the dead-letter drops. Decoded, it read

```
Day 1: Casas Military Tribunal of Honor.
Day 2: Trial of all accused begins, Casas first.
Day 3: De la Fuente accusations against Casas,
who will be present.
Security tight Day 1 and 2 with helicopters
overhead. Day 3 plus, no helicopters, or mili-
tary escort. Only civilian convoy of 2 cars,
```

```
leaving prison at random times. Authorities
want to play down military presence in front
of international press.
```

Lonsdale was pleased. Bellon's message helped him make up his mind. He would swing into action on Day 3, Wednesday, and forego the diversionary attack. With the military escort absent, his team of eight fighting men would come up against a maximum of six guards, three in each car. Manageable odds, given the element of surprise. As for the random departure times, as long as Colonel Bellon could narrow the window to a two-hour span, Lonsdale's satellite imaging capability would take care of the rest.

He had Juan drive him to the Canadian Embassy where he visited the commercial counselor and used the embassy telephone. Lonsdale pretended to call a partner in Paspebiac and then acted out the role of partner while waiting for the commercial counsellor to step out of the office. He left a message on the answering machine at the number he had called, advising that he had an appointment with the Cuban Fisheries people on Wednesday and asking if his partner would please arrange for the shipment of a refrigerated container of salted cod ready to go on a moment's notice.

Ramirez, the accountant, to whom the message was relayed as soon as it came in, interpreted it correctly to mean that the *Barbara* was to be in position just outside Cuban territorial waters within thirty-six hours, and that the Brothers to the Rescue, who had been on standby since New Year's Day, should organize the inaugural flight of the Argentine patrol on Wednesday.

Ramirez contacted the Captain of the *Barbara*, also on standby in Jamaica, and got him underway. Then he called José Basulto to advise that the Argentinean donors had arrived as planned and would like to patrol with the Brothers on Wednesday morning at daybreak from six thirty to eight thirty, after which there could be a light breakfast and a brief ceremony at the Brothers' hangar. The Argentineans would catch a plane to New York at noon where they had business.

Ramirez's last call was to a Washington unlisted number where he left a message for Patricio Patriciano, advising of the date on which the inaugural flight of the Argentine patrol would take place. Mr. Patriciano was none other than James Morton, who then arranged that two Agency people, pretending to be Argentinians, turn up at Basulto's office at the appropriate time.

Juan drove Lonsdale from the embassy back to Varadero. Just this side of Matanzas, they acted as if the cab had broken down again. They left a note on the cab's windshield and waited for the prear-ranged truck to pick them up.

Squeezed into the back of the truck with Gal, his two Israeli team leaders, and the two Cuban drivers, Lonsdale outlined his plan of attack in just under ninety minutes. The briefing was thorough, pre-cise, and graphic, illustrated with maps and photographs that were then destroyed.

By four in the afternoon, Lonsdale was back in Varadero, walk-ing on the beach with Micheline.

"What's the next move?" she asked, sounding nervous. The strain was getting to her.

"Miche, when I allowed you to talk me into bringing you here, we agreed that you will go home before the real hanky-panky starts."

She began to protest, but he cut her off. "There is no discussing it. I should have sent you home on Saturday, but I didn't, and that was a mistake—"

"OK, OK. But what now?"

"Remember I told you I had a secret escape plan just for the two of us. Well, I will be activating it for you tomorrow."

"Does that mean you are not coming with me?"

Lonsdale lifted her hand to his lips. "Hear me out darling and humor me. You remember Marie, my so-called classmate, and her husband with the sailboat?" She nodded. "Marie is no classmate. They're pros I've hired for getting you away from this place before it becomes too dangerous."

Micheline would have none of it. "I'm not leaving without you!"

"Darling, we made a deal. I've kept my side of the bargain, now you keep yours."

"But I love you."

"I know you do, sweet lady." Lonsdale pulled her toward him, his arm encircling her waist, "and I adore you, which is the very reason why I want you off this island. Besides, changing plans this late in the game would upset everything."

"How?"

"When I visited the embassy this morning I told them we wanted to sail to Nassau with our friends who were leaving by boat tomorrow. The consul called the Ministry of the Interior and arranged for our exit visas."

Micheline cut in "What are they? Why do we need them?"

"When you travel by private yacht, you have to get permission to leave this island before they let you get off it, and it is the Ministry of the Interior that grants this permission. It's called a *Permiso de Salida*."

"You said exit visas. Does that mean that you are coming with me?"

Lonsdale looked at her and smiled. "Up to a point, yes."

They walked back to the boarding house.

CHAPTER FIFTY-SEVEN

Tuesday and Wednesday, January 3 and 4
Havana, Cuba

On Tuesday morning, Lonsdale and Micheline left Cuba on board the *Vagabundo*. The vessel was intercepted, as arranged, by an Agency cigarette boat in late afternoon near the Bahamas, at Salt Key. *Vagabundo* continued her journey toward the Bahamas while the cigarette boat took Lonsdale back to Cuba under cover of darkness.

Juan picked him up in the middle of the night on the coast near Pablo de la Torriente Brau and handed him Colonel Bellon's latest message. It was laconic. "Transfer between six-thirty and eight on fifteen minutes' notice. 2 prisoners, 2 cars, 6 guards. No 'copters, no jeeps."

While Lonsdale was being driven to Havana by Juan, the maintenance truck "responded" to two breakdown calls on the outskirts of the city during which the arms, ammunition, grenades, tear gas, and other gear were distributed so that, by four a.m., all team members were fully equipped and operational.

On Wednesday at 0430 hours Lonsdale met Reuven Gal, who was driving the maintenance truck, near the entrance of *La Monumental*. He changed into battle gear and tested the electronic equipment on board. Everything was functioning perfectly.

At 0530 sharp the truck joined a military police jeep, provided by General Casas's army supporters, mobilized by Colonel Bellon. The jeep was parked on the periphery road above the northern entrance of the tunnel that links the Havana proper with the Havana del Este/

La Cabaña Prison district. The seven-hundred-and-fifty-meter-long tunnel, built by a French company in the 1920s, was wide enough to accommodate four lanes of traffic: two northbound and two south-bound. To eliminate the risk of head-on collisions, the two two-lane sections are separated by a wall that effectively divides the tunnel lengthwise.

Gal followed the jeep north on the periphery road then made a sharp right turn onto the main highway, the *Via Monumental*, leading into the tunnel.

The jeep stopped just inside the entrance. Gal drove around it and stopped the truck a hundred meters down the road where he helped Lonsdale unload two sections of "dragon's teeth" while the military policemen halted the sparse traffic. Lonsdale and Gal laid the two sections across the tunnel end-to-end and anchored them into place with giant explosive rivets so that the teeth, when deployed by radio command, would face the oncoming traffic. They repeated the operation five hundred meters further into the tunnel. Once the two barricades were in place the jeep backed out of the tunnel and parked on the soft shoulder about fifty meters from the mouth of the tunnel behind the cab containing Team A. The jeep's hood was up— yet another "mechanical breakdown."

Gal and Lonsdale exited the tunnel on the Havana side, rounded the Maximo Gomez monument and worked their way back into the tunnel, northbound this time. They saw that Team B's cab was in position on the soft shoulder of the southbound lane.

By 0615 hours the maintenance truck, lights extinguished, was once again on the periphery road above the northern entrance to the tunnel. While Gal acted as lookout, Lonsdale powered up his com-puter, which he then linked to the satellite imaging and communi-cating system. The eerie light from the LCD screen lit up the inside. Open boxes of ammunition were stacked along one wall, specially rigged smoke canisters lined the racks fastened to the rear doors. Two assault rifles and two helmets lay on the floor to Lonsdale's left.

Lonsdale, like all members of his team, was dressed in workmen's fatigues, flak jacket, workman-style boots, and a knit cap to cush-ion the fit of his helmet. A holstered, loaded Colt automatic hung on his right hip, a deployed respirator on his left. Four stun grenades adorned the front webbing of his flak jacket. In his pockets he had an Argentinean passport, fifty U.S. one hundred dollar bills, a pair of black leather gloves, and two sets of handcuffs; no personal effects, no compromising documents, no identification papers of any kind, no insignia of rank—nothing to show who he was.

The computer and the satellite imaging system were on a table that folded out from the partition separating the body of the truck from the driver. Lonsdale's seat was a one-legged stool, screwed into the floor of the truck.

The computer clicked and the screen turned blue. Lonsdale hit the exclamation mark followed by Enter. This signaled his technicians, looking at a display identical to his on board the Barbara anchored twelve miles out opposite Havana, that the mission was about to begin. A dialogue box appeared on the screen with the word "READY" at top left. Lonsdale rapped on the partition separating him from the driver. Gal eased the truck into gear and began to drive slowly toward where the periphery road intersected the Via Monumental. Lonsdale hit 1, then Enter. The screen blinked and a picture of the courtyard of La Cabaña prison, as seen from above, appeared. The resolution was good, but Lonsdale wanted a closer look. He pressed D and the camera began to zoom in on its target. A couple of clicks and Lonsdale could see the tops of two vehicles in the courtyard, parked in front of the prison building's entrance. Three dots, presumably guards and drivers, moved about, waiting for their orders.

Lonsdale fiddled with the U and D keys to adjust the picture up or down to his liking, then hit X, followed by 2, then Enter. The screen showed the northern entrance of the tunnel with the jeep and the cab parked fifty yards away from it. Lonsdale watched as the maintenance truck he was sitting in came into the picture and stopped behind the jeep. Gal got out and one of the military policemen took his place behind the wheel. He opened the right rear door of the truck and got in.

While Gal assembled and screwed the second stool into place, Lonsdale hit 3, then Enter, and an image came up of the southern tunnel entrance and the cab parked fifty meters up the road from it. He adjusted the view then went through the same routine with the picture of the western corner of Maximo Gomez Park not far from the southern entrance of the tunnel. He tested the left, right, up, and down arrows and found that by using them he could track moving objects with the satellite camera.

He now had the system calibrated so that Picture 1 showed the courtyard of La Cabaña Prison and its surroundings; Picture 2 the northern tunnel entrance area, which was near the prison; Picture 3 the southern tunnel entrance area on the Havana side; and Picture 4 a soccer field on the western corner of Maximo Gomez Park.

Lonsdale looked at his watch: 0627 hours. He dialed up Picture 1 and gave Gal the thumbs up. The Israeli put on his helmet and plugged himself into the appropriate port of the communications console in front of him. Lonsdale did likewise, then pressed the On button and cleared his throat. Gal nodded. The intercom system between him and Lonsdale was operational. Gal could hear Lonsdale, but no one else could. But everyone could hear Gal, including Lonsdale. Gal adjusted the microphone in his helmet so that it almost touched his mouth.

"A . . . check in," he said in Hebrew.

"A checking in," came the reply, also in Hebrew, from the Team A leader, who was Israeli, as was the Team B leader.

"B . . . check in," said Gal.

"B checking in," in Hebrew again. This arrangement afforded additional security. There was little likelihood of Cuban military listening posts being manned by Hebrew-speaking personnel.

Lonsdale glanced at his watch then at the screen. There were now six dots milling about the two vehicles in the courtyard. Lonsdale zoomed up. Traffic was still light on the highway, but intensifying. He zoomed back to the original setting, then hit *H*, followed by question mark, then Enter.

"Helicopter deployed, ready to go," appeared in the dialogue box.

Lonsdale hit a few more keys and then read, "Argentine Patrol overhead, has started routine patrol with hub centered on *Barbara*."

He looked at Gal and smiled. Everything was in place. All they needed now was for the Cubans to move.

That's when Lonsdale's inner voice chimed in loud and clear. *This is too easy . . . this is too perfect . . . be careful . . . watch your back . . . the Agency, the Agency . . .*

He shook his head to shut the voice up, but he kept hearing it. He loosened the straps of his flak jacket for easier access to the small, breach-loaded Berretta automatic he had taped to the inside of the garment, just in case.

The voice stopped when the dialogue box lit up: "ALERT ALERT ALERT." Lonsdale glanced at the TV screen. The dots were getting into the cars.

Lonsdale made a few more keystrokes and then nodded to Gal.

Gal spoke into his microphone in Hebrew: "Target on its way. Respirators, helmets at the ready. Turn on engines. Action in five minutes. Lock and load."

The die was cast.

CHAPTER FIFTY-EIGHT

Wednesday, January 3
La Cabaña Prison, Havana, Cuba

Casas had slept even less than usual. Things were going from bad to worse. He had been allowed to meet with his daughters, but only in the presence of two of his interrogators. The girls were in tears. They knew it would be the last time they would be allowed to speak with their father. He tried to help them by attempting to sound determined and dignified. He said he had, indeed, committed acts that had gravely harmed the Fatherland, the Revolutionary Government and Fidel Castro, and for this he deserved to be punished. He admonished them to hew to high moral and ethical standards, to choose their friends and life-partners carefully, to be unquestioningly loyal to them and to expect unquestioning loyalty in return.

He asked them to be kind to their mother and to help their paternal grandmother who was suffering greatly as a result of her son's misguided conduct. He reminded them of the many joyful occasions they'd shared with their father, and then asked them to forgive him for having caused them pain and humiliation. He had then embraced each of them, in turn, lovingly and with great tenderness and had wished them a long, happy, healthy, and productive life.

After the meeting, his interrogators told him that De la Fuente was a CIA agent and the brain behind the drug-smuggling operation. He wouldn't believe them, not even after they showed him Oscar's signed confession.

He was devastated. To have been duped so completely, to have accepted so readily that the Revolution and its leaders had been corrupted, and to have then actively striven to bring down the Revolutionary government and Fidel, his idol, now appeared to him as a preposterous act of disloyalty that nothing could justify.

He had failed as a revolutionary, and he'd betrayed his comrades by not believing in their integrity. He was accountable for his mistakes and had to pay for them—or so it seemed to him after four weeks of intense questioning, physical deprivation, and the propaganda directed against him by the State-controlled media. And the only currency with which to pay his terrible debt was his life, for even his honor had been stripped away.

On Monday, New Year's Day, they had made him put on his dress uniform and had taken him before a secret Military Tribunal of Honor, a Preliminary Court Martial, composed of forty-seven of his peers. There he confessed to all his wrongdoings.

The Military Tribunal of Honor reconvened in public at six o'clock in the evening, after five hours of deliberation, its sessions televised, as agreed by participating journalists, via two networks: Cuban National TV in Spanish and the Canadian Broadcasting Corporation in English. No other TV cameras were authorized, but journalists were welcome to attend all proceedings open to the public.

The Tribunal's verdict found him guilty of grave misconduct as an officer and revolutionary. It stripped him of the decorations and honors bestowed on him by the Party and La Patria, and reduced him to the rank of private. It then discharged him dishonorably from the Revolutionary Armed Forces. He was ordered to be held for Court Martial as soon as possible before a Special Military Tribunal.

The Special Military Tribunal convened on Tuesday morning to hear the charges against him and his co-accused. By noon, the formalities over, his trial could begin.

With a repentant and cooperative Casas on the witness stand, it took four hours of questions and answers to get to De la Fuente's role in the operation. The Court ordered a recess until Wednesday morning. The unveiling of CIA participation merited a full day of questioning.

Casas now understood why the CIA man had been so adamant in Budapest about obtaining proof positive of complicity in drug smuggling by the Cuban government. Without such proof and with De la Fuente telling all on the witness stand the CIA would look very bad.

How did Military Intelligence find out that the CIA was involved, Casas asked himself. *Is De la Fuente a double agent or only stupid? Lonsdale, must have known that De la Fuente was working for them.* Why then did he not approach De la Fuente and try to save him rather than Casas? Nothing made sense, especially not Lonsdale's assurances of friendship and promises of help.

And he had fallen for it all: Oscar's scheming, the CIA's cajoling, the glitter of gold, the feeling of security derived from having a few cents to his name. Today was the day they would expose him for the fool that he had been and nobody was going to be there to help. Certainly not Oscar De la Fuente, his erstwhile comrade-in-arms, who was now preparing to bear witness against him in court to save his own neck.

Casas reckoned that, in the final analysis, nobody helped you except yourself—and, at times, God.

CHAPTER FIFTY-NINE

Wednesday, January 3
Havana Tunnel, Havana, Cuba

At 0657 hours, Lonsdale watched the lead car leave La Cabaña and head for the *Via Monumental*. The second car did not move.

Suddenly, Lonsdale felt confused. Who was in which car? Were two prisoners in one car with guard and driver, and four men escorting them in a chase car? Or was there one prisoner per car? *Damn Bellon! Why couldn't you have been more specific?*

Was the first car a decoy, or was it a scout car, checking that the coast was clear? Or was it unobtrusively transporting two manacled prisoners in the back seat with a guard between them?

With tiny beads of perspiration on his forehead Lonsdale stared at Picture 1 and with all his might willed the second car to move—to no avail.

At 0701 hours, Lonsdale zoomed up and watched the first car reach the spot above the northeast entrance of the tunnel where he and Gal had powered up their equipment a while ago. The car stopped and waited; the second car remained still.

Lonsdale's inner voice piped up: *It's a scout car. If you don't get everyone inside the tunnel your goose is cooked.*

He leaned over the table and opened the sliding window behind the driver's head. "Drive into the tunnel *now*! Stop within five meters of the entrance. Tell your buddy in the jeep to stay put." Then he turned to Gal. "Tell Team B to back up as close to the tunnel as possible. Tell Team A to follow us into the tunnel and stop in front of the truck."

No sooner had the truck started to move than the dialogue box came to life again. "ALERT, ALERT, ALERT" it flashed. Lonsdale watched Picture 1 as the second car moved to the courtyard exit and was joined by another. He wondered if it was the two-car convoy they had been waiting for.

The convoy started off at speed toward the periphery road and reached the scout car above the tunnel entrance in minutes. As he was switching to Picture 2, Lonsdale shouted to the driver, "Tell your buddy to move as close to the tunnel entrance as possible." He glanced at the screen. The three vehicles were now proceeding as a convoy to where the periphery road intersected the Via Monumental. "Advise the teams that there are potentially three cars, not two, and that there may be as many as ten guards in the convoy," Lonsdale said to Gal. The cars were almost at the intersection. "We'll have to help take out that third car somehow."

Gal shook his head. "Too confusing at this late stage. Let the boys do their work."

The vehicles slowed down as they approached the Via Monumental. Suddenly, the lead car sped up and entered the intersection during a break in the traffic, effectively blocking the highway and doing what Lonsdale had wanted his military policemen in the jeep to do. Lonsdale yelled out to the driver. "Tell your buddy to speed through the tunnel and go home."

After a full minute's wait—to let the traffic ahead get away—the two other cars turned onto the Via Monumental and accelerated toward the tunnel.

"Action imminent," Lonsdale said to Gal who transmitted the message to the teams. Then he unlatched the truck's rear doors. Lonsdale typed on the computer's keyboard, and the dialogue box answered with "Helicopter will go within three minutes."

At 0707 hours, the two-car convoy flashed by the maintenance truck. "Team A, go!" commanded Gal as Lonsdale switched to Picture 4, which showed Maximo Gomez Park. "Go, go, go," he screamed at the driver. The truck shot forward causing the unlatched doors to snap open. Smoke canisters exploded on impact and filled the tunnel behind Lonsdale with thick, black smoke.

Lonsdale felt the bump as the truck rolled over the undeployed dragons' teeth. He slammed down on the release buttons to arm both barricades, the one behind him and the other further ahead. The dragon's teeth sprang up just as the third vehicle—the scout car— came barreling through the smoke at a hundred and fifty kilometers an hour and ripped the car's four tires to shreds. Out of control, the vehicle bounced off the left tunnel wall and slid to a halt on its rims less than ten meters from the truck, which, by then, had come to a stop at Lonsdale's command.

Two stun grenades, both thrown by Gal, exploded near the car as he and Lonsdale raced to check on its four occupants. Neither Casas nor De la Fuente were among them.

The guards began firing in Gal's direction. Lonsdale took them out with a short burst from his Galil then destroyed their communications equipment with a well-aimed second burst. Gal's Galil raked the engine and rendered it inoperable. The two returned to the truck where Lonsdale raised the *Barbara* by ultra-shortwave radio. The truck was too far inside the tunnel for the satellite system to work.

"Alpha this is Omega. Do you read? Over."

"Alpha to Omega. We read you five by five. Over."

"Omega to Alpha. I'm blind. Keep me posted. Over."

"Roger Omega. Will keep you posted. Over and out."

Lonsdale looked at this watch: 0711 hours.

The helicopter pilots timed their take-off to coincide with the Argentine Patrol's fifth sweep over the *Barbara*. The ship was being used by the aircraft of the Brothers to the Rescue as a central marker, a reference point.

As the squadron swept over the ship, the helicopter rose from the deck and flew toward Cuba alongside the Brothers' aircraft for ninety seconds. Lonsdale had devised this maneuver to confuse Cuban radar and "hide" the helicopter's ascent. The Brothers, not wanting to intrude too far into Cuban airspace, turned back. The helicopter dropped down to skim the waves to avoid radar detection. It barreled along at almost two hundred kilometers an hour toward Havana. Within six minutes it was over Maximo Gomez Park.

Meanwhile, in the tunnel the two-car convoy, with one car traveling slightly ahead of the other, reached the second barricade a few seconds after the dragon's teeth had deployed. The lead car's driver spotted them at the very last moment and had just enough time to slam on the brakes before the teeth tore into his front tires. The second car slammed into the barricade at full speed and skewed toward the lead car as both drivers battled for control. But the tires were gone and the rims had no purchase. The two vehicles spun around and hit the tunnel walls.

Before their occupants could recover from the impact, Teams A and B spilled from the cabs and surrounded them, weapons at the ready.

Resistance of any kind would have been futile.

Oscar De la Fuente died a scary and cruel death, especially because he was totally unprepared for it. Unlike Casas, he had no inkling that an attempt at extracting him would be made. Although he heard Gal's stun grenades explode and the burst of machine-gun fire, he ascribed the noise to the powerful backfiring of an ancient truck, not an uncommon phenomenon in Cuba. Thus he was taken by complete surprise when the car he was traveling in rolled over the dragon-teeth barrier and went out of control. He was sitting in the left back seat handcuffed to the roll bar. When the car, having hit the tunnel wall, spun around, the door on his side flew open and he was flung out. He was hanging from the roll bar trying to stabilize himself when the second car sideswiped him and crushed his head. Lonsdale, when he reached the scene, identified him.

In the other car, Casas, though badly shaken up, wasn't hurt. A member of Team B cut him loose with the pliers he had brought along for that purpose and Gal bundled him into the back seat of Cab A. An armed Israeli got in on each side of him and Gal jumped into the front seat beside the Cuban driver.

The five remaining Cubans dropped their gear and, clad in workmen's clothing, piled into Cab B. Lonsdale deactivated dragons teeth barrier Number Two and Cab B left for Old Havana where its occupants would melt into the crowd.

At 0716 hours Lonsdale sprinted back to the truck. "Drive to just this side of the tunnel entrance and stop. Be prepared to fight if necessary." He handed the driver a helmet and a loaded Galil assault rifle, then climbed back into the rear of the truck and sat down in front of the computer.

A minute later, the system, forty yards from the entrance, reacquired the satellite signal. Picture 4 filled the screen, showing the helicopter from the *Barbara* landing in the middle of the football field in

Maximo Gomez Park. Cab A, having rounded the Maximo Gomez monument, was approaching from the south. Out of nowhere, a military jeep carrying four armed soldiers appeared, racing in the opposite direction. Lonsdale guessed they were the advance guard of the military, alerted to the rescue operation by one of the ambushed guards in the tunnel.

The men in the jeep spotted Cab A full of armed men on the other side of the waist-high road divider and opened fire. The cab-driver, mortally wounded, lost control of his vehicle, which sped past the firing soldiers, slammed into the road divider, and overturned.

"Go, go, go," Lonsdale screamed at his driver. "Round the monu-ment and drive toward the *Malecon*." The screen now showed that someone in Cab A was returning the soldiers' fire, three of whom were crouched behind their jeep; the fourth lay motionless in front of the vehicle. Lonsdale continued to watch. The firing from the taxi was increasing in volume. More than one weapon was in action.

The maintenance truck was approaching the soldiers rapidly and Lonsdale's driver looked back at him questioningly.

"When you get within a hundred feet of the jeep, stop and turn the truck around." While the driver did so Lonsdale slammed a grenade into his launcher on the Galil. As soon as he acquired a clear line of fire he stood up and, leaning against the wall of the truck, took careful aim. He fired when the jeep was within fifty feet of him, just as one of the sol-diers, who must have heard the truck approaching, swung around and squeezed off a burst of submachine gun fire that mercifully missed.

Lonsdale's grenade hit the jeep's fuel tank, which exploded, blow-ing the soldiers away. Lonsdale vaulted the road-divider and raced over to Cab A to help Gal, Casas and the two Israelis crawl out of the overturned car. They were shaken, but otherwise unhurt, except for Casas who had a nasty gash across his forehead from broken glass. The driver was dead.

At 0720 hours, Lonsdale yelled, "Everybody into the truck," and pointed at the maintenance vehicle, which, by then, had caught up with them. They clambered on board fast and the driver floored the accelerator. The truck sped toward the soccer field.

They had almost reached the field when the dialogue box began to clatter. "ALERT, ALERT, ALERT. Bandit helicopter approach-ing from the east at 200 mph. ETA 90 seconds."

Lonsdale turned to Gal. "We'll stop the truck. You guys make a run for it. I'll cover the rear." Gal began to protest, but Lonsdale's shout cut him off. "That's an order." Then he yelled through the window "Stop now!" The driver slammed on the brakes, Casas, Gal, and the Israelis jumped out and began to sprint toward the waiting helicopter about a hundred yards away, rotors spinning.

"Stand by," Lonsdale commanded the driver and loaded another grenade into his launcher. On his screen he could see the military chopper coming up fast. He armed his weapon, released the safety, and threw himself flat on the floor of the truck. "Go, go, go," he yelled above the din of the approaching rotors. The truck shot forward like a scared jackrabbit as the rocket the copter pilot had just fired slammed into the road and exploded harmlessly where the truck had been a few moments before.

"Stop the truck," Lonsdale bellowed and the driver brought the vehicle to an abrupt halt. The pilot fought to break away, but it was too late. The chopper was almost on top of the vehicle.

Lonsdale fired his grenade at the chopper almost at point blank range through the truck's open back door then emptied a clip of ammunition into the craft's body for good measure.

The helicopter exploded. Pieces of it slammed into the front of the truck, killing the driver instantly. Lonsdale was hurled through the back door. The ammunition in the truck blew up and deafened him as he lay, face down, on the roadway. Then something hit him in the thigh. The pain was so intense that he lost consciousness.

At 0721 hours, Gal, Casas, and the two Israelis scrambled on board the *Barbara*'s helicopter, which took off just as the maintenance truck blew sky-high. Gal, leaning out of the rising craft as far as he dared, caught a glimpse of a motionless figure lying in the debris, seemingly pinned to the asphalt by a giant spear.

CHAPTER SIXTY

Wednesday, January 3
Somewhere in Havana, Cuba

Lonsdale was delirious. He believed he was snorkeling in the Caribbean, but it was kind of strange. He was swimming on his back and the snorkel tube was sticking straight up in front of his nose. He saw the shark coming and tried to get away, but the water was shallow and he couldn't use his arms because the sand was holding them down and the shark bit into his thigh and it wouldn't let go and it was hurting very much, so much so that he screamed.

He awoke to find himself strapped to a hospital bed, intravenous dripping into his right arm, an oxygen mask covering his nose and mouth, and a submachine-gun-toting Cuban Army Captain standing guard over him.

When he saw that his charge was awake, the Captain pressed the bell beside Lonsdale's bed, and a doctor appeared, his green fatigues covered by a white smock.

"*Habla Vd. Español?* Do you speak Spanish?" he asked.

Lonsdale nodded.

"You must be very thirsty."

Lonsdale nodded again.

"And you have a splitting headache."

Lonsdale nodded a third time and tried to speak, but couldn't. The mask on his face was too tight.

"We'll take the mask off in a minute and give you water and some painkillers." Lonsdale nodded again. They must have given him sodium pentothal.

The doctor turned to the captain and said something Lonsdale couldn't hear. The captain left, but returned within minutes with a major who waited while the doctor removed the mask and adjusted Lonsdale's pillow.

"My name is Arasosa Galetti," the major said. "I work for Cuban Military Intelligence and I wish to ask you some questions. Do you understand Spanish?" He sat down in the chair provided by the Captain.

"Yes I do, Major," replied Lonsdale, "but before going on could you please give me some water and something for my headache."

The major was unsympathetic. "I'm afraid that'll have to wait until after we've finished."

"You have me in your power, major." Lonsdale was matter of fact. "And you can deny me comfort and medication, but it will lead you nowhere." He licked his lips. "What happened this morning is on TV all over the world as we speak. Your government may choose or not to admit that you have captured me, but one thing is for certain. Oscar De la Fuente is dead and you'll have one hell-of-a-time explaining his demise without my help."

The major was unperturbed. "I think you're being unrealistic. Somehow I feel that, just now, you need our help more than we yours. The sooner you answer my questions, the sooner we can minister to your physical needs. May I suggest that you start cooperating?" His tone was not that of a friend.

Although his head was splitting and his thigh aflame with pain, Lonsdale managed a grin. He had just discovered two things. First, other than a damaged left thigh, he was in one piece give or take a few abrasions, and second, the major very much needed his help, in spite of his protestations to the contrary. "I would love to, and I will." Lonsdale made himself sound like reasonableness personified, "but not with you."

"Not with me what?" Arasosa Galetti was mystified. His prisoner was half-crazed with pain and dying of thirst, yet not cooperating. The interrogation was not going the way he wanted it to, and he was in a hurry.

"What I mean is that I am prepared to cooperate and answer all reasonable questions, but I will give my answers to only one man in Cuba, and that man—and I mean no disrespect to your person—is not you, Major."

"Who then?"

"The minister of the Revolutionary Armed Forces."

The major stood up. "I think I had better come back later, after you have had time to reflect on the precariousness of your position."

Lonsdale, gathering all the strength he could muster, addressed the officer in his best parade-ground voice. "I think not, major, and for two reasons. One, unless you let me speak with Raul Castro immediately you might find yourself demoted a rank or two. This is not important. What is important is that you will have caused irreparable harm to La Patria, the Party, and Fidel Castro for which you will be court-martialed and probably cashiered from the army."

"You're talking rubbish. You're making empty threats." The Major made to leave.

Lonsdale was fading fast. He had to give his adversary something to work with, or lose the initiative. "Tell Raul that the Fat Man sent me, and see what he says."

It was all Lonsdale could do not to lose consciousness before Arasosa Galetti left the room.

When Lonsdale came to again he felt much better. His headache was gone, his thigh hurt less, but his raging thirst remained. The captain with the submachine-gun was still very much present. By the light coming through the barred windows, Lonsdale estimated it was late afternoon, some twelve hours after commencement of the extraction operation and pretty well the last moment for coordinating damage control. Whether the Cuban government was interested in damage control remained to be seen.

As if on cue, the door opened and four efficient-looking sergeants appeared, armed to the teeth. They surrounded Lonsdale's bed. The captain backed up against the wall and a female lieutenant-interpreter entered to search the room and the adjoining bathroom. Satisfied, she disappeared and came back within minutes with an unassuming-looking, short, paunchy man wearing a forage cap. Everyone saluted except Lonsdale. His arms were tied to the bed.

The captain placed the chair beside Lonsdale's bed and the man in the cap sat down.

"How is the Fat Man?" he asked.

"I think, well. Quite recovered from his recent bout with food poisoning."

"You said he sent you. Explain."

Lonsdale looked at the man, his eyes hard and cold. "Gladly, provided someone first gives me a large cold glass of water for which I've been asking for the last four hours, and you untie my left arm so that I can scratch my nose, which is itching."

The man in the cap smiled frostily. "I admire your style Lonsdale, but don't push your luck." He nodded to the lieutenant who untied Lonsdale, gave him a glass of water, then scurried away. Lonsdale emptied the glass, stretched luxuriously, and scratched his nose. "Thank you, Comandante. Now that we know each other better, may I make a request for the benefit of both of us?"

"What?" The word sounded like a pistol shot. Raul Castro no longer felt like playing nice guy.

"We should have our talk in private because we may wish to touch on subjects of a very delicate nature."

The minister nodded and his entourage withdrew, except for the captain. Lonsdale remained silent and Castro became impatient. "Get on with it," he snapped.

"Not until the captain also leaves," Lonsdale said and lay back on his pillow. His thigh was beginning to hurt again.

Castro shook his head. "He stays. He's my man."

"And also the minister of the Interior's," Lonsdale bluffed. The captain turned crimson with rage, but Raul Castro had second thoughts. "Leave us," he commanded and the man withdrew.

Lonsdale got to the point immediately. "Comandante, your side and mine need to coordinate the content of a statement to the media about what happened in the tunnel this morning."

"Nothing happened. There was an accident, a number of cars caught fire, the wounded were evacuated by helicopter, and one of the helicopters crashed, killing among others Oscar De la Fuente, one of the witnesses in the Casas trial. The trial was delayed by a day, but will resume tomorrow at eight in the morning."

"And who will be your star witness?"

"General Casas, who else. Tomorrow he will continue his confession and assume total responsibility for the drug-smuggling operation to the complete exoneration of our government."

"And how will you get your hands on General Casas?"

"That's where you come in Lonsdale." Castro got up. "You go home, he comes home. I'll get you a telephone and you can make the necessary arrangements."

"No, Comandante, I won't make that call. Not after all the effort I put into this operation."

The Cuban shrugged and put on his cap. "Suit yourself. The witness on the stand tomorrow is either Casas or yourself. Neither appearance will enhance the reputation of the Agency."

Lonsdale's mind was racing. With De la Fuente dead Casas was the only one who could exonerate the Cuban government credibly. Lonsdale's testimony in a Cuban court might blacken the Agency's name, but not whitewash the Castro regime.

No, the *Comandante* was bluffing. Or was he asking for a way to save face?

"Putting me on the witness stand is good neither for your side nor ours. It's a lose-lose situation in which you are likely to lose more than we."

"How so?"

"The Agency will deny ever having heard of me. It will then reveal my true identity as a crazed ex-employee, working as a mercenary for the Medellin cartel. You will respond by vilifying poor Casas who is the least guilty of all of us. We will counter with a campaign designed to smear you by pointing out that the Revolution is an abject failure from the economic point of view, with most families depending for survival on the dollars their relatives send them from abroad."

Lonsdale took a deep breath and continued. "Incensed, you will retaliate, claiming the United States is amoral, corrupt, and oppressive of minorities; whereupon our president, reaching for the high ground, will point out that a so-called Revolutionary government, which claims to embrace high moral standards is not in a position to accuse its neighbors of immorality when its leaders—Cienfuegos, Huber Matos, Piñeda, Dorticos, Cisneiros, Abrantes, Torralba, and now, Casas and others yet unnamed—have a habit of disappearing, committing suicide, or ending up accused of corruption and treason." Lonsdale fell back on his pillows.

His little speech had exhausted him.

The comandante's reaction was laconic. "So what? Business as usual! But not for you. After your trial we will probably put you away for life, if we don't shoot you."

Lonsdale licked his lips. He was thirsty again. "Do you really believe the Cuban people will idly stand by after they discover that yet another one of their tormentors, and yours, I might add, who has been making their lives miserable all these years, is getting away scot-free?"

"What on earth are you talking about?" Raul Castro narrowed his eyes. "Casas was not tormenting the people and certainly not me. On the contrary, he was a popular hero and an excellent soldier."

"I'm not talking about Casas, but your nemesis and prime adversary, the present minister of the Interior."

"What has he got to do with all of this?" Raul Castro sat down again.

"Comandante, listen." Lonsdale could see Castro was interested. "Consider the following scenario. Oscar De la Fuente and his father-in-law, Jesus Montalba, the minister of the Interior, hatch a scheme whereby, using elements of the Cuban Army, Coast Guard, and the Ministry of the Interior, start cooperating with the Medellin Cartel in smuggling drugs into the United States. They need a high-ranking officer to help them liaise with the army, so they dupe General Casas into assisting them."

The minister did not move. Lonsdale went on: "Their scheme comes to light, Casas and De la Fuente are arrested. De la Fuente has money outside the country earmarked for saving him in case something goes wrong. He pays the Medellin cartel to get him out. The cartel retains the services of the notorious Bernard Lands, me, rogue ex-CIA agent living in Argentina, who attempts a rescue, during which De la Fuente, Lands, and one of Lands' men die, as do two of your helicopter personnel and some of your soldiers. Casas escapes and disappears, probably killed by the Colombians. Your Army

Intelligence unit, which now takes over the investigation, discovers a Panamanian bank account where Montalba's and De la Fuente's illicit profits are being accumulated. One of the transfers leads to a bank account linked to Montalba with over a million dollars in it."

Castro was mesmerized. "You can prove all this?"

"Most of it. The *Barbara*, which is the same ship the Cartel uses to smuggle drugs, was also used in the rescue attempt. Lands, me, did exist once, and I can easily provide irrefutable proof of that. As for Lands and the cartel being in cahoots and hatching the extraction scheme—well, there's a clear trail leading to proof of that. The CIA knows of the Panamanian bank account with all its relevant transactions listed, and it has details of a decade-old Montalba bank account outside Panama with corresponding entries in it. The CIA will corroborate this story and everybody will come out of this mess more or less unscathed."

"Can you give me concrete proof here and now that such a Montalba account exists?"

"Of course I can. You know damned well that I know where all the bodies are buried."

"Then why don't I just keep you here and make you sweat a little so you tell me everything you know?"

Lonsdale shrugged. "You've tried pentothal and it didn't work because my hypnotic block against it is still in place. You can try torturing me, but that'll take time. I'll hold out for three days, and even if I did break it wouldn't help. I know the general picture, but not the details. By then you will have run out of time and the press would find out about what was happening to me here, and about Montalba. The Montalba business would be given a very Cuban-government-involvement type spin, which you don't want."

"If pentothal doesn't work on you, how did I find out who you were? Notice, I called you by your name right off the bat." Raul Castro sounded self-assured.

"You did, indeed, call me by a name, a name your friend Director Smythe knows me by. He told the Fat Man who then passed it on to you."

"Which brings me to the Fat Man," said Raul Castro, musing. "With all these new developments he has become a liability."

Lonsdale said nothing.

CHAPTER SIXTY-ONE

Thursday, January 4
Washington, DC

It was half-past midnight. Morton was preparing for bed when the alarm on the hotline telephone began to wail. He picked up the handset on the second ring.

"May I speak to the Liquor Merchant please," said the well-known voice, and Morton's legs went weak. Logic had convinced him that Lonsdale was dead.

"I am the Liquor Merchant," he managed to croak, then pulled himself together and began the drill. "Who is calling please?"

"This is the Boy Scout. Do you have a first name?" The question meant Lonsdale was not being coerced into what he was doing.

"My first name is Samuel."

"Samuel the Liquor Merchant." This reconfirmed that all was well at Lonsdale's end and that "normal" conversation could commence. "How is Sparky?" Lonsdale inquired. In other words, how were things on the *Barbara*? (Sparky was the code name of the senior satellite imaging technician charged with taking over should Lonsdale fail to return.)

"He is well, but busy. The full delegation, lead by the Indian and Mr. Easter, has arrived and is being entertained as we speak." This meant that Casas, Gal, and the others were safely on board the *Barbara* and on their way to Florida where, as prearranged, they would be met by Morton's people.

"Mr. Waterhouse has lost interest in the deal, so he won't be coming." Lonsdale was telling Morton that De la Fuente was dead.

"I'm sorry to hear that. To tell the truth, I understood you were no longer interested either, but I'm glad you've changed your mind."

"It was my new business associate who revived my interest and persuaded me to call, but, of course, he will want his pound of flesh." Lonsdale was rather pleased with the metaphor.

"Can you give me some parameters?"

Lonsdale looked at Raul Castro sitting next to the interpreter who was listening in on the conversation. When the interpreter caught up, Castro nodded and Lonsdale continued.

"He is very interested in all aspects of the Belgian file. Do you have the details?" In other words, has Morton obtained all the relevant information on Montalba's Swiss bank account?

"Yes, I do. And it is quite complete."

"Good." Lonsdale let out a sigh of relief. "Bring it with you to our meeting."

"Where and when?" Morton asked, his excitement rising. Lonsdale was talking about an exchange: information for prisoners.

"In Cayman at Owen Roberts Airport at noon today. My new business associate will be with me, as will be the Russian." "The Russian" was Ivan Spiegel.

"Got it. Owen Roberts at noon. You, the Russian, and your new friend. Anything else?"

"Two things. One: your company will have to agree to refrain from commenting on certain recent events."

"No problem there."

"Two: clear things at Owen Roberts so we can talk without problems. I presume you will be flying in by company plane."

"Of course."

"Wonderful. I'll see you at noon. By the way," Lonsdale added, "it might be a good idea to bring Fred along too." This was a request to have the Agency's aircraft configured to accept a stretcher and to bring a doctor.

Morton felt the knot return to his stomach. Lonsdale must be seriously hurt. "Consider it done."

CHAPTER SIXTY-TWO

Thursday, January 4
George Town, Cayman Islands

Owen Roberts International Airport, named after a pioneer Caymanian flyer, has a separate apron for the aircraft of visiting dignitaries, and other special guests: U.S. Coast Guard planes, DEA helicopters and aircraft, Colombian Air Force jets, and so forth.

The apron is some ways off to the left of the main terminal and shielded from it by bushes.

Precisely at noon, a Cubana Airlines Ilyushin 18 landed and was guided to the apron by the "Follow Me" jeep. It made a one-hundred-and-eighty-degree in-place turn so as to face the taxiing strip. The Caymanian mechanics plugged in a generator to help run the aircraft's communications and air-conditioning systems, whereupon the engines were switched off.

A few minutes later a Bombardier Challenger with U.S. civilian markings landed and was positioned on the apron between the Cuban aircraft and the taxiing strip. Three men got out and boarded the Cubana plane, using its rear access steps.

Morton, Morton's boss, the CIA's DDO (Deputy Director for Operations), carrying a briefcase, and the CIA doctor, with his medical bag, were welcomed on board by the same army captain who had been guarding Lonsdale in the hospital. The doctor was frisked then introduced to the physician who had attended Lonsdale in Havana. Morton and the DDO were given a thorough physical search and led toward the front of the craft, past a fully armed platoon of elite Cuban Army bodyguards.

Lonsdale was lying in the business-class section of the aircraft where the seats had been removed to accommodate a stretcher. His left leg, in plaster from hip to ankle, was suspended from a stand at the foot of the stretcher. He was playing chess with Ivan Spiegel.

"Come in, come in gentlemen. You're just in time to see me get demolished by Ivan the Terrible in fewer than twenty moves." Lonsdale sounded relaxed, but tired. "Ivan, may I present my boss, James Morton, director of the Counter-Terrorism and Counter-Narcotics Division and his boss, Alexander King, the deputy director for Operations of the Central Intelligence Agency." Lonsdale presumed that Morton had brought King along to do whatever signing needed to be done on behalf of the CIA. Morton was not senior enough for that.

Lieutenant Anaya, the interpreter, appeared from nowhere and, seeing that everyone was present went forward to the first-class Cabin to fetch Raul Castro.

"Good day, gentlemen," Castro said to Morton's boss. "You're late."

"Technically you are right, Minister, and I apologize," replied the DDO. "But the reason for the few minutes' delay in my arrival is due to Caymanian air traffic control. Our two aircraft arrived overhead at the same time. Naturally, you, being the more important visitor, were cleared to land first."

Castro waved his hand. "No matter. Let us get down to business." The lieutenant rotated four seats so they faced each other on the side of the isle opposite to where Lonsdale was lying. Morton, the DDO and Castro sat down; Ivan Spiegel withdrew. The interpreter remained standing beside Lonsdale's stretcher.

"Please begin." Cuba's second most powerful man nodded at Morton who opened his file.

"Your side and ours have agreed to exchange Ivan Spiegel, a U.K. citizen, and Robert Lonsdale, a U.S. citizen, for first: information relating to a bank account in the name of Maria Teresa Montalba, which was opened by her father, Jesus Montalba, Cuba's present minister of the Interior, more than a decade ago in Zurich, Switzerland, at Bodner & Cie Banquiers, and on which Jesus Montalba is the sole signatory. Today, this bank account has a credit balance of over one million three hundred and fifty thousand U.S. dollars derived from an opening deposit of one thousand U.S. dollars in cash, and from over two dozen wire transfers in U.S. funds from the Mexican National Bank, plus two transfers from a Panamanian bank account each for half a million U.S. dollars."

Morton stopped and poured himself a glass of water from the pitcher on the side table beside him. He took a sip and continued. "Second: information relating to a bank account in Panama City, Panama, at the Bank of Credit and Commerce International, which, today, has a credit balance of over thirty million U.S. dollars after the transfer from it of one million U.S. dollars to the Montalba bank account in Switzerland." Morton looked at Lonsdale who was listening intently. "Your side and ours have agreed to divide the balance of this account equally between Department Z of the Ministry of the Interior of the Socialist Republic of Cuba and the U.S. Central Intelligence Agency."

Lonsdale almost burst out laughing. Colombian drug money was paying for everybody's expenses. "I should have asked for more," he muttered under his breath.

"Third: consent by the U.S. Central Intelligence Agency not to comment in any manner whatsoever on the events that seem to have taken place in and around the Havana Tunnel during the morning hours of January 3." Morton stopped, drained his glass and wiped his lips. "Are there any questions or observations?"

Raul Castro got up and began to pace up and down the isle. He stopped in front of Lonsdale's stretcher. "Do you know the details relating to the Montalba bank account?" he asked Lonsdale in Spanish, bypassing the interpreter.

"I do."

"Then tell me about them in Spanish."

"What do you want to know, Comandante?"

"Everything. How you found out about the account, how you got copies of it, where the Mexican transfers originated . . . everything."

It took Lonsdale twenty minutes to tell the Minister the whole story.

"What about the transfers from Mexico?" Castro asked after Lonsdale was done.

"I don't know the details."

Castro looked at Morton, who waited for the interpreter to finish before replying.

"Jesus Montalba has a sister working at the National Bank of Mexico in the foreign exchange clearing department. She is very senior. Has been there for years."

Raul Castro nodded. "I know her. Her name is also Maria Teresa, like Montalba's daughter. She was a good revolutionary, but changed allegiances and left Cuba three years after the triumph of the Revolution."

"As you say, Minister," Morton picked up where he had left off, "her name is Maria Teresa Montalba, the widow of an accountant called Sesati, who left her in dire circumstances. She wrote her brother for assistance, and he had her come to Havana where they worked out a simple way of helping her make money."

"How?" Castro was hanging on Morton's every word.

"She went back to Mexico and let it be known that she could get exit visas quickly for people wanting to leave Cuba. The cost: fifteen thousand dollars per individual and twenty-five thousand per family. She was discreet and only did three or four per year."

"I want details, not generalities." The minister was getting impatient.

"She would write letters to her brother regularly, once or twice a month. Whenever someone paid her she would say that she had a visit from such and such a person or such and such a Cuban family, whereupon Montalba would arrange the corresponding exit visas to be issued."

"And how did the money flow?"

"She was very careful. Payment had to be in cash, half up front, the other half when the visa was granted. As you know, having an exit visa is only part of the battle. It may be revoked at any time, even at the last minute at the airport just prior to departure. She was, therefore, sure to get paid the second half."

Castro was silent and Morton pushed on. "She kept the first payment for herself. When the second payment came in she took it to her workplace, slipped it into the bundle of U.S. money she was clearing on any particular day and corrected the relevant distribution slip to include a transfer to her niece's account in Switzerland."

"How much did she transfer?"

"In excess of three hundred thousand dollars over ten years."

"That's four individual visas per year at fifteen thousand dollars apiece, half of which she kept." The minister was used to counting fast. He administered a huge budget.

After that, there remained very little to be said. The DDO and Castro initialed a summary of what had been agreed at the meeting prepared by Morton on the spot and printed out on his laptop. Then Morton handed over copies of the Swiss and Panamanian bank accounts and half a dozen Banco Nacional de Mexico distribution slips that had been altered by Montalba's sister. He also gave Castro a fifteen million dollar check drawn on the Panamanian bank account.

It took six of the soldiers with occasional help from the CIA doctor and the pilots of the Challenger to transfer Lonsdale to the Agency's aircraft. They were as careful as they could be. Even so, Lonsdale would have gone crazy from the pain had the doctor not given him a massive shot of Demerol beforehand.

The Challenger took off a few minutes before four p.m.

The last thing Lonsdale heard before falling asleep was the doctor saying, "You're damn lucky. The helicopter blade fragment that pierced your thigh and nailed you to the highway missed the bone completely. You have severe muscle damage, but it will regenerate with extensive physio. Trust me. I saw the X-rays."

It was a figure of speech, which made Lonsdale smile. Perhaps it was time to begin trusting people again, and he'd start with Micheline. But, of course, that was different. He loved her very much and as soon as he could get hold of a phone he'd call her.

More than anything he wanted to hear her voice. Then he would listen to some classical and jazz guitar music and maybe start playing the instrument seriously again.

CHAPTER SIXTY-THREE

Saturday, January 6
Langley, Virginia

Acting Director of Central Intelligence Lawrence Smythe was annoyed, but not dissatisfied. Although Lonsdale had blindsided him by initiating the extraction operation at the start rather than toward the end of the Casas trial, he had achieved what the Director had so earnestly desired: preventing Oscar De la Fuente from testifying.

Reyes Puma had been furious. He had called Smythe at home during dinner on Wednesday, wanting to know how it had come to pass, as he put it, that "the manuscript was delivered so early." Although he was speaking in code, the tone of his voice made the depth of his anger obvious. Smythe had humored him by pleading ignorance. He hadn't felt threatened. His Senate Confirmation Hearing was coming up the following week and he knew that, with the president's active support and the Casas–De la Fuente fiasco swept under the rug by Lonsdale's timely action, his chances of being confirmed as DCI were excellent.

He'd telephoned Morton right away for in-depth information and had pretended being saddened to learn that, although all details weren't in, it appeared that Casas had escaped, but that De la Fuente and Lonsdale had died. Morton had promised a full briefing on Friday morning at ten in the conference room just off Smythe's office on the seventh floor. Morton's direct superior, Alexander King, the deputy director of operations had invited himself, which was only fitting since he had every right to know what was going on in his department.

Smythe looked at his watch: ten to ten. He called his secretary to ascertain that the conference room was ready. Morton had requested a blackboard, a map of Old Havana, an overhead projector, and a videocassette player.

His guests were in the process of arriving and Smythe went to greet them. He was gratified to see that his second-in-command, the deputy director of Central Intelligence, invited by the DDO, was also present.

Morton's account of the events in and around the Havana Tunnel was spellbinding. First he outlined Lonsdale's plan, illustrating his words with diagrams on the blackboard and maps of Old Havana projected on the screen. Then he showed, by means of tapes edited from real-time satellite pictures, how the operation had unfolded. For obvious reasons the action inside the tunnel couldn't be seen, but Morton recounted what Gal had told him, thereby bringing detailed realism to his narrative. "Gal last saw Lonsdale lying in the debris of what was left of the truck and the helicopter, his body pinned to the ground by what looked like a gigantic splinter off a rotor blade."

Morton sat down. "Do you gentlemen have any questions?"

"Are we absolutely sure both De la Fuente and Lonsdale are dead?" asked Smythe.

"About De la Fuente we are absolutely sure," said Morton, getting out of his chair and inserting a new cassette into the video player. "As for Lonsdale, the jury is still out. As you know, Director," Morton's eyes bore into those of Smythe like lasers, "the Cuban authorities are claiming that the rescue attempt was masterminded by a rogue CIA agent, a man named Bernard Lands, whose employment with us had been terminated decades ago and whom we believed to be dead, but who, it would appear, hired himself out to the Medellin Cartel from time to time."

He took a sip of water from the glass in his hand then glanced at a slip of paper he was holding. "The Cubans claim Lands died during what they call 'a brazen violation of Cuba's territorial integrity by criminal elements with Colombian and U.S. connections while trying to free two of their own, to spare them from having to stand trial and to bear the full weight of Revolutionary Justice."

Morton gave Smythe another hard look. "Please note that this is the only reference by the Cuban government to the United States and, obliquely, to the CIA."

"Splendid work," said Smythe, relieved. "Morton, you and your people should be highly commended. You may rest assured that your own file will bear a personal notation from me, urging that your outstanding qualities of leadership be properly and fully recognized."

"Thank you." Morton did not smile. "Now, with your permission, I would like to show you a message Lonsdale videotaped especially for you, Director, which, I am sure, you will find most interesting." He pushed the cassette into the machine and pressed Play.

A pale Lonsdale appeared on the screen, lying in a hospital bed, his left leg in traction, intravenous painkiller dripping into his arm. As the camera moved in for a close-up it became apparent that the man's face was badly bruised.

Although he looked awful, Lonsdale's voice was strong. "If you are watching this tape, Director Smythe, it means that Jim has finished his narrative of what happened in Havana on Wednesday morning. I am sure he mentioned the outstanding role Reuven Gal played in the operation, but I am also sure that he didn't tell you about Gal's equally outstanding, though unwitting, role in leading us to the discovery of high treason within the agency."

Lonsdale's battered face filled the screen. "Yes, Director, had Gal not casually mentioned your close friendship with Filberto Reyes Puma, I would never have thought of suspecting you of working for Raul Castro." Tired, Lonsdale leaned back on his pillow. "You know how it is with me, Director: I am a tenacious bulldog type. You said so yourself on many occasions. Once something starts bothering me, I won't let go until I get to the bottom of it." Lonsdale sighed. "And I did, indeed, get to the bottom of it all, and very quickly. Just watch."

Lonsdale's hospital bed was replaced on the screen by that of Reyes Puma at the clinic. Lonsdale, sitting at the Cuban's bedside and dressed in the olive-green uniform of a major in Castro's Army, appeared to be chatting with him. The quality of the sound was excellent; every word was crystal clear.

Smythe never saw the end of the video clip. When he heard Reyes Puma say "had his wife killed" he attempted to rise from his chair, but clutching his chest, fell back, his face twisted in agony.

Morton sprang to the phone to summon help, but the DDI's voice stopped him. "Put the phone down, Morton," he commanded. "Let him battle his own damn demons alone. In final defeat he won't be heaping disgrace on his country and the Agency."

CHAPTER SIXTY-FOUR

Friday, January 21
Miami, Florida

It was past ten at night and Filberto Reyes Puma was still at his office. He hated working late, but he had no choice. His practice was disintegrating.

Ever since his birthday the previous November things had been turning sour on him. The INS was treating his applications with a much heavier hand, the judges were displaying an alarming penchant for pickiness every time he appeared before them, clients were becoming ever more demanding and seemed unwilling to deal with him.

Then he really hit a rough patch a few weeks ago when the Casas rescue mission succeeded in extracting the general from Cuba. Raul Castro faulted Reyes Puma for not providing advance information about the Agency's plans and blamed him for De la Fuente's death as well. Thank God that Lands, the agent directing the mission, also got killed, otherwise, who knows, he might have tumbled onto Reyes Puma being a Castroite agent.

As if the Casas thing hadn't been enough, Senator Smythe had died at his office of a massive coronary the day after the details of the Casas rescue mission were published in the Cuban Press. All of a sudden Reyes Puma found himself with no high-level political connections, without a highly placed secret informant, and on the outs with Raul Castro.

When he tried to make fresh contacts in the Republican Party he was politely told that the new senate incumbent had a full slate of advisors and preferred not to work with members of the late Senator Smythe's entourage.

The message had been clear: Reyes Puma was no longer "in."

Damn, but it was hot. No wonder. The air conditioning in the building was being turned down for the night to save electricity—just another thing to irritate him. To save money, they were reducing service in the building, once a choice location on Brickell Boulevard near the Sheraton Towers. Hell, the cleaning service had deteriorated to the point where Reyes Puma had to complain to the landlord about it in writing.

He decided it was time to go home. As he locked up, he noted with satisfaction that his complaining had helped. A night cleaner had just finished vacuuming the carpet in front of his office and was on her way to do the same down the hall.

Briefcase in one hand, jacket held over his shoulder by the other, Reyes Puma followed the woman and resigned himself to waiting. At night the cleaners used all but one of the elevators to move their equipment and the garbage from level to level. Yet another damned aggravation. Sure enough, the woman had "parked" one of the elevators on Reyes Puma's floor and was loading her vacuum cleaner into it. She noticed the waiting lawyer and beckoned him into the lift. "C'mon. I'll take you down," she said. Grateful, Reyes Puma accepted.

"Which parking level do you want?"

"Sub-level two please." The attorney noted that the woman had a slight Latino accent. "Where are you from?"

"From Matanzas in Cuba," said the cleaner as the doors closed. "And you?"

"Also originally from Cuba, but I've been here for decades."

"You like it here?" the woman asked.

The lawyer nodded "Sure do."

"That's nice, Filberto. I sure hope you enjoyed your stay," the cleaner said and pulled a silencer-equipped Colt automatic from under her smock.

More thunderstruck than frightened, the fat man put up his hands. "What . . . what do you mean?" he managed to stammer. "And who are you anyway?"

Instead of replying, the cleaner shot Reyes Puma twice in the head at point blank range as the elevator came to a stop at sub-level five, the lowest stop in the building.

CHAPTER SIXTY-FIVE

Friday, March 31
Gander, Newfoundland, Canada

Conchita Borrego was very sad. Relations between the new, market-oriented Hungarian government and the Socialist Republic of Cuba had cooled to the point where her troupe of dancers was no longer welcome in Budapest and had been ordered to return home.

The timing for Conchita couldn't have been worse. General Casas had vanished, and she would be left to fend for herself when facing accusations of complicity in his treachery that were bound to be leveled against her in Havana.

She thought of seeking asylum in Hungary, the only country where she had a fighting chance of obtaining legitimate refugee status, but she did not speak the language and was unlikely to find a job. She had very little money and definitely didn't want to become a "stripper."

Having thought through her problem, she had her belongings—frig, stove, hi-fi, TV, furniture, and clothing—crated and sent ahead to Havana where she intended to sell most of the big-ticket items on the black market to finance the lean months she knew she would have to face.

After a tearful farewell party that stretched into the early hours of the morning, members of the troupe were driven to Ferihegy Airport where they boarded a Czechoslovak Airlines flight to Havana via Prague and Gander, Canada.

Conchita, bone weary, her mind and body exhausted, alternated between sleeping and weeping all the way to Gander. Her companions tried to cheer her up to no avail. She didn't respond to logic and none of them knew how to reach her on an emotional level. In the end, they persuaded her to disembark at Gander to stretch her legs, freshen up and to take a look at the merchandise on display in the large duty-free store, her last chance to buy high-quality goods.

While she was in the jewelry section looking at bracelets, the salesclerk, whom she had noticed watching her ever since she had entered the store, came over to her. He was an attractive-looking man with a very pale face and a pronounced limp.

"Do you speak English?" he asked. She shook her head and turned away, but he was persistent. "How about the language of José Marti?" he asked softly in Spanish. She spun around, surprised. How come a salesclerk in a godforsaken place like Gander knew about Cuba's patriot poet and could speak Spanish?

He smiled as if he had read her mind and continued in Spanish. "We have some nice silver jewelry here, as you can see, but the better quality items, made of gold, we keep in a special area in the back." He looked at her. "Would you like to see them?"

She shook her head again and laughed. The man was so pathetically eager. "I don't want to waste your time," she replied. "I have no money to spend on these things."

"You don't have to buy anything, just come and have a look. We've just received some remarkably beautiful necklaces from Africa. Gold coins exquisitely mounted to form a sort of small breastplate." He tried to illustrate what he meant by placing the palm of his left hand where his neck met his chest.

At the mention of African jewelry the image of her beloved Patricio adjusting the Angolan bracelet around her neck leapt into her mind's eye. She knew in her heart that Patricio was a good man, foolhardy perhaps, but not a traitor. His disappearance grieved her deeply. She still loved him and hoped to be reunited with him somewhere, somehow, someday.

The salesman watched her intently. She turned away to hide her tears. Too late. "Have I offended you in some way?" he asked, his voice gentle. "If so, forgive me. It was not intentional."

"No, no," she replied. "It's just that the mention of Africa brought back some very painful memories."

"Come with me, then," he said and took her by the hand. "Perhaps I can show you something that'll make you feel better—something that you'll enjoy seeing."

In spite of herself, she let him lead her to the storeroom at the back of the boutique and opened the door to let her pass.

Seated at a small desk in the far corner was a bald man wearing horn-rimmed glasses and sporting a gray beard. Dressed in an elegant, expensive dark-blue suit, custom-made shirt and beautifully matching tie, the man, tall, thin, and distinguished looking, got up when he heard them come in. The salesman was all smiles. "Señorita Borrego, may I present our expert on African jewelry, Señor Antonio Gonzales Cepeda, known until recently as General Patricio Casas Rojo, late of the Cuban Army."

Conchita Borrego, overcome by happiness, swooned into Casas's waiting arms.

With Lonsdale's help and on the strength of a letter he had with him from the INS granting Conchita refugee status in the United States, it took less than an hour to obtain a two-day Canadian transit visa for her. The three of them then flew to Montreal where a jubilant Micheline picked them up at the airport and drove them to the Four Seasons Hotel.

Although bone tired from her emotional roller coaster ride and the long trip from Budapest, Conchita nevertheless insisted on having a light dinner with the Lonsdales before going to bed.

The two couples parted a few minutes before eleven and Micheline drove Lonsdale to her apartment.

"What now?" she grinned mischievously as she inserted her key in the front door lock.

He pulled her roughly to the full length of his ready body. "My mind is focused on one thought you little devil." He danced her toward the bedroom, laughing. "Let's just do what we do so well together—let's go to bed."

ACKNOWLEDGMENTS

All together, it took twenty years to write this book.

I owe a great debt of gratitude to Adys, who gave me the material on which to base this story, and to Elaine for sweating the early manuscript. Carmen put up with my temper tantrums while I wrote and stood by me while I struggled to find my "voice."

LaFlorya contributed greatly to my understanding of how the publishing world works.

Joelle created the title for the book. Jay, my editor, and the team at Emerald Book Company, produced a polished and highly presentable package with friendly verve and great good humour.

Sarah was, is, and shall go on being, I hope, the remarkable publicist driving the marketing effort for *Havana Harvest*.

And, of course, there is my family, whose members allowed me to bore them endlessly with tales of my imaginary exploits in Cuba.

This said, let me state clearly that I assume full responsibility for any and all shortcomings, errors, and omissions in this work.

—Montreal, May 1, 2010

ABOUT THE AUTHOR

Born in Hungary, Robert Landori, whose full surname is Landori-Hoffmann, was for most of his professional life a senior public accountant, mergers and acquisitions specialist, and a trustee in bankruptcy in the Cayman Islands.

But behind the facade of the quiet man of numbers lay a life of intrigue and mystery. He traveled widely throughout South America and the Caribbean, where he came into contact with international financiers, notorious con men, well-known artists and entertainers, and members of several countries' intelligence communities.

Robert Landori also developed a highly charged and double-edged relationship with Castro's Cuba, and was, at one time, held in solitary confinement there for over two months on false accusations of espionage.

He is now a security consultant, lecturer on money laundering and terrorism, and writer of international intrigue and espionage thrillers.

He lives in Montreal, Canada.